IN THE SHADOWS, IT LISTENED.
AND WAITED.

KERSTIN ESPINOSA ROSERO

To those who kept the beacons lit
when it felt like
the entire world went dark.
To you and for you,
I am eternally grateful.

1

ABOVE REALM

14th/57R: We had set off at first light, hoping to reach home before the Hounds could ask too many questions. We failed. Now our ship is to be grounded in Port Haven until the Purge passes over the western shores. We will be granted safe passage, but being so close to the Firelands has put everyone on edge. Honestly, Elayne, I

***

The *Smuggler* lurched to the side, nearly sending Decker's quill overboard. Surprise quickly eased into relief; he had no idea how to end the letter gracefully. What was he going to write? *I miss you?* As a trader—on paper, at least—he had traveled on hundreds of ships, both air and seabound, but that one sailed a long time ago.

"The winds are bellowing!" Merc shouted from the helm. Delight widened his grin until it took up half of his face. His enormous goggles took up the other. He may have looked like a Hound, but he was as Divisoryan as they came. For one, no self-respecting

Realmborn would wear a flighter cap, even on the rare occasion they boarded an airship; the ear flaps and huge, tinted lenses were usually too much for them. But for Divisoryans who lived in the air, it became more important to protect one's eyes and ears, to keep warm against the winds—even if it meant wearing a stupid hat. "I almost forgot how sensitive the wheel was!"

Perhaps Decker shouldn't have let him steer. "Remember what Wolff said," he shouted back. "You have to treat it like a lady." *Words undoubtedly lost on him.* He snorted and shook his head. At least someone was having a good time. Then again, if anyone could find joy in fleeing a Hound-brewed firestorm and setting sail for a border checkpoint with an airship full of stolen herbs, it would be Merc. Best to live a little before you died.

He felt the *Smuggler* slow to a near halt. The gears grumbled and groused, threatened to explode. Merc shrugged. It was nothing new.

They had steered the *Smuggler* into Port Haven hundreds of times, but today, the city donned a different skin. The clouds were tinged red, tracing the outline of the towers in the distance. Shadows of the city lifted and fell, and spires rose like silent sentinels that pierced the sky.

Decker sighed. Against his better judgment, he glanced over the side of the ship. From above, the world looked nothing more than blots of orange knotted across a black tapestry. He watched the fire below grow fiercer, reaching upwards. Trails of smoke sent shivers down his spine.

Airships, he thought when he saw the shattered masts. *'Grounded' airships.*

There were portents and omens everywhere, or so Divisoryans liked to believe, but the crew had misinterpreted them big time. From tea leaves and wind patterns, they had all divined a bountiful harvest but quickly found themselves in the middle of a firestorm. As Divisoryan traders, they were allowed safe and immediate passage to the nearest checkpoint—Port Haven—and nowhere else. They had considered ignoring the orders, of course, but that was before they passed by one wrecked ship after another, black and smoldering like dying coals.

It must have been easier to make a grand escape in the *Smuggler's* prime, back when it was one of five airships in existence.

Back when there was no Valerya to burn it to the ground.

No, Decker thought grimly. *Back when there was no dragon to burn it to the ground.*

Now it was their goal to reach Port Haven as soon as possible. The Hounds rewarded obedience, and the crew was making record time. Wolff didn't even bother stopping to unload some of their more questionable cargo. Best case, they got a stamp for good behavior and could leave without much scrutiny. Worst case, they ended up stranded in Port Haven, and their goods would make them rich.

Or dead, if the Hounds found them first.

Good thing the *Smuggler* was built to hide things, even if it was constantly on the verge of collapse. Decker could only hope the underlings weren't getting high below deck. *Well, that's one way to get rid of the evidence,* he thought, snorted.

He couldn't blame them, though. Had he been their age—fresh-faced and unmarred by life's many disappointments—the prospect of force-landing at a border checkpoint, especially with the Summoner's army so close by, would have sent him crying for home.

Hell, he could use a pinch of the stuff right about now.

The *Smuggler* lurched forward.

"Move over," Decker said gruffly, tucking his journal back into his cloak pocket. Hounds and beasts and spooks or not, pondering wouldn't do anyone any good if Merc killed them all. And the sooner they landed, the sooner they would be able to leave …

***

"I'm afraid you can't leave, outsider," said the sentry the moment he and his Hound companions boarded the *Smuggler*. He threw Merc's fire-colored hair a quick glance before shifting his attention back to Decker. "Ma'am commands it."

"Commands it?" repeated Merc incredulously. His tone shattered even the slightest hope of diplomacy.

But the sentry's face did not change. He looked like he had been dealing with outsider ships all day, and no crew liked being grounded. "In the name of our King, Morian of Pyrrheas, direct descendent of Imperios, the second Trueborne son of our Guardian and …"

Decker wondered what sort of food they would be serving at the tavern that night. He threw Wolff an anguished glance, but Wolff shrugged and took a swig from his wineskin. He was thickset and strong and had been in charge of the *Smuggler* for as long as Decker could remember, but he left all the talking to the crew—especially when the Hounds were involved. He only spoke when things got ugly, which often happened when Merc opened his mouth.

Decker turned his attention back to the sentry just in time to catch the end of his speech.

"… all ships will be *grounded* until our General clears the area."

"Sorry," said Decker before Merc could respond, "but what does 'clearing the area' have to do with us? We're just traders."

"Our General, Valerya the Fireborne, first Dragon Summoner of her bloodline and commanding General of the Fire Realm, leader and …"

Damn it, thought Decker, thinking back to dinner.

"… would like to make sure no one from the villages escapes the Realm."

"Couldn't you just inspect our ships for stowaways before we take off?" asked Merc. He had a knack for distracting sentries from unlawful deeds by making them suspect other unlawful deeds. It usually worked, especially on overworked bureaucrats. Powders and leaves were harder to see when one was dead set on finding thieves and runaways.

"Traders tend to be … *eclectic,*" the sentry answered as his companions threw Decker a dark glance that spoke volumes. Decker knew they were trying not to stare at his hair, the swirls of black and brown that contrasted Merc's own. The Hound glanced back at Merc. "You will remain grounded until further notice, Outsider. Unless you want us to search your ship more *thoroughly.*"

Merc tensed, bit back an insult. He might as well have called him a half-breed. A traitor to his kind.

"Stand down," said Wolff gently, putting down his wineskin. "These men are just doing their jobs, right? What's your name?"

Decker never knew how Wolff did it. With a few soft-spoken words, he could command anyone to silence. It was all in the tone, he supposed. Or the subtle, misleading calmness that often preceded a storm.

Of course, it didn't hurt that Wolff outmatched them in size. The Hounds didn't even know he was sitting down until he rose from behind the table.

"Sunn," said the sentry reluctantly. His eyes narrowed in suspicion. It seemed as though no one had ever asked for his name before. Typical Fireborne bureaucrat.

"Well, *Sunn*," said Wolff gruffly. "How long, then?"

"Until further notice," said Sunn, this time a few shades nicer than before. "Ma'am's being productive this week. Only a couple more to go after this."

"And that's just a scare," said Sunn's companion to the right. He was small and scraggly and could probably pass for an underling without the uniform; if things went south, he'd be the easiest to bribe. "Now no one has the balls to stand up to Ma'am. Soon, she'll go after …"

"That is enough, citizen," said Sunn coldly, turning back to Wolff. "You may disembark, but you and your crew are only permitted to stay in Port Hav—"

"Yeah, we know," said Wolff brusquely. "Been here too many times." He waved a hand dismissively, signaling the Hounds' leave. Decker wondered how many crews they had checked today. The port was overflowing with ships, but it looked like some had been docked for weeks. He hoped that was reason enough to send them home.

"Long live our King," was all Sunn said. He slammed his fist against his chest before he and his posse took their leave. Once they reached land, their pace quickened.

"Well, then!" said Wolff, shaking his head. "Best take advantage of the situation. Start unloading, boys! Looks like we'll make a killing here after all."

Decker rarely sampled the fine herbs they were transporting, no matter how often Merc tried to bend his willpower. If anything, he preferred "spices"—stuff that sharpened the senses, not dulled them. All the inventory and bartering was Merc's world; Decker just steered the ship and trained the underlings.

He sighed as he turned his attention back to the torch-lit horizon. The Firelands, he thought darkly, suddenly cold. *We meet again.*

2

THE RED CITADEL
FIRE REALM

The westernmost tower was large and gloomy, paneled with dark wood and filled with austere lines of furnishing that looked cast aside from other parts of the castle.

The Citadel was built in stages, reflecting layers of history and unrest. The main keep was constructed first, and it showed: it was made of stone and timber and prone to rot when the summers turned humid. The wood was often replaced and polished to maintain its original appearance, but despite being the most primitive structure on castle grounds, it was easily the most fortified. It housed the throne room and the king's quarters, and one could not access it without passing through the other buildings first. As the Empire expanded eastward, so too did the castle; walls and towers continued to be built around the keep, embedding in their construction the spoils of war.

Still, for all the Citadel's oddities, its red color was its claim to fame. Just before the Empire fell, sandstone had been imported from the Waterlands and used to overlay the exterior. The rains had worn it down over the years, and locals claimed that over time, the fire turned it red. But it was not the bleeding stones that interested Dove, nor was it the Sun-sworn temple built after the fall of the last emperor.

She glanced over her shoulder at the passing sentries, pretending to busy herself with the barrel of rice wine in her arms. They usually left her alone, especially when it looked like she was doing the king's bidding. Often, she carried around something of his to deflect unwanted attention. An expensive-looking book, perhaps, or soap for his baths—or his favorite wine. It mostly worked, depending on who was patrolling the corridors. The big sentries only looked intimidating, but it was the small ones that liked giving her a hard time. This one threw her a nasty smirk as he passed, and she contemplated dropping the barrel on his foot.

Another time, she decided, tightening her grip on the barrel. She winced when she felt the frayed wood press against her left palm, still bandaged from previous wounds. It was worth the pain; she did not want to be sent back to the king just yet. If the changing of the guards had been any indication, she still had time before her absence became noted. She waited until the sentries were out of sight before daring another glance over the railing.

The Swordsworn patrolled the corridors in clockwork precision, but the guards changed only after the king's supper. She had to be careful there. It cleared the corridors for a few moments, but if one of them even suspected that she was not supposed to be there …

Dove relaxed and eased into the silence. *So this is it,* she thought, committing every corner to memory, every pocket that looked like a potential hiding spot. She wanted to explore the tower but did not dare linger. Beyond castle walls, it was easy to judge time by the moon's movements, but inside, she had no way of being sure. It was the rhythm of footsteps that kept her oriented, the only evidence that time still passed.

But the westernmost tower changed the game.

She had been there before, but it was not enough to predict the guards' whereabouts. Their routine was different than in the main keep, where they stood sentinel at every door. Here, the entire corridor was unmanned, though only a fool would call it unguarded. The Spades' Quarters were located one floor below, and they could probably take care of themselves.

Dove set the barrel down and winced. *Damn,* she thought when she saw dark red seep through the linen wraps. For a castle surrounded by trees, surely they could have crafted better barrels. *Then again,* she thought, reading the label. *This is Lancistierrean wine.* Of course it was. She kicked it to the side and glanced around, hoping no one was nearby. The king did not need wine, but she needed an excuse to raid the storage room in this part of the castle at precisely this moment.

It was not only the Spades who resided in the westernmost tower.

Dove slid back into the storage room and pulled the door to a near close. She had caught glimpses of the Summoner General before, but it was always in passing. From what she knew, Valerya the Fireborne spent her days in two places: her chambers, not thirty strides from where Dove was standing, or in the training halls. Aside from that, her whereabouts were a complete mystery. What she did in her free time, Dove did not know.

Any time now.

Her heart raced. It was a risky endeavor, but if there was one thing she prided herself on, it was her attention to detail. Her life depended on knowing every pattern of the castle's movements. If, for example, she had crossed paths with Greaven, the king's personal bodyguard, instead of the two sentries in the hall, her attempts at sneaking about would have been over before they started.

However, if she knew who was where at what time, maybe she could even slip past them one day …

Not if you are bleeding everywhere, she thought darkly, throwing a quick glance over her shoulder. With any luck, she would find something to redress her wounds. She had found stranger things in storage rooms, and chambermaids often kept rolls of cloth scattered throughout the castle for quick bandaging. Everyone had to follow the plan, after all. The Fireborne did not like to deviate from routine, and injuries were no excuse.

But that could wait.

Dove stood on her toes and tried to get a better look.

There! she thought in excitement when she saw the She-Jackal returning to her chambers. Her crimson cloak flowed behind her, but it was the sword slung over her shoulder that commanded onlookers to silence. Dove reckoned it was longer than she was, maybe even heavier. All for show, no doubt. At least that was what she told herself.

Gryff would be so jealous. Dove tightened her grip around the doorframe for support. *And he owes me five silver markes.* They had often wondered what the Summoner looked like, and it was he who swore by all the Sons that she was half-beast. He may have lost the bet, but Dove was disappointed when she saw that Valerya was not, in fact, three meters tall or one meter wide, nor did she bear the face of a jackal. On the contrary, she was very much human-sized, and her human face was quite pleasant to look at—if one looked past the scars.

If only he were here now.

Dove had lost track of her brother the night Myrne went up in flames, but she could feel in her bones that he was still alive. For as long as she could remember, they had been inseparable—two outcasts in a fallen, forgotten world. Surely she would have sensed if their connection was severed.

The She-Jackal stood briefly in the doorway of her chambers. For a terrifying moment, she threatened to turn, but pulled the door shut behind her with no regard for grace. Dove let out a sigh of relief and lowered herself down. She wondered what it was like being Valerya the Fireborne. The entire world was hers for the taking, and she could reduce it all to ash if she wanted—not like Dove, who did not even resist when the Swordsworn blazed through her home. The only thing she could boast of doing was not burning when it was expected of her.

Dove scrambled in the dark, taking care not to make noise as she slid her fingers over the glass containers. She had only been in the storage rooms in the main keep, but the Fireborne had a system. Cloth and leather were most readily accessible, as the Spades went through clothes like the common-folk went through bread. Wine and water lined the bottom shelves. More dangerous things were wisely kept out of reach. Dove groped along the edges of the upper shelf, counting two above her head before tapping gently on the left jar with her fingernail.

Rise and shine, she thought as the nightbloom stirred, stretching its petals as it woke from its nap. Its violet glow spilled into the gaps between the stones. Beautiful, but deadly. When crushed, its roots could knock out a horde of wild beasts, and its venom was so cold, it burned. The castle medicans used it to ease pain and cure sleepless nights.

Dove frowned when she surveyed the rest of the storage room, disappointed. She was sure she would find something to stop the bleeding. She followed the shelves to the edge of light, just where the darkness began, and felt in front of her until she touched something cold. *Wall,* she thought, frustrated. She groped blindly to the right, as far as the wall went, and felt stone turn into wood.

Door.

Its surface was rough, but not splintered. There were no cobwebs, which meant that it had not yet been sealed off. Her hands reached the handle, and she stepped to the side as she traced the keyhole with her fingertips. She had heard of locks designed to spew arrows when touched—a bit far-fetched, she knew, but it cost nothing to be cautious.

But the door was not lain with traps. In truth, it was not even closed at all. It opened soundlessly at her touch, and the breeze that followed was calm and soothing. She felt the hairs on the back of her neck bristle, but it was not fear that lifted them—it was *cold.* It bit into her skin like glass, spread across her shoulders. Slowly, it edged into excitement. Dove stood in the doorframe, wondering if she should follow it.

Either way, she was already in trouble. *Might as well keep going,* she thought with a deep sigh. She had already lingered too long. Between the king and hidden passages that could well drop her off the edge of the world, she would take her chances.

Dove slipped through the opening and pressed her back against the wall, feeling her way forward. It did not take her long to realize that she was in a winding corridor. The walls turned and twisted, and she had to stop a few times to renew her courage. She halted when sounds echoed against the walls of a wider chamber. Shadows rippled against amber-lit stone and danced along the edge of her vision. She frowned, squinted when she saw the candle sway violently to the cold. Someone else was there.

Dove held her breath. *This is ridiculous,* she thought as furnishings began to take shape. She ran her fingers over spines of old books until a scarlet glow caught her eye, brightening in intensity as she approached. When she touched it, it drew back into the symbol of a single flame. Caution screamed inside her like an alarm. She had heard of books like this. Mages often enchanted scrolls for their apprentices, but only the witchborn were known to use scarlet. *What is the worst that could happen?* she wondered, throwing vigilance to the wind. She did not believe in ghosts and spooks, and dark incantations only worked when said aloud. Probably.

She pulled the book from the shelf and leafed through the pages. It was written in old Sinthean, sharp-edged pictographs last seen in imperial times, just before Bastyan had their writing system simplified into letters. Dove squinted at the first line of characters, trying to commit them to memory. She could make out a few. The three-pronged one meant "mountain," and the triangle with upward strokes meant "fire." Or was it "horse"?

Damn it, she thought. Gryff was much better at this than she was.

Suddenly, a burst of fire lit the sconce closest to her, revealing the contents of the chamber. It was much smaller than Dove thought, but that did not stop the rush of panic that pulsed between her temples. Cold sweat pearled on her skin. *Stupid,* she scolded herself, thrusting the book into her sleeve. She knew she had overstayed her welcome. They would certainly take her back to Morian now. *Damn it, damn it, damn it ...*

But instead of a sentry, it was a woman who stood before her, draped in a cloak of dark blue that made her difficult to place. For a fleeting moment, Dove found comfort in the woman's comely appearance—until she began talking. "Curious little mouse," she said. Her voice was deep and curled under Dove's skin. "No one finds themselves here unless they're not where they're supposed to be."

Dove felt a sharp pang shoot between her ears like a crossbow, and she stumbled against the wall.

"A Fireborne then. One of us," said the woman, and the corners of her mouth turned upwards in delight. Her hair was shorn short and darker than sin, but it was her emerald eyes that revealed dark intentions. "I can always feel it. Don't worry, child. I'm not a skin-crawler. There is nothing I can sense in you aside from the Fire in your blood. But Ro-yun, on the other hand …"

The pain behind Dove's eyes exploded into white light, and her head throbbed faster than her heart. She reached for the door, but a taller figure stood in its frame, blocking her way to freedom.

"Don't torture the kid, Mina," he teased. In his eyes glowed the same deep green, and when they locked onto Dove's, they burned. "Let's have a look at you, then." He raised his arm and volleyed a blast of Fire past her, lighting another sconce. "Excuse my apprentice. She prefers the dark, though only the Sons know why. I say if you were born with the gift of Fire, you should use it from time to time."

Dove felt the pain shift, like something was scraping along the inside of her skull. A series of images flashed through her mind in rapid succession, each sharper than a stone-cutter's blade. The first thing she saw was Myrne engulfed in flames, saw it whole again. Saw a beautiful morning turn into the star-lit fields at the edge of the Dragontail, the only place she felt safe.

"Dove," she heard a familiar voice as Gryff's face swarmed into her field of vision. It was hazy at first, but the longer she stared, the more it settled in her mind like sand pouring into a glass of water. It was *him*. Every detail matched her memory, every hair that was out of place. The Ice in his blood colored his hair black, but his eyes still burned Fire.

Stay with me, she thought, but he faded back into the frays of her conscious mind, replaced by one of the Spades. She recognized him as the General's right-hand man, the one with the accent thicker than his beard. *Get out of my head,* she thought as Valerya replaced him, and the images disappeared, shattering like glass as she was ripped back into the waking world.

The pounding between her eyes stopped, and she found herself on the ground, gasping, convulsing. Something had twisted her inside out. *Skin-crawler,* she thought as the buzzing subsided. Her stomach threatened to heave. She never thought she would meet one up close, but their encounter was more than enough to break her curiosity.

Ro-yun approached again, but the images did not come. A cold wind sliced through the chambers. "What have you been up to?" he asked. His voice was calm, soothing. "Your hand is bleeding." But before Dove could feel moved by his concern, Mina broke the silence.

"Ro-yun," she said. "We could use her to ..."

"No," he said calmly, cutting her off. "This one doesn't belong to us." He reached out and grabbed Dove's face, forced her to look into his eyes. When he reached for her hand, she kicked him in the shin—a senseless maneuver against someone twice her size, but the element of surprise bought her just enough time ...

... if she had not been so disoriented from his little foray into her mind. *Damn it,* she thought as she crashed against the walls like a drunken medican.

It was Mina who grabbed her by the shoulders and pulled her back with surprising strength. "You little *bitch*," she said, and Dove felt her arm hit jagged stone. It would have drawn blood had the book not buffered its impact. She had almost forgotten it was there. The sudden glow through her sleeve reminded her.

Curious, she heard Ro-yun's voice in her head. *You have something of ours.*

I can give it back, thought Dove desperately. There was no use hiding it now.

Mina had her left arm pinned to the wall. Dove tried to use her free hand to wrench the book from her sleeve, but hope was short-lived. The pain in her skull intensified until she thought it would burst.

"What is the meaning of this?" came a voice so cold that Dove could feel the air around them tighten. She immediately felt Ro-yun's grip on her mind loosen, and even Mina drew back into a bow.

"My liege," they said in practiced unison, refusing to lift their eyes from the ground.

But the She-Jackal was in no mood for formalities. "May I remind you, skin-crawler, that she is our King's plaything, not yours. *Furthermore,*" she said before Ro-yun could say anything. "No one has authorized you to use your … *abilities* against her."

"My liege," said Ro-yun softly. "She came into this room. For all we knew, she was …"

"Two grown mages could not find other means to subdue a teen-age girl with an injured hand?" said Valerya, pointing impatiently at Dove's blood-soaked wraps. "My armor is a bigger threat."

Dove was not even insulted. She was in no position to choose her savior.

Suddenly, she felt Ro-yun's presence writhe inside her, fierce like fire. *Get out!* she thought, but the scream was stilled inside her. Morian or not, there was nothing more frightening than the feeling that her thoughts were not her own.

Valerya sighed and drew her sword, pointed it at Ro-yun's throat. "*Cease,*" she said. "Or we shall see what is underneath a skin-crawler's skin."

"It was not …" he began, but the tip of her blade had already pierced the side of his face, painting a red line across his cheek.

Valerya let her blade linger for a split-moment before withdrawing it. "Regrettably, skin-crawler, you, too, belong to our King. Otherwise, I would have your head," she said. "But the next time you disobey, I will take something else."

"We are grateful," said Mina, hoping to tear the General's attention away from Ro-yun. "We are so grateful for your mercy. We …"

"Come, girl," said Valerya, sheathing her sword. She slung it over her shoulder and took her leave without so much as a second glance.

Ro-yun lifted his gaze as Dove slipped past him, and his eyes narrowed.

Never again, she thought as she crashed against the wall once, twice, before the world around her stopped spinning. She followed the General's torch-fire through the maze of walls, past the storage room where the nightbloom still glowed.

"Stupid girl," snapped Valerya once they stepped out into the corridor. Her accent placed her far from the Citadel, but her words carried all the weight in the world. "I should have left you with those witchborn freaks. But your absence has already been noted."

The Spade with the thick beard had been standing by the doorway, but he straightened when they emerged. Valerya waved a hand dismissively, and Dove was surprised to see a trickle of blood stream from her nose.

"You'd be a fool to think I did you a favor," she said as she wiped it from her face with a piece of cloth. The corners of her lips lifted, rippling the scars on her cheek. "Valk." She turned to the Spade. "Take her back where she belongs."

"At once," he replied, and Dove's heart plummeted when she saw his expression. She had seen him often, always two steps behind Valerya the Fireborne, but no less cold. She knew she was in for a miserable evening when his face broke out into abject pity.

He gave a courteous nod. "Come on, then," he said.

Dove turned just in time to see the General head back to her chambers and sighed. The woman had saved her from the wolves and thrown her to the sharks. Dove joined the Spade, who was waiting for her to follow.

"You're small, but only marginally hopeless," he said as they walked. Dove did not know if it was meant as a comfort, but she nodded all the same. She could tell he was not from around there, but she was losing track of all the accents at the castle. "A messenger, perhaps?"

Lie. She nodded. *The less they know about you, the less they can hurt you.*

"No. A messenger rarely needs secrecy. You, on the other hand …" he continued. "You make no noise, and even now, your eyes wander. A scavenger? A pickpocket?" He paused, and Dove wondered if he could see inside her head, too. "Or maybe a sneak thief." He laughed when he saw her reaction, more courtesy than spite. "Don't look so defensive. It's only small talk."

They continued in silence. Fear swelled with each step. She was terrified of Morian, but the king had the uncanny ability to make her feel guilty about everything. Even for hating him.

Especially for hating him. Even when his blade was carving into the flesh of her palm.

Pull yourself together, she thought as phantom pain shot through her left hand.

The Spade broke the silence. "Tell me, how old are you? Fifteen? Sixteen?"

Lie. She shook her head.

A kind smile broke out across his face. He saw through her like she was made of glass. "It was only a question. In any case …" They stopped just before the arched doors decorated in iron-banded oak. "I've heard our King was in a good mood today."

Dove did not feel comforted.

"As our General says," said the Spade with a slight bow. "We must all face the consequences of our actions. Especially stupid actions."

Dove felt her heart jump when he knocked.

***

"If you wanted reading material, you should have just asked," said Morian, feigning disapproval as he paged through the book Dove forgot she had pilfered. It had stopped glowing the moment it left the witchborn chambers, and in the light, it looked tattered and torn. "Even I don't understand most of this gibberish."

He set it on his desk and poured wine into her glass. "Drink this," he said. "I don't often partake, but this bottle came all the way from Lancistierre. They make their wines sweeter in the Waterlands. Everything simply *ages* better over there."

Dove forced herself to look back into those eyes until she could see herself in them. To many, Morian was a good-looking man; his face was youthful despite nearing an age, a square jaw with a crescent smile. The Fire in his eyes charmed those he deemed worthy of his attention. Even without owning several castles and ruling over the Firelands, he had many admirers, both in and out of the Citadel.

If only they knew. There was a reason why his own men whispered "serpent king" among their ranks, spread stories of his outbursts. His eyes changed with unsettling speed. One moment, they were kind, and the next, cruel. But he chose his audience carefully. To his own people, he never let slip his insanities, but he knew Dove would never reveal his secrets. It was for that reason that she was privy to many of them.

"We can't keep going on like this," he said. "My men are always finding you in places you don't belong. Why, it's almost as if you were trying to escape." He clicked his teeth in annoyance, fussed over her appearance. He liked the deep auburn of her hair and insisted that she keep it well-kempt, but her tangles told a different story. "Is my castle not to your satisfaction? Does it not keep you safe?"

He is trying to make me feel guilty again. It was working.

"Sit," he commanded, his smile unimpaired. "Drink." He moved towards the window and pulled back the drapes. Night had turned the skies black, but torch-fire flickered like candles across the court-yard. On a good day, she could see the General's tower from the balcony.

But none of that mattered now. Dove took a reluctant sip from her wine glass as she sat. It was sweeter than honey and spread warmth across her chest, cutting off the chill from the cold. She drank some more.

"You do not approve," he said softly, more to himself than to her. Suddenly, he laughed and took the glass from her hand before she could finish it. He brought it to his own lips, took a sip. "I don't suppose you've shared many words with the She-Jackal, but do you know how she came to be here? No, I suppose not," he said before she could respond. "It's much easier believing your peasants' tales. Especially if you're from ... where are you from again? Pom's Hill?"

Dove's eyes narrowed, but she nodded. Another lie.

He laughed again and handed her the wine glass. "It may surprise you to know that Valerya came from a miserable patch of dirt, too," he said. A breath of disgust shuddered his tall frame. "The Iceborne ravaged and pillaged the border villages to the South. Honestly, I don't even think Valerya knew she was a summoner then, but I suppose watching everyone you know get *murdered* brings out the beast in you. Oh!" He smiled, pretended to be embarrassed. "Have I awakened bad memories?"

Dove took another sip and kept her face impassive. *Give him nothing,* she thought.

And just like that, his eyes turned cruel. "My father offered them peace. Helped them when their winters ravaged their fields. And how did they repay us?" His voice dripped with disdain. "And they dare *breed* with us. Did you know that children born from their unions are abominations? Some even burn in daylight. Others born with flesh that falls off at the slightest touch. *STAND.*"

Dove winced at his tone, but she obeyed. *Oh no,* she thought. Morian's demeanor had changed completely. The night would not end well for her.

"You cannot cast Fire, my dear, and you are of no use to me if you insist on getting into trouble. So I will make you a deal." He took the chain from around his neck and slammed it onto the desk in front of her. "Take this key and walk out the door. No one will stop you, not even Greaven." He took a seat, and his gaze sharpened. "But if you are not out of my sight within the next ten seconds, you will wish you had never been born."

Dove blinked. *I ... don't understand,* she thought.

"Tick, tock, Dove," he said impatiently, leaning back in his seat.

Without thinking, Dove sprang from her chair and grabbed the key, but felt herself crash against the desk. *Damn it,* she thought, shaking her head to stop everything from spinning. Her vision blurred, focusing intermittently on the shattered wine glass on the floor. Dread filled her veins, cold as ice.

Stupid, she scolded herself. *Stupid, stupid ...*

"I *might* have forgotten to tell you that Lancistierrean wine is laced with nightbloom for that extra *kick.* It doesn't affect the Waterborne much, but us ..." said Morian as his expression softened back into feigned melancholy. "Even I can only handle a sip most days."

Stupid! thought Dove, feeling her legs grow heavy. She had fallen for it. She had fallen for it big time.

And she had fallen, period.

"Dove," she heard Morian say, his voice little more than a dim echo that reverberated through her skull. She heard him rise, but felt nothing until he hoisted her up, sitting her back on the chair.

"*Time's up,*" he whispered in her ear. Then his eyes turned cruel.

3

PORT HAVEN
FIRE REALM

"I'm so bored, my life is flashing before my eyes," said Merc as he perched himself on a wall that barely came up to his waist. Occasionally, he would fling a rock into the distance, aiming for the sentinels pacing back and forth at the foot of the hill. "I bet they know I'm throwing rocks at them. But they just follow their orders all day, all day long …"

"Your aim is terrible," said Decker. "Somehow, the rocks are ending up behind us."

"Shut up." Merc untied the skin of wine slung over his shoulder and bit out the horn plug. It was his second one today. Some fine wine from the Waterlands. If there was one benefit to being confined to a port city with hundreds of traders, it was the ample supply of Lancistierrean wine—good cover, too. Piles of gold raised questions, but no one thought twice about foreign wine in a port city. It was the only commodity worth a clean barter, and they had already traded away most of their herbs.

"We've been here almost a month, now," he said as he took a swig. "I think I'm becoming one of them. Their dullness is contagious."

Merc had a point. Port Haven was a trading hub, for which reason it did not place much importance on entertainment beyond pubs and gambling rings. There used to be brothels, but as foreign traders were banned from leaving and entering the mainland, they were cleared and used as guest-keeps. Whores were compensated a portion of their pay, but they took to the streets, slept in bars. It was a mess. The locals were not at all prepared for the shiploads of outsiders grounded in their city, and they tried their best to pretend they didn't exist. Some even went out of their way to ignore them, if that made any sense, but close quarters soon simmered into resentment on all sides.

"Think we could make a break for the mainland?" asked Merc, nodding towards the sentinels. "They don't look so tough."

"And do what? Go sightseeing at the Red Citadel?" Decker took a stone from the wall and turned it over in his hand. He tossed it in the air to feel its weight. Satisfied, he reached back and aimed for the bigger sentinel's head.

PING. Both sentinels glanced around, broken from routine. They looked like they wanted to say something angry but stopped when Decker rose from the wall. He folded his arms across his chest. "Honest mistake, boys," he shouted over the winds.

"Watch it, Outsider," the smaller one warned. They glared and shook their heads in succession, muttering something about outsider scum. Decker had heard worse, especially once people found out he was from Divisorya. *Traitor. Mongrel.* He waited a moment longer, counted four grunts of disapproval.

He stretched. "C'mon, Merc," he said. "Even messing with them is useless. It's like trying to provoke a rock."

"Do you reckon that's why they have such a violent history?" asked Merc. "I mean, all that pent-up energy from doing the same thing every day …" He swung down from the wall. "I suppose that makes them very … organized in their killing?"

"Wouldn't be surprised," said Decker as they made their way back towards the half-paved roads that led back to civilization. That was one thing Valerya did, at least—restructured their army, placed commanders on the basis of merit over blood right. Where the Fireborne had once based legends on lone heroes, the She-Jackal concentrated on building killing units that favored efficiency over personal glory. *The things I learn from Merc,* thought Decker, shaking his head. No one held a candle to their organization now.

They reached the outskirts of town. Normally, he would watch his tongue in the Firelands—openly criticizing their sovereign was punishable by death—but the streets were overrun with outsiders. The Hounds, he could usually tell apart by the ink-marks on their skin. Merchants and traders often had weighing scales tattooed on their necks. Smiths were marked with hammers, fishermen with waves of water.

If only they knew. Their marking system had once been used to brand slaves. Easier to sell them that way. They were inked at sixteen, just when they began to show skill for a particular trade. After slavery was abolished from the Firelands, it remained tradition among the common-folk. Not many knew of its origins now.

"Let's go inside," said Merc, pulling his cloak over his shoulders. He eyed the tavern with good-natured mischief. "I know what'll warm your blood. And if that doesn't work, maybe some rice wine."

"I'll be fine with the rice wine, thanks," said Decker. He had almost forgotten that today was the last day of the amber star. Kiera would be there, along with several others who had docked from Lancistierre. They all bore the dark-haired, silk-skinned look of the Waterlands, and it was easy to envy them. Water allowed them to heal instantly and stay youthful longer than most people were even alive. He had met traders in their nineties who looked younger than him, saw them break bones and heal within minutes. It was not uncommon for the wealthy to live past two hundred, aging only in their final decade of life. They may not have mastered immortality, but it was close enough.

"You're one of a kind, my friend," said Merc with a heavy sigh, "but there's nothing *noble* in being faithful to a memory."

Decker let the comment roll off his back as they made their way back to the heart of the city. Port Haven was built along the harbor, with roads that twisted and turned. The shoreline formed a grotesque smile with teeth of thatched and timber roofs, but down below, it didn't look much better. It was no backwater village by far; on the contrary, its land was fertile and well walled, its people at least marginally educated.

But if we don't leave soon, I'm going to knife someone, he thought, elbowing his way through the crowd.

Finally, they reached the Hub—the sorriest looking tavern he had ever seen. It was said that secret societies used it as a meeting point for dark deeds, which didn't surprise him in the least. Just looking at it made him fear for his safety. But with the sudden influx of outsiders, most frustrated and armed to the teeth, gangsters must have disbanded for the time being. Locals had even begun to come by again. *I guess the Purge was good for one thing,* he thought when he entered. *Stranding a group of angry people drove out the first group of angry people.*

Indeed, the Hub was booming this month. Most of its patrons were like them: traders and adventurers who had spent most of their lives on ships. After nearly a month on land, they felt more like spirits wandering a city in which they didn't belong. Birds without wings.

"There she is." Merc waved. *"Kiera!"* he bellowed gracefully over the commotion. "How's life?"

"Same as yesterday, Mercuro," she answered with a faint smile, "and the day before." Her voice was even raspier than last time, and Decker suddenly felt grateful that his disdain for the Firelands was all in his mind. Kiera's body, on the other hand, actively rejected their climate. Soft rashes formed along the side of her face, and her eyes swelled with tears.

But one could see from miles away that Water flowed through her veins, and despite the rashes, she was beautiful. *For someone who could be anywhere between twenty and a hundred.* Come to think of it, she was probably closer to a hundred. The younger generation barely spoke Sinthean, and their international names were often ridiculous. Skyfall, Sugar Cane, probably the only words they knew. He had met someone named Bootstrap once.

"How's your ship holding up?" she asked, glancing at Decker.

"Still threatening mutiny," Merc answered for him. "They're going to start sacrificing the underlings if things don't pick up soon."

Her eyes sparkled in amusement as she took a sip of her wine. She was the only one in the tavern who had ordered an entire barrel. *Definitely Waterborne.* They were smaller in frame, but it took them ages to get drunk. *No wonder they prefer herbs.* It was a common saying to never share wine with a Lancistierrean, but their stint in Port Haven changed the rules. People *only* drank with Lancistierreans, or at least took advantage of their wine.

"The usual, in other words." Decker leaned in, let his voice drop to a whisper. "Any news on the Purge?" He didn't want to interrupt the pleasantries, but the question loomed over them like an executioner's blade. She was a seeker, after all. If anyone knew what was going on, it was her.

"Only that it's getting closer. I hear the Blood Queen is already setting up camp in the forest." She glanced over her shoulder.

"What else do you know about her?" asked Merc, his interest renewed.

Decker should have seen it coming. "Not again …" he groaned, but Kiera smiled it off.

"Lots of things," she said. "I like to keep updated on Valerya the Fireborne. Our lives depend on her mood."

Or so they say. But Decker knew the real reason, and it was much more terrifying. The dragon grew stronger with each life it claimed, and they needed souls to feed that … that *thing.* Valerya may have kept their realm safe, but her power came at a terrible cost.

Kiera eyed him and took a sip. "Edenn should be next."

"But that's just outside Port Haven!" Merc said.

"Tell me about it." Kiera emptied her glass and draped her shawl over her shoulders. She set her glass down, changed the topic. "Have either of you been to Sinthea?"

"Me? Nah," said Merc, jutting a thumb at Decker. "But he has."

"Once," said Decker gruffly. "It was nothing special."

Merc blinked. "It was only Valerya's *inauguration.*"

That seemed to rouse Kiera's interest. "Really, now?" she asked innocently. "I've heard a great deal about that tournament."

"Let's have it, then," said Merc, "because Decker doesn't like to talk about it."

Kiera smiled, taking gracious note of Decker's reaction. "Maybe some other time. We don't need any more reason to fear the She-Jackal tonight."

"Incoming!" the tavern-keeper shouted as he passed them two tankards of ale.

"Drink," said Kiera. "It's infused with blackwood sap. Gives it that extra *kick*."

Decker's his mind flashed back to the burning village, the scorched fields he had seen from above. Images he stored in his mind to remind him just exactly what people were capable of. All those lives, feeding into the strength of some ancient beast. He took a swig from the tankard, felt its effect almost instantly. It was so sweet, it made his teeth hurt.

"You can't cast Fire, can you?" asked Kiera. Her eyes darted to Merc's hair. It was subtle, but she cast a swift glance over Decker, searching his eyes for secrets. Her practiced glance took in everything from his hair to the way he held his glass, from the way he sat to the dagger that lay hidden underneath his cloak. He pretended not to notice.

Merc took a sip from his tankard and shrugged. "I can create small flames, but that's it. With the way things are going, I'm not really proud of it." He set his cup down with a thud.

Decker didn't know if it was the sap or his nerves, but his stomach gave an uneasy jolt. "Mads!" he shouted to the tavern-keeper. "How much do we owe you?"

Mads spat in response and shook his head. "This round's on me tonight. We're gonna need it." He pointed to the window behind them. Decker could barely make out tiny pinpricks of fire in the distance, but they swelled, raged. Soon, they would engulf everything in its path.

The entire tavern fell silent, tense like slow-cracking glass.

"Oh, *Ro-than*," Mads cursed. He poured himself a tankard and sighed. "Next round's on me, too."

4

EDENER FOREST
FIRE REALM

A dusky purple washed over the evening sky like an old bruise as amber descended with terrible slowness. Dove always liked the turn of the stars. For a few hours between every succession, they danced, painted the sky in swirls of color. Tavandir was on the rise while Riyan's glow fell into shadowed waters, giving them the appearance of molten gold.

They were headed for the Edener Forest, which, given its proximity to the sea, had been destroyed time and time again by enemy ships. The trees in the outer rim refused to grow, still splintered at the neck, for which reason the bards referred to it as the Thousand Shards. That was certainly what Dove imagined her bones to look like when a caravan wheel snagged on a rock, nearly tearing out her shoulders at the sockets.

Never again. She bit back worlds of pain when the wagon took a sharp turn. She may have been able to sneak about castle grounds when Morian turned a blind eye, but the General was a different breed of cruelty. They had caught Dove slipping out of her binds, which did not bode well for anyone. The General halted the company then and there and ordered the drudge who bound them beaten with knotted ropes to show him how they were tied. The flogged man was given a chance at redemption, and his next attempt showed no mercy: he tied Dove's wrists together, palms outwards, around the wooden post so that any unexpected movement threatened to break both her arms. His wrath was great; she was forced to stand for hours on end, following the rhythm of the caravan and praying to the gods for a smooth journey.

Twice, she was let down to sleep, but she did not recall them ever stopping to set up camp. Each time she came to, she noticed their numbers had gotten smaller. Men had fallen behind the shroud of the forest and never resurfaced. The Spades kept track of those who disappeared but did not look back; Dove assumed they would deal with them later. Bounty hunters needed something to do, and their purses would swell by dawn.

She forced her eyes open. They had definitely reached the Thousand Shards. It was the faint smell of seawater that gave it away. It caught on the winds, clung to the trees. Fog softened the torch-fire into a dim glow. It seemed like a calming night, but fear pulsed through her veins in bursts. It hit her like cold water that the end of their journey meant the end of hers.

Dove closed her eyes and sighed. She had spent a lot of time watching them, and slowly, she was able to piece together their system: the more gold lined their armor, the more certain she was that they did not belong to the General's ranks. The Spades may have been bound to the Summoner, but it did not look like they cared much for wealth. Their accents betrayed dialects, which did not reflect the upper classes. Some even bore caste-marks on their necks and foreheads. That surprised her the most.

At least one good thing came from the Purge. It had spared her that humiliation. She was supposed to have been inked with a black cross on her neck—the symbol of humility—but anyone who saw it would know what she really was: broken. A seal branded onto cripples. Gryff's affliction should have earned him one years ago, but since he worked in the Scriptorium, he bore the sign of the learned: a novice four-pointed star. She had been happy for him, of course, but envious. Being marked as deadweight was nothing to look forward to, even though her caste-mark would have had four points, too.

Occasionally, she would catch a name. Valk was easy. Skandar was the one with missing fingers and inked waves on his neck, and he took the most pity on her. He slipped her some of his own food and water through the tear in the canvas, showed kindness. The dark-skinned one with the pleasant smile trailed behind them, Sun-jo, Sun-jo he was called …

What are you doing? Dove sighed. They were escorting her to her own execution, and she was busy learning their names. Then again, it might prove useful in the afterlife. She would haunt every single one of them to their graves.

Hysterical laughter threatened to burst from her chest like a fountain, but it only renewed the pain in her bones. Finally, the wagon halted, and when she heard the men dismount and untie their saddlebags, she realized they had not just stopped to feed and water the horses.

They had arrived.

Oh. Dove leaned her head against the wooden post. It would take them more than a few precious moments to unload and set up camp. What would they do if they caught her sleeping, anyway? Execute her? She would take her chances. She relaxed her muscles as her mind drifted blissfully into the shadows, where the stars finally shone.

***

The sound of screeching iron pulled her back into the waking world. Sleep had breathed new life into her mind, and her thoughts raced like bolts of lightning. *Just a moment longer ...*

Something large crashed against the side of the caravan. Instinctively, Dove shifted her weight with the momentum, but something felt different. She tried to move her arm but found that it was already free. Rope clung weakly to her wrist, cut just before the knot.

Dove opened her eyes and saw the camp through the canvas. The Purge of Edenn had begun. She propped herself up on her elbows and scoured the crowd for the General, but Valerya was nowhere to be found.

Instead, Valk stepped into the caravan. Her muscles tensed. She may have feared him less than the others, but he was still a Hound in a sea of wolves. All his courtesy meant nothing when balanced against the edge of a sword.

"You've lasted longer than most of the Swordsworn," he said, firmly but respectfully, as he cut through the rest of her binds. The gleam of gold took her by surprise. She had tried to look for something, anything, that would give him away, but everything he wore was standard issue. There were no favors, no family name, no colors to distinguish him. It was the golden hilt of his dagger that took all the glory.

"The first wave is over," he said, lifting her to her knees. "Our General wishes to see you before the second wave begins."

That was a terrible sign. *Take me. Take me, Neva,* Dove pleaded to the goddess of mercy. She had prayed to the gods only a few times before, but she did not know how it worked. Would Neva

꧁ 40 ꧂

emerge from the trees and claim her? Or did miracles only happen after a lifetime of faith? Dove recalled all the times she had fallen asleep at the temple. *Damn it.* She had even slept through the paper-burning ceremony in Myrne, when all the villagers in the Dragontail gathered and prayed for good harvest. The night after that, the Hounds came …

Valk loosened his grip. "Nothing is broken," he said, smiled. Dove wondered when he had last dealt with civilians. Did he have a family? Maybe he had only his brothers-in-arms and their leader. She did not know much about the Spades, but it would not have been surprising.

Slowly, Dove felt warmth return to her limbs. She flexed the fingers of her right hand but did not let him see. The last thing she wanted was to give this Spade her gratitude. Valk escorted her out of the caravan, and she caught a glimpse of his face under wild tangles of brown hair. It was not as soft as his voice. Scars were chiseled onto his jaw, but he wore them well. Dark rings formed around his eyes like he had not slept in days, but the auburn in them betrayed fire.

From his accent, she guessed he was from the North. Before they took her, she had never left the Dragontail, but he did not sound like anyone she knew, so the North was as good a guess as any. It was foreign to her, but not unpleasant. Combined with his deep voice, it was almost soothing to listen to.

Valk bound her hands with cloth, but it was much looser than before. "Apologies," he said as he pulled the ends into a final knot. His gauntlets were bigger than her head, but they clung to him like a second skin. Knots posed no great challenge.

The apology caught her off-guard, but her heart warmed. It was a courtesy, nothing more, but a single candle still softened the shadows, and she needed one in her final moments. She felt her senses sharpen as she took in the last sights and smells of her life. The forest was suddenly rank with the scent of horse and sweat, and she swore she could hear whispers carry over from the farthest tent. But the stars were still shrouded in fog, and the night seemed darker, more weighted with mystery.

Dove felt the Spade's gauntlet at her back. He steered her through the swarm, glancing over his shoulder every time they turned a corner. Dove had a sinking feeling that no one was supposed to know where they were going. Not that anyone was paying attention. The drudges were busy running about while the Spades who caught her gaze turned a blind eye to their activities. It was not a comforting feeling.

Finally, they reached the General's tent, and Dove frowned. *How long was I asleep?*

The General was sharpening her sword when they entered, and Dove stared, surprised. Now that they were not in the skin-crawlers' lair, she could see the blade in all its glory. It was Fire-forged and as wide as her neck; surely it would have no trouble slicing through it. *Royal executioner indeed.* At least it would be swift.

"It must be strange seeing the killing blade," said the General without looking up. The sudden presence of company did nothing to interrupt her task, and impatience tore through her voice as though Dove had come to die too early. The General set down her whetstone and rose. "How does it look out there?"

She was talking to Valk, but her gaze was fixed on Dove. Dove felt something coil inside her, but she did not know if it was fear or admiration. Or *relief.* After all, if she was going down, it might as well be at the hands of the Blood Queen. At least no one in the afterlife could say her death was boring.

"The usual," answered Valk. "The Spades await your command, and the rest are scouring the forest for escapees."

"Tell them to cease the hunt. Our orders are to burn down the village, not hunt rats. And if the escapees are *Fireborne*," she said, turning to Dove, "they won't burn no matter how often we set them on fire. This one knows."

The air tightened with her words. *The dragon is here,* Dove realized. Sweat iced over her skin, and for a blink of an eye, a shadow hung overhead, blocked out the torchlight. Fear beat out from her chest. It was the first time she had been in such close quarters with it. Before, they had always been at the castle, with vast chambers and more people to fill out the space. In the tent, there was no one else to share its attention.

Dove felt her resolve shrink until she could almost see it vanish. There was no way anyone could win against those odds.

Valerya lifted her sword to eye level like it was made of paper. Content, she set it down. "Quickly. Before I take their heads, as well."

Dove believed it. The blade looked like it could cut through a draft horse. A few necks would warm it up some.

As much as she tried, she could not take her eyes off its gleam. And then she could not take her eyes off its wielder. The General's hair was a shade lighter than the Spade's, but less unkempt, and her face bore two scars that ran down the left side of her face. They were old but ran deep like dry riverbeds. There was no trace of softness there, and even her eyes were the color of cold, hard stone.

Fascination soon gave way to shame. *She is a murderer,* she reminded herself, *and she will murder me, too.*

Valk bowed his head. "As you command," he said. "And the girl?"

"Leave her here."

He loosened his grip on Dove's arm and bowed again, this time to signal his leave. *Come back,* she thought desperately, but he left without looking back. She closed her eyes and leaned forward, pressed her cheek against the dirt. *I will return to the ground soon,* she thought, feeling blades of grass prickle against the side of her face. *And when I do, I will haunt him first.*

Slowly, the General walked over. Five steps crunched against forest litter like a cruel countdown to her fate. Dove felt the cold touch of metal press against her cheek.

It will be quick, at least. She recalled its sharpness and held her breath. Steel forged from elemental Fire was the only thing that could cut through blackwood, and now that it had been whetted, it would slice through her like butter. It would be so easy to end the hunger, the suffering. All the thoughts in her head had become so heavy, they weighed her down like a massive boulder. With one swift movement, she would be free from it all …

Stupid, she thought. *Not like this.* She struggled to find a memory to hold onto until the bitter end, but all she could think of was how terribly, unnecessarily theatrical it was for the Summoner General to behead a village nobody from the Dragontail.

Without warning, the Blood Queen swung her blade downwards. It was swift and painless and there was no blood. Dove braced herself for the sting, but when she opened her eyes, she saw that her binds were cut. She stretched her fingers and turned her palms over in disbelief. She did not even care about the scars on her hand. At least she still had hands. Life surged back to her in waves, washed over the aches in her limbs. Fear swerved into relief, joy, and one thing became clear: she was not ready to go yet.

"Stand," the General commanded, but it was easier said than done. The best Dove could do was sit on her knees. The General crouched down until they were face-to-face, and Dove sensed it.

Her Fire. Dove had encountered Fire-casters before, but even next to the strongest, it never felt more than a tingling sensation. A spider crawl against her skin. She had felt it in Morian in his fits of rage, especially when he was close enough to touch.

With Valerya, it felt like the beast was in the tent with them, breathing down her neck. Its presence curled through her veins like smoke.

Valerya broke the silence. "Your mark," she said. "*Your caste-mark,* girl. Did your ears disappear with your voice?"

Dove shook her head, pulled her hair away from her neck.

The General contemplated her. "You're young. I suppose they would have given you a black cross. A sign of ... *humility.*"

Dove nodded.

"Oh, you're fine with that?" snapped the General as she rose. Spite tore through her voice like parchment. "Then you deserve it."

Dove stared back, shocked. She frowned. *But I am just a ...* she thought, trying to find the right words. *No one.*

"You're quick. You can outrun me and my men, and you have enough wits about you to survive as long as you did. Can you read?"

Dove reddened, nodded. She had often helped Gryff in the Scriptorium, copying manuscripts whenever his affliction prevented him from leaving the house. She hated it, but she would go back to her boring life in an instant if she had known what the alternative was.

"You can read," repeated Valerya impatiently as she sat in her chair. "You are able-bodied, sharp, and literate. And you would have let them brand you a cripple?" Her eyes narrowed as she leaned forward. "No wonder you are here now."

Dove felt cold metal against the side of her face again, but this time, it was from the General's gauntlet. "I am talking to you," she said coldly, forcing her to look up. She brushed her own hair back, revealing a hammer on the side of her neck. *The mark of a metal-smith.* Dove tried in vain to hide her surprise.

"King Avander wanted it changed when I arrived at the Citadel. A sword. Or a dragon. I refused," she said, and for a brief moment, her face threatened a smile. She nodded towards her blade. "We are either a product of our choices or the choices others have made for us. Do not allow others that power."

The General took Dove's left hand and turned it over in hers, exposing the two slashes on her palm that Morian had been particularly proud of. Warmth washed over her like a gentle bath when she felt the presence of Fire. It made her sleepy, but as quickly as it came, it vanished.

"He went easy on you," said Valerya. She paused, looked at her for a long moment. Silence bled like an open wound. Without another word, Valerya made her way to the other end of the tent and opened a cupboard. "Here," she said, handing her a piece of bread. Dove stared at it like she had never seen one before.

"It's not poison," the General snapped. "If I wanted to kill you, poison would be a stupid choice. Take it."

Dove obeyed. She had not thought about food in days, but now that it was right in front of her, the hunger returned. She bit into it, feeling the bread scratch against her throat. She coughed it out.

If the General felt anything—pity, anger, or even joy—she took great care to show none of it. Instead, she filled a cup with water and handed it to her. "Drink."

This time, Dove wasted no thought on propriety. She took the cup in her hands and drank, emptying it in three gulps. Hot water spilled from the cup, ran down her mouth. It raged through her, and she felt relief at its warmth. They drank it cold at the Citadel, but in the villages, it was usually too dirty to drink without boiling.

Dove had missed the taste.

"Some things don't change for us," said Valerya when she noticed her reaction.

Dove nodded absently as she tried to eat the bread again.

"You'll choke," was all the She-Jackal said. She kept her eyes fixed on the slashes on Dove's palm, and Dove clenched her fist to hide them from view.

"Our King brands all his squires," said Valerya. "He had the last one branded with the colors of his house."

Dove frowned. Morian's banners bore no real sigil—only colors of red and dark red.

"He did not use any ink," said the General, and it took Dove a moment to realize what that meant. The image alone almost made her retch, but she wanted to keep her last meal in her stomach.

Valerya nodded towards her blade again. "He use one of those?"

Dove nodded reluctantly. Morian's blade had not been as long— and not nearly as sharp—but it could still hack its way through trouble with the right amount of determination. Pain returned at the memory.

"Up," the General commanded, and Dove got to her feet. It suddenly got very cold, as though the gods had come valiantly to her aid, saw the She-Jackal, and retreated. Yet as frightened as she was of Valerya, she felt a bizarre urge to be near her, to be safe. It was a strange feeling to have towards one's executioner, she knew, but they had both been commoners once, torn from everything they had known.

Right, Dove. You two are practically the same, she thought, feeling foolish. *Except where Valerya lost her humanity and became the Guardian of the Realm, you lost your life and ended up food for the crows. Practically the same.*

Dove turned away, and her gaze fell on a foreign coin on the General's desk. It stood out against the solemn colors of the tent, and even without seeing it clearly, she knew what was on it: four intertwining flames carved into the center of the coin, with an outer rim cast in silver. She had only seen it once, and ages ago—in Gryff's possession.

"Do you recognize that coin?" asked the General as Dove's heart began to hammer. Panic spread to her limbs. Desperation turned into something uglier.

The General leaned forward and studied Dove's face. "This came into my possession twelve years ago. It belonged to a man far more powerful than I was," she said as the corners of her lips turned upwards into a cold smile. "I ended him."

Dove was so relieved that she did not care how terrifying her statement was. She touched the metal with her fingers and turned it over in her palm. *Where have I seen this before?* She ran through all the possibilities in her mind. Gryff had to write things for important people all the time. Could one of them have paid with it?

Dove glanced at the coin. Markings lined the silver rim, and she barely recognized it as Glasgérian. It looked like a child had carved it with a blunt blade. She knew the first word meant knowledge, but what was *mazhyr* again? She frowned, exasperated. It was an impossible language with too many consonants, and each syllable could be read three different ways.

"Knowledge means power," said the General for her. "Those who believe that don't last long in this world. As I said … the former owner of that coin was far more *powerful* than I was."

Dove wondered if Valerya was capable of saying anything that was not terrifying, but she set the coin down, wondering if the night would ever end. She knew death was waiting for her. Sharing words with her executioner did not soften the blow.

"Your parents. Are they still alive?" the General asked as she leaned back in her chair.

Dove blinked back surprise. In a normal world, the question would have been mundane, boring, but under the circumstances, it was disconcertingly intimate. She shook her head.

"Were they half-breeds?"

Dove nodded, suddenly defensive. The hairs on the back of her neck bristled. Her parents had been half-Fire, half-Ice, but blood meant nothing to her. Her true parents had left her in the forest to die, for a voiceless child was cursed in the eyes of the gods. She did not know of any culture that believed otherwise. In some villages, they even sacrificed them to prevent the curse from spreading. It was Gryff's parents who took her in, and she loved them for it.

But perhaps their belief was not all too misguided, she thought, overcome with another urge to laugh. *They are dead, my village is gone, and Gryff* ... No, he was alive. He had to be. Otherwise, what good was she?

"Dove, is it? A pretty name," said the General, and Dove realized she was mocking her. "Tell me, do you agree with the inscription?"

Dove winced as though the General had inflicted a curse upon her. The situation seemed much more intense now that she had said her name. She wanted to shake her head but had a feeling that Valerya would know she was lying.

Dove took a deep breath and nodded.

"Then tell me why Morian is sitting on the throne," said the General. "Why I hold your life in my hands. Why the carrier of that coin had to die twelve years ago." For a moment, a shade of emotion flickered across her eyes, but then it was gone. Only the cold remained.

Dove wanted nothing more than to drop her gaze and walk to her death with her head hanging, but the more she looked at the General, the harder it was to look away. The General met her gaze every time, but her expression was impossible to read. Dove had often heard that killing cleaved one's soul in two, and the next cleaved that in two, and so on, and so on, until there was nothing left. She believed it. If she had not seen it with her own eyes, she would have never believed the things that men were capable of.

And women ...

Dove did not want to know how many lives Valerya had ended, but the woman sitting across from her was difficult to reconcile with the She-Jackal she had so often heard about. It was easy to despise the villain in the Scrolls. Valerya, on the other hand ...

The General removed her right gauntlet and opened a drawer. Without warning, she rose from her chair.

Dove's fear returned. The General may have been admirable from a distance, but that was as far as she was willing to go. Children's tales or not, legends had some kernel of truth in them.

To her surprise, the General handed her a pile of clean clothes. Dove became painfully aware that she had been wearing the same rags for weeks, and she could no longer tell if it was dirt or blood that stained them.

"You were once in our King's service," said the General calmly as she sat back in her chair. "You will not die dressed as a gutter rat."

The familiarity, the wave of comfort that Dove had felt inside the General's tent, died a slow, miserable death at her words, and she stared blankly at the clothes in her hand. They were soft, like someone had actually paid a hefty sum for them. Morian had given her nice things to wear, but they were never this soft.

Surely it cannot get any worse, thought Dove, sighing. She did not want to find out what would happen if she refused the She-Jackal's offer. She placed the clothes on top of the desk, catching a quick glimpse of the map covering it. It revealed nothing of her fate.

Awkwardly at first, she reached down to remove her shirt. The General watched wordlessly, her gaze following Dove's hands. Dove pulled it over her head and closed her eyes. She found it often helped with the pain, and in truth, she had already seen her bruised and broken body enough times to know what it looked like.

Same thing, different people, she thought as she felt her fingers shake, but she forced herself to continue. Shivering, she removed everything else and opened her eyes. In her mind, she had been braver, but when the tent swarmed back into her vision, everything hit her with a vengeance. She was doomed.

"Wait," said the General, walking towards her. With her left hand, she took the shirt from Dove's hands while the right rested gently on her shoulder. It slowly moved along her contour, and Dove winced whenever she touched upon a bruise. The back of the General's hand glided back up until it reached Dove's face. It was not cold, like she had expected, and she wondered if the General could sense her fear.

It is fear, right?

Suddenly, the General pulled away and made her way to her desk. "Valk!" she shouted.

The apologetic Spade reentered the tent, never far away from his master's command. Dove suddenly felt mortified that she was bare, but he did not seem to notice. Instead, he kept a respectful distance and looked past her, like she was not even there. "General," he said and bowed his head.

"It's time for the second wave," she said as she strapped her gauntlet back on. "I do not like the feel of this forest."

"As you command," said Valk, bowing again as he took his leave. It was only when he was gone that the General looked up from her map.

"Are you uncomfortable?" she asked.

The question took Dove aback. She could think of fewer situations that were more uncomfortable. Not long ago, she was offered guest-right in the General's tent. It may have been bread and water, but it still constituted the tradition. She did not know when it all went downhill.

"Come closer," said Valerya, and Dove obeyed until she could almost feel her breath on her skin. Dove desperately avoided her gaze, but she repeated her question. "Do I make you uncomfortable?"

Dove bit her lip and nodded.

The General laughed. "Honesty. A brave man's weapon, but a fool's end. But where does the difference lie?" She thrust the garments into Dove's hands. "Get dressed."

This time, Dove made it quick before anyone else could come in. The General turned her attention back to her map. "That will be all," she said coldly. "Wait outside. You will accompany me on the second wave. You will watch Edenn burn, after which you will be put to the sword."

Dove stared at her blankly, but the General did not look back up. "*Leave*," she repeated, raising her voice so that it carried over to the farthest end of the tent. She would not say it again.

Heart pounding, Dove took her leave. Moments ago, she would

have given anything to leave the tent. But now …

Valk grabbed her arm before she got too far. She did not even see him there, though it was not surprising that he was waiting by the entrance. He had probably heard everything, too. "Apologies," he said when her body tensed. "I'm afraid I have to."

And there they stood, watching, waiting. Dove sighed and kept her eyes on the ground. *What an interesting life it has been after all,* she thought, recalling all the times she had dreamed of leaving the Dragontail. Since then, she had survived the purge of Myrne, served as squire to the king, and shared words with the General in her final moments. She knew of no one else who could say the same.

But General acted as though their encounter had never happened.

And that, strangely, felt like torture.

5

PORT HAVEN
FIRE REALM

The moment Decker stepped out of the tavern, the world began to spin. When he closed his eyes, colors wove through his mind like threads, each latching onto one of his senses. Sight sharpened. Touch exploded into shards of glass. A whisper became a shout that sawed back and forth between his ears. *Damn ale,* he thought as he tried to regain sure footing. Kiera had failed to mention how much blackwood sap Mads had added, and it wasn't until the tavern-keeper sprouted horns that he realized his mind was playing tricks on him.

Never share ale with a Lancistierrean. What should have smelled like smoke from the burning forest came to him rich and sweet like perfume. Heat clung to him like a fever where it should have been cold, and instead of fear, an unsettling calm. He could see why the sap had been popular tonight. It certainly took the edge off the sting, but it also took the edge off everything else. The others may have enjoyed shrouding their fear with bright, colorful distractions, but Decker wanted out.

Laughter drowned out all sound as he lost his balance, nearly pummeling into one of the merchants he had seen earlier in the tavern. "Byou di'a hashi," said the man in gruff Lancistierrean. The Waterborne were the only people in Port Haven *not* drunk tonight. Decker could make out their words, but none of them registered in his mind. He had studied the language briefly to get his Wings, but forgot everything after he became first helmsman ... ten years ago.

"Dou kanshi you," Decker shot back automatically, the only phrase he remembered. He had meant it as a quick apology, but the man's brows furrowed as though Decker had just insulted his mother.

Fucking ale, cursed Decker to himself, forcing his eyes shut.

"Dou kanshi you!" he repeated as he forced his way forward, but this time, it came out louder and more slurred. More laughter followed, half-cruel, half-amused. He wondered if he was saying it right, but his tones were all over the place. He wouldn't have been surprised if he insulted all their mothers.

Decker stopped and rested his hands on his knees. He recalled an old mind-trick for overcoming airsickness he had used time and time again as a boy on the *Smuggler.* How did it go again? *First, take yourself out of the town.* That was easy enough to do. No one wanted to be in Port Haven tonight. *Then out of the Realm. Then out of the world, past the sun and the stars, past the gods and the warring Fates, until your problems disappear in the clouds ...*

Decker groaned as he felt his insides lurch. *Twenty years later and you're still using that trick.* Even Nan, in all her fourteen years of wisdom, would call him a novice. Easy for her to say. As a Waterborne, she couldn't get drunk even if she tried. *Enviable.* They never got drunk. They never got sick. They never got *old.*

He staggered a few more steps before falling to his knees. Somehow, he had imagined his evening to go quite differently—not coughing and sputtering in front of the tavern like the town drunk. *Drunk, sick, and getting older.* Ten years ago, the ale would have coursed through him like water, and he would have gotten up at dawn like nothing happened. Now, he didn't even have to wait until morning to feel the weight in his limbs, and tomorrow meant a special kind of misery reserved only for those who made stupid decisions.

The doors swung open behind him as he tried to regain his bearings. "All right there?" Merc asked, amused. The effects of the Sap made his hair look so red that it looked like his head was on fire. "That seeker made me come out to see if you were still alive. Haven't you ever had the Sap before?"

"No," said Decker. "But I like to learn by doing." Blackwood was such a rare commodity outside the Firelands, and even when they had spare bottles lying around the *Smuggler,* it never interested him—precisely for this reason. Merc loved it, but Decker didn't much like losing control of his senses.

"Apparently, medicans use it in the Scarlet Cities to calm grief," said Merc, grinning. "I won't lie. A couple of sips and I feel fucking fantastic. You?"

"Slightly," Decker lied as he felt the Sap pound against his skull. There were too many things that demanded his attention, too many sounds and colors, and he had trouble focusing. "I didn't know it would work so fast."

"You didn't have to down *three.* No one downs three."

"Special circumstances," Decker said as he got to his feet with all the dignity he could muster. Ale gave him courage, and he wanted to see the dragon at least once in his life. He had slept on sheets with it embroidered across the blanket, sat in outhouses carved with its symbols, but he had never actually seen one summoned before. And if the beast's temper matched that of its summoner, at least his last memory would be glorious.

"Are you trying to get yourself killed?" Merc grabbed him by the cloak, and Decker felt the straps close around his throat. He unhooked the clasp and felt the burden lift from his shoulders as the cloak slid off his back. He felt much lighter without it, like his weight could be carried by the breeze. "*Ro-than,*" he heard Merc curse, letting it fall to the ground. "No more Sap for you, ever."

Decker ignored him and plowed through the streets. *The Empire all over again,* he thought. It had fallen centuries before their time, but he imagined it to have been just like this: terror that burned red like wine and flames that tore scars into the sky. The Sap made it feel like he was walking untouched through a nightmare. Every sound shook him to the core, but there was a certain detachment to it, like he was watching it from a distance. *Is this even real?* he wondered as he saw scarlet tear into violet and amber across the skies.

But it was the ash that brought him back to the waking world. *Ash doesn't belong with the living,* he thought as he breathed it in—and coughed. The Purge was much harder to ignore now that they were shrouded in smoke, and no amount of Sap could soften the pain in his chest.

Edenn was burning.

"Think we'll see the dragon tonight?" Merc asked beside him, and Decker could tell from the break in his voice that he was scared. Dragons were only admirable from afar; up close, they were terrifying. Nightmares personified. Just knowing one was there ran chills down his spine.

They halted just before the short wall that connected two watch-towers, that tiny strip of stone that separated Port Haven from the rest of the mainland. Great doors were set squarely in the center and clamped shut by a wooden bar. Just that morning, Decker had seen nothing but green and a sky so blue it would make a blind man cry. But now it was dry and dead, like swirls of fire had strangled the trees.

Decker's gaze fell on two sentries manning the wall. He could only make out their silhouettes, but their attention was focused on the other side. *They can see Edenn from there,* he realized. *Maybe they're waiting for the dragon too.* Avantys rarely made its appearance, but Decker supposed Valerya saw no need to keep it in the waking world for long. She was half-beast herself, and the world already belonged to her and that thing.

He would take his chances. The sentries posed no real threat, anyway. Their king had ordered all able-bodied soldiers to service and sent the scraps to man the borders. To defend the Realm, he claimed. *Horseshit.* The Hounds had always been invaders.

Decker approached the gate and ran his hand along the bar that kept it locked from the inside. It took a couple of tries, but he managed to pry it loose.

"Tell me you're joking," said Merc, not even bothering to whisper. Reproach clouded his features. "Now what? Do you mean to bludgeon the She-Jackal to death with that thing?"

Damn it, Merc, thought Decker when he saw the sentries turn. He suspected they had known they were there but chosen to ignore them—until now. Perhaps talk of assassinating their highest officer called for a different reaction. He let the bar drop. *Double damn,* he thought when he recognized their faces.

"YOU!" the sentry on the left bellowed as Decker cursed Merc's existence. To him, all Hounds looked the same, but he remembered that voice. It shouted at roughly the same level of outrage that morning, when Decker threw a stone at its owner's head. *"Get back!"*

Merc yelled back something unintelligible, but ash smothered his words. They were not off to a good start.

"What did you say?" shouted the smaller one on the right. His helm looked so big on him that it looked like it blunted his hearing, and he took it off. He was dark-skinned and looked grown, but his voice still cracked under pressure.

Decker frowned. In Divisorya, the kid would be in school, and with that accent, the girls would be all over him. They loved Realmborn accents up there, especially "original" Sinthean—not the rounded, watered-down version they spoke in the floating city. If the boy had been born in a different place, he could have been a mage or a medican in ten years. Not wasted as decoration on a wall.

"I GOT HIM!" bellowed Merc as he made his way towards Decker with all the grace of a dying ox. *"I'll bring him back!"* He let his voice drop when he approached. "What are you doing?"

"Now you're whispering?" snapped Decker.

"Get back!" the boy warned again, and Decker saw gold gleam on his armor. It took grown men years to be able to afford that sliver of gold, and for most, it was their crowning glory. This one looked born with it on his back. Wealth had gotten him up there, nothing more.

"C'mon then, boy," said his companion with a sneer. He looked older and rougher around the edges, with more than a hint of bitterness at having to patrol with a child. "Let's get rid of them." He disappeared from view, but Decker could hear him cursing all the way down. He was a big man by their standards, but he only came up to Decker's ears. This time, however, he didn't let that stop him.

"Damn, look at that rust," Decker heard Merc whisper. Merc had once apprenticed under a smith before joining the *Smuggler,* which made him critical of people's armor. In truth, he had dabbled in all sorts of trades, from baking to shipbuilding, but nothing seemed to hold his interest for long. Only alchemy, strangely enough. He knew every plant that could be used to enhance metal or cure illness. He claimed it made him a good bartender.

Decker tried to stand, but the world clashed around him in vengeful waves. *So much for a quick getaway,* he thought, reminding himself to never accept drinks from strangers—especially Lancistierrean women. If he survived this night, he would never drink again. He could already feel it swirl in his stomach.

"Seriously?" Merc asked. *"Now?"* He turned and thrust an arm out towards the sentry. "Don't come any closer!" he warned.

The sentry drew his sword. "Is that a threat?" he demanded, shoving Merc's arm aside with the side of his blade. Decker glimpsed a misshapen sword inked onto the side of his neck as though he had once belonged to another trade but covered it up when he joined the Swordsworn.

"Your loss, Captain," said Merc, shrugging. "Don't say I didn't warn you."

The sentry ignored him. "You. Glasger," he said, tapping Decker's shoulder with the flat of his blade. "What's wrong with you?"

"I'm not a Glasg—" began Decker as he felt the final lurch. Before he could stop himself, all three ales ended up on the sentry's boots, masking the rust and dirt. *Well,* thought Decker, closing his eyes as the cursing began. *At least I won't have a headache tomorrow.*

"Hey!" his companion screamed, making his way down. He was smaller and faster, with soft features and eyes that had not yet seen many evils. Even in the dark, they burned. "Wait," he said, squinting. "Hey, it's those punks from earlier!"

"What a fucking joy. I didn't notice," muttered his companion, shaking his leg. Ale splashed out in front of them, and he spat on the ground. "Our General is doing us a huge fucking service getting rid of your kind." He turned to his companion. "Maybe we should just let them cross, eh?"

The comment took his companion by surprise, and malice melted off the boy's face. *Too young for this shit,* Decker thought. Suddenly, the kid looked much too small for his armor, like someone had thrown it on him and told him to march up the wall. "That … I don't think …"

Poor pup, thought Decker, watching him squirm. Maybe they were born with hearts after all. Then they ended up like the other guy.

The boy cleared his throat, trying to reassert his authority. "They should be dealt with according to the law," he said firmly, turning to Decker. "Where are your papers?"

"In myhrrh cloarghhh," Decker managed to sputter.

"Oh, *Ro-than,*" cursed Merc. "They're in his fucking cloak."

"Where's his cloak?"

"Outside the Hub," answered Merc matter-of-factly, as though there were no other place a cloak would dare be.

"They're drunk," said the boy quickly. "Let's just throw them back in the Hub and be done with it. They won't miss us, and no one out there can escape the Blood Queen at this point." His eyes rested briefly on the bar on the ground. "Come on," he said, turning back before his companion could follow his gaze. "The sooner it's over, the sooner they'll go back to wherever they're from."

"Fine, fine, my *liege.* I swear…" muttered his companion, disappointed, as he forced Decker to stand. "Fuck," he said. "He's a heavy one."

It took all of Decker's willpower to bite back an insult. "Do you even smell the ash?" he asked before closing his eyes. Then the world around him faded to black.

6

EDENER FOREST
FIRE REALM

Dove wondered if the rumors were true. *If I am going to die anyway,* she thought, *I would love to see a dragon.* Her lips curved into a guilty smile when she imagined Gryff's face. They had always talked about what a Summoning would be like. Dove had no real concept of it. She pictured a dragon-shaped cloud, but that was as far as it got. Gryff claimed it was a fiery beast that cracked the sky in two, sending stars blazing to the ground like burning rags. He always had the more vivid imagination. If Myrne had still been standing, they would have found the highest hill in the Dragontail and watched it from afar. She had read in the Scrolls that even in its mortal form, Avantys had been shining and majestic. Beautiful.

Stupid girl. Even wolf pups were cute until they were ripping flesh off dead deer.

Valk halted, and the Swordsworn behind them followed suit. Without Valerya, he must have been in charge; the older Spades obeyed without question, and the drudges kept their distance.

For a moment, Dove wondered why they were stopping in the middle of nowhere—until she realized they were already in Edenn.

Or what was left of it, anyway. Its scorched remains wavered in the heat. Thousands of red-hot needles hung suspended in air, but when they fell, they were gentle and soft like rain.

Dove looked up, expecting stars, but even they were hiding from the Summoning. Instead, the sunless sky burned brighter than day, and it was only when she shifted her attention back to the village that she could see the destruction with razor-sharp clarity.

Dead. All of it was dead. Flames licked at what had once been the gate to the forest, and Dove understood at once why they called it the Thousand Shards. Once, a flame caught on her sleeve at the shoulder, but Valk killed it with his gauntlet. *Fire-forged,* she recalled, half-conscious of her burning surroundings. Fire could not harm him, but scalding metal could still melt the skin off his bones—unless it was Fire-forged. It had one use, at least. This was the nicest shirt she had ever worn. It would be a shame to waste such a gift before it fulfilled its purpose.

Valk pulled her past the front line of Spades who watched the burning with disinterest. He relaxed his grip on her arm, but it was not like she had anywhere to run. The Spades were behind her, and the drudges behind them. And behind *them …*

The winds around her tensed, bringing the noise around her to a deep hum as though her head had been submerged in water. *She is here.* If Dove closed her eyes and concentrated, she could even sense where. Valerya's elements were so strong that they almost called out to her.

Suddenly, Dove heard the wordless salute of twenty gauntlets slam against metal. Valk released her arm at the sound, but she wished he would hold on for a bit longer. Out of all the Spades, she liked him the most. *A Hound in a pack of wolves,* she reminded herself, *but still the lesser evil.* He looked like the type to laugh at jokes and smile if it meant being courteous, but forced niceness was better than nothing.

"Step forward," he said coldly, destroying her illusion.

And that was that. She had spent the last moments of her life with these men, memorized their faces. She liked to think they had families of their own, or nice homes, or a history of traveling to exotic, faraway lands … things she would never have. Things she had never thought about until now.

I thought the world would never touch me in Myrne, she thought as her future disappeared before her eyes. No one had heard of it outside the Dragontail, or inside the Dragontail, for that matter. *I am sorry, Gryff. I am so sorry I could not find you.*

As much as she tried to stay focused, her mind took her back to the strangest things. How the trees smelled on her tenth birthday, when her father took her out hunting for the first time. How clearly she could see the stars when she snuck Gryff out to enjoy the fresh air. How their mother nearly flogged them to death when she found out. *I will see you soon,* she promised her parents. That, at least, was a vow she could keep.

"Here, girl," the General snapped, as if commanding a dog.

Dove obeyed. There was not much else she could do.

The General turned her gaze skyward, and Dove followed. *This is it.* The spectacular show everyone had promised her. She had expected something so grandiose that she nearly missed the ball of light forming above them, unremarkable against the glow of Tavandir. It looked little more than a star, but the others stared at it like moths drawn to a flame.

The mereyn, thought Dove. It held a different meaning in every culture, but in hers, it was translated as "circle"—that ring of light that roused the dragon from its slumber. There were those who believed it controlled everything, that it brought balance to the world of the living.

But it was not the mereyn that caught her eye. The smoke and ash that covered the stars suddenly parted. It was slow at first, but after the fog broke, there was no turning back. An intense red shattered the clouds into fractures of color that danced across the trees. Whatever was breaking through to the waking world was feeding off the mereyn's energy, and before long, the mereyn itself glowed red, overshadowing the ascendant star.

The dragon had come.

Through it, fire donned a spirit, and the flames that devoured Edenn soared towards the sky. Black, red, and purple came together, but it was not the sorcery she had imagined or the blood tales children swapped in the dark. It was the elements in their purest form, a soul without a body. And it was beautiful.

Suddenly, a deep red scar flashed across the face of the sky and began to widen, opening a window into a world beyond. *The sky is tearing,* thought Dove, but just when she thought she could see beyond the wound, an earsplitting roar brought her hands to her ears. The dragon that emerged through the tear was no conjuration in the clouds. It looked real. Dove could see every scale, every flicker of fire as Avantys came to life. It shook its head, irate, as it opened its eyes. Centuries of slumber before Valerya had done nothing to soften its temper.

Suddenly, a violent rush of heat overwhelmed them. The creature spread its wings and soared high, high into the skies until its flames blocked out the moon and the stars, bathing the land around them in scarlet. Dove heard another terrible roar before she saw it descend full force onto Edenn. In a blink of an eye, both creature and village disappeared in a cacophony of sound. Flames flowed outward from where the dragon met the earth, and inside, Dove screamed.

All about her, the night came to life with a thousand bright hues that the dragon had made its own. She felt the blast of it in her bones, and the ground began to shudder. *Will it shatter like the sky?* she wondered as the night disappeared in a blazing inferno. But before the flames could reach her, they stopped, swerved. The General had cast a protective circle around them, and no matter how fierce the fire raged, they were no match for it.

Dove felt like they were encased in a glass bubble. Fire beat against the sides, demanding entry. The Swordsworn cast circles of their own, but they disappeared when the General tightened her own shield. Soon, it covered only the two of them.

At least the Summoning lived up to its reputation. Dove dared a glance at the Summoner, but even now, the General was calm. The rush of heat had blown her hair back, and fire gleamed perfectly against her armor. *She is so ... strong,* thought Dove, forgetting her fear. Valerya was fierce and unapologetic, blunt. *Everything I am not.*

Dove saw the flames swell and lash at her, and for the first time, she realized she would burn. Elements left their host after death, and her corpse would no longer be immune to fire. She shivered. For some reason, the thought of burning was scarier than dying.

"Girl," the She-Jackal's voice cut through the roar, commanding her attention like a whip. Dove felt a firm hand force her to her knees. She reached out her arms to keep herself from falling forward.

This is it, thought Dove, ignoring the pain that shot through her knees. She felt a cruel breeze against the back of her neck as she tilted her head forward. The killing moment had come.

"If Neva granted you the chance to do it all over again, would you take it?"

Dove blinked, surprised. *Of course,* she thought defiantly, wondering if she should even nod. *I do not want to be here. I should have ... I should have ...* She paused. Should have what? *Not* sacrificed herself in Myrne so that Gryff could get away? She could not burn, but her brother... the fire would have eaten him alive. Between the two of them, she had stood the better chance of survival, so she took it.

I would not be facing that thing, she thought when she saw Valerya's sword gleam red against the fire. *But then again ...* She lowered her gaze to the ground. *If not me, then him.* Dove glanced up at the She-Jackal, taking in the last face she would ever see, and shook her head. *I suppose I would not have done it differently after all.* She shook her head again, this time with more conviction.

Dove took a deep breath and closed her eyes. *So do it,* she thought as her breathing descended into faltered gasps. Her death wish bordered desperation.

"I will give you a head start," said Valerya instead.

Dove opened her eyes, and a silent cry forced the air from her lungs. For a moment, she sat as still as a statue for fear that she had heard incorrectly. The last thing she wanted was for Valerya to miss because she moved. Even when she turned her head to glance upwards, she made sure her neck stayed in the same place.

The General met her gaze. "Well?" she snapped, unimpressed.

Dove thought she had gone deaf. *Is this a trick?*

"When I lower the flames," Valerya continued, and Dove saw a faint trickle of blood stream from her nose. Flames beat furiously against the sides of her shield, faint and muffled, but the General ignored them. "I will turn. You should run."

Dove stared back dumbly. She could barely stand, let alone run. The General took something out of her side pouch and perused it carefully before stretching out her hand. "Are you voiceless or dumb?" she asked impatiently. "Take it."

The coin from the tent. Reluctantly, Dove obeyed. A strange parting gift, but there was nothing about the evening that went according to plan.

"Perhaps it will bring you more luck than it did the others," said the General, turning away. She nodded towards a path no one could see. "You see that?" she asked. Dove only saw fire but nodded anyway. "There's another entrance to the forest straight ahead. You might make it if you're not stupid enough to get caught."

Dove gaped.

"You should *run*," Valerya repeated, this time with a tone of finality. "I enjoyed your company, but if I catch you, I will show no mercy. Our King has demanded your head."

The General was no longer looking, but Dove nodded as the words settled in. She cast one last glance over her shoulder. Dark figures seemed to bleed into one another, and she became painfully aware of all the weapons they were holding. Some were armed with crossbows, but all had blades tucked behind their cloaks. If one of those arrows hit …

I should not get hit, then. She stuffed the coin into her shirt pocket.

Wordlessly, the General brought the flames down gently with her hand, like she was soothing a child. The fire died obediently, returning to the ground. "And should we meet again and I find a cross on your neck," she said coldly, "I will carve it out myself."

Dove took one last look at Valerya the Fireborne with a sense of longing she could not explain. Her spirits lifted. Suddenly, she did not care if all the crossbows in the world were pointed at her head. The General had given her a chance, and that was all she needed.

"Now."

And Dove ran.

It was like diving headfirst into the sea—the more she ran, the more difficult it became to tell up from down. Flames covered the night. They whipped at her sleeves, peeled them back from her arms. A few times she stumbled, but panic silenced the pain in her limbs.

"Find her!" she heard the General scream.

She set the dogs on me. The ringing in her ears slackened to silence, and the world around her grew dark. *Could I not for once be a normal Fireborne and cast Fire?* she thought miserably, and not for the first time.

Whatever. She would have to make do without it. There were other things to fall back on, like courage. Swiftness. Knowledge of plant-life.

They only grow where night is darkest. She felt around for a stick at her feet and tapped it against a nearby tree, once, twice …

Rise and shine, she thought, relieved when she saw the nightbloom stir. Their petals gave off just enough light for her to make out her surroundings, but they returned to slumber when she passed. She swung her stick at a rock for more light.

Once, she stumbled upon a signpost, but any town marked with a sword and crown was a bad idea. It would be just her luck to stumble into Kingsbridge, the biggest hub for aspiring Swordsworn. Sinthea was too far and much too close to the Citadel for her liking, so that left one possibility: Pot Have.

No. She frowned and wiped away the mud with her finger. *Port Haven.*

It was as good a gamble as any. She was a walking target by herself, and the adrenaline was beginning to wear off. It was though her body suddenly remembered it was broken, and she felt every bruise, every pang of hunger, eat into her reserves.

The first rays of daylight beat through the clouds, but the skies were far from blue. She continued until dirt gave way to cobblestone, which meant that Port Haven must have been close by. The stone path was her best bet; they were well traveled, and if anyone approached, at least she would be able to hear them from afar.

She reached a short wall and rested. Just beyond it lay the gate to the city. Her heart jumped when she saw the watchtowers—and plummeted. First, she had to get past the gate, and sentries were ordered to turn away outsiders during the Purge.

She cursed her appearance. She was covered in ash and smelled of smoke; there was no way in this life or the next that they would believe she was anything but an escaped convict. All they had to do was demand her name and she would be doomed.

Them or them. If the sentries did not cut her down, the men behind her would. She took a deep breath and raised her arms in surrender as she moved cautiously towards the towers. She waited for yelling, a warning shout, but there was nothing.

Then she saw that the watchtowers were empty.

For a moment, she stared. After Morian, she felt like all good signs were traps in disguise. She even half-expected him to step out from behind one of the towers, his stupid, perfect hair unburdened by a crown—he never wore a crown—with eyes that signaled joy or malice, whichever he felt that day.

She walked up to the gate and pressed her hands against the doors. It had looked smaller from afar, but now it towered over her in judgment, no doubt locked from the inside. Her hands found the handle. *I am so close,* she thought as she leaned against it for support …

And fell forward when it opened. She opened her eyes and looked around for signs of life, but no one manned the gates. Her gaze fell on the wooden bar on the ground. Someone must have unlocked the gate, and … what, killed the guards? There were certainly signs of a struggle, footprints forced into the dirt. Dried vomit.

She shut the doors behind her. When she heard them click into place, she felt a wave of relief course through her like water. At least there was a wall separating her from the wolves now, and soon she would walk among the common-folk again—people who walked in plainclothes, not armor, and carried tools of their trade, not weapons. With a little luck and a bit of soap, she could even pass off for one of them.

And then what?

Dove recalled the General's words. *'Should we meet and I find a black cross on your neck, I will carve it out myself.'* No, she would not live out her days as an invalid. She had to get as far away from here as possible. If she had any hope of finding Gryff, she had to survive first.

She took a step forward, and then another, and another, until walking became easy again. The streets were wide, black, and empty. It seemed that all life had gone to the local tavern, which was overflowing with patrons. Another blessing—it would provide the perfect cover from the General's men, and maybe she could find something to eat. *They might even take this as payment,* she thought, feeling the coin through her shirt pocket. It was foreign, but everyone in the tavern looked like an outsider. One of them was bound to recognize it.

She clenched it in her fist. *No,* she thought. She would not part with it.

Dove took a deep breath, but before she could open the door, a brawl erupted in the tavern. She would have missed the orange-haired man, but his voice was loud enough to drown out the sound of breaking glass. *One of us?* He looked more like a Fireborne than she did, but his clothing was too foreign, too eccentric. Goggles dangled from his neck.

Divisoryan, she thought, excited. She had seen drawings of their kind, the strange people who had made the sky their own. It would explain why he was struggling against two armed sentries, though upon closer look, they were forcing him to stay, not leave. The red stripes on their shoulders meant border sentries.

Solves that mystery, thought Dove, hiding from sight. But these outsiders had saved her life in more ways than one—they had to have come from somewhere, after all. Somewhere with big ships and big sails that would take her far, far away.

Dove continued along the main path. Outsiders did not care much for the Purge, and they looked away when they saw her. No one would touch her there. She continued until she saw land disappear into water. Grounded ships loomed in the harbor. Trader ships, no doubt, and mostly foreign. Only the flying ones led to Divisorya.

Most of the ships were painted in proud colors of gold or red or blue. Some of the bigger ones bore beasts as sigils, but there was one that did not. In fact, it was not painted at all, and instead of dragons and jackals, it bore the sign of winged messengers. Dove's eyes quickly passed over the name of the ship: *Smuggler.*

Good enough, she thought, deciding quickly. There was no turning back even if she wanted to. The instant she stepped onto the gangway, she was immediately swept along the current of travelers. Times were lean. No one wanted to spend another second in the Firelands if they could help it. They were smart to get out while they could.

When she reached the ramp to the *Smuggler,* she lunged to the side as if grabbing at a piece of driftwood. Crates and mountains of bags were piled near the entrance. Two cargo handlers were playing cards, doing their best to ignore them. One of them sensed her approach.

"Get lost," he said dismissively, "and don't even think about it." They looked like they could handle themselves, and neither looked up from their game. Her silent, desperate presence must have screamed pickpocket.

No turning back, she told herself. One was dark-skinned and looked to be roughly her age, and the other was tall and heavyset, with a round face that made him look like an overgrown child. His nose looked to be broken in three places, like it was carved of wood.

"All right. Enough is enough." The tall one sighed and tossed his cards on the table. His eyes widened when he turned to her. Pity softened his anger. He looked ready to give her a few coins, and for a moment, he was as voiceless as she was.

"You two. Inside," came a gruff voice from inside the ship.

The man who came out looked like he was fully capable of handling trouble, or had been, once. He was thick-set, but what was once hard muscle had given way to drink and idle days. If she had to hazard a guess, she would have placed him in the Icelands. He and Gryff shared the same wild, black curls of the Glasgers, and he was easily the biggest man on the gangway.

"Forget them," he growled as the handlers scrambled back onto the airship. Scars formed cracks on his face when he talked, and he spoke Sinthean like it was bound to him. "They were raised by bears." When he stepped forward, she drew back. He looked a bit like a bear himself, but his expression softened, or at least tried to. "Let's have a look at you, then."

Dove could tell he had seen thousands of travelers pass through the airship, but none quite like her. The dragon had burned holes into her clothes, and she smelled of smoke. Her entire left side was black and blue.

But it was her unburned skin that gave her away.

"You're one of *them*," he said. "Thought they wanted to get rid of outsiders, not their own." He spat on the ground and cursed when he saw the crates near the entrance. "Useless boys …" he muttered. "Well, no use talking about it. Let's get you cleaned up." He extended an arm, but Dove hesitated when she saw the scars on his hand. They ran down his sleeve and up the side of his neck like someone had tried to cleave him in two. The skin that formed around them had hardened into hide.

To her surprise, the man laughed. "Don't look it, but I was pretty in my day." He slapped her on the back, and she felt the wind leave her lungs. "Maybe you'll get on better with Bright Eyes over there. Hey!" he called, and Dove glanced over her shoulder. "What took you so long?"

Dove blinked, and then blinked some more. Two men were approaching the airship: one was the orange-haired Divisoryan she had seen in the tavern, the one who had saved her from the fury of a thousand arrows. From the way he carried himself, it had been far from the first brawl.

The other was different from anyone she had ever seen. He was tall, perhaps of a height with the scarred man, but somehow … *flawless.* His skin looked as though it had never torn or calloused, but he did not look like a stranger to hard times. *Lancistierrean?* His face matched the descriptions she had read of their kind, but everything else screamed Glasger. Even the way the two of them stood was foreign.

It was easy to see who the scarred man meant when the taller one glanced down at her. Bright Eyes frowned, tried to piece together her presence. "I saw the village burn," he said. He had a deep, pleasant voice, but his first words were dark and bitter.

"And you're going to toss her back, or what?" asked the scarred man, breaking his intense gaze. "Get her inside before the dogs come."

"What makes you so sure she's not dangerous?" asked the orange-haired man as he pointed to her wrist burns. "What if she's a serial killer? Remember what happened when Zan …?"

"Shut up, Merc," the scarred man snapped. "Just for that, she's your responsibility." He yelled a few foreign words at people who stopped to stare. They jolted, continued on their way. "Think carefully, kid," he said, dropping his voice to a near-whisper. "Traders are always looking for quick money, and some of them have probably alerted the bounty hunters by now. There's no going back for you."

"Damn, Wolff. Ease up on the drama," said the traveler in blue. "If she survived *that,* I'm sure she can handle herself." He placed a hand on Dove's back. It made her uncomfortable, but he was worlds better than Greaven. Just recalling his breath against her neck made her skin crawl. It always smelled of rotting meat and ale. "Come on, then. This place will be teeming with your kind soon." He turned to the orange-haired man. "What about you, Merc?"

Merc laughed. "I gave Nan the run-down last time. It's your turn to take in the runt."

The man in blue sighed and steered her inside, away from the scary man with the scarred face, away from the scary men and their Jackal Queen.

The inside of the *Smuggler* was not a friendly place. For an airship, it smelled strangely of seaweed and saltwater, but it was a palace compared to the caravan. She could live with it.

Her bruises stung in protest as she followed him through the corridors, but she did not let them slow her down. These people were saving her life, and she did not want to be a burden. There was so much she wanted to know about them, about the Fireborne with the weird accent, about the man in the blue cloak with the other weird accent.

"Is there anyone who can take you in?" asked the man, slowing his pace. "Any relatives in the Realm?"

The question hit her hard, and she shook her head. There was only Gryff. But before she could even think about looking for him, she had to make sure no one was looking for *her*.

She sighed. Her brother had to be on his own for now. Despite his ailment, he was actually quite resourceful. He understood the way things worked just by looking at them, and his head was full of useful things, unlike her. It was only his temper that got him into trouble, but it never led to anything serious.

The man in blue took a sharp turn. One stride of his equaled two of hers. "Quickly now," he said, glancing back over his shoulder. "Can you write?"

Dove nodded as she struggled to keep up, running her hands along the walls to guide her.

"What's your name? Keep up."

Dove traced a D with her finger before the man turned again.

"Danea? Devina? Dalianna?"

Dalianna...? Dove frowned. She drew an O in the air.

The man paused. "Didn't think so. Doreen? Donella?"

He is playing with me, thought Dove when she saw a quick smile flicker across his face. But it was not like Morian's games. She actually felt her spirits lift, not plummet. The man in blue disappeared into the stairwell. "Keep up!" he shouted over his shoulder. "I thought you were quick, Doroteya."

Dove glared but quickened her pace. What was *his* name, then? Probably something she could not pronounce. Lancistierrean was easily the most complicated language she had ever encountered in the Scriptorium, which was probably why their people never aged. They needed at least hundred years to master it, and their names were equally absurd.

"Well?" he said, glancing over his shoulder again as she climbed down after him.

She halted as pain surged into the base of her spine. Now that her body sensed it was safe, the strength it had borrowed from her reserves was being paid back tenfold.

"You're not from Edenn. Your wounds look like they took weeks to make." He extended his hand and helped her steady herself. "Where are you really from?"

Dove sighed, exasperated. She traced a D on the wall with her finger.

The man laughed. "Never mind," he said. "But I'll still have your name."

Dove drew a V in the air.

"Dove," he said, letting it settle on his lips. "Pleased to meet you."

What about you? she asked with her eyes as she pointed at him.

"Me?" He kept his elbow extended for her to lean on as they

continued down the corridor. "My name is ..." He drew a D in the air. He smiled when Dove glared daggers at him. "Decker," he said, tired but courteous. "The loudmouth with the orange hair is Merc, and the bear is Wolff. Surely you can guess where we're from."

Dove sighed as she raised her hand once more. *D* ...

"Divisorya, you're right. What gave it away?"

Everything, thought Dove. She could think of no other situation where a Glasger, a Lancistierrean, and a loudmouth Fireborne would take in a stowaway. They came from a nation of stowaways.

He gave her a faint smile. "Seems not all Hounds are dim."

Dove was too tired to react. In truth, she was not even insulted. She had learned more about the rest of the world in one morning than a lifetime in the Scriptorium. Before, Summoners and Glasgers and floating cities were just words on parchment—yet in the blink of an eye, she faced all that and found her way onto a Divisoryan trader ship. *Me of all people,* she thought, strangely proud. *And I am still alive.*

"You should get some rest," said Decker as they stopped in front of the washroom. "Nan will help you settle in. She's ... *interesting.* I'm sure you'll get along." He nodded towards the door. "Let me know if you need anything," he said and took his leave.

***

Interesting was an understatement. If Dove did not believe in the grand mereyn, that bringer of balance in the world, she did now: where she was silent, Nan more than made up for it by never shutting up. She darted back and forth like a hummingbird, going on about her past travels at full-speed while Dove sat helplessly in a copper tub. Nan tried not to notice the bruising but shot her curious glances between pauses.

Finally, she could no longer contain herself. "Did a boy do that to you?" she asked, edging closer to the basin. Her hair fell neatly over her shoulders when she spoke, and even before she opened her mouth, Dove knew she was Waterborne. Her accent was heavy and she spoke in tones. Occasionally she forgot words, but she did not let that stop her.

Her question took Dove by surprise. She had a hard time classifying Greaven as a *boy,* but Nan could not have been older than fourteen. Dove played along, nodded.

Nan cursed. She was good at that. "Merc can teach you how to throw a punch," she suggested helpfully. "He's the … loud, fire-haired one. He taught me how, and now I beat up the boys on a daily basis. Except Decker, of course …" She reddened.

Dove tried to imagine what would happen if she took a swing at Greaven. He would probably break her in half.

"I can try healing you," Nan offered, cutting off her own line of thought. "My elements aren't that strong, but I can try. Wolff made me heal Ieon's nose after I broke it, and now it looks good as new!"

Dove's mind flashed back to the boy with the misshapen nose. *Wait …*

"And I bet you've never seen Water before!" Nan's eyes widened. "C'mon, it won't hurt. And you've got nothing to lose! If it fails, it'll just be the same as before. Hold out your hands!"

Reluctantly, Dove lifted her arms out of the water. Some of the cuts from the splinters had reopened, and a wooden needle was still lodged in her arm. She had not noticed it before, but just seeing it made it hurt.

Nan took her hands in hers. "This won't hurt a bit," she promised as determination crossed her face.

Dove felt her muscles relax. Water seeped into her bones, cushioned her body against the sides of the tub. Some of her cuts closed and scarred as though they had healed weeks in seconds, and she no longer felt the edge of the basin dig into her shoulder blades.

"I can't do anything about the splinter," Nan said. "Elayne can do much better. But at least it hurts less?" She glanced at Dove, seeking approval, and Dove nodded. Nan smiled. "You might want to see Decker about that! He can stitch you up in no time. Like a … rag doll." She rose and darted to the back of the washroom, taking some clothes out of the cabinet. "These used to be Elayne's," she said and set them next to the basin. "I'll see if Decker is around to fix your arm. Take your time, though! It's not like any of the boys take baths, anyway."

Just watching Nan run out the door made Dove tired. She knew there was a time she felt like that—bright, energetic, and happy to be alive—but that felt like a lifetime ago.

Gods, she thought, sinking back into the water. *What a life.*

***

The Ice spread and crackled as it wrapped itself around her arm. One of the Glasgers had cast it, and she felt her hand numb instantly. Decker used the opportunity to slide the splinter out. It was roughly the length of her wrist, but she could barely feel the pressure beneath the cold.

"Nan did a good job," he said, turning her arm over. "She's

getting better." He held out a needle. "Merc, if you will."

Merc snapped his fingers and created a ball of Fire that floated steadily above his palm. Dove watched, captivated, as Decker waved the needle over it. She did not even flinch when he began sewing up her wound. Instead, she eyed Merc curiously as he left the room. She wondered if he had ever burned himself.

"Dove," said Decker when they were both alone. "Who did this to you?"

Damn, thought Dove. Ice kept her arm pinned to the table. There was nowhere to go.

Decker cut the string. "We all have secrets, but Nan found this in the pocket of your shirt." He took out a coin from his own pocket and pressed it against her palm. Dove blinked in surprise. She had forgotten all about that. It was the only connection she had left to her past life, to … *her.*

"If I were you, I'd be more careful with that." Decker rose from his chair. He turned as though he wanted to say more but decided against it. "Good night, Dove. We'll talk in the morning."

When he left, Dove was surprised to see that it had grown dark outside. She realized she had not slept since the caravan, and when she rose, she felt the weight of the world press down on her shoulders. *I am alive,* she told herself again. Everything else could wait until morning.

She opened the door to the cabin that had once been Elayne's and collapsed on the bed. Sleep claimed her at once, and her dreams were full of fire.

7

THE RED CITADEL
FIRE REALM

They're the invaders, not us.
They killed our men first.
They raped our women second.
They butchered our children to close the loop.
They brought down the Empire.

Those foreign dogs. They dragged his people down to their level and forced them to join the Realms. *Fire Realm.* It sounded so banal, humiliating. The Scarlet Cities had once been the heart and soul of the Empire, but they were just cities now, rebuilt upon the bones of his ancestors. Their blood still whispered along the cold walls, and no one would ever know of their sacrifice. Emperors and empresses became kings and queens who bowed to weakness, and slowly, even the dragons disappeared. No wonder. Sintheans had become fragile. Weak. Buried their heads in the flock like sheep when they had once been wolves among men.

A sharp smile grazed Morian's lips. *But the dragon did come.* And it needed blood.

Morian returned to his desk and sat in thoughtful silence. He had been perusing the map all day, running a magnifying glass over each mountain, each river that branched to and from civilization. There were over a thousand villages in the Firelands alone. From the Brethren Wastes that separated the North from the rest of the mainland to the Greenwood in the South, he knew all their names by heart. He had to now, more than ever. Reports of dissent were sweeping the country, and he had to close in on traitors quickly. Not everyone liked the idea of an empire, and he had no use for cowards who feared strength.

They don't want us to prey on the weak, he thought, smiling at the irony, *so their solution is for everyone to be equally weak.* Their logic was astounding.

Normally, he would get a few reports a month, and rogue dissenters would be dead by nightfall. Bounty hunters were easy to tempt, and those in the outskirts craved a challenge. But now, reports came in almost weekly, and mercenaries came back empty-handed. Rebels hid like the roaches they were, and they were getting better at it. The Red Spears, they were calling themselves now. They lay low in forgotten villages, but there was only one way to stop the disease from spreading. *Kill the infected.*

The blood-stained shirt broke his concentration.

"I take it Edenn is history?" he asked, not bothering to look up from his work. It was important that he finish going over all the names. It was part of his nightly ritual, and if he hesitated, he would have to start all over again. He placed a wooden Hound figure where Edenn once stood and sighed to fill the silence. He was not used to being ignored.

Impatiently, he looked up from his map, prepared to send the messenger to the gallows. Instead, he was surprised to see Valerya standing before him. Her blade was still slung across her back, and he could smell the smoke and horse and blood on her. It was like having a night-wolf on a leash, and it pleased him. She even looked the part. Over the years, her face had toughened into a permanent scowl, pale brown skin the color of dead wheat. She looked human, but her eyes were like dark skies where the stars had long gone.

The beast must have taken over some part of her, there was no other explanation. But there was something alluring about that savagery, that primal aversion to weakness that could only come from daughters of the gods. *Even then,* he thought. Even when she was a nobody.

He put on his best smile. "Valerya," he said, pretending he had expected her all along. "Normally you would have one of your drudges deliver the news." He took a dagger from his drawer and picked up the shirt with its blade. The cloth writhed and twisted against the candlelight. "Ah," he said with a sad smile. "Good memories." He pushed the tip deeper until it pierced the cloth, and for a fleeting moment, his heart was filled with sadness.

Morian cleared his throat. *No, no.* There was no need to overreact. Yet he couldn't help but wonder, yet again, if it was a good idea to have his squire executed.

Of course it was a good idea, he thought, laughing to himself. *It was mine, after all.* Still, he had grown quite fond of her. Where others had screamed and pleaded for their lives, she withstood his demands without a single word of complaint. And sharp, too, not like the last ones. Hollow as an echo, they had been, and dull as dust. Playing with Dove was never dull, and the girl even knew how to write.

But, as the Fates would have it, the voiceless were cursed even more than bastards, and there was no room for them in his castle.

But her blood was pure ...
Voiceless! She would have cursed your line.
She should have lived.
She had to die.

Morian sighed. Arguing with himself was a hassle. Ending her was an act of mercy, nothing more. As much as he hated spilling Fireborne blood, all voiceless bastards were nobodies. Even in the First Scrolls, it had been that way, and a thousand years of history could not have been wrong. He wouldn't be so cruel as to send her back to her miserable life.

He never laid a hand on her. At least not in the way most people thought, though he often felt the urge to. She was young and untouched, with just enough comeliness to have made it worthwhile. But he was, first and foremost, a gentleman. That, and it was cursed to lie with the voiceless. The gods only knew what would have happened, the abominations they would have brought into this world.

Morian frowned, suddenly troubled. But it only lasted a blink of an eye.

"It is done," said the General solemnly.

The corners of his lips forced his mouth into a smile. "Tell me how it happened," he said with as much propriety as he could muster. If Valerya had been a common messenger, she would have been singing by now. Or hanging.

But Valerya considered words valuable. On a good day, she spoke in complete sentences, but most of the time, she hardly spoke at all.

Morian wondered if she did it on purpose. He never had to question her loyalty, but she was a thinker, which put him on edge whenever he saw it in her eyes. He almost preferred the sort that either talked too much—or didn't talk at all.

Finally, the General broke the silence. "Most of the village was decimated in the first wave. The second wiped out the rest."

"That bores me," Morian said, waving a hand dismissively. "Did she like it?"

The General raised her eyebrows in mild surprise, but that, too, lasted a blink of an eye. "She didn't *say*," she said. Most would have considered the response brazen, but Morian respected her power enough to let her get away with honest answers.

Most of the time.

"I liked her," he said wistfully. "She was self-sacrificing. Working for me is demanding, but she did it without a word of protest."

The General said nothing.

"Just like that!" he beamed. "Not the talkative type, I'm afraid." He scrutinized her face for a moment, wondering if he had cracked her mask. *Such a perfect specimen,* he mused sadly. *Shame she isn't one of us.* In most manners of the Citadel, she was as much a noble lady as a wild boar was a prized horse. After twenty years, it had not changed.

A lone survivor pulled from the ashes. The coincidence amused him. There was not much that separated her from Dove once. But Valerya was strong, and those who had taken from her paid with their lives. The Glasgers who raided her village had doomed the Icelands to a terrible fate. Valerya's blood campaign decimated half their population, blazed through their fields, and introduced to them to a new wave of terror. He knew no one who had a bigger score to settle.

They drove us back like cattle and slaughtered those who didn't leave, he thought, eyeing her hungrily. *Now we will take it back.*

"I bet it was stunning," Morian answered for her, taking care to look humble as he twisted the bloodied shirt with his blade. Try as he might, he could not bring himself to part with it. Instead, he wrapped it around the dagger and set it aside. Valerya's presence demanded his attention now.

"You know, squires are a pleasure," he said, hiding his distaste. It was such a display of bad manners. Sometimes, being around the woman was like holding a monologue. It was exhausting maintaining a conversation by himself. "I don't know why you don't have one."

Valerya's mouth made a thin line. "I don't need assistance," she said.

"Assistance?" asked Morian. Clearly, she had no concept of what squires were for. "Who said anything about assistance?" He leaned back in his chair. *Twenty years and I still have to teach her everything.* He bit back envy. *But father always had a soft spot for her.* As the first summoner in centuries, she had foregone the usual customs, earning titles faster than his father could grant them. But in the end, she threw them away to join the ranks.

No imagination, he thought. *But it worked out in the end.* Instead, he smiled. "I've decided to award you a squire for your hard work and … dedication. Tell me, what trait do you value most in a servant?"

The General looked as though he had just offered her rat poison.

"Or I could resort to old methods," he suggested, almost hopefully. "We could weed out the strongest, most clever …"

"One who can write," said the General abruptly.

Morian grinned. "As you wish. You know, it's a shame you didn't ask earlier. You could have just taken my old one if that was all you wanted."

That's it, he thought when he saw the nerve he hit. It flickered across her face for a fraction of a second, but it was better than nothing.

"Your Highness," she said instead, but he knew she wanted

nothing more than to withdraw to her quarters. *No imagination at all.* It must have been boring. She may have been glorious on the battlefield, but at the Citadel, she mostly stayed in her chambers, emerging only to flog a few novices or train with those hyenas she called Spades. Gods, even the company she kept was embarrassing.

"Will that be all?" she asked, interrupting his thoughts.

Of course not, he thought, pleased that she asked. He had been wondering when to bring up bad news. "The lord of Kingsbridge reports that his second son has died of fever," he said. "He has no heir, so his estate will go to his nephew … if his daughter doesn't kill the boy first." He watched her intently. "*We're* dying out." He took care to emphasize the first word. She may have come from the lowest rungs of his kingdom, but her blood was still pure. Not like the rats that invaded and bred.

"The boy was always sickly. It was a mercy," said Valerya, ever so gracious with condolences. But he could see in her eyes that this was a dance she was familiar with. She knew what he was going for.

"Why don't you stay a while?" he asked.

Another nerve, he mused. Two in one conversation. Valerya's gaze didn't waver, but for a moment, he saw the skin around her jaw tighten. Instead, she straightened and gave the same answer she always did. "I take my sworn duties seriously."

Morian had expected that, but he still felt a twinge of disappointment shoot down his spine. *Such a perfect specimen,* he thought again. He could look past the scars. Usually, he liked them soft, but he could overlook that, too. She was still a woman; they all felt the same where it counted, and their children would bear the blood of kings and summoners.

But how would that even work? he found himself wondering,

trying to imagine how they would couple. They were of a height, and no doubt even underneath the armor she was harder and more muscled than he was. Still, she wasn't ugly. In a certain light, her face could even pass for pleasant.

Morian put on his most winning smile. "Then that will be all." *For now.* Their conversation was far from over. There was no shortage of noble ladies he could wed, but none of them could summon dragons. "And do take care of that nosebleed," he said.

Wordlessly, Valerya wiped a light stream of blood from her lips.

The dragon is getting restless, he mused. She only got nose-bleeds when it was feeling prickly, and it was happening almost every day now.

"You know, now that I think about it," said Morian, halting her in her tracks. He opened his drawer and pulled out the book the girl had stupidly pilfered from the storage room. "Be a dear and give this back to Ro-yun for me, will you?"

The General took it in her hands, and he tried not to smile. He knew she despised the mages and their magic; she probably thought the book would unleash the plague. Instead, Valerya bowed her head. "Your Highness," she said as she took her leave.

When he heard the doors shut, he sighed. He took the dagger bundled up in Dove's old shirt and placed it in his drawer, next to his blood-stained glove.

8

ABOVE REALM

Dove thought she had awoken to the sound of a baby crying but realized it was just the noise she was making in her head. It was not far from how she really felt, but there was not much she could do but lie in bed and wait for the hammering behind her eyes to stop.

Everything hurt. Pain tore into muscles she did not know she had, distorting her reality into something vile. It all felt wrong. Of course, she was on a ship hovering in the air—she had already come to terms with that—but she never saw the same thing twice when she looked out the window. One moment, they were flying over lush forests, and the next, the cracked and sunbaked face of the wastelands.

Only one thing kept her grounded in reality.

She brought her hands to her face. Her arms were still wrapped in bandages, but some of the wounds had reopened while she slept. She sighed in relief when she saw that was the only thing she had done. A few nights ago, one of the younger boys from the next cabin came in to rouse her from a nightmare, but by then, she had already clawed out her stitches. Still, that was better than when Decker found her trying to tear herself open, convinced in half-sleep that Ro-yun had found his way inside her mind.

No wonder everything hurt.

"It's not normal," Decker had said that night as he redressed her wounds, "but not altogether strange. Most folks on the *Smuggler* are running from something, but it's only a matter of time before their ghosts catch up to them. Demons have wings, too."

Flashbacks, she recalled him saying. *Night terrors.* Those were the words he used to describe being catapulted into a bad memory. At times, they were so vivid, so intense, that they felt like part of her new reality.

Dove sighed and turned to her side as quietly as she could. Nan had begun sleeping there in case Dove's night terrors got worse, but the girl was often out and about by the first signs of dawn. Today, she had slept through the early afternoon, curled up under the covers. Dove inhaled and smelled ale and poor decisions.

Dove's lips parted into a strained smile. Nan could live to be two hundred and fifty; she could afford more than a few nights of poor decisions, and even at her worst, she looked flawless. Dove could not help but envy her.

Dove sat up with effort, careful not to wake her companion, and swore she heard her bones crack in protest. *I feel two hundred and fifty,* she thought glumly, trying to ignore the cold numbness that rolled down her spine like dripping wax.

The *Smuggler* did not help much. She had never been on a normal sea-boat before, let alone an airship, but magestone was harder to steer than a canoe in a storm. It elevated whatever it touched, and whoever was at the helm had the supreme joy of controlling the masts to respond to the winds. Suddenly, she understood why Merc was no longer allowed at the helm.

Dove groaned. Even her stomach had lost its sense of balance, and it lurched forward and back with the ship's movements. *Good thing Morian never coupled with me,* she thought, suddenly nauseated. *At least I know I am not with child.* She had not even bled the past few months, but she supposed her body needed all the resources it could get.

Slowly, she forced herself to rise and made her way to the door.

"Where are you going?"

Dove's heart leapt as Nan turned. A soft smile lined her features as she rubbed the sleep from her eyes. "I'm a light sleeper," she said. "Unlike you. You sleep like a … like a …" She paused, struggled to find the right words. "A dead thing."

Dove blinked. *Close enough.*

"Did your wounds reopen?" asked Nan when she saw Dove's bandages. "You should see Decker about that. They say it's bad luck to use Water on the same wound twice, so I probably shouldn't …" She reddened when she laughed, a sweet sound. "You must think our superstitions are strange. But we are riding on a flying heap of wood, so you can't blame us for being cautious."

Dove smiled to herself. They were indeed superstitious—even more superstitious than the Fireborne. A bird that flew against the wind was considered an ill sign, and no one whistled for fear it would attract bad weather. Up here, they made omens out of anything.

And what did they say about the voiceless? Her smile faded. Even her own people thought she was cursed. The villagers she grew up with would have fed her to the wolves.

"Decker's probably steering," said Nan, stretching her arms. She arched her back. "You can find your own way up, right? You might catch lunch at the … kiln? I don't know what you call it. I think I had too much to drink last night …" She laughed again, this time guiltily. "I'm probably not as tired as you. I mean, it's normal to feel like dead in your case, and we're taking bets to see how long it'll take for you to recover."

Dove wondered if that was supposed to make her feel better, but she kept her face impassive. Nan always took Dove's change in demeanor as a new point of conversation, and she could talk all day if she had the chance.

Instead, Dove nodded absently and closed the door behind her. It had been a while since she stood on her own, and the ground beneath her feet felt uneven and dislodged. *One foot in front of the other,* she told herself as she stumbled her way to the deck. *Nan drank all night, but I am the one staggering like a fool.* She opened the hatch to the outside world.

The first thing she noticed before her eyes adjusted to daylight was the air. It was thin up here, but fresh like the start of spring. She stretched out her hand until it covered the sun and flexed her fingers, feeling the wind pass gently between them. Blue sky eased into the corners of her vision, giving shape to the helm and the crewmen. And the kiln, as Nan called it: a giant, wide-rimmed iron pot over a burning furnace. Judging by the wisps of smoke that curled upward from dying coals, lunch had not been too long ago. Cushions were still strewn about on deck; the underlings would clean them up later.

Dove stared at it, fascinated. Gathering around it was the crew's favorite pastime. The airship was their community, and whatever differences they had by day disappeared when they ate together. They threw everything in that pot and let it boil. Dove had not been able to join them, but Nan or Merc would bring down a bowl whenever she felt well enough to eat. Whenever Nan was in charge, the soup was so spicy, it burned.

No wonder I feel nauseated, she thought, narrowing her eyes when she saw the helm. Merc was steering, not Decker. The ground shook.

She let her eyes wander, taking in the sights and sounds of the waking world until she found Decker writing in his journal. He always had that thing around, and it did not seem to bother him that his leg was dangling precariously over the side of the ship—even with Merc's steering.

"Ten days," he said without looking up. "Impressive. But I suppose you have questions, so let's have them." He flipped to a blank page and handed her his journal.

Dove's eyes widened, and she took it cautiously. He may as well have given her his soul. "Keep your eyes on the horizon," he said, following his own advice. "It helps."

She glanced over the railing and saw gray earth that looked made of bone dust, trees that lay bent and broken and weeping.

The Brethren Wastes, she thought as she felt a chill that no current could carry.

"If you look closely, the Wastes are just one massive labyrinth," said Decker. His eyes squinted against the sun. "Hundreds of paths, but only seven that lead to the northern provinces. The others, on the other hand ..." He smiled, shrugged.

Dove gripped the journal tightly and sat down, taking care to put enough distance between them. He was kind enough, but so was Morian on his good days. A well-crafted smile hid the darkest intentions, and his piercing stare made her want to get into his good graces. *Definitely Lancistierrean,* she thought when she saw the golden threads that weaved across the blue in his eyes. Nan's eyes were dark, but they had the same gleam—an eternal mark.

"You've met her, I take it," said Decker. His eyes met hers, and for a moment they narrowed. "Valerya. Strange to say, I haven't met many people who have. They're either trying to kill me, or they're already dead. One day, you must tell me your secret."

He hates us, she realized. She supposed it came as no surprise that they were not well liked; she barely liked her own realm, and she was born there. But Decker was open about his animosity. He did not want her there, that much was certain. She could tell that when he looked at her, he saw the destruction of the world.

"That coin of yours," he said. "Can I see it?"

Instinctively, Dove clutched the coin through her shirt pocket. It had not been away from her since her first night there, but she handed it to him. He had saved her, after all; that warranted at least a modicum of trust.

Decker ran his finger over the engravings. "Whoever owned this coin must have been very powerful."

She is. Dove turned away. *And so was its previous owner.*

"Who gave it to you?"

She drew in a deep breath. Valerya had given it to her. It was the only thing that connected her to the Firelands now, and it felt like betrayal to hand it over so freely. These outsiders may have saved her life, but she was a Fireborne. Her people had forged a cruel world, but she could not forget her origins.

For the first time, a shadow of concern played across Decker's face. "The world is tearing at the seams, Dove. Soon, you will have to decide which side you want to be on. Ours ..." He nodded grimly towards the shadowlands. "Or theirs." He handed her the coin and rose. Stretched his arms. "Come. Let's take a walk."

Dove held onto the railing as she followed, pretending to use it for support. In truth, she felt like throwing up over the side of the ship, right into daybreak's bouquet of red, orange, and gold.

Why did Gryff have a coin like this? she wondered. His affliction kept him indoors, and he was more interested in studying the elements than using them. He loved *books.* Most of his coppers were spent on ink and candlesticks to get through long nights at the Scriptorium.

She turned to the horizon as if expecting to find him in the distance. *There are so many things I do not know about him.* What exactly did he do in the Scriptorium so late at night?

"Thinking of someone?" asked Decker.

Dove sighed. She turned to Decker and nodded.

"Aren't we all?" He gave her a tired smile, halting before the door that led below deck. "We'll speak later. In the meantime, relax and breathe in the fresh air. We dock soon." He took a courteous bow. "And if you're feeling charitable, find Nan. I think she has a bit of a crush on you. It's not often we get girls onboard, so she won't shut up about you."

Does she ever shut up about anything?

"Oh, and before I forget," said Decker, his grin uncharacteristically boyish. "Ten days. If you see Merc, tell him he owes me ten crowns."

It took Dove a moment to realize what he meant, but by that time, Decker had already gone back to his ledge. She wondered how many others placed a bet on her survival.

Ten crowns. So it was true about the Divisoryans. No wonder they were prime targets for pickpockets down below. If they were lucky, Dove and Gryff survived on one a month, and that was *with* his ailment. That was pocket money for this crew.

As soon she saw the high towers in the sky, held together by magic strings, the world felt frighteningly large. Through the air, life gained a new dimension.

Divisorya, she thought as the airship began to slow.

From a distance, it was less impressive than Dove had imagined, but Divisorya was not meant to be lived in. The winds were dry, the air thin, and the city was designed by mages, not artesans. Nobody built a research center with aesthetics in mind. Still, there was something reassuring about its silhouette against the setting sun, far, far away from the Firelands.

Decker stood at the helm as he prepared to steer into port, which explained why the voyage had suddenly gotten smoother. "Once we land, we're sending for the Prefect!" he yelled from the helm.

"Rey will know what to do with you," said Merc, collecting his cards. And coins. Dove frowned; she recalled him warning her about gambling. "He and Wolff go way back."

"Wouldn't worry about him, though," said Wolff as they soared closer to the port. The gears of the *Smuggler* slowed to a halt. "You'll love him. He's a goddamn *puppy*."

They were hovering now, swaying slowly from side to side, but she felt sick for other reasons. She did not want to meet any more officials. Kings and prefects were all the same, but a floating city did not provide many chances for escape. Even if she got far enough, the only way to go was down.

Decker hopped down from the helm, grinning from ear to ear. He was finally home. "Welcome to Divisorya," he said.

9

THE RED CITADEL
FIRE REALM

"Fire!" said the boy, gasping for air. "I'm a citizen! Let me go!" His voice had just barely begun to deepen, but it no longer cracked. It would set in another year or so, but nothing would correct his small frame, his crooked posture. An abomination. A mongrel abomination. And they brought him to her.

Valerya wondered which drudge she would hang first. Civilian matters were not her concern. She thought she made that clear the last time they brought in a citizen accused of a crime. He was the son of some baron who paid to murder a street whore. As the sole heir to an old house, he expected a scolding and a slap on the wrist. She castrated him herself, ending his bloodline with a single swipe of her blade. No one had bothered her since.

"Take him to the Sun-sworn," she snapped. The priests passed judgment at the Citadel, not her. They called it the Reckoning, and based on the whelp's voice, he couldn't have done more than steal a loaf of bread from the royal storages. *Stupid boy.* His breathing reeked of weakness. She tried to sense the air around him, but his elements wavered pitifully like a candle flame in the wind.

A mongrel indeed.

He would be better off with the Sun-sworn. They would demand a few fingers at most, and she had better things to do than put down strays.

The drudges released the boy's arms, and he crumpled to the ground like paper. "Please," he begged, cowering before the torch. "It's too bright."

I'll take his hands, I swear, thought Valerya, slamming the book shut. She had decided to keep it a while longer to try to make sense of the red symbols. It was probably full of witchborn magic, but there had to be something of note. *Unless the girl was a complete idiot and I've made a mistake in letting her go,* she thought, sighing. She'd had every tome on ancient scripts brought to her from the library and would have deciphered the entire book by now if they hadn't kept interrupting her. Perhaps if she skinned this one alive, it would set an example.

She looked up, ready to draw blood, but frowned when she saw him. The last thing the boy needed was a flaying. His skin was already peeling, curling before the light.

"He's not one of us," she said to the guards, ready to separate them from their sorry hides. "Let this night-walker out in the sun if he has committed treachery." *Feed him to the dogs, for all I care.* One less useless mouth to feed. "Why have you brought him here?"

"Our King has ordered that a squire be brought to your service," the noseless one replied. He said it firmly, without hesitation. His life depended on a satisfactory answer. She knew she had seen him before, but her list of campaigns was long, the list of drudges even longer.

"Have all the Fireborne burned?" she asked impatiently. "Have we resorted to taking half-breeds captive?"

"His … your command was to find one who could write," said his companion, a woman—one of the few swordmaidens at the Citadel. She was sturdy and built well for this life, but her hesitation would kill her later. "We would've burned him on the spot, but he was writing and releasing the birds when we found him."

Fuck. Valerya hadn't expected any of the villagers to be able to read or write.

She had always wondered why they bothered teaching the highborn how to write in the first place. It was considered in poor taste for them to draft their own letters, and rich people could afford scribes. Eithan the Archemage had forced her to learn at seventeen, and to this day, her letters still looked forced and uneven. It was Valk who handled the falcons.

"Releasing *birds?*" she asked, torn between amusement and annoyance. Of all the things to die for—yet it was the very thing that saved his life.

Suddenly, Valerya rose. She took the torch from the swordmaiden and held it to the boy's face, searching for any trace of Fire in those foreign eyes. But his hair was short and dark, his skin so white that she wondered if his veins had run dry. *Sickly,* she thought, disgusted. A freak with no color. She had cut down men and women all over the Realms, each praying to whatever deities existed in their little worlds, but no god would allow creatures like this to live and call it mercy. The skin along the boy's jawline began to tear. Deep red blotches raced across his face. There was a faint crackling sound, like a rabbit being roasted over an open spit.

She frowned. As much as she hated the idea of taking on a squire, she had hoped for at least little better. One who could stand and face her, at least. Not this abomination. Even the girl, Morian's plaything, would have done better. She may have dangled at the mercy of the gods, but there was Fire in her, and it burned fierce. This one, however …

"Please," the boy repeated, begged. "It's too bright."

Valerya sighed and handed the torch back to the swordmaiden. She held a hand to the boy's face and concentrated, sensing the air around him. *There it is,* she thought, feeling the connection. There was Fire in him too, but it was barely there, muddled with something else. "Fire," she said, ignoring his pleas. "And the other?"

"Ice," he gasped, struggling to breathe.

Ice. Of course it was. Morian was playing one of his games, and instead of finding a Fireborne to torment her all day, he would stick her with this *Glasger.* Even his face reminded her of one of them. It was still rounded by youth, but in a few years, it would mature. They all looked like birds to her: angular faces, sharp noses. White like snow owls with slits for eyes.

Avantys stirred inside her, felt her scorn. *Not now,* she thought. She would summon it soon, no doubt, but not here, and not for this whelp. It calmed, but its presence had already been felt. The drudges bowed their heads in fear, and the boy stopped his whining. *Perhaps I should summon it after all.* If she wiped them all out now, she might decipher the book before breakfast.

Enough of this nonsense. "Leave us," she said.

The drudges bowed hastily and took their leave, grateful for the reprieve. When the doors closed, the tension shifted. Now all her attention was focused on the boy, this *useless* thing that was keeping her from an even more useless exercise in symbology.

The evening was not going the way she had planned. She had thought to get through a few pages before hitting the training grounds, but the symbols proved to be more interesting than she thought. At times, they disappeared from the pages completely, depending on who was around. Now, they had definitely disappeared.

Valerya cursed and flung the tomes from her desk with a swipe of her arm.

"What do you make of a book where the words keep changing?" she asked as the boy stared open-mouthed, wondering whether to pick them up. For a moment, the question took his attention away from his peeling skin. "Quickly, now. Your answer could save your life." She leaned back in her seat and watched him intently, removing her right glove as she stretched her arm towards the torch-fire. As she lowered it, the flames dimmed. *"Talk."*

The boy's breathing steadied, and when he looked up, Valerya saw that half his face had already melted off. She had heard of people who scarred in the daylight, but she had never encountered a night-walker up close before. Fire was as necessary to her as breathing, if not more so, and the thought of burning without being touched by it was incomprehensible.

"I ..." he began. His expression was hard to read. "Dark magic."

"A half-wit could have said the same. Try again."

"What color are the letters?"

Interesting, thought Valerya. "Dark red."

"High mages," he said between gasps. "Different orders used different colors under the Empire. Purple was used by alchemist mages ... emerald by warriors ... black by enhancers, and blue for... for healers." He regained his breath. "Dark red was used by the Fifth Order."

"Skin-crawlers," said Valerya. She had gathered that from Ro-yun and Mina, but perhaps the boy had his uses, after all.

"Blood mages," he said.

"How did you come across this knowledge?"

"I read about it," he answered nervously.

It was pitiful, but it made sense. Even when she worked at the smithy as a girl, Valerya had come across boys who could break him like glass. They were built like oxen, too—all brawn and no brain. It never occurred to her that the opposite could be true, too. There was certainly little brawn in this one. She could probably snap him in half with her bare hands.

"Can you handle a blade?" she asked.

"No, I ..."

"Ever picked one up?"

"No, but ..."

"You can't defend yourself. You burn in daylight, and even if I let you go, you wouldn't make it past dawn." She leaned forward. "What makes you think you'll be better off here?"

"Because I ..." he began, choosing his words carefully. "I have nothing to lose."

Those eyes, thought Valerya. That was where the Fire raged. He may have been on the lowest rung of the ladder, but he had survived the onslaught. It was better than nothing, she supposed, and with a bit of luck, he would get himself killed at the Citadel in no time. The other boys would see to that. There were more than a few who would kill to train under the Summoner General. They would pick his bones clean if they had the chance.

"I expect loyalty and obedience," she said, ignoring his answer. "Weakness is no excuse, and the swordsmasters will show you no mercy. Either you meet my expectations or die in training. I have no use for weaklings, deadweight, and empty claims."

The boy's face softened into surprise and something else.

There it is again, she thought. That look. Rumors of her origin had reached her ears over the years. Stories of fire-wielding elves and dark magic, which somehow involved soul-trapping gems. She didn't know where the elf came from, but it was still her favorite rumor. And this one believed it.

"Keep staring and I will pluck out your eyes," she snapped, and he lowered his gaze. *Stupid boy.* She wanted nothing more than to melt the Ice off his bones, but watching him writhe in the torchlight gave her pause. She had killed thousands on her blood campaigns, but prolonging their pain was Morian's flavor. She was a firm believer in swift deaths.

She grimaced. Now that the boy wasn't burning alive, the Ice was unmistakable. He had their look, but his stature betrayed his mix: he was smaller than the typical Glasger, but she didn't know if he was naturally weak or underfed. She guessed him to be a few shades under twenty, not too far from her youngest Spade. Old enough to know better.

Silently, she cursed Morian and the drudges who brought him there.

"I'm sure you're clever enough to evaluate your situation," she said. "It would be stupid to fight, and I'm tired." She sighed before he could look too relieved. "But don't think you're getting off easy. You haven't met our swordsmaster yet."

She smiled to herself. Perhaps she would let him live after all. "I suppose we should get the formalities over with," she said. "Do you have a name?"

The boy cleared his throat. A red line had run from his left temple to his jaw; it would likely scar. When he glanced to the side to avoid her gaze, she could see the mark on his neck: a four-pointed star.

Finally, he found his voice.

"Gryff," he said, coughing. "My name is Gryff."

10

DIVISORYA

Dove could not imagine anyone less puppy-like than Rey of Divisorya.

She had imagined someone with soft features and more flesh around the middle. Bureaucrats were not exactly known for their physique. The higher ups may have been warriors once, but the lifetime of luxury that followed was quick to soften muscle and resolve. For a floating city that placed more value on research than brute force, she was not expecting much.

So when the beast of a man walked in, she wondered if he had eaten Rey. Based on the Scrolls, she knew right away that he was one of them: a Thunderborne. A *Thoryn*. She did not know much else; airships could not brave the winds that surrounded the island, and cartographers had failed time and time again to pinpoint its location.

But based on the Prefect alone, she suddenly understood why they had never been conquered. Rey was a head taller than even Decker with twice the girth, and his face was toughened, not weakened, by age. His hair was tied back, blue strands in a sea of gray.

Wolff had kept Decker and Merc behind while the others disembarked, and all four of them were waiting in a cabin below deck when the Prefect arrived with his personal guard. Dove wondered if the guard was a Thoryn too, but she could not see much under his helm.

Rey threw her a dark look. "You brought one of *them* here," he growled.

The guard straightened when he saw her. His eyes shifted to her hair.

"Hospitable as ever," grunted Wolff. "For a former Guardian, you're a shit politician."

Dove wondered what he meant, but no one looked in the mood for questions. Wolff and Rey eyed each other with suspicion, and she did not want to get caught in the crossfire.

The Thunderborne ignored him. "I didn't know you were so keen on breaking the Stalemate. Bringing a war to our doorstep."

"*That* kid?" said Wolff, amused. His reaction was so smug that she almost felt insulted.

"Her *Sovereign* would. And his guard dog would for even less. They can paint the Blackstone red with all the blood on their hands. And the She-Jackal hates mages." He gave a bitter half-chuckle. "The woman can talk to dead dragons but hates *magic*. I don't understand your kind at all."

Dove did not know why, but his words stung. She had lived her whole life among the Hounds, but it had not been all bad. Away from the Citadel, people were kind and hearty in their own way. Not everyone aspired to kill outsiders. Most preferred a quiet existence in the fields.

Rey overlooked her reaction. "Fifty years it took to build peace with the Hounds. Then you come in, trails blazing, with one of *them*. She's cute now, but just wait a few more years." He leaned back and turned to his guard. His mood soured. "Dann. Wait outside."

The guard raised two fingers to his forehead in what Dove assumed to be a salute, and she felt her face redden when he just turned and left. She shot Rey a nervous glance, but he did not seem to care. Not one muscle twitched. He did not even bat an eye.

Valerya would have killed the guard.

"You're wondering why Dann didn't bow," said Rey, sensing her discomfort. "But do you know where bowing comes from? Your *Empire*." He straightened his shoulders, doubled in breadth. "It was never meant as a sign of respect. It just made it easier for your emperor to punish his subjects."

Dove blinked. She did not follow.

"*Bowing* leaves your neck exposed. Messengers would present him with news, and then bow before their liege. And if it didn't please him ..." He brought a hand to his neck and made a swift cutting motion. "People kept doing it after the Empire fell. No one wanted any trouble."

Dove tried her best to maintain eye contact, but Rey made it difficult. He looked at her like she was the bad news. And it did not please him.

"Times are changing," said Wolff, breaking the tension. "Even down below."

"I see this *change*. The Empire is cleansing itself from the inside now." His words made everyone in the cabin uncomfortable, but no one else spoke. "But that's their problem."

"How long do you think before it reaches home?" countered Wolff. "We can't run anywhere. We're on a floating rock."

"They'd need magestone to reach us first."

"Or a *dragon*," said Wolff. "I imagine magestone wouldn't be too much of a problem. The largest reserve is off the coast of Glasgérios, and they're no match for the Hounds. Especially after what happened."

He placed his hands on the table and leaned forward. "But that's not what's bothering you though, is it?"

"Mm," was all Rey said. He threw a sharp glance at the door, making sure it was fully closed. He pulled out a piece of parchment from his pocket and passed it to Wolff. "A messenger from Glasgérios came by this morning with a message. And a coin."

Dove had a sinking feeling she knew what kind of coin it was.

Wolff frowned. "That's not possible."

"It is," said Decker. She had almost forgotten he was there. After Rey and Wolff, his voice sounded soft and meek. It was no match for his elders. "The kid has one too."

Dove stared at it, mortified. She had been so close to slipping past the Prefect's attention, but with a few words, Decker had dragged her back to the center.

Rey's eyes narrowed when he saw her. "You brought one of *them* here," he said, bristling. Dove saw muscles tense underneath his sleeves. His knuckles whitened around the table, and for a moment, she feared he would fling it across the cabin. "We want nothing to do with your kind. You call yourself a Falcon, but you're not worthy of the name."

A what?

"C'mon, she wasn't even alive then," said Decker.

"But even she knows the story of Elder Eithander." Rey's voice was as cold as a winter breeze. Her presence in the cabin had become only marginally tolerable now.

Dove nodded. The story was a village favorite. The common-folk loved scandal, especially if a highborn got disgraced. Even the coal boys sang songs of King Eithander, who made it to eighty-three, and his affair with one of the seven Glasgérian princesses. She still knew the words. *Elder Eithander, was proud the tales told, he ne'er succumbed, 'twas a sight to behold, until that one day, when he turned eighty-threes, he met a Cat, and bent both knees.* It was mundane enough, she supposed, but when the truth of it was discovered, he went and got himself killed in the war that followed. If anything, the consequences were more severe than the crime—the throne passed on to his younger brother, who would later go on to spawn Morian.

Thanks a lot, Eithander, she thought bitterly.

"Of course you do," Rey said. "How do you think their affair was discovered?"

Dove shrugged. She had always assumed it was a chambermaid or a jealous sentry. Or the stable boy. It was probably the stable boy.

"Falcons aren't supposed to meddle," said Rey. "They live and die in the shadows, serving knowledge above all else. If we lost every single one of them today, the world would never know of their service. Or their sacrifice."

Dove stared blankly. She had been hoping for the stable boy. *Instead, this whole thing started because ...* She could not find the right word for it. Espionage sounded too dramatic, but the way he talked about dying in the shadows left no alternative.

"You can imagine the chaos that ensued. No one knew what they stood for anymore, so most of them vanished. *Most.*" Rey glared. "Until they returned. But this time, under a new cause. Calling themselves the Red Spears now."

For a moment, it was quiet. No one wanted to anger the Thoryn. "This *coin* is an order to regroup," said the Prefect. "Insurgents used it hundreds of years ago. Now the Spears are using it, too."

"Regroup where?" asked Merc with all the tact of a bull in a porcelain shop. He had been uncharacteristically quiet, but talk of open rebellion roused his interest.

"Glasgérios," said Rey. "Where the Order began."

"If we do nothing, the Realmlands will eat each other alive," said Wolff before Merc could open his mouth. As far as he was concerned, Merc was done talking. "What good is knowledge if it stays hidden? Do you want to start another Purge?"

Wait. Dove frowned. Did they know about the Purge before it started?

"Falcons—*true* Falcons—pass along information. Nothing more. This new generation can go and die however they want."

Wolff glared. "You can bury your head in the sand if that's what you've become. But I can't stand by and watch as the world tears itself apart. Not again."

"You're forgetting your role in this, *friend.* If it hadn't been for …" Rey caught himself in time. He straightened, regained composure. "Every time we try to save a few, we doom thousands."

"We've all paid the price," said Wolff. "But imagine if that package had fallen into the wrong hands. And don't pretend you don't know what I'm talking about. Your act might work up here in the clouds, but you know what we've done."

At least one of us does, thought Dove, relieved when she saw the confusion on Decker's face. She was not alone. Merc had stopped following completely.

Rey's lips drew back into a thin line. "And things got so much better after that, did they?" he asked. "Tell me. What exactly did we contribute to the Realmlands?"

"A chance," Wolff snapped, and Dove braced herself. They were both abnormally large, and if they lunged at each other, she would get crushed between them.

Wolff rose from his chair, spurred by the Prefect's coldness. "We can't just sit and …"

Rey stood, knocking his chair over backwards. It tumbled, cracked against the wall. Dove jumped at the noise. "I cannot risk the lives of …"

"I KNOW WHAT THE RISKS ARE," Wolff bellowed. "More than *you*."

Dove expected fists to fly, or at least for Rey to shout back. In truth, she would have preferred broken chairs and screams to the quiet that followed. She did not know who won the fight. Words cut deeper than blades, but the wounds they left behind were silent.

After an uncomfortable pause, Rey gave a solemn nod. "I will not lend my support," he said, "but perhaps you will find more sympathy with the Glasgérian messenger. A mysterious man, to say the least, but he should be of great help." He extended his right arm. "I regret that we must part this way. But I wish you luck on your journey, old friend."

Wolff nodded and clasped it below the elbow. "Until the tides, then."

"Until the tides."

No further words were exchanged. Even after the Prefect took his leave, the silence could be pierced with a knife.

"What the *hell* was that?" Merc demanded when Wolff rose from his chair.

Wolff laughed and shook his head in disbelief. "Well, off to the Blackstone. I've got a niece to visit." He slapped Merc on the back. "Don't look so sullen. This is all part of it!"

Welcome to Divisorya, Dove thought glumly as Merc grumbled to himself. What had she gotten herself into? Was it too late to get dropped off in the Firelands?

Wolff grinned when she passed him. "What did I say?" he asked before she could look too dismayed. "Like a goddamn puppy!"

11

THE RED CITADEL
FIRE REALM

G ryff's face felt like it was on fire again. Blood pounded in his ears and trickled down his chin in spurts. *Keep going,* he thought. He might die tonight if the gods were cruel—or merciful—but if by some chance he survived this fifth layer of hell, perhaps he could finally get out, or at least see life beyond the training hall.

All he had to do was lock horns with the bull.

"Again," it spoke. It had a name, but Diante didn't seem befitting for a swordsmaster. Jagger, maybe, or Melhor. A name with muscles. Diante was a name bred for nobility, finesse. The swordsmaster didn't seem like he cared for either, but he was probably born into wealth. In the castle, most of them were—here, even servants and sweepers hailed from respectable families. They ate more than stale bread for breakfast and slept on actual beds, never having to worry about lice and filth. Luxury had a different definition in the capital.

Gryff picked up his stick, feeling his spirit wane. It was much lighter than steel, but after two hours of training, it might as well have been a bag of bricks. He had often dreamt of fighting along-side the Swordsworn, but out in the open, with daylight streaming across his face. It didn't have to be anything glorious—a real sword at most, and maybe a long moment or two of sunshine. His hopes died quickly in the training hall.

"Again!" it spoke, commanding him to his feet for the hundredth time.

Gryff kept his curses silent. Pain seared through his legs as he stood, but it was a small price to pay. He only had to close his eyes to imagine all the boys and girls in the Firelands who would kill to be where he was—*him,* of all people. Training at the Citadel was almost as prestigious as growing up in the training villages. In some ways, it was even better; here, he had private training, and when he was done, all he had to do was complete tasks for the Summoner General. Mostly, they entailed writing, but that had been his livelihood. He had a scribe's handwriting of which he was especially proud, and he could remember everything Valerya dictated to him with crystal clarity. It worked to their mutual advantage: she didn't seem the type to repeat herself, and he could retire to his chambers early.

He gripped his stick and prepared to attack. As much as he liked being there, it didn't stop him from wanting to punch Diante in the face. Not that it would have changed much. The man was missing several teeth, and his cheekbones looked like they had already been knocked into place. As swordsmaster, he was responsible for making freshlings into better men, but he set no good example. He was the lowest of six masters, responsible for incoming novices. The better they got, the more quickly they moved through the ranks. The head swordsmaster, Domnic, was said to be patient and kind, but it would take years to reach him—maybe even a lifetime for Gryff. That is, if they made it that far without being dispatched to the outskirts. Domnic trained only the most advanced students, and after they went through him, Valerya took over.

Finally, with a desperate burst of energy, Gryff swung his stick upwards.

Diante stepped to the side and swiped at his legs with his own stick. He was smaller than average, but faster than Gryff could anticipate.

Gryff's knees buckled without protest, and he found himself back on the floor.

I'll just stay down this time. He didn't have much use for his legs, anyway. He was a scribe, after all. Prior to this, the heaviest thing he'd had to lift was a quill or the occasional manuscript at the Scriptorium. Hells, his muscles ached after a night of reshelving. Asking him to fight was like asking Valerya to bake pastries.

Pull yourself together. What would Dove think? he wondered as he lay there, bleeding. Thinking about it hurt more than a blade to the knees. *She would think I was a coward.*

Gryff tried to imagine her face. She may have moved as quietly as a shadow, but she never could hide what she felt. He had to fight to remember, because the longer he stayed at the Citadel, the more her fine-lined features—every blemish, every freckle over the bridge of her nose—blurred into one. Any trace of her memory turned hollow and colorless in his mind.

She survived, he told himself firmly. *The Fireborne can't burn, and she's one of them.* He bit back a smile as he recalled all the times she thrust her arms into the fire when they were children. There was not much else to do in the village.

"Are you waiting for a bedtime story?" Diante hissed, throwing him a dummy sword. "On your feet, mongrel!"

Mongrel. Fresh anger coursed through his veins. *Mongrel.* The reason he couldn't do anything when they blazed through his village. When Dove pushed him aside and …

Gryff braced himself, ready to sacrifice the last of his strength, when he heard the doors swing open.

"What are you doing?" a voice echoed through the hall. It was calm, composed, but demanded the right answer.

Even Diante was taken aback. "My General," he said with a practiced bow. "I am training your squire in swordsmanship."

"With a dummy *greatsword?*" Her words were accented, its edges sharpened by the South. Gryff felt the air tense and tighten around his throat as she drew near. "He can't even lift a stick."

"General …" The swordsmaster shifted uncomfortably to Gryff's amusement. It gave him immense satisfaction watching Diante squirm.

One way or another, people get what they give, he thought. *Though if that were the case, I wonder what that says about me.* Perhaps he had done something in a past life that he was paying dearly for in this one.

Diante chose his words carefully. "I was ordered …"

"Yes, ordered. By me," the General interrupted him coldly.

Gryff winced at her tone. He had spent most of his childhood sickly and bedridden, but even he had heard the stories. Back then, they were the only things that allowed him a window into the outside world, especially when he and Dove read them together. He used to like the ones that kept him up at night, back when Valerya was just a character in them. It was Dove who hated the blood tales. She always wanted to skip the scary parts, and now Gryff understood why. The She-Jackal who flung the bodies of men, women, and children from spired towers was much less terrifying when she wasn't standing right in front of him.

"Leave us, swordsmaster," Valerya commanded. She was taller than Diante, but he shrank even more under her gaze.

The swordsmaster bowed. Gryff stared on in disgust as he took his leave. Had Diante been a dog, his tail would have been so far between his legs, it would have reached his nose. Not that Gryff would have fared any better, but he wasn't a master of sword.

Valerya turned her full attention to Gryff. Her eyes narrowed as though she had just spotted an insect.

Come back! he found himself begging silently after the swordsmaster.

"Stand," she commanded.

Gryff obeyed. He could swear he heard his knees rupture when he stood, and he felt warm blood trickle down his leg. At least, he hoped it was blood.

The General approached and drew her sword. He stepped back instinctively as she held it in front of him.

"Take it," she ordered.

It was hard not to imagine the blood of thousands dripping from the blade, how many times it must have been scrubbed clean after one of her campaigns. There were more drawings of it in the Scrolls than there were of Valerya herself, though he had read that she refused to sit still for likenesses. Any existing portraits of her were painted from memory, for which reason they were often inconsistent or exaggerated. It was not hard to see where the rumors came from. Often, artesans drew her to resemble a beast or a jackal. Those who had never met her didn't know what she looked like, so they made it up as they went along.

Gryff wrapped his fingers around the handle. Easy enough, he supposed. It was overlaid in black leather that felt freshly changed, and he found that he could grip it easily. But the glory was short-lived; it was much heavier than he had anticipated, and when she let go, he let it fall clumsily to the floor. The sword's weight took with it his sure footing, and he collapsed to his knees.

If they didn't rupture before ...

It was the worst pain he had ever felt, and that was including the time the village medican extracted two of his teeth without anything to numb the pain. He knew it wasn't going to be easy; the road to the top was always rocky, braved only by the best. Even youths in the training villages suffered long years and sacrificed their childhoods before getting anywhere, but at least they had actual opponents.

Gryff was bested by a sword that hadn't even attacked him.

Get up. He clenched his fists, but the rest of his body wouldn't listen. For a brief moment, his life flashed before his eyes. He wasn't supposed to die this way. Boys of his kind died as they had lived: quietly, peacefully, forgettably. They weren't meant to survive the Purge, and they certainly weren't meant for high society. Class systems still ran deep in this part of the Firelands. They could tell he wasn't one of them just from the way he breathed.

The General neither laughed nor sighed. "I just handed you the most powerful sword in the Four Realms," she said, picking it up effortlessly off the ground. She leaned it against the wall. "But what good is power if you're too weak to wield it?"

Humiliated, Gryff grabbed at his wooden sword.

"First lesson, boy," she said, kicking it aside. "Know your strengths."

She tossed him the stick. It was pitiful compared to the other one, but he lifted it without much effort.

"Better?" she asked, but Gryff doubted she expected an answer. Whenever she spoke, she spoke past him, never to him. She spoke that way to everyone, save for that Spade who trailed behind her all day. His presence was sorely missed.

"Attack me," she commanded.

Gryff ran at her and swung with all the strength he could muster. With her arms behind her back, the General sidestepped and kicked his legs out from under him, sending him sprawling. A white light burst across his vision, like a mountain had collided against the side of his skull. He swore he heard his knees pop when they hit the ground.

Just cut my fucking legs off, thought Gryff, hoping the gods would listen to his plea this time. Had it been Diante, he would have surrendered and suffered the blows, but he couldn't give up in front of *her.* He had a feeling she would not let him rise again.

He clambered to his feet and plunged forward.

"But more importantly," said the General curtly. She grabbed his wrist and forced the stick out of his hand. When she let go, he fell to the floor, clutching his arm. "Know your weaknesses." She tossed him the stick. "I suppose a sword does feel different than a pen," she said. "Which is your sword hand?"

"M-my left," Gryff stammered. He wished he could sound more intimidating, but the air had left him when he hit the ground.

The General ignored his sputtering. "Then your right is your element hand."

Gryff blinked, confused. He could barely freeze an ant, let alone cast Ice at will. A shield would have been a better use for his free hand.

It was only when the General picked up the dummy sword that Gryff realized she had not been armed. "Again," she said.

Still, he forced himself forward, lunging with everything he had. The adrenaline drove his momentum, if only for a moment.

With a swipe of her wrist, her sword forced his stick to the ground. He braced himself for another world of pain, but she grabbed his arm before he could fall and hoisted him back up.

That didn't even last a second, he realized.

"I'll switch hands," she said, tossing the sword to her left. "Again."

Gryff attacked again. And again. And again.

He wondered if he was dead and this was the afterlife the Fates had designed for him: an eternal battle against Valerya the Fireborne. Each time he advanced, the General forced him back. She seemed to know exactly where he was fated to fall and stopped him from hitting the ground. "The stones don't need more of your blood," she said coldly. It was humiliating.

Soon, he began attacking out of desperation, like a cornered dog. But the General had no mercy for motive and beat him down each time.

"You're distracted," she said impatiently. "Don't make me use actual force."

Gryff's face reddened. "I ... I can't," he said. His body had abandoned him.

He was met with silence. His fear tensed, but the General didn't command him to his feet. Instead, she said, "I suppose it's hard to go on after watching your family burn in the fire."

Gryff's heart stopped. "I'm sorry?"

"Or slaughtered by the Swordsworn," she continued, indifferent to his shock. "I don't command my men to kill runaways, but some just have a natural taste for blood. Once they reach the forests, they're like unleashed dogs."

The sharp pain in his bones dulled when he imagined Dove in a gutter somewhere, cut in half or worse. Whatever fear that lingered in the back of his mind turned to something uglier. He threw himself at her full force. He didn't care if he looked desperate. All he could think of was a fully armed Swordsworn beating down a girl half his size …

"Your parents?" she asked, forcing him back. "A girl?" She blocked his sword, and her lips curled into a thin smile. "A boy?"

And when the General knocked him to the ground, the floor burst into Ice.

Unfazed, she lunged forward and melted it away in a blast of Fire. "Concentrate!" she said as the flames died down. She crouched over him with her sword aimed at his throat.

"I … I didn't …" Gryff stammered, gasping for breath. "It just …"

"Control your emotions," said the General. "In real combat, they will say worse things. Do worse things. Don't lose yourself to their taunts."

She's testing me, he thought between breaths. His rage subsided, replaced by pain. He stayed down. *And I failed.*

"What should I have done?" he asked, taken aback by his own brazenness. "I was being attacked, and …"

"I have men for killing," said the General, cutting him off. "Men who like it. Men who live for it. Men who joined our ranks just so they could do it. Are you one of them?"

Slowly, Gryff shook his head. "No, I … I'm not."

"Your objective is not to kill, but to stay alive." She approached him and pressed the sword in his hand. "Know your strengths, Glasger. I have no use for you dead."

Gryff realized with a mix of admiration and horror that she hadn't even been trying. She barely wasted her breath while he gasped for air like a fish washed ashore.

As he lay on the cold stone, his mind flashed to Ice. He had never cast it before—at least not to this extent—but it felt natural, almost *intimate,* like they had known each other for years. Could the General sense it in him? Dove could, and she spent their childhood trying to scare him into casting it. The farthest he got was cooling a tankard of water, and that was on a good day. Not at all like what had just happened.

By the time he looked up, the General was already headed for the door. "We'll see about your element hand in the future," she said before opening it. "Valk!"

So he's been out there all along, thought Gryff, reddening. He wondered if the Spade had heard every fall, every stammer and misstep that characterized his attempts at fighting.

A familiar shadow appeared in the doorframe. It bowed.

The General handed Valk the dummy sword. "Six seconds should do," she told him. "Once he lasts more than that, his training is over for the day."

Valerya took her leave without looking back, and Gryff slowly forced himself to his knees. She was done with him. For someone who was supposed to be her squire, he only saw her for brief moments at a time. He had no idea what she did with the rest of her day. She trained elites, he knew, but where?

"Gryff, is it?" asked the Spade, taking his stance. He was bigger than Diante, but more refined in his movements. Maybe Gryff stood a chance, after all. "Don't worry," he said. "It should be over soon."

***

It took over two hours to last six-and-a-half seconds. Of course, Gryff had spent most of it on the ground, resting and catching his breath.

Valk was unlike Diante and the General, as he quickly came to realize. He was silent all throughout and let Gryff attack and defend as he pleased. Whenever Gryff staggered, the Spade waited for him to regain sure footing.

Had Gryff not grown up with Dove, he would have found the silence unsettling, but it was a comfort to him now. It helped that his opponent was patient; it was only after Gryff lasted six-and-a-half seconds that he even opened his mouth.

"Well done," he said.

"Six-and-a-half seconds," muttered Gryff as he rubbed his arm. "Six-and-a-half."

"Much can happen in six-and-a-half seconds," said Valk encouragingly, leading him back to his quarters. His accent was even stronger than the General's, and Gryff had to concentrate to understand him. "When our General first started training at the Citadel, she could last only three."

Gryff stopped. "Really?" he asked.

Valk tried to smile. "No," he admitted. "Sorry."

Gryff sighed. "How well did you do?"

"I was never much good at being a swordsman. I wanted to be a scholar and study the stars," said Valk with a laugh. "I was ill-suited for this life, but in this line of work, you learn quickly. Experience is the best teacher, no matter what *Diante* would have you believe."

"A scholar?" Gryff raised an eyebrow. He wouldn't have considered it a Spade's aspiration, but he supposed it wasn't too surprising. Valk was highborn and educated at the Academy—the most renowned training village in the Scarlet Cities. Even among the elites, it was exclusive, but that only meant that Gryff had to exercise caution. Valk may have been courteous, but he could burn down the entire Citadel if he wanted.

"Yes," said Valk, unfazed by his reaction. "But duty called. The stars could wait for better men."

They won't have to wait much longer if Valerya continues her blood campaign, thought Gryff, but Valk seemed to know exactly what he was thinking.

"As ... *cold* ... as our General is, she will save your life, one way or another," he said, to Gryff's surprise. "Whether you hate her or love her for it is up to you."

They continued down the corridor in silence. It must have been close to nightfall now. During the day, Valerya ordered every window leading from his quarters to the training hall to be closed and curtained, but no one paid much attention once the sun went down. When the drapes hung that lazily, it meant the day had ended.

Good, thought Gryff. The excitement of the evening was dying down, leaving him to feel every bit as bloodied and exhausted as he looked. He wanted nothing more than to collapse in his bed. That, at least, was a comfort. He may have been lower than a servant in the castle, but he still enjoyed its perks. A full meal and a soft bed made all the difference in the world.

Valk stopped in front of the doors that led to the library. "Sleep well then, Glasger."

Gryff winced. "I was born in the Firelands," he said coolly.

The corner of Valk's mouth turned upwards into a somber smile. "Your loyalty to the Fireborne is most admirable," he said, "despite troubling times that have befallen the Realm." He bowed slightly. "All the same, I meant no offense."

Gryff stood there dumbly as Valk took his leave. Why had Gryff been so quick to identify as one of them? They wanted to burn him, to eliminate his kind. The only reason he was alive was because they saw him writing.

Fly. It was a simple message, but one that would have had him burned on the spot. It kept the Spears one step ahead of the flames. Gryff was not one of them, but he had his list of promises. One of them was to pass the message along when he received it, no questions asked. He sorely regretted not having asked any questions.

Gryff opened the doors to his quarters, which consisted of a side table and a bed placed in the corner of the library. At first, he had been overjoyed; there were stacks and shelves of manuscripts spread over chambers the size of grand halls, accessible only to nobility and high-ranking Swordsworn. But with training every night, he didn't even have the energy to open a book cover. The only thing he explored was the path that led from the doorway to his bed.

Will it ever get better? he wondered as he lay sprawled on the mattress. His body felt stitched together, every movement a blade to his ribs. Soon, he would come apart at the seams.

Still, it didn't bother him today. None of it did, because he had something to show for it. *Ice.* Dove would be impressed. Finally, there was something he could do that she couldn't. Something the rest of the castle couldn't, only him. It was part of him now, and once he regained his strength, he would try again. It was weak, but it would get stronger. One day, he might even be able to control it.

Gryff barely noticed the moon spill into the library until he saw the shadows darken. It was the only kind of light he could brave, the only time he could go outside. Maybe if he got better at his training, he would walk through the gardens after dark. *Whenever that may be.* Dove always hated going out at night, but she did it for his sake. If he got really strong, he could even find her and bring her back to the castle. She probably wouldn't like the capital much, but she would pretend to—for his sake.

He sighed and forced his eyes shut. He couldn't even go one day without thinking about her.

If only I had a distraction ...

Then the courier falcon came.

Fuck, he thought. Anything but that. Gryff prided himself on his way with words, but there was no way he could explain the bird's presence in his chambers. It would be just his luck if Greaven stopped by. If he saw the falcon, Gryff's head would soar clean above the gardens. Then again, he thought bitterly, *at least I'd get to see them before I die.*

Gryff swung his legs to the side and got to his feet. "Where did you—?"

The falcon flew past him when he drew near. It was a peregrine of solid black, the choice falcon for those who could afford it. It cost more than a horse, so the common-folk didn't bother. It didn't cost extra to send harmless messages. *The harmful ones, however ...* Better to get a bird that wouldn't fail. Every time Gryff saw one, his life changed for the worse.

"No, come *here,*" he hissed, but it soared through the library and landed on a bookshelf on the second floor. Definitely a courier falcon. The ribbon tied to its leg was black, almost impossible to see in the darkness, but moonlight gleamed off the silk.

Everyone in the Citadel is trying to break me, thought Gryff as he hobbled up the flight of stairs. *Even the fucking chicken.* He extended his arm, but the falcon flew deeper into the library.

Intrigue kept him on his feet. Even when the peregrine soared past the elemental sciences and into an even smaller chamber, Gryff trailed behind it.

He brushed cobwebs off his shoulder and coughed. The falcon flew several shelves higher until it hovered in front of a tattered book squeezed between Glasgérian dictionaries. *No wonder,* he thought. No one wanted to learn the language of the Icelands. No one wanted to learn other languages in general. Sinthean had been the imperial language, and purists considered it an insult tainting it with foreign sounds.

He pulled the book from the shelf and blew the dust off its cover. As he examined it, the peregrine bit his finger and flew off.

"Fuck!" His hand shot up to his mouth. The bird had drawn blood, but it tickled in light of his bruised ribs and wounded pride. *I can't wait for this night to end.* He made his way back to the bed and held the book against the moonlight. The title was written in old Glasgérian, but he had studied enough to understand:

***

JOURNAL

***

Specific. He turned the page.

***

EITHAN OF SYNTH, SON OF MATHIEU THE TRUEBORNE FOR MY APPRENTICE, KAYNE

***

The Archemage. Gryff's heart leapt in his throat. *The Archemage who taught Valerya everything. The Archemage she executed …*

His finger traced along the word "Trueborne." It didn't get much nobler than that, except it was a nobility born from strength, not wealth. Summoners did not always hail from the upper classes, but their descendants carried with them the Trueborne name. If Valerya ever spawned children—gods forbid—they would be considered Trueborne too, even though she herself rejected the title.

He sighed and turned the page. He squinted when he saw a note scribbled hastily in the top margin.

***

I write this from the darkcells as a testimony to my final days. With these confessions, I pray not for the salvation of my soul, but for the safety of the Realm.

***

Oh, thought Gryff, all exhaustion forgotten. *It looks like I won't sleep tonight after all.*

12

DIVISORYA

Not even Divisoryans knew what the mages were up to in the Blackstone. Once in a while, green smoke misted from its windows and the ground shook beneath their feet, but no one seemed overly concerned. People lived their lives around it, like a giant tree had been planted in the middle of their city.

At the edge of the world, the clouds were clear and crisp. Dove could see the emerald rays of Salandra force out what was left of Tavandir. The ascendants clashed in the middle, twisting into a thousand unbound embers. But despite the hostile takeover, the colors stayed stagnant. She felt like she could reach out and touch them. Each star looked freshly forged, piercing through the night like arrows.

Must be magic, she thought.

That, too, seemed to be lost on Divisoryans. Mages from all over the world came to study their craft there, for which reason they created splendid things. Ships that flew. A city that floated. They had answers for everything, too. Their houses were warmer without fire, their food was better preserved, and it was not uncommon to speak three or four languages.

I do not even speak one, thought Dove with a sigh.

She did not know how long she had been there; they must have been looking for her now. It would be easier if they looked up, but they probably did not think to search the roofs of the guard towers that bridged city walls. She was not, strictly speaking, supposed to be there. Not that she had planned on staying long, but she did not expect to catch the turn of the stars.

Dove curled her hands around the edge of the roof and lowered herself down to the window. The chill wound around her neck and bit into her bones. It was colder up here, which was all the more reason to move quickly. Her body was not used to the altitude, and she did not want to lose feeling in her fingers—or her lungs.

Shivering, she pressed onward. From the rooftops, she could see that people were still out and about in the inner streets of the city, but crowds thinned as they stretched to the Blackstone. That was how she knew they were coming: bright orange hair and blue cloaks were hard to miss, even when green and purple conquered the skies.

The sights were less spectacular when she reached the ground. Red, graffiti-lined walls guarded houses as far as the eye could see, and vendors had already begun closing down shop along the main roads. She turned her gaze back to the stars.

"Told you there was nothing to worry about," she heard Merc's voice. She shoved her hands into her pockets, hiding grime from the wall that clung to her fingers. "We were taking bets on whether you'd take the next flight back."

Decker smirked. "Who'd want to go back after that?" he asked, nodding towards the sky. "Mages say that the spirits of dragons live beyond the light and that ascendant stars are their connection to this world. A beautiful concept, I'm sure."

"Shut up, both of you," muttered Wolff. "I don't want to hear any more about dragons and spooks. Stars have nothing to do with magic." He threw Dove a sharp glance as if forcing her to agree. "Come on, then. If you're into sorcery, you'll love the Blackstone."

They headed up a rugged slope and began their ascent.

For all its man-made wonders, the Blackstone looked like it was built on cliffs. It was the only thing in the floating city that looked more impressive from the ground up, and Dove wondered if that was where the locals had hidden all their magestone. There were five towers, not one, but Dove could not see them all from the airship. The mist started halfway up the main tower, hiding them from view.

The only way to reach the main gate was to cross an upward bridge that connected the towers, spilling formations over the sides like dripping candle wax. The bridge was Divisorya's claim to fame, because no one could explain how it was made. They had invited builders from all over the world to guess, but in the end, only one answer remained: magic.

They were met with a sullen-faced mage at the entrance. He was not what came to mind when Dove thought of sorcery—his dark red robes made him look more like a Sun-sworn priest than a mage, and he gazed blankly into the distance, waiting for his shift to end. Wisps of silver wafted across his forehead, and his cheeks looked as gaunt as the circles around his eyes.

But when his face broke out into a forced smile, Dove saw that he was younger than she thought. She saw old eyes but no wrinkles, blue that bordered on white. It was impossible to determine his age. For a moment, curiosity outweighed fear. *Is this part of their sorcery?*

"*Segnes,*" he said with a quick bow.

"*Segnes,*" replied Wolff. "We seek to enter."

"Are you in need of guidance in the elements?" asked the mage, glancing at Dove with an intensity that indicated he was sensing her. He must have seen countless apprentices, many of whom harbored power beyond their control, but he would be disappointed with her. She could feel him trying to piece together what she was. "A Fireborne," he said, amused. "And a Realmborn, I see. It's been a while since we've had that combination."

"Watch yourself," warned Wolff. "Skin-crawling is outlawed up here."

Dove froze. Terror turned her legs to stone. The Citadel that had seemed so far away came rushing back in waves. *Ro-yun,* she remembered, his name as clear as day. *Mina.* She tensed, trying to sense a presence in her mind that was not hers.

"I don't need *skin-crawling* to see," said the mage, but his voice betrayed resentment. He did not like that word. "I can always tell a Realmborn from the way they move." He straightened. "I see I'm not the first you've met of my kind. Who was he? She?"

"I need to speak with Elayne," interrupted Wolff. "Urgent business."

"There is nothing barring non-mages from entering the premises," said the man as he turned to Decker, much to Dove's relief. She felt a great burden lift when their connection broke, like a cloak falling from her shoulders. "But I'm afraid weapons aren't allowed inside."

Decker nodded and removed his blade from its scabbard. She could tell he was not pleased, but none of them seemed willing to deal with a skin-crawler.

"It will be safe here," the mage reassured him, but Dove did not believe him. After seeing what his kind could do, she would never trust them with anything—especially promises.

He stepped aside to reveal a circle cut crudely into the stone; inside, there was a triangle pointing downwards. He held his hand against it, whispered words she did not recognize. For a moment, it became so quiet that Dove could hear the winds change.

Suddenly, blue flames shot out between the lines, crackling like the mouth of a furnace. They traced along the sides of the triangle and spread to the circle around it, and when both ends met, the symbol glowed.

Slabs of stone gave way to a dark entrance, and Dove took a step back. She turned to her companions, expecting the same reaction— any reaction, really—but it must have been their hundredth time in the Blackstone. Decker was not even paying attention; he was too busy sizing up the skin-crawler while Merc stared blankly into the horizon.

"May you find what you seek," said the mage.

The hall that greeted them was a warm relief from the bleak welcome they had received. Walls vaulted over them, displaying painted scenes of the tower's history, but unlike the Citadel, they were not of dragons or great battles with armored warriors. Instead, she saw robed mages and icons, each to be read with layers of meaning. *Perhaps they were artesans after all.* She tried to get a good look at the figures, but there were none she recognized. Whatever truths the Divisoryans believed, they reflected a reality much different than her own.

Bookcases lined the walls, occasionally interrupted by wooden doors so high that they looked like gates to a stronghold. It even smelled of parchment. She recognized the scent from the Scriptorium, from the long hours she and Gryff spent illuminating manuscripts. She liked that. It was Gryff who had a poet's handwriting, but she enjoyed turning letters into gold.

"Red robes. Skin-crawler," Wolff growled under his breath. "Hate 'em."

"Come on, Uncle," Dove heard a voice descend into the hall. It was deep and pleasant, not at all like that of the sentry mage. She allowed herself a little hope. "Bastian's a dear. Or *Ro-yan,* as soon as he passes his Rites."

Dove turned. Elayne bore the same solemn demeanor as Bastian, but it softened at the sight of them. She was dark-skinned and golden-eyed, something Dove had never seen before. She never would have guessed that she and Wolff were related.

"How did you—" began Wolff, but the hard lines had melted from his face.

"I practically live in the library," she said. Her eyes were tired, but they glowed like embers. Like Bastian, she wore long robes, but they were soft blue, the color of her Order. "I can see people coming up the bridge from miles away." She pulled away and embraced Merc.

"So you're a Healer now," said Decker, clearing his throat. "But it's only been ..."

"Eight years!" Elayne interrupted him with a punch to the shoulder. "What, you didn't think I'd be an apprentice forever, did you?"

"You should have written," said Decker indignantly. "I would have ..."

"What, come back for my Rites?" she teased. "I know you better than that, Deklan."

Dove tried not to let her amusement show at Decker's true name, especially when it made him cringe. It sounded so formal, like the name of some stodgy Realmborn noble. Or a bureaucrat. Not at all like the first helmsman of a smuggler ship.

Before Decker could respond, Elayne cut him off. "Responsibilities, I know," she said, smiling. "I have them now too, officially. Protect the weak, the sick, and the injured. La, la, la." She held up a thin chain around her neck from which three rings hung: one of silver, one of gold, and one that looked made of crystal.

Dove had no idea what they meant, but if a coin could protect her from the General's wrath and get her all the way to the floating city, she could not imagine what rings could do. Three of them, for that matter.

"Let's see … gold is Lancistierre, silver is Divisorya … and what, Glasgérios?" asked Merc, grinning ear to ear. "All you need now is iron from Sinthea and bronze from Thoryngald."

"I'd have better luck besieging a cave troll," said Elayne as she threw her arms around Decker. It took her a moment longer to break away. "Should we speak in my quarters?"

Dove kept her hands clenched in her pockets, but Elayne smiled when she saw the grime marks on Dove's shirt. "I have a feeling we'll get along," she said playfully. "After traveling with this crew, I'm sure you wouldn't mind different company. And I don't blame you for climbing the wall to get away from them."

***

As they ascended the winding staircase that wrapped along the inside of the residence halls, Elayne rattled off quick facts about the Blackstone. It was mostly for Dove's sake. The others heard it all before, and they seemed accustomed to the long climb. *Lucky for them,* she thought. Her legs were burning by the eighth floor, and by the twelfth, her pride was taking a hit.

Apprentices were practicing spells in the common areas, and they snickered when they saw her struggle. Some of them came closer, curious about their potential classmate. She was surprised to see that many of them were around her age, but she supposed white-haired scholars had to have started somewhere. Some were novices who had not yet earned their robes, but that did not stop them from trying. They pretended to work when Elayne passed by, and occasionally, she would scold some of the younger ones for dueling. Elayne kept her face stern but smiled softly when they left. She did not seem the type to tolerate nonsense from fledglings, but at the Blackstone, she was home.

Gryff would kill to be here. Dove remembered the countless hours he had spent studying Ad'ami so he could understand the mages' scrolls, and he would translate them back to her in great detail. The mages could fill a library with his imagination. He would do well here.

As they continued up the steps, Dove felt her attention wane. It was hard to listen when everything around her was so new and foreign. She had never seen *students* before—young people, like her—learning their craft, not having to worry about survival. Their families must have spent their entire livelihoods to have them educated here. It was not too different from the training villages in the Firelands, she supposed, but those were designed to train fighters. Killers. Here, it was all about the elements. There was no weapon in sight.

"There are five archemages here, one for each Order," said Elayne. "Before, it was customary for one to preside over the Blackstone. You might have heard of a few of them."

Dove nodded, in agony. *I cannot believe she came down to greet us,* she thought. *I would have sent a falcon from the rooftop and told them to come up.* The steps were high and uneven, and Dove wondered if she would have had an easier time scaling the sides of the tower. She had always been a strong climber, but stairs were no fun.

"Eithan studied here," Elayne continued. "Came with dreams of being an alchemist mage and ended up being educated in three Orders. He became the youngest archemage in the history of the Blackstone, but he ended up returning to the Firelands." She grimaced. "He served as the King's advisor and was later executed by Valerya the Fireborne."

Instinctively, Dove's hand shot up to the coin in her pocket. *No wonder Decker does not like me,* she thought. *He associates me with Valerya.* And Valerya killed their hero. Everyone knew that. It was one of the rare truths believed by both sides.

Elayne waited a few more steps before continuing. "The other archemage I'm thinking of was centuries before our time, but you've probably heard of him. He once went by Vinzent, but when he presided over the Blackstone, he changed his name to Ro-than."

The hairs on the back of Dove's neck bristled. Gryff had always tried to get her to read the blood tales with him, especially on stormy nights, but she hated those stories the most.

"Don't scare the kid," Merc protested. "I barely sleep at night because of him."

Elayne ignored him gracefully. "Ro-than didn't always have dark intentions. But somewhere along the line, he got it in his head to induce his own powers by … *absorbing* them from others. While they were still alive. He …" She stopped herself when Wolff cleared his throat. "Well, let's not get into blood tales. His findings completely changed how we understood the elements, but his means were atrocious. The sacrifice was too great."

By the time they passed through the twin doors at the top, Dove barely noticed the ache in her legs. In truth, she could not feel them at all. They had turned wobbly and weak. She could not imagine having to climb those steps every day.

"Nothing to be afraid of. Mages are harmless," said Elayne, mistaking her discomfort for fear. Dove wondered if Elayne even remembered the first time she had climbed those steps.

Dove nodded, but she was surprised. She had not expected the Tower of the Mages to be so … *academic*. There was nothing bloodcurdling about bookcases and rolls of parchment, nor was there anything intimidating about rows of burnt-out candles from long nights of study. She assumed sorcerers just dueled in their spare time or turned each other into unnatural beings.

Elayne's quarters barely had enough room for a bed and a desk. Warm-toned wood did nothing to soften its austerity. Books were strewn across the sheets as though she had done some light reading before bed, but they were written in scripts that Dove could not understand. She wondered how anyone could make sense of all the lines and squares and circles.

"All right," said Elayne after everyone crammed themselves inside. Dove found herself next to Decker, much too close for comfort. She could smell the ale and smoke on him, the smell of a tavern. To her dismay, Elayne closed the window. "What's this all about, Uncle?"

Wolff pressed against the door to make sure it was shut. "Some of the birds were sent to fly," he said softly. There was no room to move, no room for extra words.

Elayne raised an eyebrow. "That's not possible," she said, throwing Dove a suspicious glance. *Now she thinks I am a traitor, too,* thought Dove miserably. Making new friends was harder than she thought. Her past followed her everywhere. "She's one of them, then? One of the Silent Messengers?"

"Nah, she's not sworn to silence. She's just silent," said Wolff, "but she survived the Purge and found her way onto our ship."

"A remarkable girl then, and a long way from home," said Elayne. It was not meant unkindly, but suspicion still burned in those golden eyes. "I wonder how many of your *friends* are looking for you. The skies aren't safe for birds these days."

"She's not one of them. Not one of the dogs, either."

"And you trust her so readily?" Elayne asked. "She, who shows up on your ship just as the command was given to flee. The only living survivor of the Purge—tell me, did Valerya let you go, then?"

A thief, a spy, and a liar. A traitor. Dove's list of titles was growing, and Elayne did not even know about the coin. No wonder Decker had been skeptical. When she said it like that, even saints would see the worst in her.

"No," said Wolff for her.

"How do you know?"

"Why else would you put Bastian at the entrance? If she was one of them, he would have smelled it on her. Even without crawling too deeply."

"Don't say that word."

"All I know is that the beacons haven't been lit in over a hundred years and suddenly, here we are. There's something else at work here, and my hunch is never wrong," said Wolff. "Rey is arranging a meeting with a Falcon tonight. Maybe this Glasger can tell us more about it."

That got Elayne's attention. "You two are talking again? As in, with words?"

"More like *fighting*," interrupted Merc impatiently. "Care to tell us what that was about?"

Wolff turned to the window. "Old wounds, heh." He gave a short chuckle, but Dove could tell it was not a good memory. "Just something we delivered for King Avander. Didn't know him personally, but he seemed like a good man. Desperate. Lost his family to the mystery illness, and can you imagine having Morian as your only comfort in life?"

He paused to let the thought unsettle everyone in the room. It worked. Dove would have swallowed a bottle of crushed nightbloom before she let it come to that.

"Get to the point, old man," Merc said with a frustrated sigh. "Was it the Scepter? Tell me it was the Scepter."

"Shut up, Merc," snapped Wolff, but he looked away. "This world is built on secrets. Let one unravel, and it'll all come crashing down."

"What's done is done," said Elayne firmly. For someone who spent her life around spells, she did not want to hear about magic scepters. "Whatever you did, it doesn't *matter.*"

"No," said Wolff. "We created a ripple and we have to make things right."

"What, so you're going to Glasgérios to join the fun?" asked Elayne. "You're not one of them anymore, Uncle. They're *insurgents* now. Traitors, and they're doomed. Leave the Realms to the Fates, *especially* the Firelands."

"You know I can't do that," said Wolff softly.

Elayne turned to Decker and Merc. "And what do you have to say about all this?" she growled. Dove had almost forgotten that Elayne grew up on the *Smuggler* until she saw them cower before her wrath. Old habits died hard.

"If it comes down to it, I'll go to Glasgérios," said Decker firmly.

"If it comes down to it." Elayne's eyes narrowed. "So you've joined *them,* then?" Buried resentment broke through the surface. The slight chill in her chambers suddenly became as cruel as a dry, cold wind. "So typical. Always at the front lines, never thinking about anyone else …"

If Decker felt affronted, he hid it well. "Them?" he asked calmly.

"Those … Red Spears," said Elayne. She kept her voice steady, but her gaze cut daggers. Suddenly, Dove did not want to know what curses and incantations she was capable of. "Passing notes like children, regrouping in the Icelands like vigilantes …"

"Elayne," said Wolff softly. "I'm not demanding your help. I'm asking for it. This journey will be a dangerous one."

Elayne opened her mouth to speak, but no words came out. Those amber-lit eyes narrowed when she turned to Dove. "And what is your part in all this?" she demanded.

Dove was glad she was standing next to Decker. She pushed him forward.

"She *survived,*" said Decker, coming to her aid. "And she will continue to do so, even if it means fighting."

Fighting, thought Dove. A strange word to associate with her. In times of conflict, she ran or climbed. She did not *fight.*

"She's a child," Elayne said, but the sharpness in her tone had dulled.

She cannot say no to him, Dove realized, throwing them a curious glance.

"Not after what she's seen," said Decker.

"And Rey didn't try talking you out of it?"

"He did," said Wolff, "but he's an old goat. You're smarter and more sensible."

"And we need a sorceress on the field," Merc cut in.

Elayne threw him a dark look. She lowered her hood, revealing black waves that fell about her shoulders. They framed her face, sharpened her features. "Don't say that word." Her tone brooked no patience, but after a long silence, she sighed. "Where is that Glasger?"

***

The Glasger came and went like a shadow, and life went on like nothing happened.

They were sitting in the Chimera, a tavern just off the main plaza. Dove wondered if it was wise to continue their discussion in such a populated area, especially with a Healer in the group, but the five went unnoticed. Too many guests had been drinking from dawn until dusk, and it was easy enough slipping into an empty corner, away from prying ears.

Dove had never been inside a tavern before. The closest had been the guest-keep in Myrne, but it attracted the dregs of the surrounding villages. She could not imagine a place more filled with mutual dislike. The boys who had strived to make her life miserable grew into brutish men who continued their tradition of fistfights and slurred insults. One or two claimed to have had her, as it was considered a brave undertaking to bed the voiceless. Rumors, of course, but it did not stop their friends from trying. It was not a happy place.

Dove glanced around the table and saw that she was not alone in her thoughts. Her companions sat in silence. She sat next to Wolff on one side; the other three sat on the other.

That was how the Glasger found them.

He had been watching them from across the tavern, and Dove wondered how they could have possibly missed him. Even at a distance, he stood out from the locals: he was tall and robed like a wraith, with skin so pale he did not seem human. Sort of like Gryff, but at least Gryff had warm features. This one looked carved from ice, and his presence was no less cold.

When the Glasger approached, Dove half-expected him to pull out a knife and slit their throats. Instead, he waved a hand at the candle before them, freezing the flame in its wick. He pulled down his face-guard, revealing silver eyes that were only slightly darker than his hair.

"Evening," he said raspily. His voice was coarse like he had not spoken in years, and his words sounded strained and unnatural.

"*Segnes,*" greeted Wolff.

The man took out a coin and put it on the table. "Sirian *kraehmys,*" he said. "I've been holding onto this for a long time, waiting … just waiting," he said. He struggled with Sinthean, but spoke it with a confidence that no one dared question.

"*Segnes,* Sirian," said Wolff, dropping his voice to a half-whisper. "I was told you might be able to—"

"No explanation," said Sirian dismissively, but not unkindly.

Elayne's eyes narrowed in suspicion while Decker suppressed a laugh behind his cup. They had been anticipating meeting the Glasger since they left the Blackstone, expecting more of a challenge to win him over. Rey wanted them to squirm before extending his help.

"Old goat …" Wolff whispered, but only Dove could hear.

"We go to Glasgérios," said Sirian firmly.

"I apologize, Sirian *kraehmys,*" said Elayne. "But how do we get across the border?"

"Easy," said Sirian. "I am *kraehmys*. I take you with me." He cast a sharp glance at the others. "Three strong men, escort."

"Escort?" asked Merc.

Sirian gave an impatient nod towards Dove.

"Hold on," said Wolff. "Kid hasn't even decided yet."

"Not safe. Eyes and ears everywhere," said the Glasger, looking around to see if anyone had been listening. He did not seem to be aware of it, either. He wore distrust like a second skin. "The Prefect can draw up the order. She must go. It is the will of the … *domeras.*"

"The shadow god?" asked Merc. His interest peaked.

"The shadows," Sirian corrected him. "No gods." Without another word, he extended his arm to Wolff. "We have committed the same sins," he said. "But there is hope yet."

Wolff clasped just beneath Sirian's elbow and nodded, but his frown indicated he had never seen the Glasger before in his life.

Great, thought Dove. *We are relying on a lunatic.*

Sirian turned his attention to Dove, and she screamed inside. "May the *domeras* guide you," he rasped.

And with that, Sirian *kraehmys* took his leave, slithering past scores of drunken patrons who did not notice him, and back into the shadows that embraced him.

***

Dove twisted and turned in her bed. She was glad Nan was not there. Most of the crew had opted for the nearest guest-keep in Divisorya, but Dove decided to stay behind. With everything going on, she did not think she could handle another change. A stupid idea, in retrospect. She may have been in the same bed, but now she could not sleep.

She crept out into the corridor of the *Smuggler,* her ears primed to detect the tiniest of sounds. Now that most of the passengers disembarked, it was the sort of silence that reeked of fear. The next voyage would be unlike the others, and Wolff had made it clear that those who wanted no part in it could stay behind. Not many did.

Dove glanced over her shoulder before continuing. Skulking about the airship would not raise too many questions, but she did not want anyone to know she was sneaking off by herself. For a silent stowaway, she had already attracted too much attention. The last thing she needed was for Wolff and the others to chain her to the ship.

The crew was huddling around the kiln for a late-night meal. Some had brought their Divisoryan friends—or "friends"—onboard, and ale was aplenty. She darted past them easily enough, and once she saw the lure of stable ground, she made a mad dash for freedom.

Damn, she thought, slowing her pace. She was still not used to the altitude. If she kept running, she would lose consciousness before reaching the entry gate.

At least the Prefect had made good on his word: she was allowed in and out without too much scrutiny, with even more ease than Wolff and the other traders. It came as no great surprise. After their quarrel, Rey looked like he wanted nothing more than to have Wolff banned from Divisorya.

Not like there was much to patrol in the city. Life migrated to the docks at this time of night. Dying starlight revealed endless paths before her, but there was only one that remained of interest to her—one where she knew no one would be lingering about.

As she wandered the streets in darkness, events of the day played in her mind, warped by terror and uncertainty. So many things demanded her attention. The Falcons, the Hounds, the mages, the non-mages... and none of it made sense. The Firelands were bad, but Valerya let her live. Divisoryans were good, but they wanted her gone. Smugglers were good-for-nothing, often likened to thieves, but they had taken her in. It was impossible to choose.

Before long, she found herself facing the Blackstone. Its jagged silhouette cut into the moonlight, shooting up as far as the eye could see ...

Candlelight.

A blood sacrifice? she wondered, scaring herself.

Still, now that it was there, she had to know. Even if someone had just forgotten to put it out, exploring the Blackstone was better than a sleepless night on an airship.

When she reached the other end of the bridge, she pressed her body against the side of the tower. *Concentrate.* She held her breath, trying to sense in the dark. *Fire.* Fire pacing back and forth in front of the main entrance. There was no way she could pass without raising questions.

Unless ...

She looked up, and a smile formed upon her lips. It was higher than anything she had ever climbed, and she knew no one who could claim they had snuck into the Blackstone at night.

Well, if there is one advantage in all of this, she thought after what seemed like an eternity of grabbing at shadows, *at least I cannot see the ground.* The air was so thin that it scraped against the insides of her lungs, but she moved steadily, using her legs to push her upwards. It did not bother her that there was nothing but gravity on either side; in truth, she had missed the feeling of flying. Not in the way the city was flying, but being away from the ground, from everyone else. Down below, the voiceless were easy targets, but up here, past the break in the cloud cover where silence spoke louder than words, she was home.

Colors of the ascendant stars swirled about her, so delicately constructed that it seemed a light rain might wash it all away. They revealed footholds in the stone that blazed a trail to the skies. She followed them all the way to the window and rested a knee on the ledge, already dreading the moment she would have to climb down.

Dove observed the candlelight until she was sure no one was near the window. She peered inside.

Nothing. No one was there. Only a candle burned softly near the ledge, nearing the end of its wick. She drew in a deep breath and propelled the rest of her body inside.

The library, she realized, both pleased and dismayed. Pleased that she had not stumbled into some sacrificial Bloodborne altar, dismayed that there were so many bookcases, some tilted to fit inside the chamber. She did not like libraries anymore.

No, better to sit at the edge of the world. She hopped back onto the ledge and glanced out into the distance, watching colors breathe life into the clouds.

"Impressive," a familiar voice rang from the library, nearly knocking her off the ledge.

How long has he been sitting there? She felt stone dig into her palms. It suddenly occurred to her how high up she was.

"It's a long way up," said Decker, barely glancing up from his journal.

And an even longer way down, she wanted to scream at him. She jumped back inside and felt blood rush to her face.

"Are you hiding, too?" he asked as his lips parted into a thin smile. The candlelight dwindled, and shadows crept into the circles around his eyes. She dropped her gaze. To her, he looked tired and broken, and she feared that if she looked into his eyes for too long, she would see her own broken face reflected back at her.

Dove nodded.

Decker's quill stopped halfway across the page. The tension between them weakened. "I was hiding, you know. But I suppose my plans have been foiled now."

Dove threw him a curious glance.

"I used to come here often," he said. "The only place the archemages never went after dark. Too high up for a night stroll." He laughed at her disbelief. "I know. Me and elemental science. But it's fascinating, really. It reduces all of us to simple, interconnected parts."

Dove shrugged. It did not seem too far-fetched.

"If that's true, can you imagine being Valerya the Fireborne?" he asked. "Having power so immense you can summon *dragons*."

Decker rose from his chair and moved closer to the window. Dove cringed despite herself. It was a strange feeling. She was not threatened by him, but he made her uneasy. She did not know if it was his elements, but something about him put her on the defensive.

"That Sirian is a strange fellow," he said, peering out the window as the wash of colors began to fade, "but he can grant us safe passage to Glasgérios. Coldest place in the world."

Dove shifted in the shadowed corner. She did not even know what snow looked like. The Scrolls spoke of winds as sharp as blades, of ice that burned like fire.

"You could stay in Divisorya if you wanted. Or you could go back to the Firelands. To Sinthea, maybe," he said.

Dove shivered. She winced at the thought of being closer to the Citadel.

"I see," said Decker softly when he saw her reaction. "We all assumed you were from Edenn, but I'm guessing you've made your king's acquaintance long before then. He doesn't seem like the kind who gets his hands dirty, so he must have given you to his guard dog. Tell me, how was Valerya the Fireborne?" He nodded towards her wrist, and his fingers brushed against her arm. "Did she do all that to you?"

Instinctively, Dove pulled back. *No, she did not,* she thought, feeling her muscles tense. *She let me live. She ...*

Even in her head, it sounded ridiculous. The woman could summon the spirit of the largest dragon that ever lived and command it to burn the world to the ground. Valerya the Fireborne was not nurturing. There was no way she wasted a single thought on Dove.

Dove shook her head. The truth hurt.

They stood in uncomfortable silence until Decker nodded. "That was ... poor of me," he said. "Sorry, Dove. There is very little about your world that I understand." Though his mouth did not move, his eyes relaxed into a smile. "You know, I used to come up here whenever something troubled me. And when I was your age, I was troubled quite a lot."

Dove blinked. She could not imagine the tower being a place of comfort. It was a massive structure of cold, lifeless stone. Rock jutted from the sides of the tower, but there were no lines of mortar that indicated something human had built it. Its imperfections were planned.

"Not because of the tower," he said, reading her face. "Look outside."

Dove did not even notice the sky shimmer, closing the seams between their world and the next. She stood there until dawn kissed the edge of darkness. Light cut holes into the clouds.

"Once you think about it, we're standing at the edge of time," said Decker. "When the sun stirs or the stars change, we're always the first to know." They stood in silence, watching the clouds lift. "Have you decided?"

Dove would have laughed had it not been so sad. Her Realm had betrayed her in every way possible. Gryff was the only person living that connected her to her old life in Myrne, and she did not even know where he was.

She turned to Decker and nodded.

I have to find him, she thought, realizing for the first time that she could not do it alone. *I just hope he gets himself as far away from the capital as possible before it's too late.*

13

THE RED CITADEL
FIRE REALM

Eight seconds before the dummy sword sent him sprawling. If someone had told him weeks ago that he would get used to the pain, he would have laughed, but the more he practiced the movements, the better he learned how to fall. *Again,* he told himself, propping himself up against the wall. He could not quit. He may have been making progress, but great strides meant nothing if his opponent was always two steps ahead.

Valk had become merciless in his training. Gone were the days he stood by and waited for Gryff to attack at his own pace. Now, he did not even bother waiting for him to stand.

'Not much of a swordsman,' Gryff recalled bitterly. He didn't even want to know what the other Spades were capable of. He mostly saw them in the dining hall, but they kept to their own, occasionally flexing their muscles to scare the novices. The other Hounds avoided them, but the feeling was mutual. There seemed to be great animosity between the Spades and the King's Command, and those who fell in between offered no comment. He suspected it was difficult to choose between saviors.

Saviors. That was one word for it, he supposed.

He leapt back before the sword could hit him a second time. *Not bad,* he thought, pleased with himself. The past few weeks had lined his arms with a hint of brawn, and his wrists bulged with muscles he didn't know he had. Even his hair seemed fuller—it grew in every direction and prickled his face when he turned. He had always kept it short to avoid lice, but that wasn't too much of a problem at the Citadel.

"Novices make the mistake of focusing on the most immediate threat. The *weapon,*" said Valk as he lunged forward. Instinctively, Gryff brought up his blade and rolled to the side. It was a lost cause and he knew it, but if he didn't at least try, it would have hurt worlds more. In the training hall, failure was reprimanded, but surrender was punished. Severely.

Gryff braced himself, but the blow never came. Normally, Valk would have taken advantage of the opening and gone for the knee, but his hesitation confirmed Gryff's suspicions: something else was on his mind.

"They panic and shut out their surroundings." Valk raised his voice. "Pay attention!" He lunged again as Gryff advanced, and his sword hit the nape of Gryff's neck. It was more of a reprimand than an attack, but a sheet of Ice washed over the ground all the same. "*Beheaded,*" said Valk, his tone sharp with disapproval. "Concentrate!"

"It's a bit difficult to concentrate on anything else," Gryff muttered. Instinctively, he ran his fingers along the back of his neck until he felt it sting. It would likely bruise.

"It is imperative that you concentrate on *everything* else," the Spade insisted. "Your opponent's eyes, his build, his defenses ..."

"Defenses?"

"My armor is infused with blackwood," Valk said, pointing to his breastplate. "It cannot burn, and neither can I. Any novice knows that. Any *child* growing up in the Firelands knows that. We are sparring with sticks, but it may be useful to know what I can do to you without them."

Gryff fell silent, suddenly feeling foolish. *Why does he even need blackwood armor?* he wondered. Valk couldn't burn even if he wanted to. If anything, Gryff needed it.

"Let's stop for the day," said Valk, half-irritated. It was the first time Gryff saw a crack in his demeanor. It wasn't much, but he didn't want to stretch the Spade's patience any further. "You must learn to control your elements. And your mind."

Gryff relaxed his element hand and watched color return to his fingers. His power was becoming unpredictable. His fear often frosted the room, but it was anger that turned it to Ice, sharper and colder than any blade.

"Eight seconds," said Gryff, trying to diffuse the tension. "I'm getting better."

He had meant it as a joke, but Valk wasn't the type to partake. No wonder he was the General's right-hand man. Gryff reckoned no words were wasted between them.

Instead, Valk nodded. "You'll continue to improve if you look beyond your sword," he said, but there was a hard edge to his tone. "Tomorrow, we aim for ten. Make sure you've gathered your wits about you. Otherwise, I swear I'll get Diante to finish your training."

He threw down his dummy sword and took his leave.

Gryff frowned. Their sessions were getting shorter, and Valk had stopped accompanying him to his quarters. In truth, it was a bit spooky; once the Spade left the training hall, he seemed to vanish. No matter how quickly Gryff regained his strength and scrambled after him, the corridors that greeted him were empty, cold.

And dark.

The curtains were loose, but no light came through them. It was the only time he could roam castle grounds, and no one gave him any trouble. Being squire to the Summoner General meant he could go where he pleased—which usually meant the kitchens after hours—so he stood tall and regained strength quickly. He didn't know if his good treatment was a result of Morian wanting to annoy Valerya, or Valerya wanting to annoy Morian, but he couldn't complain. It certainly attracted the attention of the chambermaids and the occasional serving boy. They were especially nice to him, hoping to gain favor.

It was the first time girls looked at him, really looked. They didn't know of his origins—all they saw was an aspiring Swordsworn who had fallen in the Summoner General's good graces and the glory that came with it. But as tempted as he was to talk to them, he could only think of Dove when he opened his mouth. *They may shine with jewels, but they pale compared to her.* Wealth meant nothing without substance.

Gryff sighed in relief when he reached the doors to the library. Valk had assumed correctly. His mind was elsewhere, on Eithan's journal. Most of it was names and places that left Gryff's mind as quickly and quietly as they entered. But some parts …

He glanced over his shoulder, making sure the door was closed. He opened the book to the page with the folded corner.

***

MEREYN SHIELD

***

Eithan had clearly been an alchemist mage. Some of the pages were filled with spells and potions he had never heard of, but the mereyn shield intrigued him the most. He knew that strong casters could create a shield using the elements, but someone had scribbled *"Otherworld"* next to the name. He did not know what that meant.

He closed his eyes and concentrated. *First, press my hands together ...* That was easy enough. *Then cast the elements against each other.* If he did it correctly, the force would push his hands apart, and he could use the concentrated energy to cut a circle in the air, then a triangle inside the circle. Someone had drawn the motions in the margins. It couldn't have been that hard.

He sighed and opened his eyes when nothing happened. Maybe he needed more elements.

Or maybe it only works with Fire. He ran through the lines with his finger. *No.* There was no reason it couldn't work for Ice. He just needed to concentrate harder. He drew in a deep breath, closed his eyes. *I need to think of something.*

Usually, it was panic or fear that drew his elements to the surface, but he wasn't afraid of anything. Of Valerya, sure, but she wasn't standing in front of him. *She can probably cast a mereyn shield,* he realized. Maybe she could teach him.

He slammed the journal shut. *Enough.* He should be thinking of ways to get out, not ways to stay in, and nothing good ever came from the words of ghosts.

A knock at the door jolted him to his senses.

Gryff threw the journal under his pillow and tried to think of something else. He may have been better than Dove at hiding his thoughts, but the Hounds were good at sniffing out lies.

Valk, he thought when he heard a second knock. He was the only one who bothered knocking. Still, Valk opened the door without asking. Some of the color had returned to his face since that morning, but that didn't make him any less stern. "Our General wishes to speak with you," he said, a veiled command.

Gryff felt his insides deflate, and he rose without sound. He didn't even bother asking why. Nothing good ever happened when Valerya had him summoned.

The walk to her chambers made him uneasy. On good days, Valerya ignored him. On bad days, which heavily outweighed the good, it wasn't just her he was dealing with. Sometimes, he could feel the dragon's presence around him. It was always faint, but it grumbled beneath the surface like a volcano in bad temper. He didn't know if one influenced the other, but it certainly seemed to sharpen Valerya's mood.

Not that it needs any sharpening, thought Gryff. He prayed for a good day.

They turned into a corridor lit by torches that lined the walls, but they burned out one by one as Valk passed. Occasionally, Gryff glanced behind him in wonder. Valerya didn't seem the type to care for worldly possessions, but she had most of the upper floor of the tower to herself. Once called the God's End because of the Sun-sworn temple that bordered it, it was now fondly referred to by servants as the Godsend: Valerya forbade them to enter and clean without permission, so they rarely came by. A single serving girl—Sian, she was called—brought hot water for her baths, but aside from that, Valerya preferred to maintain her own quarters.

Gryff counted three main chambers and a slew of smaller rooms, but he didn't know what they were for. He only saw the insides of the chamber where she worked; the rest were a complete mystery.

His eyes fell on the open door across the atrium. This part of the castle didn't seem particularly forgiving towards negligence, and it struck his eyes like a blade in the dark.

"What's that?" he asked.

Valk followed his gaze and sighed. "We really must get that door fixed," he said. "Nothing good ever comes out of there."

"Is that one of our General's rooms?"

"I dare you to ask her," Valk laughed. "But no, let's keep you alive a bit longer. That's where the alchemists work."

"That doesn't sound so bad."

"Our *King's* alchemists," said Valk. "They tend towards the more ... shall we say, unnatural side of the elements."

"You mean like ... the witchborn?"

"Ah, I forget they still call them that in the villages," said Valk, chuckling to himself. "That door used to lead to the mages' chambers, but after Eithan, our King moved in some of his own. But make no mistake. They are no friend to us."

After Valerya killed him, you mean, thought Gryff, but he kept it to himself. Instead, he turned his attention to the iron doors, painstakingly hand-forged with flowered designs he knew the General despised. He had always assumed the door came with the quarters. She'd had thorns added, at least, to stave off the impression that anyone else could live there.

The Spade knocked, and at the General's command, they entered. Valk bowed his head, and Gryff dropped to his good knee.

With a swift gesture, Valerya motioned him forward. "Valk tells me you're improving, and I don't have to worry about you dying on the battlefield for eight seconds," she said.

Gryff blinked. It was the highest compliment she had ever paid him.

"You will continue until you can best the worst of us," she said, her expression unwavering. "Most of the threats we face come from fishermen and farmers' boys. Surely you can best a pitchfork?"

Gryff reddened. He had been proud of his progress, but his skills were far from presentable. "I will try," he said, hiding his own disappointment.

"Try harder," the General said, casting his response aside. "He also tells me your rage is blinding you."

Gryff struggled to find the right words, but his protests were caught in his throat. *Excuses are a weak man's armor,* the Spades always said, so he said nothing. Better to accept responsibility than deflect it like a novice. The General's men loved their sayings, and most of them involved fighting.

"You're not a Swordsworn. You are under *my* guidance, whether you and I like it or not. And I need my own to see," she said. "You cannot see if you are blind, correct?"

"I can see, General," said Gryff, deciding that agreeing was the safer option.

"Then tell me," she said, finally glancing up. "What do my doors look like?"

He paused, confused. "They're … made of iron, with rose designs, and thorns added in later." He knew he sounded like a fool the moment the words left his lips, but most people wouldn't have noticed the design in the first place.

If his aim was to disappoint her, he did not disappoint.

"Valk," she commanded.

The Spade stepped forward. "The doors were likely a gift from King Avander after our General's induction into the Swordsworn, which is why they were never changed. He had likely had Eithan the Archemage infuse them with blackwood, for it was he who first discovered the technique. From that, we can deduce that our General had an amicable, if not jesting, relationship with the former king."

It all seemed painfully obvious now that Valk had said it, except for one thing. "Jesting?" Gryff asked despite himself.

"Do I look like I enjoy flowers, boy?" snapped the General. "Valk got all that on his first day at the Citadel." She rose from her chair. "You burn. You're weak. I've got boys half your age with twice the skill. I need you to use your wits, not your emotions. Otherwise, what good are you to me?"

Gryff fell silent, and his heart twisted inside him. *They're acting like I volunteered to do this,* he thought. *Like I wanted to.* He paused, guiltily. He didn't though, did he?

"Speak freely," said the General, to his surprise. He must have let it show, because soon after, she sighed. "I'm not Morian. You may speak freely."

"I …" Gryff began. Facing the She-Jackal often stopped his thoughts before they could form words. He took a deep breath before he spoke. "I didn't want …"

"This glorified lifestyle?" asked the General. Her laughter came as a shock. "What makes you resist us so much?"

There was no turning back, and Gryff should have seen it coming. Years of isolation had done nothing to improve his subtlety. "Because … so many lives have been taken. Innocents."

"And if you had the power, what would you have the Sword-sworn do?"

"Surrender to peace," answered Gryff with as much dignity as he could muster. He knew it sounded like a childish fantasy, but no one had ever asked him before.

"*Peace,*" repeated the General, and his confidence plummeted at her tone. "Listen well, Glasger. War doesn't breed heroes like you hear in the legends. It brings out the absolute worst in us." She leaned back in her chair and contemplated him for a long moment.

"Did you lose family in the fire?"

"My parents died years ago," said Gryff.

"Siblings? A wife?"

"A friend." The word dropped and thudded in his mind with such force, he almost buckled under its weight. "I don't know where she is."

It was the first time since Myrne that he had spoken of her. The tatters of her memory came to life, a thousand disjointed bits pouring into him with frightening intensity. The grey, hollow eyes that had haunted him for months turned dark auburn. *Dove,* he thought.

He was dimly aware that the General's eyes were on him, but there was no way of knowing whether his words had fallen on sympathetic ears.

She nodded, uninterested in the details. "Now imagine that one of my men hunted your friend down and drove a sword through her heart. And let's say I had him brought before you to these very chambers. Would you accept terms of peace then?"

Gryff frowned. "But you're eliminating an entire people from the histories," he said. *People like me,* he wanted to say.

"An entire people?" she asked, amused. "I burned down a few villages and slaughtered insurgents in each one. Your Sovereign had a faster, more *violent* suggestion, but I had no desire to set fire to the Scarlet Cities." Her lips twisted into a bitter smile. "Power means a constant battle of choosing the lesser evil. Imagine what worse your *Sovereign* would do if I weren't around. Remember what the Iceborne have done."

"But … we attacked them first," Gryff said.

"And who attacked us before that?" she asked. "Hundreds of years ago, the Lancistierrans kept us as slaves. The Glasgers *sold* us as slaves, and the Thoryns ignored our cries for help. Do not delude yourself, boy. These … *victims* that you feel so sorry for were at the top once, and they too did atrocious things."

"So you agree with our Sovereign?" asked Gryff, feeling bold.

He could sense cold amusement lurking beneath the surface. "I am bound, for better or worse, to the safety of the Realm." She waved a hand dismissively. "I ask you again. What would you do to the Swordsworn who murdered your friend?"

"I would …" he began, looking at his hands for counsel. The question embedded in his imagination a thousand gruesome possibilities. He could almost see the Ice emanating from his fingertips.

The General nodded solemnly, and Gryff had a horrible feeling that she understood him better than most. "Valk informs me that your powers are getting erratic," she said, changing the subject. She glanced at his hands as if expecting him to prove her point.

"They come and go," said Gryff. "Mostly frost, bits of Ice here and there …"

The General cut him off. "I have no use for snowmen, boy," she said coldly. "You must learn to control them."

Gryff held his breath. "Will you teach me?" he asked. For a split-moment, he wanted to ask about the mereyn shield.

The General laughed, much to his embarrassment. "I would rather endure a lifetime of tea with Morian than see Ice on a daily basis." She waved a hand. "Now get out of my sight."

Gryff bowed hastily and turned to Valk, but the Spade didn't look like he had been paying attention. He stood in silence, waiting until he was needed. Even Valerya went back to her scrolls. They were done for the evening, so Gryff could go back to being invisible.

He let out a sigh of relief when the doors closed behind him. His body felt as small as his courage, but without the dragon's presence, he felt free. He felt the sudden urge to run to his quarters, but something else lingered in the back of his mind.

A presence draws near, a voice whispered, smooth and soft like silk.

"Who's there?" demanded Gryff. He whirled about, unable to trace its source.

The Summoner's lackey, another replied, a woman.

A sound startled him. It was barely audible, but in the cold, stone halls, it had the power of a scream. He took a deep breath and forced himself to step forward. Their voices left an echo in his mind that did not sound human, but it stayed, hauntingly beautiful—yet he saw no one. He drew back, pressed his hands to his ears. *Is this ...*

Don't be scared, said the woman, and he jumped. Gryff could almost feel her voice under his skin. *I won't slip into your mind. Ma'am will get upset.*

"Who are you?" Gryff asked again, but it was barely a shade above a whisper. He turned his attention to the door across the atrium, but it had closed. He considered knocking at the General's door but decided against it. The last thing he needed was to be branded a coward, a believer of blood tales. "Get out of my head!"

Truly? Child of the night, said the man, darkly seductive. *I see what's inside you. I sense what flows in your veins. I sense many things.*

Gryff took another deep breath as he quickened his pace. Skin-crawlers, he thought. The whispers fell farther and farther behind as he walked, and he felt the spell lift.

When he reached his chambers, he let out another sigh of relief. Between skin-crawlers and the She-Jackal, it was easy to feel trapped. He glanced at his hands. *But then again ...* He made sure the door was shut before he closed his eyes and breathed in the cold. He pressed his palms together. *What would I do?*

He bit his lip. *No. What would I have done?* He remembered that night in Myrne, when Dove shoved him aside and surrendered herself to the Hounds. He tried to go after her, but the light from the fire stopped him. *I couldn't do anything.*

Anger pulsed through him, and he felt his jaw clench. *But I can now.*

A burst of Ice exploded between his hands, forcing them apart. Surprise broke his concentration, and in an instant, it was gone. It wasn't a mereyn shield, but it was a start.

Before he could try again, movement grazed the edge of his vision. He turned to face it. Even without the light, he could sense where it was. He had spent his life in darkness and wore its shroud like a second skin. The hairs on the back of his neck bristled.

"Show yourself!" he commanded.

"Don't be angry, m'lord!" a voice called meekly from the corner. Gryff couldn't make out its source's features, but its figure was thin, gangly, and warded off fear. He lowered his guard and frowned.

"Who's there?" he asked.

"It's Marcus, m'lord! The tailor's 'prentice," he said dutifully, stepping out into the moonlight with his arms raised. He didn't look to be much older than Gryff, but he seemed to be stuck in perpetual adolescence: all limbs with no fat to warm his bones. He didn't speak with the refined accent of the highborn, which meant he probably slept in the capital and commuted up the hill whenever he was needed. Valerya didn't much like the castle smiths and tailors and often preferred to summon her own.

"The tailor's 'prentice," Marcus repeated proudly. "Our General has ordered me to take m'lord's measurements."

"I'm not a lord," said Gryff, though he did like the sound of it. He had often been mistaken for a lordling at the Scriptorium because of his pale skin, which—rightfully—looked like it had never seen daylight.

Until Valerya burned half my face off. "Why are you sitting in the dark?" he asked.

"Had to wait for m'lord. Didn't want to burn out the candles."

"What for?" he asked.

"I'm not supposed to say, m'lord," answered Marcus. "All I know from my master is that it has to shield m'lord from the sun."

"Isn't it a bit dark?" asked Gryff. "I mean, couldn't this wait until morning?"

Marcus smiled good-naturedly. "Salandra is enough for my eyes, and I work quick."

Gryff felt a twinge of excitement shoot down his spine. If anything, at least it was a welcome change from the rest of the evening. "Sorry," he said. "Please begin."

14

THE GREENWOOD
FIRE REALM

The hooves of his impossibly large horse clashed hard against stone as they fled, probably attracting every Swordsuit within a five-mile radius. Dancer had an even bigger horse, but she knew how to ride, steering instead into decades of leaf mold and rich earth that stilled footfall.

He had imagined their escape to be grander, somehow.

Ever since the First Warriors saw fit to claim destriers as their steed, the common-folk thought that made them the vessels of heroes, inseparable and loyal when they charged the killing fields. But the legends were lies. These monstrosities made for terrible getaway horses, and they grew tired after long distances. They may have inspired fear under the command of dragon-summoning generals, but they seemed to attract trouble everywhere else.

Especially in the company of two fugitives who had left twenty men spattered in violence without so much as the dignity of a second glance. Of course, that spilled blood was not their doing.

Not all of it, at least.

"Bard!" called Dancer, halting her steed. "Watch where you're going!" He did well to remember that the sweet ring of her voice led to the undoing of an entire Swordsuit convoy, no less than her ivory skin was capable of inspiring thousands of songs.

Battle songs.

Terrifying, blood-crazed battle songs.

She was no more a Dancer than he a Bard, but that was how they had introduced themselves. Two death-bound fugitives escaping from a prison caravan amid smoke and fire had neither time nor need for human connection, so names were useless.

It didn't look like it was the first time she had gotten herself into this sort of mess, either, and she handled imprisonment with the utmost poise. People like her didn't get caught—not unless, of course, they willed it, and Bard was certain he was smitten from the moment she threw him that charming smile that said: *touch me and die.*

Bard hadn't exactly gotten caught, himself. He had been trudging through the forest when he heard the clamor of Swordsuits marching east, which was where he was headed. Sitting in a caravan seemed much more comfortable than walking the last stretch of the journey, so he joined them.

There had been a third. Smith, they called him. Whether iron or steel was of little importance, as neither came to his aid when the blood came spurting from his throat. Still, he had been an enjoyable fellow.

Shame, really, that he had to go like that.

They had been held up on the way to the capital by a troupe of plunderers. If he had been a real bard, he would have sung of it, and she would have danced. Instead, they stared in silent amusement as the Swordsuits tried to fend them off. It was that look, that spark of mischief in her eyes, that convinced him they would make great friends.

Until they parted, at least. For such was the life of nomads and adventurers.

It should have been an easy battle, but these were no ordinary bandits. They were probably part of the insurgent movement that was spreading to the outskirts, outsiders who sought to destroy every Hound they could find. One of those rogue brotherhoods Bard had been hearing about, and the reason he was heading east.

Flames gave way to Ice, and it was to Bard's advantage that he and Dancer looked nothing like the sun-shat bastards of the Firelands. He wasn't sure if it was his dark blue—no, *azure*—hair or eyes of perfect, indeterminate color that gave him away.

It was the hair, most likely.

Still, by the end of it, not all the Swordsuits were marked with blood. Two were left standing, looking positively pleased with themselves. They were the biggest of the lot, absolute beasts who decimated the herd. Surely the kind who thought destriers made for good steeds. They had brought their greatswords down upon their assailants, separating limb from body with a single stroke. Headless corpses fell to the ground like sacks of meat.

One of them had regrettably been Smith, who ran when one of the bandits—bless his soul—tried to free them. He didn't quite get the mercy of a quick end, but it was better than what the Fates had in store for the remaining plunderers, who had to endure all sorts of flying appendages before death claimed them.

Spurred by bloodlust, the Swordsuits needed something softer to break. It didn't take them long before they set their eyes on Dancer.

"Sing us a song!" they demanded, drunk from adrenaline.

Dancer simply smiled and obeyed. Her voice was sweet, but fearless, and she sang to challenge, not to obey. Even Bard lost himself in her song, if only for a moment, and it didn't seem to be in a language he recognized.

Sweet, beautiful Dancer. She could have passed for a true Waterborne if it weren't for her eyes. Her long, dark hair spilled over her shoulder like rows of silk, deceptively mesmerizing, but her eyes betrayed Fire. He had caught himself staring on a number of occasions, but it was those two who couldn't keep their eyes off her: the fragile porcelain doll.

And it was Dancer who ended them.

It started with the smaller of the two, as Bard had anticipated. The man had already been restless since they caught her on the Queensroad, and after the thrill of taking on a horde of bandits, he was practically bulging in his breeches.

Should I be concerned? Bard wondered for a split-moment, but he held himself back as the man cut her binds, intent on breaking her. With lightning speed, she wrested the dagger from him and slit his throat. Bard watched, impressed, as the edge of the knife split open soft flesh, spraying the sides of the caravan with warm blood. Some of it had even gotten on Dancer, but she simply groaned, inconvenienced, and hopped down from the caravan. She didn't even wait for the poor bastard to die properly.

It happened faster than his beast of a companion could process, and Dancer allowed him a moment to think. When he realized what had happened, she straightened, ready for the next round. It was almost comical seeing her confront him like that, like a fairy princess who had just woken up from a nap to take on an ogre.

She tossed the dagger back in the caravan, just beyond Bard's reach. She was unarmed and facing a giant with nothing but blood smears on her skin that reminded him of red war paint.

No matter, thought Bard, shrugging it off. He was there if things went awry. Even in a proper swordfight, he could still pose a challenge to the Hound, and he had already lost count of all the ruffians he had slain on his travels. Granted, his hands were still tied, but such details could be overlooked under the correct circumstances.

Grinning, the Swordsuit dropped his sword, clearly pining for his dead companion. "I'm going to *murder* you," he said. Malice formed on his already unsightly face. "But before that, I'm going to fuck you until you *scream.*"

Crude, thought Bard disapprovingly. There were a million and more threats the man could have given, some with even a modicum of good taste, and he chose poorly.

The Swordsuit charged forward. Without a moment's hesitation, Dancer swung her right arm around the man's neck. His own arm grabbed at it instinctively as his other hand hooked behind her head. For a wild moment, it looked like the man would fall forward and crush her, but she thrust herself forward, her body providing just enough counterweight to keep balance.

That gave her the leverage she needed. She lifted her lower body up, wrapped her legs around his arms and left shoulder, and clung on for dear life. The man's head was caught behind her leg now, and the pressure of her weight, tiny as she was, brought him down to one knee.

She had him.

With her legs still wrapped around his shoulder, forcing his arms in place, she reached an arm out in front of his leg, which was supporting most of their combined weight. Bard saw her take a deep breath as she thrust her arm back, punching his leg out from under him.

The man tumbled forward with her legs still around him. She had him pinned.

Surely that was not what he was expecting, thought Bard, grinning to himself. Under vastly different circumstances, this might have been considered foreplay.

Dancer had no time to spare. Her legs were holding him down, but he could still break free if she hesitated. She threw her body back, still holding onto his arm, until …

SNAP.

Bard didn't know which was louder: the sickening crack of the man's arm as it was wrenched free from its socket, or the stream of curses that followed. She had just incapacitated his element hand.

As a mercy, Dancer wrapped her leg around the man's neck and held. His other arm flailed about wildly, but it did nothing to hinder his fate. If she hesitated, even in the slightest, Bard was certain the Swordsuit would have thought to burn her. But when faced with death, Bard often found that bestial instincts took over even the bravest of men.

And two seconds was all one needed to lose.

Soon, the man's flailing and gargled protests stopped for good.

Even Bard held his breath, careful not to interrupt the silence that followed. If the man feigned death, not even Bard could react fast enough to save her.

Dancer stayed in that position for a while, making sure he was dead. She lay back, exhausted.

Bard's lips curled into an amused smile. "I don't suppose I could trouble you to cut me loose, could I?" he asked.

The thought of moving seemed to displease her, and she threw him a playful glance. "Who are we kidding, Bard?" she asked breathlessly, her legs still curled around the dead man. Her face was spattered with blood. "You look like you can handle yourself."

Good girl, he thought, still smiling as a surge of Storm burst from his wrists and exploded through his binds.

***

If love existed like it did in the legends, Bard would have likely been balls deep in it. In the figurative sense, of course. But he was older, wiser, and aware that she was fully capable of murdering him in his sleep.

Sometimes, they spoke, but neither seemed particularly keen on revealing secrets. So they kept it to mindless banter, cutting out their past lives from their present, enjoying each other's lies. He was good at it, but she was better, and he bought every word.

He was headed to the Glasgérios, but first, he had to make a stop in Genovel. Dancer just wanted to get out of the Realm. That much they agreed on: they would part at the border, probably after wiping out the border sentries, if no other possibility presented itself.

Bard knew it couldn't have been very far, but the setback had disoriented him somewhat, and he found himself uncertain of his surroundings. Still, they marched on. On some mornings, irritation ate at their nerves, and tempers flared under the pettiest of arguments. There were stretches of time where they simply refused to speak to each another. Still, they got along great, given the circumstances.

And at least it was an irritation born of idleness, not hunger.

Bard was an excellent huntsman, and he had snatched longswords from two of the Swordsuits they left behind. Dancer had refused to carry one, claiming that swords were the lowest form of attack—weapons wielded by trolls and barbarians and Hounds.

"Don't tell me you're a pacifist," he had teased, but that was before he turned back and saw her pilfering a crossbow.

Together, they caught more than enough food to stave off hunger.

The Greenwood was infamously vast, and at times, there was no way of telling where they were headed. As a precaution, they kept their hoods up, as their foreign appearances would warrant suspicion anywhere.

The black demon-horses didn't help much in that regard.

Dancer was prone to rashes, signs of her bodily resistance to the Firelands, but they washed away when she drank from the streams. She had sustained all manners of scrapes and bruises along the way, especially after that face-off with the beast of a Hound, but they, too, faded over time. Bard wondered how many things had marred that beautiful face, how many scars she had hidden from sight. She was still a half-breed, a bastard in the eyes of the Firelands, but Water ran true in her veins.

They encountered single huts and guest-keeps along the way, but they never lingered for more than a day. The last thing they needed was a horde of Swordsuits on their tails, especially after the carnage they left behind. Anyone who chanced upon the two travelers may have assumed that *Bard* had slaughtered those twenty men, the way he was built. He was the one with the broad shoulders, a strapping chest, and muscles carved into his arms and legs from years of brawls and aimless wandering. No one would ever suspect his Lancistierran companion of causing all that chaos, especially when she smiled, or told them he was guilty.

Bard was relieved when he saw the stone houses. It wasn't Genovel, but after weeks of navigating through forests and countless ravines, he was beginning to doubt they would ever find traces of human settlement again.

"I would skin you alive for a shower," grumbled Dancer next to him. "Where are we?"

Her tender words melted his heart.

"This should be Waird," he answered. In truth, he had no idea and said the first name that came to mind. If they weren't allowed to have names, then villages weren't, either.

The thought of a cold shower and a warm meal that someone else killed appealed to him. Perhaps they could stop here for the night if they avoided the guest-keep, where the loud-mouthed and travel-weary gathered like moths to a flame. He supposed the two of them would draw attention to themselves no matter where they went, but he didn't feel like a fist fight on an empty stomach. He glanced at Dancer and saw in mild surprise that she wasn't quite feeling up to the challenge, either.

Bard was getting old.

"Follow me," he said. "I know a good place to rest, and we can find some Hounds to thrash about in the morning."

***

"A brothel," said Dancer, feigning indignity as the chambermaid scuttled out of the room. The sight of a Thunderborne traveling with a blood-soaked nymph seemed to unsettle her, especially when they were armed to the teeth with blades and a crossbow.

They had tied the destriers to the stables. There were a few others, which meant that the pubs and guest-keeps were likely teeming with self-important—or newly forged—Swordsuits.

"What?" asked Bard with all the innocence he could muster as she propped her crossbow against the wall. "You wanted a bed and a shower, right?"

She eyed the mattress skeptically. The sheets would likely undo any effects of a cleansing bath, but it was still better than another cold night huddled in a cave. And as far as brothels went, it showed only the occasional hint of dark deeds. It even had a washroom for its patrons. Given what they charged for an evening, they should have had goddamn servants.

It was a good thing those plunderers had been heavy with coin.

A thought of a more mundane sort seemed to cross her mind, and she frowned. "You don't think that chambermaid will tell, do you?"

"Of course not." Bard yawned. "These girls get roughed up all the time. They appreciate a little brawn to scare away overzealous patrons."

He unstrapped his scabbards, not bothering to put his weaponry anywhere discreet. They were in a brothel, not a monastery. He stretched his arms before he began undoing the straps of his leather breastplate. It boasted several features he had never used, like knife sheaths sewn onto the front, but he wore it like a second skin—a token from days past. It had looked much more intimidating before he lost his pauldrons in a pub wager, but he honestly hadn't expected the Crimson King to push through on his threat to cleanse the Realm. *A stupid bet.* He sighed. *In retrospect, at least.* He liked those pauldrons.

After a long moment, Dancer decided their accommodations were adequate. When she left to find the washroom, he found himself wishing he could join her.

Damn, it's been a while. He tried not to imagine her slipping naked into a warm bath. He even tried not to imagine her caressing her own skin as she washed the blood and dirt from her body, and he definitely tried not to imagine her hands moving down, down, after such a long journey, sliding between her ...

His attempts were futile.

He removed his mud-caked boots and kicked them to the side. He'd had his fair share of adventures with pretty women on his travels, mostly tavern wenches with forgettable names who left his touch with nothing more than a romp and a memory. And he never turned down the opportunity to visit a good brothel every now and then.

But none of it meant anything. Not anymore, at least.

He was sprawled on the bed, exhausted from all that thinking, when Dancer returned. "Pathetic," she said, throwing her blood-stained garb at him. She was wearing a fresh linen shirt that went down to her knees and nothing underneath, it seemed.

"Where'd you get that?"

"Swiped it," she replied nonchalantly, smelling of fresh lavender. "I'm tired of sleeping in the blood of Fire Hounds."

Marry me, he thought. "Glad you feel so at home," he said instead.

She sat on the edge of the bed. "What, you think I've never been to a brothel before?" she asked, raising an eyebrow. She lay on her stomach and eyed him playfully, almost daring him to make the next move. Those dark eyes betrayed a myriad of secrets, but she seemed the kind to take them, not give them—and mercy to those who tried to take them from her.

Significantly more interesting than a tavern wench.

Bard had a witty retort crafted perfectly upon his lips, but she crawled on top of him before it could escape his mouth. Waves of dark brown spilled onto his chest. Her mouth moved to his throat, and she kissed it, swiftly but passionately, and he breathed her in.

If he hadn't seen her take down a Swordsuit twice her size with her bare hands, he would have thought there was an unspoiled sweetness about her—but alas, he had seen that side of savagery in her, that passion that likely spilled into other, perhaps *unspoken* parts of her life.

Or so he hoped.

He closed his eyes and dug both hands into her hair.

"Damn it," she cursed softly into his ear, perhaps her idea of sweet nothings. "I see I don't have to tell you to play along." She shifted her weight, feeling him underneath her. "Maybe one day, we'll make this real."

Bard blinked in confusion. "What?" he asked.

It was the only thing that could have ruined the moment, even more than a dagger to his throat, but she said it anyway: "I saw some Suits in the hallway. The chambermaid squealed."

And as though the gods lived to spite him with unfortunate timing, there was a knock at the door. *"Open up!"* a voice shouted from outside.

"What?" demanded Bard, his frustration genuine. He turned back to Dancer, and that gleam of mischief in her eyes was enough to melt his heart. He grinned, and both chuckled to themselves. *Well done,* he thought.

It was in that compromising situation that the Swordsuits found them. When they barged through the door, Dancer rolled off Bard in feigned terror and crouched against the wall. "Pl ... please don't hurt me," she whimpered, with a foreign accent she pulled out of thin air.

Unbelievable, thought Bard. He supposed it was useless trying to intimidate them when a rather excited part of him bulged through his breeches, but his irritation was authentic. "What is the meaning of this?" he said with the exaggerated outrage of a nobleman whose tea ceremony had just been interrupted. They may have shared the same milk-tongue, but he tried to imitate their accent, which only made him sound like a half-wit.

Dancer hugged a pillow close to her chest, hiding her face, but he knew she was laughing at him behind it.

"We got word that some suspicious folks have been sneaking about this part of town," the smaller one answered, strutting about the room until his eyes fell on the pile of leather armor and weaponry on the floor.

They were both common foot-soldiers, from the looks of it, clad in steel and wielding swords that were too heavy for them. Destrier-riders, most likely. But solid Fire-casters, judging by the steel in their armor. One of them even had a bow slung about his shoulder and a quiver full of unused arrows.

Why is it always the smaller one that talks first? Bard mused. Instead, he said, "I, sir, am a respectable client of this fine establishment."

"Take a look at *this* one," said the one with the bow. He reached Dancer and wrenched the pillow from her grasp. Bard saw her glance back at them with those big, innocent eyes.

They're doomed, he thought.

"How about I take his turn?" the Swordsuit asked, shooting her a nasty grin that revealed a wonderful array of missing teeth. "He hasn't used you yet."

"I am appalled," said Dancer most unconvincingly. "Is this how you treat the good citizens of Waird?"

Bard wanted nothing more than to burst into laughter.

The man frowned, but when he saw Dancer's blood-stained garb on the floor, his confusion gave way to alarm. He drew his sword and pointed it at Bard. "On your feet!" he commanded as his companion followed suit. He turned to Dancer, wondering what to make of her part in all this.

Dancer simply smiled at him. "I like your bow," she said.

***

"Good thing I took a bath," muttered Dancer as they continued trudging through the Greenwood under the guise of night. Not only had she incurred more bloodstains than their previous encounter, but they were both covered in ash.

It was the most spectacularly unsubtle exit of his life. The two Swordsuits didn't go down without a fight, and Dancer refused to end them quickly. On the contrary, she had given them ample chances to live, but they simply refused to be bested by a brothel whore. Not the smartest duo in the Swordsuit army, to be sure, and by the end of the scuffle, their room had gone up in flames. To their good fortune, they managed to sneak off into the night unnoticed, hidden in the mass of screaming paramours and panicking whoremongers.

Where have all the clever Swordsuits gone? The Hounds weren't all beast-born brutes, he knew, but the Purge had turned most of them into crazed dogs.

"At least you got a bow out of it," said Bard, and he half-expected to hear her aim an arrow at the back of his head. Instead, he could almost feel her smile.

Listening to Dancer's horse plod along beside him brought a grin to his own face. He hadn't had this much fun in years.

They reached Genovel just as the skies turned purple, preparing for the sun's return, but halted their horses before they could interrupt the sleepy pastures of the village. Bard had been here enough times to watch it rebuild itself from the ground up. Like any village reborn from the ashes, it had likely been restored by nomads, perhaps even the hunter clans, seeking to bring their wandering days to an end.

There were still some huts made of wood and straw, but the lands were fertile, the crops plentiful. If he hadn't seen it once burnt to cinders, he wouldn't have guessed that it was restored. The only thing that gave it away was the stone. Bricks had not yet collapsed into each other, and the houses still looked untouched by time. Trees edged in cautiously on all sides as if shying away from the village, and if travelers didn't know exactly where they were going, they wouldn't have even known it existed in the heart of the Greenwood.

Beautiful. Untouched. No one would have ever guessed that this was where Valerya the Fireborne was born.

Bard had always taken care to stop and admire the view before ruining it with his presence. He could sense Dancer breathe it in next to him. He knew little about her past, but he liked to think the sight of it brought her a similar sense of peace. Try as he might, he couldn't imagine her returning home to play the harp or whatever it was that Lancistierreans expected of her. Hers was a life wrought with scars, and not the kind her body could heal.

"What say you, Dancer?" he asked as she rode up beside him.

They had agreed to go their separate ways once they reached the border, and Genovel was only half a day's ride away from it. He would have rued any day she decided to leave, but it was customary in this life to part ways. Not once had it been different. In truth, there was only a handful of people who knew of his existence, and even fewer who knew he was still alive.

"Until the tides, friend," she said solemnly, extending her arm.

"Until the tides," he answered. Disappointment twisted knives into his heart.

"I don't actually know what that means," said Dancer with the slightest hint of a smile. "But I'm going with you."

Bard grinned despite himself. *Infinitely more interesting than a tavern wench,* he thought as he urged his horse forward.

It was such a picturesque little village to be marred by the arrival of two black destriers carrying hooded strangers, and they didn't bother heading to the stables. They tied their horses to a tree next to a house built entirely of stone. Bard had always hated it, but he supposed it made the most sense. Its inhabitants had a history of setting things ablaze, so it would have been madness to build walls of timber.

"So tell me about this friend of yours," said Dancer when she dismounted. "Is he anything like you?"

"Who, Artis?" asked Bard absent-mindedly, tying the reins of his horse into a double knot. "He's an old friend. Raised me, in a way."

"An older version of you?" asked Dancer, amused. "I might just die."

"Not exactly," said Bard, knocking at the door. "Artis!" he called. "It's Bard!"

They waited a courtesy pause before they were greeted by a kind voice. "Bard now, is it?" it asked. "I lost track years ago. About the last time I saw you."

Bard didn't know which would have been more amusing to Dancer: an older version of himself, or the complete opposite of himself. Even by appearance, Artis was the gentlest man he had ever known, his soft features constantly etched with concern.

When he spoke, it was with the refined confidence of a man who treated even the basest of vagrants with respect—but knew how to handle himself when the niceties backfired. He was a Fireborne in every sense of the word, even if he didn't act like one. He only came up to Bard's shoulder, but he could definitely roast him alive if he wanted.

Still, he had aged considerably since the last time they met. His hair was milk-white where iron-gray swirls had once been, and time had creased his face into folds. He wasn't intimidating by far, and that had often led to the undoing of thugs looking to rob an elderly gent.

Bard supposed Artis and Dancer had that much in common.

He reached out and embraced the old man, and the years melted away between them.

"Let's not forget common courtesy," scolded Artis good-naturedly. He turned to Dancer. "Who might you be?"

Dancer reddened, much to Bard's amusement. If Artis had a way of making him feel like a little boy, he wondered what effect he had on her.

"Dancer," she answered. This time, her sweetness wasn't feigned.

Artis clasped her hand in his. "Absolutely charmed. I hope you didn't have to endure much of Bard's drivel along the way."

Dancer threw Bard a winning smile that said: *I like him already.*

"You both must be exhausted. Come in," said Artis, and Bard was saddened to see him struggle to the door. Old bones grew weak, especially after breaking and healing in so many different places. Artis had never been the adventuring kind, but trouble had clearly attracted him in his younger days.

"Quickly." Artis ushered them inside. "The villagers might see you, and we might get stuck talking to them for hours."

He closed the door behind them. "If you would be so kind as to remove your shoes," he said, completely ignoring the swords and bows strapped to their bodies and the bloodstains that peered out from beneath their cloaks. Dancer threw Bard a playful glance over Artis' shoulder. She was absolutely enthralled.

"Excellent timing," said Artis, more to himself than to present company. He made his way to the window on the far wall. "I'm expecting someone, too. And there he is."

Bard frowned. The old man loved speaking in riddles, but Bard was too tired to guess. "Who?" he asked as Artis extended his arm out the window.

And then the black peregrine came.

15

THE RED CITADEL
FIRE REALM

Even before the clouds broke, his armor gleamed. Its infused blackwood beat back the advances of a new dawn. It wouldn't be long until daylight came, and for the first time in his life, he would be able to see it. He would see colors, people—not just his captors or the Swordsworn, but *people* living in and around the Citadel. People like him.

The castle may have been a dark and primal place, but not today. Even when Marcus tightened the straps, cutting off all blood to his arms, Gryff didn't care. His hands were fitted into gauntlets that shielded his wrists from light, and a light cuirass was strapped to his torso. It was a bit loose, but General expected him to get bulkier.

"The helm was a challenge, m'lord," said Marcus. "Took the smith a long time to make."

Indeed, the helm came in different parts, and it didn't seem like Marcus knew how to put them together. "I'm just the tailor's 'prentice, m'lord," he apologized, placing random pieces on Gryff's head and replacing them with irritating frequency. "I ... sew and mend."

Why are you here? "Why isn't the smith here?" asked Gryff.

Lukan used to be one of the swordsmasters at the Citadel, but now he forged most of the steel for the General's men. Strangely, Gryff had never seen him on castle grounds.

"Master Lukan doesn't really leave the Ironhands, m'lord," said Marcus, concluding that the bowl-shaped piece belonged on top. "Don't much like it at the castle." He fastened the visor and cheek-guards in place, but in the wrong order, and for a moment, Gryff saw nothing at all. It was only when Valk entered that Marcus stopped trying.

"That will be all, Marcus," said Valk. Amusement lifted his tone. "I will take it from here. Go tend to your master."

"M'lord!" said Marcus, relieved. Gryff heard the sound of fading footsteps.

"Poor boy," said Valk as he unfastened the cheek-guards. Clanking magnified tenfold in Gryff's ears, followed by a dull hum that drowned out all but the Spade's voice. "Loves it at the Citadel, but I'm afraid the Citadel isn't too fond of him."

Gryff pulled off the helm, trying to unclog his ears. He blinked twice to make sure his eyes weren't playing tricks on him.

He almost didn't recognize the Spade without the armor.

Gryff supposed it made sense. They couldn't possibly walk around in it all the time, but seeing the man in plainclothes was like seeing Valerya in a gown.

Valk dropped a second helm next to the first. "The boy brought the iron prototype the smith presented to our General," said Valk, unfazed. "She thought it was too heavy and … complicated. Hard to put on quickly in times of emergency. Even when it isn't an emergency." He lifted a hand, commanding Gryff to his feet. "Let's have a look at you, then."

Gryff faced himself in the mirror. He swelled with pride but tried not to let it show. At first glance, it looked standard-issue, but he could see how much care had been placed into making sure there were no gaps that light could reach. His elbows were protected by guards that folded into each other when he moved.

Valk brought his attention back to the helm. "You open it this way." He swung the hinged plate guarding the lower face upward. "It connects at this point here, which is also where this visor pivots." His boyish grin took Gryff by surprise. "Our General and I were playing around with this all morning. Absolutely ingenious. We must find a way to reward Lyra."

The image was oddly comical, and Gryff tried to hide a smile. "Lyra? I thought the smith's name was Lukan." He paused, confused. "I thought the smith was a man."

"Lukan did all the forging, yes," said Valk as he pulled the helm over Gryff's head, "but his apprentice designed it." He snapped the helm shut and lifted the visor. "How does it feel?"

"Brilliant."

"Should be. It's Fire-forged." Valk nodded. "Well, let's go, then. Daylight is coming."

Gryff's smile died on his lips. *Daylight?* It seemed like a great idea that morning, but now that it was becoming a quick reality, it had lost its appeal. "Yes," he said, hoping it would strengthen his resolve. It didn't.

He had seen daylight once before but couldn't remember it. His mother told him years later that he was born in the summer sun. It had been a difficult birth; his parents had to force him out, but when they did, his skin started to peel. They threw the bloodied sheets in front of the window until he stopped screaming, and there they stayed until his first night. The medican claimed the struggle corrupted her womb, and it would nurture no more children after that. *Probably why they were so eager to take in Dove.* His mother had always wanted a girl, and a voiceless daughter was better than none.

I disappointed my mother with my birth, and I disappointed her with my life, he thought. *Dove was the child she wanted, not me.* As a boy, he wanted to hate Dove, but she loved him. Even when she could barely walk, she followed him everywhere, and everything she owned, she shared. No one could fault her for his own short-comings.

As they stepped out into the corridor, Gryff could see traces of daylight beat furiously against the curtains. A few rays managed to slip through the gaps. They would only get brighter. Valk positioned him in front of an arched window. "My favorite view from the castle," he said.

"Trees?" asked Gryff, trying to make out what lay beyond the waters of the Sinth.

"Patience," said Valk sharply.

And that was where Gryff found himself, overlooking the blackwoods to face the rising sun. The sky had paled from purple to gray, bringing with it the promises of a new day. To most, it signified a new beginning, a reprieve from sorrows that grew fat and heavy at night. But to Gryff, it had always meant a world of pain, of punishment.

And when the sun cast its first rays on the horizon, approaching them like a horde of wild beasts, all he could think about was how long it would take for his skin to melt off his bones.

"Your face-guard," Valk reminded him, and Gryff pulled down his visor, thinking grim thoughts about his life. His heart hammered furiously against his cuirass.

Daylight hit him as it spilled into every crevice of the Citadel.

Oh, he thought. *That wasn't so bad.*

And then a burst of light exploded in his skull, blazing through his retinas.

It wasn't the kind of fire that swallowed men whole or reduced villages to cinders. It was the burn of seeing light for the first time in eighteen years. His eyes had gotten so used to the shadows that they hid from the sun, but he forced them open, blinking tears from his eyes. Instinctively, he flung his arms out in front of him as though it would deter the rays.

He blinked once, twice, until his eyes adjusted. His vision slid in and out of focus as if trying to make sense of what was happening, but then it settled. The slit of his helm was narrow, but it was enough to see life wash over the blackwoods, painting the skies in a thousand colors he had never seen before. It was so overwhelming, he was glad Valk couldn't see his face. Tears streamed down his cheeks, and it wasn't just from the pain.

So this is what people see when they open their eyes. What they saw when they dreamed.

Only the blackwoods didn't change.

"Brace yourself," said Valk.

Gryff barely had time to turn. A blast of Fire hit him square in the chest, but the plates that protected his body swallowed it whole. They blackened upon impact, but the metal felt cooler than before.

Valk nodded. "Absolutely *ingenious,*" he said again. He lifted Gryff's arm and examined the elbow-guard enviously. "No light got through?"

"None at all," said Gryff, glad he was still alive.

"Then follow me," said Valk, slapping him on the back. Gryff stumbled forward and straightened before Valk could notice, but the Spade was already three strides ahead of him. He took him down corridors where the windows weren't covered, where light breathed new life into the Citadel. It had never occurred to Gryff how big the castle was or how many people were in it. Swordsworn, nobles, errand boys, serving girls … and they all smiled at him when they passed.

"Jonath," said Valk, halting. Gryff stopped beside him.

"Segnes," a boy answered. His blade looked too expensive for his age, but he moved with the certainty of knowing how to use it. But it was his cloak that got Gryff's attention. "Call me Jack. I hate Jonath."

"Congratulations, Jack," said Valk, extending his arm. "We heard about your work with the Second Cloaks. Welcome to the Spades."

"Thank you," said the boy as he clasped Valk's arm at the elbow. He threw Gryff a curious glance, but Gryff found him equally fascinating. He was dark-skinned with true-black hair—and the flowing, crimson cloak of the Spades. "I just had a chat with our General."

No wonder he looks so terrified. Valk's presence probably didn't help much.

"Your blade got a bit of an upgrade then, I take it," said Valk.

"It appears so!" Jack relaxed his shoulders. He was charming, with a quick smile and cunning eyes.

"Why don't you introduce yourself to the others? I trust you can find your way around. It's a bit different from the shipyards, but you get used to it."

"I think I'll manage," said Jack. Mischief seeped into the creases of his smile. "I've been waiting for this moment for half my life."

"A good ten years then, if that much," said Valk. "We'll talk later, Spade."

"Segnes," said Jack, turning to Gryff as he passed. "Nice helm."

Gryff waited until Jack was out of earshot before he opened his mouth. "I didn't know Second Cloaks existed."

"That boy is a First Cloak now. A Spade," said Valk as he continued forward. "Of course there are Second Cloaks. And Third, and Fourth." He frowned, confused. "What, you didn't expect our General to have just fourteen men loyal to her?"

"No, I've just … I've never seen them."

"Our General likes to keep them away from the Citadel," said Valk with a quick laugh. "The Second Cloaks are the Diamonds, commanding our ships in the North. Then we have the Clubs. They stay within the Realm, and the Hearts are scattered all over the world."

It made sense now that Gryff thought about it. Of course the Summoner General had the loyalty of over fourteen men. With that naming scheme, it was no wonder outsiders still called them Suits.

They stopped in front of the General's quarters.

"This is where I leave you," said the Spade, knocking. "But don't despair. I don't intend on being long."

"What?" asked Gryff, but the man had already turned. His mood spiraled downwards.

"*In,*" came the command. It wasn't particularly loud, but it was sharp enough to break the silence into small, jagged slivers. Gryff took a deep breath and entered, dropping to one knee.

"On your feet," said the General, and he obeyed.

Valerya wasn't even looking at him. She was signing her name on different pieces of parchment, and each one weighed down on her patience. Finally, she set her quill aside and watched him in silence, but he could swear he saw amusement flicker across her face. "I feel like I'm talking to a box," she said, looking at his helm as though she couldn't place his eyes.

She rose and tapped his shoulder-guard. There were three or four layers of blackwood and metal between them, but it was the closest he had ever come to her presence. Still, it felt cold, distant. He was glad she couldn't see his eyes widen at the smith-mark on her neck.

"If you're to be of any use to me, you should get well acquainted with the Citadel. All parts of it," she said, snapping him back to reality. "In times of battle, I doubt I will ask you to fetch a book from the library."

Gryff reddened inside his helm. Silence clenched between his teeth. *So it's true.* He wondered why she had never had the mark removed or altered. *I would have changed it to a dragon,* he mused, thinking back to his own four-pointed star. *In a heartbeat.*

"I have a package to pick up from the city," she continued, turning back to her desk. "Valk will show you around. If you are to make today's training, I suggest you take the horses."

It had been months since he had been outdoors, but a single word smothered his excitement.

Horses?

* * *

"I must admit, I find the backwards nature of our circumstances hilarious," said Valk. He had taken the reins while Gryff held on for dear life, threatening to slide off the horse whenever they hit a patch of rough terrain. For all his Fire-forged armor, it was Gryff's first time on one.

But if Gryff was a sheep in wolf's clothing, Valk was a wolf masquerading as a lamb. There was no way in this life or the next the Spade would have passed for one of them. Even the way he laughed commanded respect, and for the commoner he was pretending to be, he was extremely well-dressed. Not extravagant, of course—it looked like he had gone through great pains to dress as simply as possible—but neat. Orderly. There were no creases on his sleeves, and his shoes looked scrubbed and shined.

"I've never ridden a horse before," Gryff admitted.

"Never would have guessed."

As much as Gryff hated riding, he had missed the forest. The trees had a different scent in Sinthea. The blackwood they imported from the North was dry and rough like sand, but at least it didn't smell like stone. It could not be cut by a normal blade, so it was left to grow as it pleased.

The rest of the forest told a different story. Road builders had cut deep into its flesh, pouring its wounds with sand and brick. Whenever it tried to heal itself, it was forced back down to keep the paths clear. Trees leaned in grotesquely from the edge of the road.

If trees could talk, thought Gryff, shifting uncomfortably.

The castle had a smithy, but Valerya preferred the services of the Ironhands not too far from the city wall. The lower half of the capital housed the butchers and meat vendors, and the smell of blood clung to them like bad perfume. Sintheans were definitely meat-eaters, and it showed: they were bigger and bulkier and looked to be of good health. It was the first time Gryff had ever seen them walking about, how hectic the city was. During the Empire, it was said to have been the grandest in the world, even grander than the Scarlet Cities; after its fall, it was rebuilt quickly with no regard for aesthetics.

They turned away from the busy street and halted. Gryff's

method of dismounting consisted of sliding awkwardly from the back of the horse, but Valk had mastered the art of not reacting to unpleasant situations. Valk swung down from his saddle and held out the reins.

A boy no older than nine ran up and gave the Spade a clumsy bow and a toothless grin. He took the reins and led the horse away, throwing them shy glances over his shoulder. Gryff realized he hadn't seen children in months. They were at least fifteen when they got to the castle, almost grown. Physically, at least.

"Lukan," greeted Valk as they approached the smithy.

"Spade," said the man at the grindstone. His tone was as rough as his face, but familiarity smoothed it at the edges. He threw Gryff half a nod, and Gryff tried to catch a glimpse of his caste-mark.

Lukan didn't have one. Perhaps the years had rubbed it dry, but Gryff could tell he was born a smith. His hands were coarse and calloused, and he handled his blade like a newborn.

"Lyra!" Lukan shouted over his shoulder. "The Spade is here!"

Gryff heard a clamor in the background. Its source lowered its hood and smiled.

So that's Lyra, he thought. Even if the gods plucked her from the skies and dropped her anywhere else in the world, her connection to Fire was undeniable. Her auburn hair was on the brink of orange, and her eyes burned red flames.

Eagerly, she grabbed a long package from the workbench and made her way to the front. "Careful, now," hissed Lukan disapprovingly. "That's not a toy."

She ignored him. "Spade!" she said, unable to hide a grin that dug dimples into her cheeks. She saw Gryff and her eyes brightened. "Is that ...?" She reached towards him as if wanting to open his helm, and he took an instinctive step back.

"You've really outdone yourself, Lyra," said Valk, diffusing any awkwardness that might have ensued. "The helm is ingenious. Our General commends your work."

Lyra looked as though he had paid her highest compliment. "See? I *told* you," she turned to Lukan, and her eyes glimmered with happiness. "And she should know! I mean ..." She threw Valk an apologetic glance. "I didn't mean to offend ... uhh ..."

Valk laughed, not unkindly. "I doubt she is ashamed of her origins. I'm sure there are more embarrassing things to be known for than forging weapons and armor." He smiled. "You've given no offense."

Old and weathered as he was, Lukan did little to suppress his own pride. "Lyra is a natural. I'll go see about that other package, now."

Lyra crouched, allowing Lukan to place his arm around her shoulders. She helped him to his feet. "I was third swordsmaster of the Citadel for twenty-one years." He spat. "Can't even get off my chair now."

"Papa," Lyra scolded. "I told you not to spit in front of company."

Inside his helm, Gryff gaped. He tried to imagine Diante and Lukan standing side-by-side. The latter could barely stand, but he exuded an authority that could break the other in half. Gryff wouldn't mind training under him.

When her father was gone, Lyra turned her attention back to the Spade. "Valk," she whispered. "Did I do good?"

"Brilliant," said Valk. "The elbow-guards were a nice touch. I want a set."

"You're too kind," said the girl, reddening.

"Spade!" called Lukan from the back, sparing her from further embarrassment. "May we speak in private?"

"If you'll excuse me," said Valk, not sounding like a civilian at all. No one was ever that courteous. Even when he tried to change his accent, he failed.

"What's your name?" she asked once the Spade was out of earshot.

"Gryff."

"I'm sorry, Gryff. I should've helped you with your armor earlier, but Papa thought it would be improper for a … for a girl to go alone," she said, but her face told another truth. *He wants her nowhere near Morian.* "We sent Marcus instead, and he told me it was a disaster. Well, yeah, I mean, he brought the wrong helm …"

She smiled shyly.

Gryff found his voice. "This is excellent," he said awkwardly.

"Is it?" she beamed. Her eyes reflected blue skies like a windowpane.

Gods, those dimples.

"Isn't it a bit rare for girls to apprentice to smiths?" he asked.

"Yes, m'lord … Gryff. That's what Papa said. He almost sent me to work at the guest-keep, but our General forced him to take me on." She grinned, and he saw admiration flicker in those Fire-kissed eyes.

"I think our General knows more than most that girls can be just as good as boys in some things," said Gryff before he could stop himself.

Did I just compliment the Blood Queen?

"In *all* things!" said Lyra. "I bet I can even cast stronger Fire than you!" She had meant it in jest, but her eyes widened. "Sorry. I shouldn't have said that. To a Spade and all."

"It's all right," said Gryff, trying to mend the situation, but she was already furiously gathering tools splayed across the counter.

Without thinking, he placed a hand on her arm.

She stared at him, unsure of what to do.

Thank the gods for Valk, thought Gryff bitterly as the Spade reemerged with Lukan hobbling beside him. In his arm, he clutched a smaller package wrapped in linens.

Talking with Dove had never been a problem, but that was the problem. Gryff never expected girls to actually talk back. With words.

"Spade!" said Lyra, who seemed equally grateful for Valk's appearance. "Here's the other one our General ordered." She hoisted the long package onto the counter and unwrapped it, revealing a Fire-forged sword. The blade was narrower than the typical Sword-sworn blade, but it gleamed all the same. Gryff wondered what use Valk could possibly have for it. "Forgive me," she said, not looking sorry at all. "I got a bit carried away with the hilt …"

Indeed, the quillon was shaped into an S, and its ends were crafted to look like the head and tail of a dragon. *A dragon for the General's men. An S for the Sinthean Empire.* Gryff shook his head. *No. S for Spade. Or Swordsworn,* he told himself. *Not the Empire.*

"Our General informed us that m'lord required a lighter blade, so I did what I could," Lyra continued. "I almost went with the knuckle-guard, but she asked for gauntlets, so …"

She let her gaze drop, tired of answering unasked questions.

Valk turned to Gryff. "Well, what are you waiting for?" he asked sharply, reprimanding him for bad manners. "Try it out."

Me? thought Gryff, gaping behind his helm. He pulled the blade out of the linen folds and held it to his face. It was much lighter than the sticks and dummy swords he had been practicing with, and he could see the care that had gone into every detail.

"Brilliant," he thought out loud.

The word brought color back to Lyra's face, and she smiled again.

"We thank you for your fine work and implore you to reconsider," said Valk, bowing his head. Lukan nodded, and Lyra bowed for him.

"Reconsider?" asked Gryff once they were out of earshot.

"Smiths of the Citadel used to reside in the castle. Once the girl is ready, she can do the same. Her talents would, I dare say, be wasted on anything else. I can't imagine her weaving." Valk placed the smaller package in the horse's side satchel.

Gryff made sure no one was watching before he grabbed onto his arm and hoisted himself up. Once they entered the heart of the blackwoods, they spoke freely.

"So, Lukan was the former swordsmaster at the Citadel ..." Gryff began.

Valk sighed. He knew where this was going. "He is of the Castellans. He and Lyra may spit and slur and drink like seafarers on leave, but they've never been far from the Crown. Lyra was even educated at the castle until she decided to work at the smithy."

"Really," said Gryff, pretending not to be surprised. He would never have guessed that Lyra was a *lady*. Lukan's hands were as gnarled and gritty as a peasant's, and she ...

"Tell me about your *friend*," the Spade said, and Gryff remembered that Valk had witnessed his less-than-spectacular exchange with the General not too long ago. He sounded amused. "Is she anyone special?"

So he had been listening. "I ..." said Gryff and paused. "We've never ... yes. I think so. Maybe."

"To be young again," said Valk, shaking his head. He almost laughed.

"What about you, then?" asked Gryff, half-irritated, but his tone gave way to genuine curiosity. He knew nothing about Valk outside the Citadel. The Spade never spoke of his private life. "Don't tell me you have a wife and children?"

"I don't."

"Never wanted to marry?" Gryff was sure Valk could find someone easily, even now. Women threw themselves at Spades, and Valk was one of the better-looking ones. He was kind and born of wealth; they would probably spread their legs for him if he asked politely.

"I didn't say that," Valk answered.

"So there *was* someone?"

"There was one, yes. I was a young man too, once."

"Tell me about her."

"She was … polite, obedient, and hated attention. A typical court girl who knew her poetry, the harp, and all the songs of the Realms combined in four different languages."

"Didn't take you for a man who liked poetry and songs," said Gryff. He frowned. If Valk asked him to describe Dove, he would have a million things to say, and none of them would have anything to do with poetry and songs, or *typical*.

"I'm not. I confess I don't think much of them, but as it turned out, neither did she."

"I don't follow."

"Her words were rehearsed, her movements practiced, but she was so *typical* that it wasn't real. I saw her at every social gathering I was forced to attend, but it took us years to speak in private. She was like …" He paused for a long moment. "Like a candle in a lit hall, but the only one that burned when it went dark. When we were alone, her smile shone as bright as the stars, and she meant it only for me."

Not much of a swordsman, and you don't like poetry. "You loved her, then."

"I did."

"What happened to her?"

"She was wed to a traitor and died for it," said Valk curtly. "That's all you need to know." There was no trace of bitterness in his voice, but he always stressed the last word when he was done talking.

They rode on in silence as Gryff tried to imagine a young Valk—or gods forbid, a *laughing* Valk—pining after a ghost. Gryff wondered what she must have been like. *The only candle that burned when it grew dark.* He liked that.

Suddenly, Valk halted the horse. "Shh," he said, holding up a hand before Gryff could ask. "Remember, boy. I'm a civilian today." He pulled his hood up, and through the narrow slit, Gryff could see three figures standing before them. They were young and clad in standard armor that didn't quite fit—trainees, from the looks of it. They weren't normally allowed to leave castle grounds during training periods, but occasionally, a few of them broke free.

"That's him," said the smallest of the three, pointing at Gryff. "That's the Glasger. I saw him. I saw him cast Ice."

"What's the meaning of this?" asked Valk.

"Stay out of this, old man," said the one in the middle with clearly no inkling of who he was talking to. His sword had replaced his common sense with confidence.

"Another lesson, boy," Valk whispered to Gryff. "Avoiding bloodshed." He dismounted, and Gryff followed suit. Fear drove self-consciousness from his mind, and he was able to swing down from the saddle without stumbling.

It was then that Gryff understood what the General had meant by seeing. If any of them had seen the sword gleaming beneath Valk's cloak, they would have gathered that he was very clearly a Spade—not some random civilian giving a Swordsworn a ride.

They look younger than me. Gryff realized they were the first boys his age who had ever talked to him at the Citadel. And just like in the Dragontail, they were already picking on him.

Valk stepped to the side and nodded, encouraging him to handle the situation.

"What seems to be the problem?" asked Gryff with all the courage he could muster.

"That's some fancy armor you've got on," said the gangly one, steadying his element hand. "Meant for fancy elements. Go on then, show us what you got!"

"Hardly seems fair," said Gryff coolly. "Three against one?"

"You've got blackwood on," said the small one, pointing at Valk. "And this poor sod. I'd say we're even."

The man's patience is unwavering, thought Gryff when he glanced at his companion's composure. He wondered if Valk was even listening; he just stood there like a shadow bear watching cubs swat at each other.

But this wasn't roughhousing. Cruel boys always grew into cruel men, and it was the same here, in the Dragontail, everywhere. And he had been too weak to stop them. Even his father had been ashamed that his only son couldn't stand up for himself, and loved Dove because she fought his battles for him. Even when she failed spectacularly, his father loved her. *I wanted to hate her* … But she chose him over everyone else, always coming to his rescue, and for that, they made her life hell, too. He couldn't hate her. On the contrary …

'I don't command my men to kill runaways, but some just have

a natural taste for blood.' The General's words rang in his ears, clear as day. His mind flashed to the image of one of them opening Dove's throat with his sword.

Before he knew it, the gangly one sent a blast of Fire to his face. It didn't burn, but its impact knocked him to the ground. Valk observed silently, but Gryff could see his hand move towards the hilt of his sword.

"Stop," said Gryff breathlessly, raising an arm in surrender. "My fight isn't with you."

Who is it with, then? he thought. He had convinced himself over and over that Dove was alive, hiding out in the forest until the coast was clear, but facing these future killers had dashed those hopes. Perhaps the Swordsworn had cornered her, just like this. Perhaps she had even raised her arms in surrender, just like this.

A natural taste for blood.

"C'mon, he can't burn with that thing on!" he heard one of them complain.

There will be no mercy for me, Gryff realized. The strong would always overpower the weak, and the weak would always allow it. *But I am not weak anymore.*

Something exploded in his chest, blind but unstoppable. He braced himself for impact, but the punches never came.

Instead, when he opened his eyes, he saw two of them lying on the ground at odd angles. Shards of Ice stuck out like splinters from their chests. One had hit the small one in the face, splitting his mouth in two. Needles skewered the other. Streams of red soaked the earth below.

Valk had melted the Ice before it could reach him and the horse.

"I ... I didn't mean to ..." sputtered Gryff, but that was a lie. He *wanted* to.

"If you let him live, he will spill your secrets," said Valk, nodding towards the third.

Gryff followed his gaze and saw the gangly one struggle to support himself against a tree. His face was a ruin, his breaths short and panicked. A single blade of Ice jutted from his chest. Blood trickled down the tree's bark like ink.

"Please," the boy begged, coughing up blood. "I ... surrender. I won't ... won't tell."

Gryff turned to his companion. "What should I do?" he asked. He was aware the question made him sound like a child, but he'd never had to make this decision before.

"That is entirely up to you," answered the Spade solemnly. "Save a life, and you may doom hundreds more to die. End him and you may live with his shadow for the rest of yours."

There was a time Gryff would have let him live. But he saw in those eyes a monster, the lives it would silence forever. Maybe he had done no harm to girls like Dove, but he would. "Our General asked me what I would do to the men who cut down my friend," he said softly. His skin shivered with rage. "Do you remember?"

He didn't wait for Valk's answer. When the edge of his blade pierced the boy's heart, he took care to twist it. The *S* gleamed in the sun, the head of the dragon smiled back at him ...

The boy's eyes widened and relaxed as his last threads to life were severed.

Valk contemplated him. "That was a jag," he said softly.

"A what?"

"A jag. A block of Ice that breaks into shards," said Valk, suddenly troubled. "You will not speak of this to anyone. You will not so much as *mention* jags at the Citadel, not even to our General. *Especially* not to our General. Do you understand?"

"I just killed someone," said Gryff, aware that he was talking to a seasoned killer. The shock of it still trembled in his hands.

"A necessary action, to some."

"What would you have done?" asked Gryff. "Would you have killed the ones who … murdered the girl you loved?"

"I let him live," said Valk. "But I live with shadows of a different sort." He gathered the reins and stroked the neck of his horse to calm it down. "Let's go."

Gryff opened his mouth, but fear silenced the words in his throat.

It didn't scare him that he had killed three people. They had attacked first, after all, and two of those deaths were accidental. It didn't scare him that he couldn't control the Ice in his blood. It didn't even scare him that he ended the third boy while he was begging for his life.

What scared him was that, after the shock wore off, he felt nothing at all.

16

GLASGÉRIOS
ICE REALM

I ce in this part of the world did not melt. No matter how many fires
they set, it only seemed to get colder. The chill bit into her bones
and settled, rushing back to life whenever she moved. The days were
slow and long and painful; she breathed in daggers and exhaled mist.
Even the kiln was put to rest until kinder days.

Glasgérios meant "glass mountain" and was built inside the tallest
crag. She wondered if it was made of Ice or ice, but no one was able
to give her a straight answer. It was considered their longest-kept
secret, much like the Divisoryans and their bridges. A Hound like
her was not worthy of the answer, but she figured it was Ice. Its
black core probably warded off fire.

The surrounding area was cold, desolate, and thinly peopled.
The snow lay undisturbed, and not a single path had been dug.
And this is their capital. In Sinthea, people were living on top of
each other. It was not uncommon for four or five families to cram
into a single commune, for which reason the elderly loved to retire
to the villages. In Glasgérios, the only thing that signaled human
settlement was the towering bastion that protruded from the peak of

the mountain: a gleaming monument of arches that looked wrought with silver crystals. They reflected back the light like a thousand landbound stars.

Everything was so *clean*. Dove had expected to see dirt or tracks in the snow—anything that pointed to signs of life that had made the cold peaks their home. Instead, she saw another world, one in which the sky shone brighter than the sun, where an endless winter did not melt.

It was almost enough to make her forget why the city was so empty.

Dove shivered. She tried not to imagine her people marching into their capital and massacring every living thing they could find, but it was hard when faced with a city of ghosts.

Outsiders would die here. She was wrapped in three cloaks and several pelts, but her face was red and raw from the dry wind. At least no one could see her suffer. Merc had refused to come out, muttering something about ice monkeys, and Decker stayed in his cabin, electing to write instead of admiring the view. They already knew what they were missing out on.

Dove, however, had never even seen snow before. Nights were cold in the Dragontail, but in Glasgérios, it was enough to stretch minutes into days. Suddenly, she realized why no one ever wanted to rule *in* the glass mountains. Their capital had been ransacked time and time again, but its conquerors always marched home and ruled from afar. Only disgraced Swordsworn were sent here, but it was more of a punishment than a necessity. They did not last very long.

Dove's ears perked when she heard the hatch open. Every so often, Sirian came up to check on her. At first, his presence made her uneasy, but as they sat and watched the approaching towers of Glashaven, she found that she did not mind. He wore the same light robes he had donned in the Chimera, but he did not so much as shiver, let alone acknowledge the howling of the winds. This was home to him. Dove held her cloaks tightly and despaired.

"Now you know how I feel when I see your kind walk through fire," he said, pulling back his sleeve. Burns embedded craters into his arms, and his skin stretched and grew over them like a badly stitched tapestry. "You're silent," he said after a while. "Like a *domerys.*"

Dove rather liked being compared to a shadow guard. There were not many left in the Icelands, and most works that chronicled their existence were torched when the Summoner razed through their ranks. It was not easy isolating fact from myth when the victors controlled the Scrolls. No one recalls that they existed now.

Sirian watched the city with sadness. He saw something different in those cold peaks, something no Scroll could ever describe.

"*Ro-than,*" she heard Decker curse behind them. "You look like a stuffed bear."

Since their exchange in the Blackstone, pleasantries had been somewhat forced between them. Dove was not used to confiding in strangers, but he had seen everything that night. It was worse than being bare; revealed secrets could not be covered up so easily.

Decker unfastened the clasps of his cloak and draped it around her shoulders. Her anger melted away with the cold, and she felt blood rush back to her fingers. She pressed her hands against the inside of his cloak. It was as warm and slick as fever. Quickly, she pulled the hood over her head. Now she understood why Decker never left the ship without it.

"You should have said you were coming up. I could have given it to you earlier," he said. He looked smaller without it, but he still dwarfed most people onboard. "Glasger elk. They can't survive outside Glasgérian wastelands, and their hide protects them from the cold."

Not that he needs it, she thought, not feeling sorry at all for taking it. Decker did not look like he minded much. The cold must have been with him his entire life, and he bore it with poise.

Sirian nodded next to her, taking in the strained beauty of his homeland. "We will dock soon. You remember what I told you about the Glasgers," he said. "They are a superstitious people. They believe that winds carry voices. It is akin to sacrilege to speak in the open."

Finally. Somewhere I belong.

"There is still bad blood between the Realms. Most of us don't even speak the common tongue." He seemed to have trouble calling it Sinthean. "Keep your hair hidden. Always."

"A view for the gods," said Elayne behind them, amused. Dove realized that she was the only one bundled in layers; from behind, she must have looked like a heap of clothing. She turned, annoyed that Elayne was not wearing anything against the cold, either. "You might want to get rid of a few layers if you want to pass off as one of us."

That tone.

Whenever they used that tone, it was obvious that they wanted to discuss something without her there. Still, she was hardly in the mood to be outnumbered. She made her way below-deck and entered her cabin.

"Are we landing?" Nan was still curled up under the covers, but she opened her eyes at the sound of the door. She rarely went to her own room anymore. "Is that Decker's cloak?" she asked, pretending to stretch. She concealed her feelings well.

Dove pulled off the cloak and was suddenly hit by a blast of cold. Her eyes screamed for help as she fumbled with the other clasps.

Nan crawled out of bed, barely dressed. *Why do these people even use covers?* thought Dove bitterly.

Nan's eyes darted to the auburn strands of Dove's hair. "You should hide that when we land," she said, but her tone was seeped with regret. She had always been fascinated with Dove's hair. It was the only thing, appearance-wise, that made her stand out from the others, and the first thing they told her to hide. Nan stroked it gently before continuing.

They spent a few absurd moments stripping off layer after layer until Dove could move again. Nan slung Decker's cloak back over her shoulders. "Is that better?" she asked, pulling the hood over Dove's ears. Her hands were enviably warm.

This will never get old. Dove nodded when she felt the cold fade.

"It's cold inside the crag," said Nan. "Wolff says only you and the others are allowed, but Ieon reckons he can get us in." She grinned. Nothing could go wrong with this plan. "I've never been there. I heard it was ... something. I mean, yeah, it's not beautiful or anything, but it used to be filled with domerics and all. I wonder what they're like. Do you think they're all gone?"

Nan was talking to herself again. They made their way back on deck where the others had already gathered. No one talked to preserve heat, but Dove was relieved to see that some of them had at least donned Glasger cloaks.

"Dove!" said Elayne from across the mob, raising a hand. "Over here!"

Nan held out a hand to stop her. "Just you wait," she whispered, grinning. Her hair fell neatly on her shoulders when she turned to the glass mountains. The Water in her blood added color to her face. "We'll see each other soon. And don't worry, they'll take care of you! I guess."

Dove slipped past the crew and made her way to Elayne. She almost did not recognize Merc sulking next to her. He had wrapped a bandanna around his head, and his cloak was two sizes too small. He picked up a piece of wood and broke it into smaller pieces. He did not look pleased to be there. "I fucking hate heights," he muttered, smashing.

They had landed in the water, but Glashaven itself was located on a cliff. They would have to climb into Glashaven by crossing a high jetty, and only she had the advantage of being small, quick, and unafraid of heights.

At the other end of the jetty stood sentries wrapped in black-scale armor that looked like silk. It conformed to their every movement, unlike the plates they wore in the Firelands, and there were no gaps to let in the cold. Bows slung over their shoulders like dark snakes.

"You be careful," said Wolff to his niece, but he did not seem too concerned. Elayne looked perfectly capable of handling herself, and Healers were held in high regard no matter where they came from. Dove was not so sure about Sirian, though. He was one of them, but he was so thin, so intense in movement, that the Ice in his bones looked like it might snap.

Wolff pounded up the jetty, and the rest trailed behind him cautiously. Dove scoured the crowd one last time for Nan, but the girl had disappeared. Dove felt a sharp sadness that took her by surprise. It had been a while since she had friends, someone close to her in age. The men were kind enough, but they were cautious around her. It was Nan who showed genuine interest, who lowered her guard. *We will see each other again,* Dove thought firmly. *She said so.* And Nan seemed like the type to get what she wanted, one way or another.

Decker glanced behind him too, but he was looking for Elayne.

He made sure she found Sirian before he stepped onto the jetty. Fear flashed across his features, and each step was laden with tension.

It was funny to Dove that three grown men who flew airships for a living were afraid of high places. The dark did not faze them, and neither did the prospect of open rebellion. But up here, where they were safe and sound between the railings, they were terrified. *Traders are so weird,* she thought. They lived on a flying rock and worked on flying ships, but they were afraid of falling.

When Dove reached the other end, the sentry on the left extended his arm, and for a moment, she wondered if he wanted her to clasp it. Before she could embarrass herself, Wolff handed him a few pieces of paper stamped with the Divisoryan seal.

Still, she had no idea what the Glasgers were thinking. Their faces reminded her of Gryff, but there was no trace of him in their eyes. In fact, she looked into them and saw nothing—two sets of voids that soaked in all light. Yet when they looked into hers, they saw everything.

They straightened, and Dove felt her heart fall back into place. She did not know them, but she was afraid of them. They were tall with cold features, and quiet. Not quiet like she was quiet; it was more than that. She could not even hear them breathe.

With a stiff bow, the sentries stepped to the side. They closed the gap when Dove passed, but she felt their eyes follow her. *They know,* she thought, but did not look back. *They hear lies in the silence.*

She was not alone. Her companions quickened their pace until they reached the edge of town, passing through another set of sentries. She did not even look at them this time. She did not want to see those pale eyes sharpen when they closed in on her, reminding her she was a thousand leagues from home.

Glasgérios was connected to the port city through a journey up a mountain. The snow looked untouched, but that was a lie. Sirian had told her that horses and travelers came up and down the mountain at all hours of the day, but the snow always found a way to repair itself. People were said to fall through soft spots in the snow, never to be seen again. Locals claimed they were eaten by the mountain god they called Dakraemu. Dove refused to believe that.

Still, she would not say no to taking horses.

"All right, you three," grumbled Wolff when they reached the stables. He glanced around, but the stablemaster was nowhere to be found. "Let's just take three horses and run."

Merc's face lit up at the prospect of doing something unlawful, and Decker put his face-guard on. "You ride with me," he said to Dove as though Wolff had not just suggested committing a crime.

They walked out to the stalls and passed by the more massive beasts without a second glance. "Never, ever ride a destrier up a mountain," said Decker through his face-guard. "Trust me on this."

Dove nodded. She had only seen one person ride one on a regular basis, but Valerya the Fireborne could do whatever the hell she wanted.

They stopped in front of a much smaller horse and made sure no one was around. "Are you ready?" he asked as he threw a blanket over its back. It barely reacted, like it was already used to getting stolen. Decker placed a saddle on top of the blanket and extended his arm.

Do I have a choice? she thought before getting on.

***

Dove decided that she disliked horses. She was in no real danger; she was cushioned between Decker's arms and her only task was to not fall, but she found it unnatural how she could see its eyes despite being positioned directly behind its head.

It was Wolff who took the lead. Decker followed with Merc close behind. They charged at full speed, interrupted by occasional swerves. The Hounds had destroyed the main roads to cut off supplies in the last siege, leaving behind only a difficult trail that snaked between the trees. Dove tried to look for soft spots people might have fallen through and heard Decker chuckle behind her. "*Dakraemu,*" he teased in her ear.

When they finally reached the crag, she hopped off eagerly and landed without sound—unlike Decker, who hit the snow with an ungraceful thud.

"First time on a horse?" asked Merc as he dismounted, not even bothering to lower his voice. A few Glasgers who were unsaddling their own horses stopped to glare at him.

Dove nodded. She had taken caravans and coaches, but not once had she sat on the demon creatures that pulled them along.

He laughed. "We'll make a rider of you yet."

From the outside, Glasgérios looked like a typical crag. The city was no stranger to siege, but before Valerya, the bastion had never been taken by force. Only the She-Jackal and her company were able to storm the castle, ending the Battle of the Shadows once and for all. *Maybe one day, I will find out how she did it.* There were too many conflicting accounts, and for an event that had caused so much destruction, it was poorly recorded in the Scrolls.

From the inside, Glasgérios was, quite simply, a city encased in rock. A soaring display of stone figures lined the sides of the mountain. *Domerics,* she thought when she saw the insignia of a falcon cradling the moon in its wings. Historians recalled in shame how the Swordsworn beheaded all the statues after they won, and she felt blood rush to her face when she saw that their heads were shades paler than their bodies. *Reconstructed.* Like everything else. She pulled her hood forward. Merc adjusted his bandanna.

A single road spiraled up to the castle, dividing the city into layers. Houses lined the base of the mountain, varying so greatly in height and form that they looked like they may have been built on patches of quicksand. Lampposts were spread out over broken roads, but their flames were surrounded by tinted glass. Maybe Glasgers burned in daylight, too.

"Don't get too close to the castle," muttered Wolff next to her. "The last thing we need is for them to arrest you."

They walked until they stopped in front of what she assumed was the main plaza. She wondered how a main plaza would even function here. Morian had only taken her to the one in Sinthea once, but she distinctly remembered … *sounds.* Vendors shouting. Children laughing. But here, it was difficult to imagine any of that without talking.

And at the far side, gleaming ivory in the tinted lamplight …

The Court of Queens.

Dove could not make out the Glasgérian letters, but it was the only building that still looked a million years old. The Swordsworn may have desecrated the statues after the war, but Valerya had ordered them specifically not to touch it. It was, according to the Scrolls, the oldest place of worship on the mainland, and Valerya was not one to anger foreign gods.

But the Glasgérians worshipped only one thing, and that was Shadow. The *domeras.* The Conqueror of Light. It sounded terrifying, but for a nation of people who burned in daylight, she could see why the *domeras* was their savior.

They entered, and Dove was surprised that it was so ... *empty*. The walls were almost entirely made of marble, but it was sparsely decorated. There was no one around save for a hooded figure kneeling before a statue.

"It is ill fortune to enter the Court of Queens once the sun has set," he rasped in flawless Sinthean. After hours of silence, his voice made Dove flinch. She remembered that they were inside now, where voices no longer carried.

Slowly and soundlessly, the hooded man got to his feet, his back still to them. "I count three large men. Am I correct?"

Merc glanced uncomfortably at his companions, but Wolff remained unfazed. Decker's hand moved to the hilt of his sword.

"The one on the left reaches for his sword. The one on the right looks about nervously. Am I correct?" the man continued.

Reluctantly, Decker stayed his sword hand.

"He relaxes. But something else feels different in this hall." The man paused. "Someone else is with you. Am I correct?"

Dove stood as still as a statue, unsure of what to do.

"When one cannot see in the daylight, one must learn to hear in the shadows," said the man as he turned to face them. "I am rarely wrong." As he approached them he seemed to glide, and he drew back his hood.

Dove gaped. It was the ugliest, and most beautiful face, she had ever seen. At first, it looked flawless—pure white, only a shade darker than snow, that extended to the tips of his short, tousled hair. His face had bled and healed with such constancy that the scars faded into his skin, save for one that slashed horizontally under his right eye. When he turned to her companions, she saw that part of his face had been badly burned.

"I was worshipping the *domeras*," he said, answering the question he saw on her face. "It's been a while since anyone has gotten past my ears. I must pay more attention in the future."

"Wh … who are you?" asked Merc, shifting nervously.

"You haven't told them about me?" he asked Wolff, feigning surprise. His voice was raspy, like Sirian's, but deep. Soothing.

Merc's eyes widened. "You *know* each other?"

"It's been a while," said Wolff, extending his arm. "The times haven't been good to you."

The man chuckled. "It's true," he said as he clasped Wolff's elbow. "But I see the times have been excellent to you."

Both laughed but made sure it was not loud enough for outsiders to hear.

"We fight on the side of the Shadows, now," the man answered, turning to the others. "My name is Tomá. I am one of the last surviving domerics in the Four Realms."

17

GENOVEL
FIRE REALM

It was a strange thing, the feel of a man freshly severed from the waking world. His body bent and twisted but didn't break, and for having just parted with something so immense, it felt absurdly heavy.

Bard spent a few moments trying to place the dead man's face, but he had never seen it before. Not that it made a difference; Bard was sure he had several running bounties on his head, and it was hard to keep track of who wanted which reward. But this man was a professional. A seeker, by the looks of it. His clothes were marred by travel, his cloak besmirched with red stains that had long since turned black. Seekers loved to target rich, soft men who went down easy. It took a special breed of hooligan to hunt down hooligans.

Bard sifted through the seeker's satchel, but its contents betrayed nothing of his origins. A few coins from everywhere. A list of locations with some crossed out. The only possession he had of value was a dagger that lay at his side, now dripping with his scarlet mistake.

The seeker had come at night while the entire village slept, on the rare occasion that Bard decided to wallow in self-reflection.

And ale.

The destriers must have given him away. No one rode them out in the woodlands, and they were too expensive for this part of the world. Bard had wanted to cut them loose, but Dancer refused, threatening to cut something else loose. He was standing behind the house, dulled by drink and musing the mysteries of the universe when the seeker found him.

"I have a message for you," the seeker had said as he unsheathed his dagger. His words were tainted by his thick accent, but more intelligible than Bard's slurred "whohasthmessage?"

Bard had seen the dagger, but he liked to give people the benefit of the doubt. Ending them was such a final thing, and unlike Dancer, who didn't discriminate, he only raised a hand in defense. He was a pacifist, after all. Only the weak started fights, and only cowards attacked the unarmed. Dancer had a much more lenient definition of *defense,* but he supposed she had more to guard than a few drops of blood and a handful of coins.

Of course, that didn't mean he couldn't finish fights. He wasn't about to go seek a duel with the Blood Queen—once had been enough to last a lifetime—but he had never gotten himself into a situation he couldn't handle without blood, steel, or Storm.

Except for that one time ... he mused, taking a swig of ale. *And that other time ...*

The man saw an opening and lunged, blade in hand. Bard bristled, more irritated at being interrupted mid-memory than attacked by a foreign assassin.

Well, he thought. *At least he isn't a common street thug.* Thugs wielded blades that were sharper than their minds and attacked wildly under the belief that weapons made them more dangerous.

This one was calm, though. He kept the knife close to his body instead of flailing it around like a drowning man grabbing at driftwood.

Still, his best efforts were in vain. *I was trained, too,* thought Bard in distaste. As much as he hated the Swordsworn, it was often their training that kept him alive. *Repetition, repetition, repetition.* They practiced simple maneuvers for hours until their instincts burned into his memory. Back when he was posted in Sinthea, they had treated him like one of their own: mercilessly. He couldn't even clasp someone's arm without feeling the urge to break it, couldn't see a dawn without remembering how Lukan made them rise early to balance buckets of water on their shoulders.

Bard staggered outside of the man's elbows, hitting the back of his hand and forcing it to swing forward. *Impressive,* thought Bard when the seeker held onto the blade, but that didn't stop Bard from kicking his leg out from under him and punching him in the face.

Dancer might have been able to make it look elegant, but Bard was gifted with neither speed nor patience. He had lost count of the times he had won tavern brawls by simply pummeling into his opponents.

In truth, he would have liked nothing more than to fry the man to a crisp had he attacked in kind, but Bard had vowed only to counter like with like. A hit for a punch. A flame for a surge. That was what Artis had taught him, at least.

That, and thinking about Dancer made him strive to be more poised in his brutality.

Good thing he rarely thought about her.

"Who are you?" demanded Bard in ale-inspired fury, holding the man down by the throat. His knee pressed against the wrist of the man's knife hand. As enraged as he was, he took care to keep his voice to a whisper. Fistfights and murder held less weight on his conscience than waking up Artis in the middle of the night.

"*Fraehkhaerazyshaeryas*," the man gasped, sputtering blood through fresh gaps in his teeth.

That wasn't what the man said, but that was what Bard understood. He knew it was Glasgérian but didn't know it well enough to tell if the attacker was from the Icelands. It was extremely angry-sounding, and Bard scoffed. Why was his *attacker* mad?

Bard shifted more weight to his knee until the outsider dropped his blade, and Bard picked it up with his free hand.

Steel.

It didn't gleam with the craftsmanship of the Hounds, but it had still been forged with care. No doubt the man intended to open Bard's throat with it, but Bard was feeling generous today—just like Dancer when she faced the Swordsworn in the brothel. He got up slowly, throwing the man a menacing glare that he hoped said: *Run, you bastard.*

It must have said: *Attack me, I'm drunk,* because the man hurled himself at Bard once he regained control of his limbs. Bard almost grunted, but his mind flashed to the old man sleeping in his bed. Instead, Bard threw his assailant off and with a single stroke painted a line of red across his throat.

The outsider could barely shout past a whisper, his slit windpipe no longer capable of human sound. Bard stepped back as blood speckled across the sleeve of his shirt. With a gurgle, the man fell to his knees. It almost made Bard want to stab him in the heart to quicken his fate.

Dancer would have definitely done better.

Sorry, Artis, thought Bard as he dragged the body inside. The last thing he needed was a dead outsider sprawled behind Artis' house. The old man was an outsider to the village, which made him a constant object of speculation in Genovel. Even after ten years, they still spoke of him as the Sinthean, the city-dweller. He didn't need more fodder for village gossip.

Bard's first impulse was to tell Dancer they were no longer alone.

He made sure the seeker was dead before heading back into the guest room, stumbling, it seemed, into everything that wasn't in his path. It hadn't been his finest killing. Adrenaline pumped in his veins and drummed in his ears, but his grip softened when he opened the door.

Bard had slept in that room many times over the years, and every time he entered, it felt like home. There were two beds, twice the luxury most villagers couldn't afford. Artis wasn't an extravagant man by far, but he wanted his guests to be comfortable. Normally, Bard took the one close to the window, but Dancer liked to look at the stars before sleeping. They were unfathomable to her: just billions of balls of light swimming in a black sea. Yet for all their chaos, they were the only things in the world that never changed.

He sat at the edge of her bed, wondering if she would knife him if he woke her.

"Bard," she murmured sleepily beside him, her tone so gentle that it almost stirred in him memories of other places, better times. Bard couldn't tell if she was really awake. She probably was, knowing how lightly she slept. If the past several weeks in her company had been any indication, she had likely heard his struggle with the seeker but couldn't be bothered to move.

It was Artis' voice from the outer room that pierced through the silence. "Why is there a dead man on my floor?"

The words "dead man" pulled Dancer from feigned sleep faster than anything Bard could have done, and she shot up, bright-eyed and rejuvenated. "Dead man?" she echoed, giving him a sleepy smile. "What have you done, Bard?"

He lit the candle next to her bed. "Nothing," he answered, but his unconvincing tone prompted her to follow Artis' voice out into the hallway.

At first, it looked like torches lit the ceiling, but Artis had cast a ball of Fire above them. Bard hated it when he did that. It made anything they discussed seem like some sort of conspiracy. It sent a chill through him every time.

But the deepened lines on Artis' face betrayed neither fear nor urgency—only concern. He turned to Dancer. "My dear, did this man attack you?" he asked.

"No," she answered, approaching the body. Around it, dark red had already begun to spread, and she didn't even wince when she stepped in the puddle. With an air of solemnity that Bard wasn't accustomed to seeing, she knelt, forcing the man's lifeless eyes to stare into hers.

"A seeker, from the looks of it," she said. "I've been hunted down by enough of these bast—sorry, Artis—*hoodlums* to recognize them." She smiled, almost nostalgically. Bard imagined with glee the list of bounties she must have incurred on her travels.

Dancer turned her attention back to the body. "Not a very good one. Was he armed?"

"He had this on him," answered Bard, handing her the dagger before throwing Artis an indignant glance. "And I'm fine, thanks."

Dancer examined it and wiped it clean on the dead man's cloak before slipping it into her own knife sheath. "What? It's good steel," she said innocently. "Not like the other one."

The beauty of a thing sculpted so perfectly to its purpose.

Bard didn't even care that she stole it from him. He contemplated the handful of half-jesting answers he might have offered, then reconsidered and ate them. There would be time for that later.

"I fear it is no longer safe for you here, Bard," said the old man. A gentle smile replaced unease. "But at least now, you aren't alone. My dear, you look like someone who can handle herself."

Dancer blushed.

"I advise you two to pack your things and ride at the break of dawn."

"What about you?" asked Dancer, her voice wrought with genuine concern.

Bard laughed to himself. His Storm could wipe out entire troops of Fireborne soldiers, so much so that he had incurred a ban on casting it in his homeland. Naturally, he had once cast it out of spite but was quickly taken down by a swarm of Thunderborne sentries. To him, there was nothing more unpleasant than being imprisoned by guards resistant to Storm, and it took them ages to set him free.

Artis could beat back his powers blindfolded.

Still, Bard could see that he was touched by Dancer's concern. "No need to worry about me. An old man has spent his entire life paving the path to his grave," said Artis. He turned to Bard. "And *you*. I advise you to *mind the black peregrine*."

Bard hated it when Artis was being cryptic. He had blissfully forgotten about the damn bird, and when Dancer went to gather their things, he threw Artis a spiteful glance. "Do you think that maybe, just once, you could just tell me what you mean?" he asked. The bird hadn't been in good shape when it arrived—its feathers were ruffled, its beak smeared with dried blood. Even its message had been less than spectacular:

***

BACK TO THE ROOTS.

***

Bard was tired of riddles. Black peregrines were never a good sign. They were bringers of misfortune, and whenever he saw one, even in passing, things took a considerable turn for the worse. He still remembered the first one he saw, back when he was fresh-faced and stationed in Sinthea. Even then, crime lords and thieves were hesitant to try their luck against a Thunderborne, so he was assigned to guard all sorts of important people. He could barely remember who they were now.

Fuck me, has it been that long? he wondered, anguished. It was hard to believe that an outsider like him could hold such an esteemed position in the Firelands, but times were different under Avander. There were no purges, no blood campaigns. Simpler times.

For a week, at least. That was the amount of time he was at the Citadel before he received his first peregrine. In its talons, it bore a message with a single word:

***

MASSACRE

***

A day under eighteen and Morian had already waged his war against the Glasgers. And when they retaliated and attacked Genovel, it was to Bard's ill fortune that he was at the border, accompanying Glasgérian officials out of the Realm. Avander had thought it prudent to get them out of the Firelands quickly.

Bard would never forget the wave of fear that swept through the convoy like wildfire when he saw it for the first time. Even the clouds tried to part, but they were too slow. The dragon had torn a hole in the sky, red and fierce like the dawn.

He had seen it from miles away. It stained the sunrise with the color of bad blood, and he remembered how much he dreaded meeting the new Summoner. The Scrolls loved chronicling how terrible they had been. As the saying went, there were three types of heroes in the Scrolls: brave, insane, and heartless. Summoners were inevitably two of the three.

But when he saw the girl for the first time, he let his guard down. She was big for her age, sure, but nowhere near what he had imagined. *She's just a kid,* he remembered himself thinking. That was his first mistake.

He had stayed in the capital for a while, and she seemed to take a liking to him. Even then, she had been a serious girl, but at least she laughed. For a time, that is. Bard liked to think it was her last dream to return to the borderlands, and when it became clear that she couldn't leave, she stopped.

They were a few years apart, and save for one other, she didn't talk to anyone else. Bard had even taught her how to fight, for all the good that did the Realms, and when his duties summoned him elsewhere, he thought he had left their capital in better shape than when he found it. His second mistake.

The gods are bastards. He spat at the dead man.

The second peregrine came years later, when Bard was seated in the Highlands—that miserable patch of land where all four realms intersected. Avander was dead. Morian had just ascended the throne and ordered his father's inner circle killed for treason—including Lucien, the only Hound Bard had ever considered friend.

If it were up to Bard, he would roast every peregrine in the Realms and eat them for dinner. It had been the most liberating day of his life, when he walked away from the path laid out for him. Not that his wasted, nomadic existence was anything to brag about, but it was better than seeing just exactly what blood had built.

That is, until he received the message to fly.

Artis patted him on the back, bringing him back to reality. "In good time," he said with a quiet smile, as though he knew exactly where Bard's mind had taken him. "Are you still following the path you chose, boy?"

Bard shrugged it off. He was well over forty, but he supposed anyone was a child compared to Artis. In truth, Bard couldn't imagine a time when Artis didn't exist. He was just there, like a mountain was there. "Do I have a choice?" Bard asked.

"Always," said Artis. "And many, many consequences."

Dancer came back out, yawning. The excitement of the dead seeker had already died down inside her. "Consequences?" she asked sleepily, her longbow slung about her shoulder. "What are those?"

The memory of her bounty list was clearly long gone.

"I'm going to Glasgérios," said Bard firmly. He turned to Dancer, and before he could stop himself, he opened his stupid mouth. "Will you join me?"

It was impossible to tell who was more surprised: Dancer or Artis. Or Bard.

Dancer suppressed a smile. "I *do* have people looking for me, and seekers *are* coming after us," she said with the air of a lord's daughter trying to decide which gown to buy. Finally, she shrugged. "But I've got a new dagger to try out, and it would be boring to get caught alone."

A rapid spectrum of feelings swept over Bard, most of them overwhelmingly positive, but he limited his expression to one: excitement, in all meanings of the word.

Artis shook his head and chuckled to himself. "Ah, to be young again," he said.

"Will you be all right, Artis?" asked Dancer. "I'm surprised you live alone. You're such a sweet man."

It was like watching a tigress calling a night-wolf sweet.

Artis smiled it off. "I was born into a wealthy family, lamentably. I didn't marry for love, but for convenience." He laughed at Dancer's reaction. "But don't feel bad for me. Little did I know, I would meet the love of my life later, when my wife bore her."

Dancer threw Bard an enchanted glance that said: *I want to keep him.*

Bard grinned and extended his arm. "Until the tides, old man."

"Until the tides, dear boy."

"Oh," said Dancer. "So that's what that means."

They clasped arms, sealing the paths before them. Bard wondered when they would meet again, or if he would ever return to the Firelands. As much as Bard hated it, he always found himself coming back—but would the old man still be there?

Bard and Dancer went out to re-saddle the destriers, throwing all their belongings into the side satchels. It didn't take long; most of it was food and water, and a few Glasger cloaks that Artis had dug out of his wardrobe. Anything else they could pick up along the road.

The sun had begun its climb, and by dawn, they resigned to what should have been obvious from the beginning: they were bound together, whether they liked it or not. He should have known it from the moment they left behind a trailing blaze of dead Hounds.

Now, there was nowhere to go but south—until things died down, at least. Not that he was complaining. A change in scene had been long overdue.

Dancer had the rare and invaluable talent of knowing which information was meant for her, so she didn't even bother asking about the peregrine. Artis had simply told her it was from his daughter, and she chose to believe his lies. *How wonderful it must be to be unburdened by truth.* She kept her eyes on the road ahead.

To Bard's dismay, the ale had worn off, and with it his excuses for poor behavior. Not that he needed them around Dancer, but he never knew what manner of highborn he would offend along the way. Artis would be disappointed if trouble found him strides away from his house.

The color of dawn drained from the sky and left it a vivid blue, and light poked holes in the towering trees. Dancer pulled up beside him. She seemed well rested today, despite the dead seeker. Her mood in the morning was a coin toss most days, but it usually leveled out by noon.

It was then that she decided to break their unspoken rule of asking about the past.

"How did you and Artis meet?"

The question took him aback, and he blinked the glaze from his eyes. It seemed so personal, *so intimate.*

"Do I get a question too?" he asked.

"Might."

Good enough.

"We met in the Greenwood a long time ago," he began, unconvincingly. *Not even a week after I'd renounced my duties.* "He was adventuring, too, can you imagine? Fifty years old, and me half his age." *He still kicked my ass, though.* "He was traveling with a companion, and we fought our way through the Greenwood. For a time."

Bard decided he wasn't very good at storytelling. "I suppose after a lifetime of wandering, settling down in a tiny village must have been an ideal alternative." *It seems like the worst fucking idea.*

Dancer smiled. "*You're* almost fifty," she teased.

Bard sighed. It stung more when someone else said it. "How old are you?"

"Is that your question?"

"No." He was sorely tempted to make it his, though. She could have been over a hundred, for all he knew. Her life left no scars, but her eyes told a different story. "I suppose I can't trouble you for a name."

"A name is present," she said. "We're uncovering the past, you and I."

"Damn." Bard rode on, deep in thought. "Well, then, I'll pose a philosophical question."

"If you dare."

Oh, but I do. "What happened to you?"

Dancer paused, contemplating an equally philosophical answer. "I lost something. I don't mean someone close to me died. I just mean I lost something."

Bard didn't like this game very much. He wasn't proud of his past, and most times, it was easier not knowing. Surely he could grant her the same courtesy.

And so they continued, entertained by trivial questions that passed the time. He discovered that she had once ended a man in three moves, but never with a sword. He revealed his childhood dreams of being a sea captain before he realized he was afraid of the sea.

After an hour or so, Dancer rode ahead, much to Bard's confusion. She halted the horse before a bout of thick shrubbery sheltered between two trees and swung down from her saddle.

"We can't be there already," he said, frowning, but Dancer brought a finger to her lips. She crept forward to the leaves, stepping without sound and peering past the twigs and brambles.

Bard dismounted with less grace and followed her lead. With his finger, he moved a few twigs that blocked his view.

Tents.

Lines and lines of Swordsuit tents.

What the hell? He glanced at Dancer and saw the same question lingering on her face.

"*How many?*" she mouthed to him.

"*Twenty-six,*" he whispered, not even bothering to guess. It was the first number that came to mind.

Bard turned his attention back to the Swordsworn. One quick glance told him everything he needed to know: their armor looked custom-made, not like the goons they had encountered in Waird. They lacked the sigil of the Suits, which meant that Valerya wasn't anywhere close by.

King's Command?

"*Should we ride around them?*" asked Dancer, who had likely realized that twenty-six Fire-casters might pose a challenge.

"*Where's your sense of adventure?*" countered Bard, feigning disappointment. "*Don't you at least want to know what they're up to?*"

The Suits didn't seem to be doing anything important. Some played cards while others drank ale, and a particularly hefty one had removed his armor to spar with a golden-haired Northerner half his size. If Bard had to guess, the Northerner would pose the biggest threat—he wasn't inconveniently large like his sparring companion, but not fresh-faced like a trainee.

And he was good-looking.

It was always the good-looking ones who did everything they could to protect their faces, even if it meant exercising caution and—gods forbid, strategy—in combat.

Bard watched one of the Suits step away from the camps to take a piss in the trees. He met Dancer's gaze and felt his heart warm when he saw that familiar sparkle return to her eyes.

He could have kissed her right then and there.

Dancer smiled at him. "*I like his armor,*" she said.

18

GLASGÉRIOS
ICE REALM

The Ice shot up from the table, right between her fingers. It was colder than the side of a blade and would have sliced through her hands if she had moved in the slightest. Dove fell back from her chair in surprise. Tomá watched without sound as the others hid their faces behind their tankards, trying not to laugh. The children were less successful.

"Again," said Tomá.

Dove had been trying and failing to anticipate his movement all evening, even when he told her exactly what he was planning to do. It was embarrassing, but she could not help it. It was the first time she had encountered Ice in its cast form, and its presence felt so *wrong*. It made the air she breathed feel foreign. Traces of it clawed at her chest on the way down, casting thin veins across the insides of her lungs.

The Fire in her blood did not take it well. Sweat poured over her brow, and her heart beat furiously to pump the foreign element out of her system. Her arms itched and threatened rashes; her eyes watered. Her body was rejecting him. For a moment, she wished she could cast Fire to show that she could do powerful things, too, but decided against it when she saw the burns on his face. *He would kill me,* she decided. *In an instant.*

Stifled laughter reminded her that she was on the losing side.

Dove shrugged it off. After journeying with the airship crew, jests no longer boiled her blood. She positioned her chair upright and placed her hands on the table like Tomá had told her: forefingers and thumbs together to form a diamond.

"Remember, the Ice will hit here," said the domeric, pointing to the center. His fingers were as cold as the elements he cast, but they were nothing compared to his eyes. Inside rings of silver, they were so black they looked like holes.

Focus. She turned her attention back to her hands.

They were in the belly of the Underground, a web of tunnels that led to a guest-keep just below the Court of Queens. Fires kept it well lit, and warm air moved through spaces in the floor and walls. The heat from the tunnels was said to warm Glasgérios above-ground. It made Dove never want to leave.

The tunnels themselves branched into chambers that ranged from small to cavernous, and each was filled with messengers. None were from the Firelands. No one looked like her, and from all the accents she had heard in passing, none of them sounded like home. She considered that a good thing but kept her hood up all the same. Even in their world, red was a disease.

The first Falcons had been domerics, so navigating through the darkness had come easily to them. It was not surprising that they designed the Underground accordingly. Not many braved the tunnels alone, but Dove could find her way with ease—one of the perks of growing up with Gryff, who used to beg her for late-night walks. She had to know the forest in the dark, know each trail like she had carved it out herself. After that, caves and tunnels came easy.

The entrance was located behind the statue that Tomá was worshipping, and there were others scattered throughout the city—one, as rumors had it, underneath the queen's throne. The punishment for sneaking around the castle was sudden death, so no one had the courage to find out. *Maybe if we were at the Citadel,* thought Dove, tempted. But Glasgers were different. Their ears noticed any change in movement, and she was not sure she could sneak past them unnoticed.

The blast of Ice shattered her concentration. Unwillingly, Dove's hands broke apart, and they gripped the edge of the table. There it was again. That feeling. *Ice.*

Damn it. No wonder their people were always fighting. If this was any indication, she did not want to imagine what elemental warfare was like. The constant presence of Fire and Ice was enough to drive both sides insane.

"You know exactly where I will attack," said the domeric, ignoring her reaction as Merc snorted. "There's no need to panic if you can anticipate your surroundings. Nothing kills faster than impulse. Except, maybe, hesitation." He reached over and grabbed her hands despite silent protests, forcing them back into position. "Once you know your enemy's moves, you own them."

A blade of Ice more jagged than the others shot up between her hands. Its edges threatened to saw through her fingers, but she forced them to stay together.

Merc cleared his throat like a fresh-faced actor preparing for a grand speech. "Splendid, m'lady!" he said as Dove stared, suddenly homesick. The core of the Ice was black, but it reflected colors across the table—colors that reminded her of the stars in the Dragontail. Decker had promised that they shone over Glasgérios too, but the fog was too strong for them to see.

"You have the makings of a domeric," said Tomá. It was meant as encouragement, albeit in the most frightening way possible. She never knew what he was thinking, and the more time she spent in his presence, the emptier she felt. She wondered if that was Tomá's secret. She could not quite explain it, but there was something dark in him, one that could only fill something that was already empty to begin with.

Still, Dove found him fascinating. She only wished he did not find her equally so.

"Next you know, we'll have you shooting arrows," said Tomá, rising.

Dove beamed.

"That was not a joke. Come. Follow me."

Her smile died a painful death on her lips. She rose reluctantly and threw Merc a desperate glance, but he had his eyes set on the golden-haired bar maiden across the guest-keep.

Dove did not know if it was the bar maiden or the tankard in her hand he was eyeing. Most likely he would be drunk within the next hour and embarrass himself, and Decker would not even be around to laugh at him for it. She rarely saw one without the other, but Decker had excused himself from their company as soon as they arrived.

Smart man, thought Dove as she and Tomá entered the tunnels. The domeric moved so silently, she did not know where he was half the time. *A domerys,* she reminded herself. Midnight forged.

"Sirian *kraehmys* seems to be under the impression that the *domeras* has willed your presence," he said after a long silence.

He was nothing more than a voice in the dark, but at least now she could follow its sound. "I trust his judgment. As *strange* as he is."

Dove did not think Tomá had the right to call anyone else strange, but she kept it to herself. Occasionally, he would toss a stone so she could follow its echo, but she had given up trying to map her surroundings. If she lost track of him, she would probably die in the tunnels.

Torch-fire renewed her hopes.

They reached what looked to be a training hall. The pell posts in the corner looked untouched, but the wall on the far end was lined with targets. "Outsiders must be trained in the art of arrows," said Tomá. "It is nature. Falcons attack in the air."

He pointed to the pell posts. "Swords are an art reserved for Fire and Thunder. I only use my greatsword against your Swordsworn."

It was strange imagining Tomá wielding a greatsword. He was lean and refined in movement, but he could probably wield a battle-axe if he wanted. Two.

A pair of young messengers with ash-black hair was shooting arrows. They were Glasgers, from the looks of it: dark hair, sharp features. There was an ample supply of practice bows available, but when they saw the domeric, they bowed and moved aside.

"*Domerys,*" the taller one said. He kept his eyes fixed on the ground and offered his bow with both hands.

Respect commanded through silence. Perhaps Dove had been born in the wrong realm.

Tomá nodded in silent gratitude.

The practice bow was nothing special; it was splintered and frayed and looked like it had passed through a thousand hands, but the domeric handled it like a newborn.

He turned to her, contemplated her build. Dove would have

found it strangely intrusive had he been anyone else, but Tomá did not seem to harbor any human desire—at least, none that she was familiar with.

"You're a climber," he said after a long silence. "Am I correct?" Dove nodded.

"Then your arms and shoulders should be used to strain. I see your right is your dominant side." He placed the bow in her right hand. She curled her fingers around its grip, wondering how ridiculous she looked. He might as well have handed her his greatsword.

"*Vambraehs,*" he said in a commanding tone, and one of the youths unstrapped his bracer in obedience. Tomá buckled it around Dove's right forearm. "*Faehas.*"

The taller one handed him a single arrow.

Tomá struggled to find the words native to Dove's ears. "*Draehar,*" he said, holding her right arm towards the target and fitting the arrow in its rest. He stepped behind her, and with ice-cold hands moved her arms up, drawing the bowstring back for her at the same time. She felt his breath on her neck, the only part of him that was warm, and she was surprised to hear a heartbeat. For every one of his, Dove's beat three times. "*Vraehar.* Aim now," he whispered softly, letting go. "But don't linger."

Without him, it was infinitely more difficult to keep the arrow drawn. She let go almost immediately, and the arrow soared past its target. It would have been a close one if her target had been the ceiling.

Dove expected snickers to come from their two spectators, but no one made a sound. One of the messengers presented another arrow to Tomá. "Again," he said. "*Faehas min aehas.* Where the eye goes, the arrow follows. Don't keep it drawn."

Faehas min aehas. Dove tried again, this time taking care not to linger. When she drew the bowstring back, she released as soon as she brought the bow up to her face.

Again, the arrow whizzed past its target, but somehow, it earned Tomá's approval—or so she liked to believe. There was no way to read his face. The crease in his brow that had deepened at dawn showed no signs of letting up, and his features reacted to nothing.

One of the boys presented her with another arrow, and she tried again. And again. And again, until missing became less embarrassing. She liked the feel of it. Her sense of space and balance came easy to her after a lifetime of climbing; all she had to do now was get her arms used to the movements.

After a few clumsy attempts, Tomá placed a hand on her shoulder. He bowed as he whispered in her ear. "What do you see when you close your eyes?" he asked softly. "Someone you hate?"

Someone I hate ... Hot sweat pearled on her forehead despite being surrounded by ice. She closed her eyes and raised the bow, imagining Morian standing before her. It had been a while since she thought of him, but fresh anger pulsed through her veins.

And when she opened her eyes, it was the closest she had come to hitting the target.

Given present company, Dove tried not to grin like a child on her birthday, but it slipped through despite her best efforts. She concluded that the Glasgers smiled only for the sake of outsiders, and even then, it looked strained, practiced.

Tomá did not even bother trying, but his eyes betrayed approval. "It always helps to think of your foes riddled with arrows," he said, ruining the moment. He gently took the bow from her and aimed.

Until that moment, Dove was not aware that air could be sliced. She barely saw him raise the bow; all she heard was the sound of the arrow whistling through the air like a dart. Cutting bread would have made more noise.

To no one's surprise, the arrow hit the center of the target. "Perhaps it is someone who has offended you," he said, taking another arrow and shooting again.

Slice.

"Someone who has wronged you."

Slice.

"Someone who has hurt you a thousand times and more."

Slice.

He took a deep breath as the youth presented him with his last arrow.

"Mine is your Blood Queen."

Slice.

Dove's eyes widened as it splintered through the others. His resolve filled her with dread.

Tomá stepped back as the messengers collected the arrows. His face was still contorted in a grimace, his features twisted with bitterness that betrayed his years.

She knew that look too well. Tomá had fallen headfirst into a memory that trapped him in his own prison of pain. Suddenly, she knew what human desire drove him. Revenge came at him like a thousand swords, each one a separate note of misery.

But more than his face and his thirst for revenge, it terrified her how well she understood him. She felt a stab of dismay when he pointed to the gash below his eye, the hideous burn that had marred his face. "I have a score to settle with your Summoner," he said, forcing half a smile. She had not seen it before, but she glimpsed the scorched skin that ran down his neck. Burns razed through his upper body, and she did not know where they ended.

But it was not the scars that had ruined his face.

The hall was caught in a wave of silence that no one but he dared to break. "Keep practicing with these two," he said. "I must attend to another matter." He turned to the others. "*Maehstrar'ys faehlar.*" The words were as ugly as his mood.

"*Domerys,*" they said, bowing. All they did was bow. Dove wondered what would happen if she bowed, too.

When Tomá took his leave, the Falcons looked at each other uncomfortably. It was uncomfortable for her, too; one tried positioning her arms while the other spoke wildly at her, which only served to confuse her more.

Language of the wolves, she thought with a sigh. As she took a deep breath, she thought of her own scarred hand gripping the bowstring. That dungeon of pain. How many like her had already trapped themselves in their own graves?

She raised her bow.

All because of Fire.

She aimed.

All because of him.

She released.

Slice.

It was far from the center, but it hit the outer ring of the target. The hall became silent, distant. Her bow hand was shaking, and her body no longer felt like her own. She shivered uncontrollably, and the cold had nothing to do with it.

"*Graehes!*" said the two, reminding her that she was not alone. They balled their hands into fists and raised them to their stoic faces. A passerby would not have known whether they were cheering or preparing to attack, but it did not matter. She was broken.

She stared at the target in disbelief, and the awe wore off as she came to her senses. The bow clattered to the floor and she unstrapped her bracer, much to the surprise of her companions. The messenger closest to her took it from her and glanced at his companion. The other shrugged.

Without a second glance, Dove took her leave.

Vengeance had taken her down a dark path, if only for a moment. Dove could see now that it had poisoned Tomá's soul, spreading through every vein until it had driven out all else.

She found herself surrounded by tunnels, each uninviting in its own way. The paths ahead presented a choice between dark and cold, dark and narrow, and dark and smelly. Without thinking, she chose the first. She needed some time alone.

It took a good three turns before she regretted her decision.

The tunnels were not torch-lit, and she soon found herself unable to tell where one ended and another began. She kept her hands pressed against the walls; the warmer they were, the closer she was to the main chambers, to human life. But soon, they all ran cold. She sighed and continued along, wondering if she should throw things to make noise. She pried a loose rock from the wall and flung it as far as she could.

The rock smashed against more rock, which she had expected. The low growl that followed, however, was the last thing she wanted to hear. She could not place its source, but echoes told her it was much bigger than a wolf. She held her breath. *Now you have done it,* she thought, trying to balance the thin line that bordered on panic. *Now you have gone and angered the mountain god Dakman or Dakraena or whatever the hell his name is.*

"*Baehr?*" a voice called. It spoke that hideous tongue, but given the circumstances, it was the most beautiful thing she had ever heard. Torch-light spilled into the crevices of the tunnel and pooled in high places on the floor. It was followed by two silhouettes: one that was decidedly human, and another she could not attribute to anything she had ever seen.

It was its red eyes that she saw first: two glowing pinpricks that indicated she was no longer staring at a shadow. Its hide was dark and tough, if one could even call it skin. Upon second glance, she realized to her dismay that it had no fur—only muscle that looked painted black. She had wished it was some sort of dog, but it moved like the shadows, like its limbs were made of liquid. She had never seen one up close before, but she knew what it was: a night-wolf.

"*Graevyhr!*" the other figure screamed, and she did not know if he was talking to her or the night-wolf. "*Graev—*"

He paused as the night-wolf charged.

Dove closed her eyes, wondering where her life went wrong. Out of all the things that could have possibly ended her, it was a night-wolf that would succeed. A night-wolf. In the belly of the Underground. Even if she could scream, no one would hear it.

"Get down!" the voice attempted again, this time more urgently.

Dove did not know if that meant to sit or kneel, but she threw herself on the ground all the same. She kept her face pressed against her arm so that she did not have to see the night-wolf's teeth tear into her bones.

But the pain never came. The night-wolf stopped in front of her, lowering its head to sniff at her hood. Its snout brushed against the back of her hand, and she was surprised that its skin was as rough as sand. Its growl turned into labored breathing as it relaxed.

Finally, when the only thing she could hear was the beast's breathing, she opened her eyes and slowly lifted her face from the ground.

The night-wolf was staring back at her—or rather, staring in her direction. It did not seem to be able to see her; it was only when she moved that it reacted, but the man next to him kept him at bay. He was thin, younger than Decker and Merc, but not much older than she was. His tongue was unmistakably Glasgérian, but his mixed features hinted at Fire. He pointed at a strand of her hair. *"Sintger?"* he asked, almost amused. "You're far from home, Sinthean."

She wanted to punch him, but his friend would not approve.

"Don't worry. Bear is not dangerous. He only gets excited sometimes," he said. His words were accented, but fluent. As long as she could understand him, she did not care. "You can stand, you know. Now that he knows you, you don't have to be afraid." He extended a hand.

I can do it myself, thought Dove indignantly, getting to her knees.

"I'm Marv," he said.

Dove raised an eyebrow. She could not see his features clearly in the torch-light, but he did not look like a Marv.

"Well, *Marvynhr.* If that's better."

I have no idea how to say that. Even in my mind, thought Dove, sighing. *Marv it is.*

"Not a lot of *Sintger* come to the Underground. This part, especially. Actually, people avoid this part."

Dove nodded towards the night-wolf. *Is that why?* she asked with her eyes.

"Night-wolves are misunderstood creatures. They're very … what's the word? Noble." He laughed, but it was not in a mean way. It was a nice sound that gently brought down the walls between them. "They only attack when provoked. The only predators that prey on other predators. How much better our world would be if humans behaved that way."

He is insane, she thought as he patted the side of the night-wolf's neck. *There is no other explanation. I have stumbled into the tunnels and encountered a madman.*

"I am a … *sunmaehrys.* I don't know what the Sintger word for that is. I suppose you can say I study creatures from all over the world. Just be glad you didn't wander any further. I have a few glow-flies loose, and they can get vicious." He drew back, suddenly self-conscious.

Dove suddenly realized why his features were so hard to see. The fire from his torch was encased in darkened glass. He was one of them. One of the night-walkers, like Gryff. For a bizarre moment, it comforted her.

Marv rose slowly, and Dove followed suit. He was thin and gangly and had short, messy hair, but that was the only thing she could tell from the shadows. "Well, Sintger, you should stop by some time. I think maybe you know what it's like to feel different. And misunderstood." He smiled. "Come, *Baehr.*"

The night-wolf had been standing in silent attention, but it turned when it heard its name.

Wait! Dove waved an arm. She pointed at the vast darkness behind her and moved her arms in a circle. *How do I get out of here? This … void of complete and utter misery?*

She was not sure he got all that, but he laughed again. "The walls are actually marked with arrows that lead to the central cavern. From there, simply … follow the falcons." He paused and brought the torch next to Dove's face. "Take this." He pressed it into her hands. "Don't worry, I don't need it. Just do me a favor and …" The short silence spoke volumes. "Don't take off the glass until I leave."

He turned and walked until he disappeared into the darkness. "Oh, and Sintger!" she heard him yell from the other side of the tunnel. "I was just joking about the glow-flies!"

Dove smiled despite herself and waited until she could no longer hear his footsteps. Bear made no sound as he trailed behind him. Finally, when she was sure he was no longer there, she removed the glass.

Fire cast light across the walls, and she saw arrows painted along the ceiling, like Marv had said. Tears of joy threatened to burst through her eyelids. But before she followed the signs, she wedged a rock into a gap in the wall. *Just in case,* she thought. Seeing beasties did sound appealing to her, but the night-wolf had been enough for one night. It would warn her if she got lost and found herself in the same place.

She continued, singing songs in her head to pass the time. She tried not to think of Marv, because then she would have to think of Gryff. It seemed like they had exchanged worlds; while he was out there, she was down here, where the sun never shone.

Dove did not know how long she had been walking, but when she saw a soft glow at the end of the tunnel, she expected to find another hole, another void. The only thing that filled it was a voice, deep and solemn.

She crept closer for a better look and took care not to gasp too loudly.

She had stumbled into a cavern lit by gaps in the ceiling, glittering off crystal-covered walls. Stone bowed to the river that flowed through it, giving it the impression that it was on fire, dancing in turquoise-green flames. Beautiful formations from the ceiling and ground met in the middle, and light filtered down in dusty columns.

And then a familiar shade of blue.

He is everywhere, she thought, half-irritated when she saw Decker sitting on a rock next to the river, writing in his journal.

Gods, how many pages does that thing even have?

She supposed she could not be too angry. It was a talent of his to find the one place not teeming with people. They had that much in common, at least.

He smiled courteously as she approached, much to her disappointment. She thought they had gotten past that point. That smile of his was impossible to breach. "We should stop meeting like this," he said, reaching into his satchel.

She took a seat next to him and glanced around for the voice.

"They call these the song caves," he said, reading her face. "You remember what they say about speaking out in the open. They say the winds carry outside voices here, to these caverns."

Dove glanced around, looking for the gaps in the rock where voices could fit.

"They're right to be cautious. The first Falcons carved out these caves to hear messages from the outside world. I bet they didn't know they would create such beautiful things. Peaceful," he said. Each word added to the weight under his eyes.

Dove felt herself relax to the sounds of the river. She could not imagine peace anywhere. Even her life in Myrne had been an illusion.

"What should we call it, then?" he asked, smiling. "Song cave isn't good enough. This one needs to stand out from the others. All we need is a name."

Dove threw him a playful glance, grateful for the reprieve. She pretended to think. She placed a hand under her chin, as she had seen Gryff do many times when he found himself faced with a problem he could not solve.

"The Beard it is, then," said Decker, closing his journal. "A name to intimidate the fiercest of plunderers."

Dove smiled. After a courtesy pause, she threw a curious glance at his journal.

"You're wondering what I'm writing about," he said, and she nodded.

"I suppose you can call them memories, though I don't quite know how true they are." He threw her half a smile. "A lot of it is a blur. But I don't like to think of the past much."

At his words, Dove swore she could feel the beating of their hearts align, and she realized that perhaps she and Decker had more in common than she thought.

"Well, you're with us, now," said Decker. He made a move to slap her on the back, realized she wasn't Merc, and retreated to an awkward pat. "It's the will of the *domeras* and all." He laughed. "That Sirian. Wolff asked him if it was wise getting us involved, and that was all he kept saying. *'It is the will of the domeras.'* He's even got Tomá saying it. Drives me crazy."

Sirian and Tomá may have been most similar in appearance, but imagining them spending time together, *speaking* to one other, was comical.

"And you?" asked Decker. "Do you believe the great *domeras* is pulling our strings?"

Dove shook her head slowly. At least, she hoped not. What would that have said, then, about how the *domeras* felt about her?

"Best keep that to yourself," he said. "You never know what they're thinking."

Dove smiled uncertainly. She agreed.

"Come on, then," he said, rising. "Let's find the others."

Dove nodded and stood.

"Let's meet here again one day," he said. "Promise?"

She smiled. She missed having a secret place. She and Gryff

used to hide coins in the forest all the time. After their parents died, they became easy targets. Village drunkards tried breaking into their home time and time again, so they needed a quick getaway.

Decker made his way back through the maze, and Dove wondered if the Ice in his blood helped him see in the dark. For someone so big, he was skillful at not crashing into walls.

All kinds of thoughts shot through Dove's mind as they walked, most revolving around Tomá and the Falcons, and it was only until they were back in the guest-keep that she realized how deftly Decker had avoided her question. Perhaps he had not been entirely truthful about the voices in the tunnels.

19

THE RED CITADEL
FIRE REALM

Morian was of the humble opinion that he had been spending too much time in his quarters. The longer he spent indoors, the more intense his visions became. He could almost touch the sounds, see every detail of the world that would one day be his. He saw the Empire how it must have been: Sintheans ruled as far as the eye could see, and the blood of their enemies rushed the fields like dark rivers, feeding their crops.

The sun greeted him with a blinding glare when he stepped out onto the balcony. Its sharp rays peeled back the clouds, revealing what the Empire had become: half-hearted houses that sprang up to form a sea of rust-red roofs beyond the forest. He squinted, disgusted.

Morian used to enjoy the view, but now that he knew the glory it had once been, all he felt was anger. On most days, it was bearable, but today, it was so sharp and intense that he did not wish for a better world for anyone. Not for the foreign dogs who ruined his country. Not for his people who let it happen. Many fought valiantly in the name of their realm, but their efforts were dragged down by weaklings. *Mongrels.* Outsiders who poisoned their blood until it became something grotesque. Unnatural. *Useless.*

No one will escape the Reckoning. His fingers clenched around the railing.

But they're your people.

They are not worthy of my protection.

An oath was sworn.

Morian laughed to himself. The oath only made sense to those worth saving. His father had once said that even the lowest dregs of society deserved a chance, that peasants and kings were connected through some unseen balance in the elements. That was a farce. The ugly truth was that some people could disappear, simply slip off into the abyss that lay beyond the waking world, and no one would bat an eye.

And now it is time to rebuild. Not the houses and castles the foreign dogs tore down, but the idea, the spirit, that had given rise to the red dawn. Valerya had already begun paving its foundation in blood. She knew where the last emperor was a fool and avoided his mistakes. Where Bastyan conquered Lancistierre and Thoryngald first, bent on mining their resources, she strengthened her command over the mainland. Where he placed his family and high lords in command of regional armies, she destroyed the class system in the ranks altogether.

Some things, however, she brought back with a vengeance. The training villages had been in a pitiful state before she took over. Now, they were overflowing with talent, morale. Young people who didn't make it into the villages were still encouraged to patrol their communes, and they gave it their all. Now that they had a Summoner General, failure brought shame to their families. *She strengthened our core until we were strong enough to expand,* he thought. *And expand we will.* Now all he had to do was get rid of the mongrels.

Some said it was they who brought with them the mystery illness that had swept through the Firelands. The alchemists traced it back to a Glasger ship docked in Port Haven, to a half-breed trader who just couldn't die alone. *These freaks of nature killed thousands.* The Citadel with all its riches and medicans and Sun-sworn priests couldn't keep them safe. A third of their population was wiped out in a fortnight. His sister Elarya had gone first. Then his queen mother. *A child and a queen, all because of them and their bastard gods.*

"Your Highness," said a voice behind him.

"Make it fast, Greaven," said Morian, annoyed. Greaven must have finished his patrol early, which often meant there were few dark deeds in the city today. A good sign to anyone but Greaven. To Morian, he was loyal, obedient—so obedient that Morian often forgot what he really was. Only few saw the beast behind the smile, but as long as he enjoyed his ... *tendencies* in a way that kept his streets safe, Morian turned a blind eye to the complaints. *But that also means he's hungry now.* Morian sighed, shrugged it off. There were surely some young inmates in the dungeons that no one would miss too terribly. He could have those if he wanted.

"They've set up camp in the Greenwood, close to the border," Greaven said. Morian liked how his intonation changed. He would dance and sing if Morian commanded him to and take it out on someone else later. "More have been assembled and are ready at your command."

"Excellent, Greaven," said Morian, breathing in the fresh air. It smelled significantly less like peasant since he had new waterways built for the aqueducts. Half the city was still shrouded in scaffolding.

He still remembered how the peasants cheered as if he had done it for them, but in truth, he couldn't stand the way the arches were going lopsided. Symmetry calmed him, and clean water from the Sinth put them one step ahead of the Thoryns. The streets and side alleys stretched in perfect order, and they were working on paving out the stones. "Remember, I want this to be a small endeavor. A pebble, so to speak. A mere foray into the vast wilderness."

Morian liked being poetic. If anything, it broke the monotony that had swept over the castle as of late. He had even resorted to creating his own fun at the Citadel, but his side experiment with the three trainees had turned out most unexpectedly. They were only supposed to pick at the Glasger, perhaps even whack at him with a few branches if they wanted—not draw their swords, especially with the General's lackey by his side.

Stupid boys. Granted, he did not expect Venn or Vait or whatever his name was to let the half-breed stab them all with sticks. The lower castellan had called in their bodies, and the medicans rushed to show their corpses to eager students. Ice-inflicted wounds were a novelty in the castle, and they could not be reproduced by any weapon forged in the Firelands. Some wounds looked like cat scratches from afar, but some had punctured deep, stilling their hearts. It wasn't a significant loss; Morian had chosen the dumbest and most useless of the lower castes, but he had at least expected them to ward off the half-breed's attacks.

Greaven stared, but Morian knew what he was thinking. *Beast, indeed.*

"How is our General doing, then?" Morian asked, feigning nonchalance. "Still not privy to our plans, I hope?"

"Surely not, your Highness," answered Greaven. "Your Highness has been most discreet."

Too many words.

Morian hated it when people used too many words. Flattery was full of them, words as ugly and lopsided as the aqueducts had once been.

Thirty men wouldn't make much of a difference. Valerya had reported scores of aspiring trainees pouring into the Citadel. Their ranks had reached a record high, and they were having enough trouble producing enough to feed and clothe them. The Icelands, decimated as they were, had only a fraction of that, but they would likely forge an alliance with the Lancistierreans should the Stalemate end.

And those blue-haired shits from Thoryngald ...

His Realm may be able take on Glasgérios and Lancistierre, but if the Thoryns came running back, he wouldn't be foolish enough to battle three fronts.

Which is why we've gotten help ...

We don't need them.

They've already agreed.

Get them to un-agree ...

Either that or we take the Huntsmen Woods.

No.

Morian shook his head. Anything would be better than working with savages. He cast a sweeping glance across the courtyard, desperate for distraction, but it only depressed him more. Sentries marched in circles, caravans went in and out, but nothing remarkable happened.

And then a flash of auburn.

Dove?

Morian's heart leapt and fell when he realized that the girl's hair was a shade lighter than his former squire's, her face more exuberant and full of life. He didn't remember Dove ever smiling, not once.

"Greaven," he said. "Who's that?"

"The smith's daughter, your Highness. She was asked to come to the Citadel to discuss some new designs."

She looks just like her. Morian squinted. *From afar.*

"She's going to our General, yes?" he asked.

"Yes, your Highness."

"Will she stay long?"

"Not likely, your Highness."

"Greaven," said Morian, irritated. "From now on, simply answer with 'yes, your Highness.' Can you do that?"

"Yes, your Highness."

"Good man," said Morian. "Keep an eye on her for me." Whoever she was, she was refreshingly glib. He needed more cheer in his life. "Oh, and Greaven," he said before turning. "I'd like to extend the Citadel's warm welcome to our General's squire. It's about time I got to know who's been following her around all day."

"Yes, your Highness."

***

In old Sinthean, the moon was referred to as *madra,* the Mother, who protected those who walked the path of righteousness. When it revealed itself in its full form, people knew to be wary; it meant She was watching, searching for hidden truths. Fear of Her wrath had reached every corner of the Firelands—even forgotten piss corners of the world like Genovel.

Valerya hated poetry. She had almost refused to learn how to read once she heard its flowery words, its emphasis on colors.

She didn't care why a flower was blue; it only mattered to her if it was poisonous. The only tale she had taken note of was that of the Mother, but only because her own mother had told her of it—and because of how wrong it was.

The Mother could have been a guardian or a god, but She cared nothing for Her children down below. Wayfarers begged Her for safe passage, and some of the Swordsworn still kept to the old faith, but it was nonsense praying to something in which she no longer believed. The Mother only graced the Firelands once a month, but She never failed to cast a somber shadow on Valerya's mood, bringing her back to days long gone.

Protect the line.

The Mother was watching then, listening to Avander's last words. Avander. The closest thing she'd had to a father since her own was taken from her. It was so long ago that she barely remembered what that felt like, but she still heard his words after all these years, sharp like glass.

Protect the line.

Valerya sighed. Children were idiots, and she had been no exception. She had naively thought it noble to honor the wishes of a dying man, and others had lauded her decision to head the Swordsworn after her own commander was put to the sword.

But what others were quick to praise as glorious was nothing but a blood-torn battlefield, cratered and desolate as the Mother herself—the guardian who did nothing but stand by and watch as her children burned. There was nothing *glorious* about crouching in the cold, surrounded by dead comrades. How quickly a sky that had once burned with a fiery intensity blended into spilled blood, into the smoke that colored it the shade of old bones.

And the sounds.

Brave cries descended into something else when the tides turned. It wasn't uncommon for grown men to cry out for their mothers. Wet nurses. She had signed so many messages to families left behind that her sympathies turned as black and diluted as the ink on her quill.

And then Morian decided to attack his own castle.

If she could, Valerya would spit at the moon. Her guardian. Her enemy. How the Citadel burned that night. The Cleansing, they called it afterwards. It started with her rank, butchered like animals in their own beds. Valerya was spared, along with a few others who would later form the head of the Spades. Lucien had fought them off valiantly—Lucien, who had been part of the convoy that found her in Genovel—but it was Greaven, of all people, who managed to cut him down.

Greaven. Big as an ox, but uglier.

Hasn't changed. In the mass confusion, she and Valk had found themselves barging into Lucien's quarters. It was the first time she had ever seen Valk in a rage, flying at the beast of a man and *winning,* but it was her voice that steadied him, warned him to back down.

Lucien, or what was left of him, was apprehended like the others and put to the sword. Morian had even set his guard dogs on their families. He wanted all traces of them destroyed. Them, their brats, everyone. She knew nothing of Morian's plans until Eithan told her, but it was only because she was in charge of his execution. Her mentor. He who had taught her everything she knew about Fire and dragons.

Morian hadn't changed. The Citadel was still full of his toys.

He couldn't even leave my squire alone. Valerya had been wondering when the boy would meet their sovereign. Still, Morian must have been well rested today. The boy had only sustained minor burns and welts.

Perhaps the king thought it unwise to break Valerya's things.

Her squire was recovering in the infirmary now, more shocked than injured. *Stupid boy.* Killing him would have been the greater mercy, but this was Morian, after all.

I didn't come up here to think of them. Every so often, she would send the sentries to do some mundane task so she could climb the steps and think in silence. It amused her to no end how ardently they went about doing it. Last time, she sent them to polish the horseshoes of every steed in the stable. They *glistened* on the training grounds the next day.

Tonight, she just sent them to patrol the gardens. She didn't need much time—only a break from the blank, vacant expressions she had been dealing with all day.

Valerya felt the creature stir inside her, responding to her anger. *Calm yourself.* It seemed to grow restless with each passing day, thirsty for Glasger blood. Especially when she thought of that night. *Lucien.* Lucien was the only reason she joined the fucking Cloaks in the first place. Their first task had been to rid the border of Glasgérian fanatics, and she accepted with pleasure. Each Summoning had soothed the beast, bound it to her for eternity.

Now there she was, fifteen years later, with a Glasgérian half-breed for a squire.

A soft mist washed over the moon as she heard an all too familiar voice behind her. It sliced through her head like a newly sharpened blade.

"Absolutely beautiful, isn't She?" it asked, nearly singing with jubilation.

"Your Highness."

The voice laughed.

That laugh, she thought icily, and her head began to throb.

"Always so serious, General," it said.

Valerya turned and bowed with decades of strained obedience. It didn't hurt her to play along. "Forgive me, your Highness."

"No matter." Morian waved a hand dismissively. "I hope you don't mind that I borrowed your squire on such short notice. You killed mine, after all."

It was ill timing that Morian decided to show himself just as she was recalling Lucien's demise, and it took extra effort not to react when he spoke so openly of his cruelties.

"I dread imagining you, your squire, and mine in the same room. The silence would be deafening," he said as he approached her. "And how is your squire recovering? I admit, I didn't actually think he would burn in daylight, but I had to find out for myself."

Valerya's face remained impassive. *Gods be damned,* she cursed to herself when she thought of Dove and Gryff. *I'm safekeeping Morian's playthings.*

Morian smiled. "I told him to hurry back to his quarters. I didn't know his kind could run so fast." He sighed, disappointed. "But I suppose the Mother guards us all tonight. He wasn't hurt too badly." He paused thoughtfully and clicked his tongue in feigned remorse as he tucked a lock of her hair behind her ear.

With an upward slash, I can cut off his hand with my dagger, she thought as his hand glided down her cheek, running over her scars. She had thought about it on countless occasions. It was enough to keep her going in dark times.

"Such a waste," said Morian. "Do you remember the first time you came to the Citadel?" He drew back his hand. "The news had already reached us by then. First Summoner in a century, they said.

And squirted from a *peasant,* can you believe it?"

Valerya remembered the day all too well, but it was unsettling how Morian recalled it with the same clarity. *Even back then, he was a cunt.*

"By the time you came, I expected a bear of a girl. The Scrolls always spoke of half-beasts and bulls, so I was curious." He sighed. "Imagine my surprise when I saw a peasant girl with nothing to her name. *Nothing.*"

The playfulness had gone from his voice. As much as she hated their talks when he was being jovial, it was better than when he was serious. She knew where this was going.

"Have you ever wondered what life outside the command would be like?" he asked.

Valerya blinked in mild surprise. He had never been this direct before.

"Servitude, ordering thousands, killing even more … it must get tiring."

"I fight for the good of the Realm," she answered, growing tired of his rhetoric. The throbs intensified.

"As always," he said, almost absently. "But you could do *far* more." He moved towards the ledge, watching the Mother over the railing. Whatever gods existed, they paled next to the exquisite cruelty carved into his smile.

Finally, he said, "I need a queen."

"The Firelands has many suitable *ladies,* your Highness. You can create powerful alliances in the South."

"I don't need a lady," he said, turning to her. "I don't *need* alliances in the South. Those hog farmers are loyal to me whether I like it or not. You may only be a *Fireborne,* but …"

Valerya cringed, for a great many reasons. She had not gone

back to Genovel since it was burned to the ground, but hearing Morian speak of her people as hog farmers made her regret he was her sovereign. Then again, it could be interesting. After all the blood campaigns, at least regicide would have been something new.

"I take my sworn duties seriously," she said. The answer was so engrained in her mind that she could say it in her sleep.

Morian's face softened in mock surprise. Melody returned to his voice. "Sometimes, *Valerya,* I really must wonder whose side you're on."

"As always, your *Highness,* I fight for the good of the Realm."

"You fight for *me,"* he said, raising his voice.

Perhaps not so well rested after all. For a split-moment, she hoped he would get into one of his moods. At least then she would have an excuse to knock him out, and he would wake up the next morning with no memory of it.

In the past, she had considered wedding the king, bearing him a son or daughter, and then promptly slaughtering the king, protecting his bloodline in other ways. But whenever she thought about his hands on her, his mouth on hers, she was overcome with the urge to vomit. Even for Avander, there were some things she would not do.

But Morian regained composure before she could ball her hand into a fist. "There will be war, General," he said softly. "One way or another." He looked as though he wanted to say something else but decided against it. "Leave me," he snapped instead, straightening. "Go tend to your mongrel squire."

"Your Highness." Valerya bowed and took her leave with slow, deliberate steps. Any quicker, and he would have been under the impression that he held power over her. Indeed, he had been more erratic than usual, but that was a satisfaction he would never enjoy.

It was only when Valerya reached her chambers that she realized how tired she was. She was used to long marches across the country, but nothing drained her more than one of Morian's talks, especially those involving her as queen.

His queen. Taking on an entire army of Thoryns by herself seemed a more appealing prospect than mothering his brats. Even now, she kept her surname out of spite. Many highborn families had offered to make her their heir, but she didn't want to forget where she came from. That, and Smith irritated Morian to no end.

Valerya had Valk summon the Glasger to her chambers. His wounds weren't serious, as the graces reported, but she wanted him out of the infirmary. When she was new to the castle, she spent more time there than she would have liked. Her fainting spells had been cause for concern, and there was a time she had actually lost courtyard brawls. She hated the infirmary.

Especially with those old crones.

None of the graces had the stomach to treat a Glasger at the Citadel, especially one who had been so marked with the king's approval. But they ultimately decided that they feared the She-Jackal's wrath more than their ruler's "mercy" and bandaged the boy up like a broken doll.

And when Valk entered her chambers with her squire at his heels, she could see the linen wraps around his torso, barely visible beneath his shirt.

"On your feet," she said, and he obeyed.

Not a whelp anymore. She recalled the first time he was brought to her chambers, whimpering and cowering like a beaten dog. Months of hard training had turned the soft-faced scribe into a somewhat passable soldier, even if it meant dangling at the lowest ranks, and he was at the age where he seemed to be growing with each passing sunrise. He was still shorter than Valk, but he still had time.

Valerya cared nothing for false pleasantries. She was aware that burns hurt—to ask if they did would have been stupid. Instead, she went straight for the heart. "What were you thinking?"

The boy blinked, confused.

"I don't ..." he began.

"I meant with the trainees," said Valerya impatiently. She grew tired of seeing his dumb, dazed expression every time she asked a question.

"They attacked me, General."

"So you killed them all?"

"It wasn't intentional," he said, keeping his head bowed.

If there was one thing to be had, at least, it was that the boy stopped being defiant towards *her*. She cared nothing for sycophants, but she couldn't stand empty convictions.

"But you wanted to," she said. "Eyes to me."

A pause as he obeyed, contemplated his answer. "Yes," he said firmly.

"Why?"

The conviction in his eyes was unmistakable. "Justice," he said. *Idiot.*

"Justice." She didn't bother hiding her distaste. "What do you know of justice?"

The boy struggled to find the words. "It means giving the enemy what they deserve."

"Did you give them a chance?"

"No, but ..."

"Justice without the possibility of mercy is simply vengeance," said Valerya. "You'll do well to remember that, Glasger. I care little for motive, but I will not have you strutting about and acting under a misguided notion of *justice*. You must at least know the truth of why you fight. That way, you cannot delude yourself."

"Vengeance," he repeated. "But the Scrolls say that you …"

Valerya's headache was coming back. She didn't know why she bothered. "The Scrolls say many things. They say the last emperor was cruel, that the outsiders were heroes for destroying the Empire. But tell me, do you know why they all say the same thing about us?" she snapped, not bothering to wait for an answer. "Because we *lost*. The Scrolls are always kind to the victors. The Glasgers who ransacked the city weren't *merciful*. They weren't heroes. They threw our children from the towers of the highest keep, fed their corpses to the hounds. They say some of their officers began a killing competition to see how many of us they could slaughter."

The boy paused. "I've never read about …"

"Of course you haven't." Valerya felt her patience reach its limit. Perhaps she would burn the boy herself and say he died in the infirmary. He probably even enjoyed poetry. "It's not written in any of your precious Scrolls."

It was like talking to a piece of furniture. A wardrobe with a faulty door that creaked when it opened and never closed. Valerya cut him off before he could say more. "In the meantime, you must learn to control your powers."

The boy reddened. "I'm trying," he said. "But I can't …"

"I will find a suitable arrangement. Now leave me." Her head was splitting now. She had lost count of all the voices she had silenced, and with them thousands upon thousands of dreams.

All in the name of justice.

Vengeance.

Mercy.

The boy glanced at her reluctantly, and she saw questions forming upon his lips. Instead, he swallowed his words and bowed. When he took his leave, Valk shut the door.

"You know what I have in mind." Valerya's tone softened. She showed no weakness in front of the others, but Valk was allowed to see her suffer a headache. "Speak plainly."

"General." Valk approached cautiously. "Is it … *wise* to send the boy there?"

"He is no longer safe here."

"How will you explain his absence?"

Valerya handed him a message. "A falcon came today," she said. "There's been a chain of attacks in the Greenwood. Most likely bandits and marauders, but the Swordsworn patrolling the area think it's the work of the Red Spears." She almost laughed. "There's an attack that's left twenty dead. Half a brothel was burned to the ground. And dead seekers have turned up along the southern border."

Genovel.

The name was almost foreign to her now, and she thought of it with the detachment of a child reciting old houses and their histories. It loomed over her like a half-remembered dream.

"Officially, you and the boy have gone to investigate. For all our King knows, I grew tired of his presence and made him *your* squire."

She knew the Spade well enough to know that underneath his stoic expression, Valk was suppressing a smile. "Alone?" he asked.

"Anyone with half a brain knows that one of you is worth a hundred Swordsworn." *And to me, the entire army.* The only friend she had left after Morian killed them all. The other Spades were loyal, but none had braved quite as many battles with her as Valk, nor had they offered her counsel in dark times.

And no one else had gotten to see her suffer a headache.

As much as she didn't want to send him away, there was no one she would trust more with the task—especially now.

"I have something for you," said Valerya, taking something from her desk drawer. It was the other package that he and the boy had picked up from Sinthea. "I trust you know what it is?"

"I admit, I don't," said Valk. He took it in his hands and un-wrapped it from its linen folds, staring, frozen, at its contents. He dropped the linen in shock, taking the golden hilt of the dagger in his hand. It bore the Lukan's mark, clearly re-forged—but even from afar, its gleam was unmistakable.

"Lucien's dagger," he said softly, turning the blade in his hand. "How did you ...?"

"Whenever Avander marched into battle, he carried Eithander's old dagger with him," said Valerya, cutting him off. "He never used it, of course, but he was convinced that the dead watched over him. Like ..." She sighed, but there was no other word for it. She had trapped herself. "*Guardians.* These are precarious times, Valk. We need all the protection we can get."

Valerya could see the man's grip on the hilt tighten. "Do you still remember that night?" he asked softly.

"Always." She nodded solemnly. "Now leave me. We have long days ahead of us."

Valk nodded and bowed. "General." He stopped before his hand reached the handle. "Is it justice that stays your hand when it comes to the boy?"

"No." Valerya sighed again. The throbbing had turned into ham-mers beating white lights into her eyelids. No doubt she would have another nosebleed soon. "It's mercy."

20

THE GREENWOOD
FIRE REALM

"I can't believe I let you talk me into this," Dancer muttered as she tousled her hair in a vain attempt to look haggard. Even with dirt smeared across her face, she looked like she had just woken up from a nap. Not at all like the stone-cold killer she was supposed to play.

Focus, Bard thought to himself as she tore her shirt at the side.

No one would ever believe that Dancer was apprehended—yet again—for attacking a convoy and subdued by Bard, who now went by Franco. It seemed like a proper name for a Hound, and he was thinking of keeping it forever until Dancer threatened to go by Brunhilda.

Bard cleared his throat like an actor preparing for a big debut. As he pulled the helm over his head, all he could think about was how unnatural it felt. He had never worn a helm voluntarily, even—or especially—when it was required of him. It was bulky and limited the scope of his vision, so he always managed without one. But now, it was the only thing that concealed the blue strands that swept through his hair, which had grown out into rough, uneven waves.

It covered most of his head, leaving a Y-shaped opening for his eyes and mouth. Dancer had all too gladly offered to shave the stubble off his face with her new dagger, but the blue in his beard was just dark enough to pass off as black.

And as much trust as he placed in her ability to handle a blade, he much preferred not to see her approaching his throat with one.

She needed even less to subdue the Swordsuits.

All Dancer had to do to was throw one of them a playful smile and lift up her shirt when he went to take a piss. He came to her willingly, dropping his weaponry and taking the utmost care in not letting his comrades know. If Bard had tried the same thing, the man would have alerted all twenty-plus soldiers to his side, weapons drawn and Fire at the ready.

The man had even unstrapped his armor without being told, the fool. Bard reckoned it must have been months since he had seen a female civilian—*decades* since one willingly spread her legs for him. He might as well have slit his own throat.

But to the Suit's good fortune, Dancer had been in one of her existential moods as of late, questioning her place in the world.

"I'm tired of leaving a trail of dead behind," she sighed as she punched the Suit in the jaw. His face snapped to the side, and he crumpled to the ground like a stringless puppet.

Bard stared, enthralled.

It was a difficult thing, knocking a man out cold with one blow. Most assumed that brute force was enough to do the trick, but Dancer knew just how to send the man's brain rattling against the sides of his skull.

"Let's play another game," she said as though she had just grown tired of counting marbles. "The first person who kills, loses."

"What does the winner get, then?" asked Bard, unconvinced she would win. And if by some unforeseen miracle she did, he wasn't sure her newly donned pacifism matched her current goal. In a clash between Storm and Fire, she would be at the greatest disadvantage.

The corners of her lips drew back into a shy smile. "Oh, I don't know," she teased. Her safety was secondary to her amusement. "A secret. And one that matters."

Bard almost laughed as he strapped on the soldier's cuirass. It was remarkably light for Hound armor, and not nearly as cumbersome as it looked. It was a shade too small, but if he let the straps dangle, he found that he could breathe again. "And what's to make me believe you won't start screaming about how blue my hair is?"

Dancer cursed, her plan foiled. She continued tearing at her clothing as she pondered, pausing thoughtfully between rips. "Then we can't sabotage each other," she said decisively, smearing more dirt on her face. "The one who sabotages forfeits the game."

Bard found it oddly endearing that she was contemplating the lives of thirty men like they were part of some jousting tourney. Then again, the men had the horses for it, but to his dismay, Bard had counted only two destriers.

In fact, this particular group of soldiers wielded longswords and rapiers, clearly bent on attacking the unarmed and unarmored. Only the ox of a man wielded a greatsword, which did nothing to convince him that these were novices.

Nothing more discouraging than appropriately sized swords. Fresh-faced trainees may choose embarrassingly large weapons and massive steeds over function, but it took a true master to recognize the power of subtlety.

And there was only one person he knew who could wield a greatsword with ease, coincidentally the only convincing destrier-rider in the world.

Bard grimaced underneath his helm. His mind had been full of two women as of late, and they would surely not get along.

"What's our story again?" asked Dancer, interrupting his thoughts. She had grown tired of tearing at her skirt and resorted to looting the Hound's body.

"I'm a dashing Swordsuit," said Bard confidently, dark times forgotten. He had run through this scenario many times in his head, except in his glorious rendition, he had envisioned himself charging them in a fiery battlefield—not rushing to join them.

But such details could be overlooked, given the right company.

"And me?" she asked, distracted by the coins she had swiped from the man's satchel. She tossed the dravs aside and pocketed the rest.

"You're the seeker who tried to assassinate me along the way." Bard shrugged. His dream did not include an accomplice, much less a Waterborne with an aptitude for deviating from the plan, but try as he might, he couldn't come up with a more convincing story for her.

"I suppose I can try."

Bard found her reluctance endearing, especially after seeing her knock out a Suit with a single blow to the jaw.

Dancer frowned. "Why didn't you just end me, then ... *Franco?*"

"It's considered improper for a man of the King's Command to lay a hand on a woman after she's been properly disarmed." Bard knew the words sounded stupid before they left his mouth, but Morian never did things that made sense.

Killing her, on the other hand ...

Fortunately for Dancer, most men found relief in desires of the flesh rather than in scarring it, so she would likely be safe as long as she didn't reveal their plans.

Or rather, the *men* would likely be safe as long as she didn't reveal their plans, for Dancer was neither helpless nor someone who could be properly disarmed.

Pleased with his answer and not bothering to ask how he knew it, Dancer smiled and resumed tearing at improbable parts of her clothing. "What do you think? Do I look like a hag?"

Bard didn't have the heart to tell her that she looked like she had just stumbled out of a tavern, so he nodded. Even at her worst, she owned him.

When they were properly disguised, Bard bound her wrists with rope from the horse's saddlebags, trying to suppress a stupid grin. He failed, of course, but she shrugged it off with grace. In truth, she didn't seem like she was paying much attention. He suspected she was still in one of her moods and couldn't be bothered to think of trivial things, like survival.

"Ready?" He unrolled the rope until it dangled to the ground. She was to follow him on foot as he rode valiantly into camp, letting him bask in the rare glory of having the upper hand.

"You insult me," she said playfully, smiling and holding up her bound wrists. "Remember the last time a Suit cut my binds?"

Bard raised an eyebrow. "You don't want to lose the game that badly, do you?"

"You're just going to have to save me, then," she said, feigning concern. "You wouldn't let me die at the hands of a Hound, would you?"

Bard knew he was going to lose.

"Come on, then," he said as he mounted the destrier, rope in hand. "Time is of the essence!"

Six Suits were playing cards in a circle, but they rose, alarmed, when they heard the hooves of the demon-horse clang heavily against stone.

Bard vowed to buy a pony when he had the means.

"Whoa," said the smallest of the group, as Bard had anticipated. The Suit wasn't young, but he was all limbs and reminded Bard vaguely of twig-bugs he had once seen in Lancistierre. It was a hard image to unsee after that. Twigs held up a hand in a half-hearted attempt at a warning. "What's going on here?"

"Greetings," said Bard with all the misguided confidence of a destrier-rider. "My name is Franco. I was riding here under the orders of our King, but this seeker tried to pick me off on my way here. Burned down a brothel and everything." He jabbed a thumb behind him, wondering if Dancer looked even mildly convincing as a captive. She certainly looked despondent enough for it, but he suspected it was because he had confiscated her dagger. He pulled it out of his sheath and let it fall to the ground, hoping beyond hope that she wouldn't scream in protest.

Bard coughed, allergic to his own lies.

"Where are you from?" asked Twigs as his companions straightened, prepared for all manner of possible outcomes. It was at this point, Bard found, that most brutes and boors would flex their muscles or puff their chests in an attempt to look intimidating. Sort of like bulls in mating season.

This man and his companions did nothing of the sort.

Another bad sign.

"I hail from Waird," said Bard, this time more convincingly. He had heard enough Hounds on his adventures to know how they talked, and any deviation from standard Sinthean could be blamed on coming from a village that no one had ever heard of.

The man eyed him suspiciously.

Bard coughed again.

"Strange that our King sent you," said the man. He threw a quick glance at Dancer, trying to piece together what could have possibly happened on the road to warrant such unconvincing dirt-marks. "Then I'm sure you wouldn't mind answering a few questions."

"Why, I certainly don't!" said Bard, echoing what he thought a Franco would say.

The man spat, unconvinced. There was nothing remarkable about his face, but the way he contorted it into grotesque shapes was impressive. "Here's an easy one," he said. "Who's the head swordsmaster at the Citadel?"

Bard paused thoughtfully. The swordsmaster had probably changed in the past twenty years, but he would never forget the man who trained him when he was posted in Sinthea. He was a fierce man who had given up his claim to a gold mine to teach thousands of Swordsuits how to stab things effectively. Even now, Bard doubted he could best him.

"Lukan," he answered. He could almost see the Fates above him flipping a coin. "I trained under him."

To his relief, the Suit laughed. Bard was surprised to see that all of his teeth were still intact. "Yeah, that's right. Most of them went to shit after that. Now they have masters like Diante ..." He spat again.

What the fuck kind of a name is Diante? thought Bard, but he couldn't even frown under the weight of his helm.

"C'mon, that's too easy," one of his companions jeered. He looked like a fresh recruit, and freckled, like the sun shat on his face. His fire-colored hair only made Bard all too aware of his own blue locks.

Freckles stepped closer and squinted, trying to look into Bard's eyes. "This is one that only a King's Command soldier would know."

Now you're talking, thought Bard, preparing to unleash a fury of events with a single word. Oh, how the real bards would sing if this single-handedly led to the end of the Stalemate.

"Lukan is the swordsmaster, yes." Freckles smiled, as if eager to get to the punchline of a joke. "But who first trained Valerya the Fireborne in the art of sword-fighting?"

Bard felt his face harden when he recalled the ghosts of fallen allies. "Lucien," he said softly, and wondered if he should push his luck; he was down to his last card anyway, and he supposed it would be interesting to force the Fates to play their hand. *Why not,* he thought, grinning to himself. "And that Thoryn prick. I forget his name."

He could hear Dancer stir in surprise. With just a few words, he had betrayed a part of his past that he hoped she would never see. Knowing the name of the swordsmaster may have been rare for an outsider, but not unheard of.

But knowing—even *being*—the devil in the details ...

Freckles frowned, clearly too young to remember, and he turned to his companions. "Is that right, Martyn?"

Bard was insulted. Surely no one wanted to hear of the outsider who thrust a sword in Valerya's hand, but to be erased from their histories completely? That hurt.

The oldest of the group—Martyn, he presumed—cleared his throat. "Yeah. That blue-haired shit."

A poor choice of words.

I don't remember you, thought Bard. But he made sure he would in the future.

The answer sent a wave of mixed responses from the group, especially from Bard. Some shook their heads while others remained stone-faced. Among them, Freckles maintained his dumb, confused demeanor. Bard had no doubt that Dancer could stay calm in the face of stampeding trolls, but her silence was the most unsettling of all.

"Tie up your horse, then," said Freckles before turning to Dancer. A vicious grin masked any trace of youth on his face. "And then tie up this wench."

This Bard had to see.

He glanced at Dancer, who stared at the man. Her mouth contorted into feigned fear, but eyes locked onto his.

Poor Freckles, thought Bard sadly. *He had only just begun to live.*

Bard threw them his most winning smile and urged his destrier forward until he reached a tree located behind the tents. "Here we are," he said as he dismounted, trying to sound as jolly as possible. He counted a total of ten times Dancer could have ended him between "tavern wench" and the tree, but she had her heart set on winning the game.

As he tied her to the trunk, he loosened her binds. "Is that all right?" he asked, taken aback by his own concern.

Dancer smiled. "Go run and play with the other boys."

Bard almost blushed as he tied the knot. He was sad she couldn't see it.

He tied the horse to the tree and strutted back to the tents, taking in every detail as he walked. There were the six Suits they had encountered up ahead, two sparring off to the left, and the rest, either watching the fight or resting in their tents. It looked like they had been there for a little less than a week; they had set up cooking spits but barely unpacked their belongings.

Whatever reason drove them there, they didn't plan on staying long.

"Hey, Franco!" said Freckles, offering him a wineskin. "Drink makes the time go faster."

Bard took it, his gratitude authentic, and bit off the horn plug.

"Name's Gerry," he said as Bard took a swig, though Bard preferred Freckles. "That's Martyn, David, David, Lorenz, and Robian."

The others gave a half-hearted wave as Bard proceeded to forget all of their names, opting instead for Freckles, Martyn, Twigs, Flowing-Hair, Stalwart, and Baby-Faced.

"Take off your helm, eh?" laughed Stalwart to his left, slapping it from the side. A reverberating gong shot through Bard's skull, and he nearly spat out his wine.

"Can't," said Bard gruffly once the ringing died down. "I plan on taking on that beast over there once pretty-boy is done." It was meant as an excuse, but Bard could see the possibility looming dangerously above him.

The others laughed. "You want to take on *Vet?*" asked Freckles.

Bard threw Vet a curious glance. The man was built like a draft horse, and his arms bulged and flexed as he warded off his opponent's advances. Bard could see every muscle ripple with effort, and he wore a face-guard strapped around the back of his head. It didn't look like it was meant for protective purposes.

Perhaps Bard had spoken too soon.

"*Vet?*" he repeated, refusing to show any trace of doubt. He cried inside.

"Hard to recognize without the armor, isn't he?" asked Freckles, and Bard decided that he talked far too much for his own liking. "Venturon. Named after a *bird*. Gods, I wonder what his parents were thinking. And he used to be a Spade before he joined us, can you believe it?"

Bard recognized the name but couldn't place it. Instead, he shook his head. "I wonder what it was like serving under the She-Jackal," he said.

"Don't know. Vet's not really the talkative type," said Flowing-Hair, returning to his round of cards with Baby-Faced. "I'm sure he'll show you when you're fighting him, though."

"I don't doubt it," said Bard, growing bored of Hound banter. He felt his intelligence sink. "How long have you been here?"

"Almost a week, now." Freckles spat. "Just waiting for our King's signal. My sword itches for Glasger blood."

So there it is.

Anyone with half a brain could have guessed that soldiers setting up camp so close to the border were up to no good, especially those under the King's Command.

"So what's she like?" asked Twigs, and for a split-moment, Bard was confused. Then he saw the man nod towards Dancer. Bard almost laughed when he saw her bored, glum expression.

"Wouldn't know. Doesn't talk much, but who needs her for *talking?*" said Bard matter-of-factly as he took another swig of wine, recalling with diminishing clarity the Hounds they had warded off in the brothel. Crude, all of them.

The men laughed, except Baby-Faced.

Bard stared, trying to make sense of his face. Baby-Faced looked like he had once been a beautiful child whose quest for glory became marred by the onset of puberty. His skin blemished and blistered in the most inconvenient places, and scraggly hairs about his chin formed an ill-advised attempt at a beard. He sulked like a man who wouldn't age well. Still, though his looks had gone elsewhere, he may have wielded all the honor and integrity in his group of companions.

Bard made a mental note to spare him should the circumstance arise. He considered himself a good judge of character and had no mind to kill boys—decent ones, especially, who had a chance at bettering the Realms.

"What's your name again?" he asked.

"Robian," answered Baby-Faced.

"Robian here doesn't know a good jest when he hears it," said Freckles.

"I find it crude," insisted Robian. "We're guards of the Realm. Not whoremongers."

"Listen to *him*," said Martyn, taking a swig from his own skin. "Whelp. At this point, I'd mount the She-Jackal if I could."

Robian sulked and rose. He took a flask and made his way to Dancer. As much as Bard wanted to see her reaction, he kept his attention focused on the others. Twigs wouldn't be too difficult to pick off, and Freckles looked like he had never seen battle up close before. Flowing-Hair didn't seem particularly attached to his longsword; it lay at his feet, dull and neglected.

Strong Fire-caster, Bard noted.

That left Martyn, who might pose a challenge with a sword.

Bard contemplated his situation and chose his words carefully. "Any word on when the attack is set to occur?" he asked, feeling the wine settle in his stomach.

"Nope," said Flowing-Hair, irritated at having lost a few markes. "Reinforcements are set to come soon, though. Truth be told, we thought you were part of it."

"Nope," Bard echoed. "I was just sent to see how you were doing." With each gulp, he found it increasingly difficult to maintain their ridiculous accent.

I really must stop drinking, he thought, taking another swig.

He glanced back at Dancer, who endured the pup's companionship with grace. She even *smiled* at him when he offered her the flask, and not in a murderous way.

"Franco," said Freckles. "Franco. *Franco!*"

Bard turned back to his companions and frowned. He knew the name sounded familiar, but it had taken him a moment to remember why. He blinked.

"Mhh?" he asked, irritated.

"Did you come directly from the Citadel?"

"Nope. I was heading east with a convoy of Suits when we were ambushed by a horde of bandits." Bard spat, marveling at how easily storytelling came to him. "Three of us slaughtered them and made our way to a nearby village when she attacked us. She cut down the other two and burned half the brothel to the ground."

The men laughed. "A brothel, eh?" asked Flowing-Hair, raising his flask in respect. "Well done."

"Have some more." Freckles handed him another skin. Malice carved lines into his face. He threw a quick glance at Martyn and nodded, and Bard saw the older man nod in return.

Fucking wine, thought Bard.

"Who was it who sent you again?" asked Martyn.

"The king sent me," said Bard, setting down the skin.

He realized at once that his conversational foray had suffered a spectacular misfire when he was met with a stony silence. It was only when Stalwart turned to him that Bard realized his grave mistake.

"Don't you mean … *our* King?" he asked. "Without a convoy of … *Suits?*"

Damn it, Franco, thought Bard, cursing Franco's stupidity.

"You see, it's funny," said Freckles as Martyn drew his blade. "Martyn and I were in a tavern not too long ago. In a village not too far away," he said. "A little chambermaid ran in and told us that a Thoryn and his blood-stained whore had come to the brothel."

Bard sighed. The wine had seeped into his muscles, and the

prospect of taking on a horde of King's Command soldiers seemed far less appealing with a belly full of drink. He suddenly knew how Dancer felt when she couldn't be bothered to move.

"Does that look like a blood-stained whore to you?" he slurred, pointing to the tree behind him. But instead of Dancer, he saw Robian tied to its trunk, clearly unconscious.

Unbelievable, Bard found himself musing, enamored. He almost forgot that he was surrounded by Hounds who had just exposed his lies.

"On your feet," commanded Martyn as Flowing-Hair and Stalwart rose. "David, Lorenz, find the whore."

Bard wondered if it would have been easier to just follow the shouts that erupted from the tents. They were stilled quickly—not nearly loud enough to reach the sparring Swordsuits and their on-lookers, but not quiet enough for his current companions to ignore. Flowing-Hair and Stalwart grabbed their blades and rushed toward the tents, ready to spill outsider blood.

One might have laughed at how unconvincing the duo looked.

Bard rose, pretending to be significantly drunker than he was. In truth, a drop more of the stuff would have likely been his end, but he used it to his advantage and stumbled sideways. "I dunno-where …" he slurred, grabbing onto the side of the cooking spit.

"Grab him," commanded Martyn, and Freckles drew his sword.

"Let's not be toohastyfriends." Bard raised an arm towards them. He might have been able to take on the two, but doing it without killing them?

Cast your Fire, he thought, challenging them with a glare. They weren't wearing much armor, and he had been itching to cast Storm for weeks. His mind went through all sorts of amusing scenarios that ranged from knocking out Freckles with the back of his gauntlet to lightly shocking the men into unconsciousness.

And then somewhere, a tent went up in flames.

That, at least, caught the attention of the Suits watching the sparring match, and they ran toward the tent as soon as they realized it was on fire.

Bard watched as all his plans fell through.

Back-hand slap it is, then, he thought, sighing, as he raised a hand and flung it across Freckles' face.

Freckles staggered to the floor, and his hands shot up to his mouth. As he screamed, Bard could see streams of red trailing down his fingers. "'uck!" he managed to half-curse through missing teeth and a splintered jaw.

Martyn drew his sword and advanced, and Bard wondered if he had been trained by Lukan. He hoped so; his own training at the Citadel was now backed by his mercenary years. He had once fought with the propriety and honor of the *Temereyna* but could resort to the tactics of a common street brawler should the need arise.

Bard took care to kick Freckles in the face before drawing his own sword.

Meanwhile, more tents were catching ablaze, and he hoped Dancer had donned Fire-forged armor before foraying into the heart of the camp. As he turned his attention to the flames, Martyn ungraciously took the first swing.

Martyn was surprisingly agile for a man of his age, but Bard saw everything well before it came. As the old man lunged, Bard charged ahead, and their swords met in an ear-splitting screech. Bard forced his way forward until he swore he heard the sound of their hilts scraping.

He cringed as Lukan's voice rang in his ears. *"High guard, boy!"* *"Not the edge, you fool!"* *"Are you trying to dull your blade?"* Bard realized that these men hadn't been the spectacular swordsmen he had previously thought, which only meant one thing.

Morian had sent them to their deaths.

Come on, old man, thought Bard, not knowing if he was referring to Martyn or himself.

It was to Bard's advantage that many of his brawls had been ale-inspired, but Martyn used his dulled reflexes to gain the upper hand. The man was on him, hacking away like a woodsman with a battle-axe, and Bard was disgusted with his own sluggishness.

It was difficult trying to figure out how not to kill a man when Martyn's sword constantly threatened to slice Bard's face in half. It was all Bard could do to beat back the man's parries and buy himself more time, only marginally distracted by the distant shouting.

How the hell did Dancer do it?

Bard almost laughed at the stupidity of his question. *Without swords.*

Martyn swung again, and Bard had just the presence of mind to duck. He dropped his sword and heaved himself forward, crashing into the old man full-force. Bard's sword-hand fist rammed into Martyn's ribs and twisted the man sideways, and both found themselves sprawled on the ground.

Bard rolled clumsily to the side, colliding with the side of the cooking spit. His helm slipped down and blocked his vision, and his hand fished behind him as the old man rose, sword in hand. Bard's fingers closed around the rim of the cooking pot, and before the Martyn could react, he flung its contents at his head.

Perhaps it would have been more effective had it been cooking, thought Bard ruefully, realizing he had just thrown cold soup in an old man's face.

Still, two seconds was all one needed to lose.

Bard scrambled to his feet, using the Suit's surprise to his own advantage. Bard balled his hands into fists and pressed them together as his body twisted to the side. Finally, he took a deep breath and flung upwards, feeling his elbow crunch against Martyn's jaw.

Martyn staggered to his knees, shouting in agony as his mouth sprayed blood.

It was a sight Bard would have liked to see, but his stupid helm kept sliding down. Frustrated, he pulled it off, and with one decisive swing, bludgeoned Martyn's head with it. Bard took particular pleasure in the gong that boomed when metal hit jaw, grateful that it was no longer ringing in *his* ears.

Martyn keeled over instantly, and in a panic, Bard laid a hand on the man's throat. He sighed in relief when he felt a slow pulse.

Bard stood tall, congratulating himself on incapacitating two Swordsuits, when he turned and saw half the camp in flames.

Cursing, he pulled his helm back on as he picked up his sword and staggered towards the fire. Chaos had spread out over the field, and Bard could barely tell what was happening. Not that he had an idea before, but now things were visually confusing.

"Dancer!" he shouted, realizing he sounded stupid as he navigated his way through the confusion. "Brunhilda!"

He reached an arm out, halting a Suit in his tracks. "What happened?" he asked.

The young pup was covered in a layer of ash, and burnt remnants of his garb clung vainly to his side. "I'm armoring up!" he said, caught up in the excitement. "There's an insane whore running around looting everyone!"

"Did they catch her?" asked Bard.

"Not yet!" answered the boy breathlessly. "We can't even find her!"

"Okay. Thanks," said Bard courteously before his fist met the boy's face, feeling his nose crunch against metal. He took the dagger strapped to the boy's waist and felt for a pulse.

"Franco!" he heard a voice bellow behind him.

"Stalwart!" answered Bard jovially, spinning around. "Where's Flowing-Hair?"

"Burning, for all I care. Fucking bitch," snarled Stalwart, clearly unaware of Bard's naming scheme. "And if not, just *wait* until I get my hands on her." Blood was dripping down the side of his face, and Bard could see that Dancer had already slipped through his fingers once.

Stalwart drew his sword, and Bard groaned.

Couldn't they resume the fight *after* he knew where Dancer was?

Before he knew it, Bard and Stalwart were smashing their way through the burning tents in a spectacularly inefficient brawl, one not quite managing to kill, and the other trying desperately not to. Stalwart was in his way, plain and simple, and needed to be put in his place: in the ground.

Or at least on it, if Bard was to win the game.

Bard stumbled against a table, half-resolved to get rid of his armor once he was through with Stalwart. Then again, it wasn't all steel; it may have been heavy, but it was the ale that turned his body into bricks.

There were unconscious bodies strewn about on the floor, their emptied satchels clearly of Dancer's doing. Bard backed into one of them as Stalwart advanced, and his boot slipped on a shoulder just as Stalwart's sword lurched forward to meet his throat. Bard fell in a momentary tangle with the unconscious soldier, and he kicked out Stalwart's legs from under him.

Stalwart fell forward, presumably a combination of thrusting his blade out and the sound of his shin splintering.

Bard grabbed onto Stalwart's wrist and slammed the man's hand back until he heard the bones of his forearm crack. Stalwart gave an inhuman squeal, almost like a baby crying. Bard would have never expected it to come from such a solidly built individual.

Bard grunted as he rose to his feet. He pushed his helm back up and collected his own sword from the ground. For good measure, he back-handed his opponent across the face.

Stalwart was down.

Bard spat on the ground next to him and knelt to feel his pulse. *Good.* He unstrapped his cuirass as soon as he left the tent and pulled his helm off, letting both fall to the ground. *Breathe!* he thought to his skin before setting his sights back to the burning horizon.

The fire didn't scare him any more than the Hounds did, but he would fight every last one of them if they had somehow managed to get their hands on Dancer. He trudged out into the open, cursing his limp. He had taken on an entire band of Suits, but it was slipping on a shoulder that had twisted his ankle.

"Franco!"

Her voice sang melodies in his ear.

He spun around and saw a confusing array of metal strapped onto a human body. The pieces of armor Dancer had looted from the tents seemed to swallow her whole, yet they didn't deter her at all from the sack of stolen goods she carried her back—or the bow she had slung over her shoulder. "What took you so long?" she snapped, making her way towards him.

"I didn't expect you to take out Baby-Faced!" he protested. His relief took a wild swerve into indignity.

"*Baby-Faced?*" Dancer glared. "What, are you chums with the Hounds, now?"

"Are you … are you *angry?*" asked Bard incredulously as they walked past flames that seared through the tents like paper. It may have been a spectacular sight, but Bard was too busy being insulted. "I was trying to find you!"

"I don't need to be found!" she shouted back.

They made their way out into the open, bickering into the swarm of remaining Suits. "I didn't know where you were!" he screamed above the clamor of soldiers who had just located the cause of their camp's demise.

The Suits came at them clumsily, weighed down by ale and wine and adrenaline. They knocked over cards and coins as they fumbled to get their weapons out. It was almost as though they were competing to see who could stab Bard first.

It was to a particularly rotund solder's ill fortune that he decided to charge Bard at such an inopportune moment. Irritated, Bard beat back his advances with ease and punched him in the face. "Can't you wait a second?" he hissed. His fight with Dancer was far more pressing.

But instead of waiting, the man stumbled back and tripped on a fallen branch. His head hit a rock with an ominous crack, and Dancer stopped arguing to stare at it open-mouthed.

"I … I didn't …" began Bard, but Dancer had already rushed forward to feel his pulse. Her anger gave way to playfulness in a way that no one but he could understand.

"You killed him," she said triumphantly. She smiled, choosing to ignore the Suits that were gathering around them.

"What? That … that doesn't count!" sputtered Bard. He had put in so much effort into sparing his foes, even tolerating their crudeness and ridiculous sense of battle talk. Surely he was not to be outdone by a branch.

But one look at the dead man and he knew he had lost.

And thus, the kill ban was lifted.

Bard blinked. "Where were we?" he asked, trying to remember where they had left off.

"I was doing just fine!" Dancer's rage returned as she dropped her sack. She unsheathed a dagger and flung it at his face.

Bard jerked his head to the side, and the blade cut into the charging soldier behind him.

"You could have waited for me!" said Bard, thrusting his fist towards her face. She ducked, and it crunched against the nose of the Suit behind her.

"Damn it, *Franco,*" she said, aiming an arrow at his head. "Don't you see? It's every woman for herself." She released just as Bard sidestepped, and it clipped a Suit thirty meters away. It knocked the man back with force.

Bard didn't even have time to be impressed.

"Fuck!" He didn't know who to be angry at, so he cursed the world around him. "Come here!" He pulled her close as he cast a shield of Storm around them, warding off the flames that rushed at them from all sides. He knew this was coming. There was no way it could have ended otherwise.

Dancer stared at the dancing snakes of blue that surrounded them, hissing when they met the flames. Fire and Storm never mixed, not once in the histories. They had always spoken of Ice and Fire being mortal enemies, but never the chaos caused by Storm. It was rarely mentioned in the mainland Scrolls. As far as the other Realms were concerned, Thoryngald didn't even exist.

The deep hum was a comfort to Bard's ears. Until this point, it was starting to feel like a bitter, pointless sort of life—but once his elements aligned, seeping into every hole of his meaningless existence, it felt like home.

So much for discreet. Storm had all but disappeared from the mainland since Thoryngald withdrew from the Realms. Casting a surge or two may have gone unnoticed, but there was no way he could talk his way out of this one. He stared at the Storm around them and saw the Stalemate shatter before his very eyes.

Bard cast a cursory glance across the field for Vet and his sparring companion, but they were nowhere to be found. Instead, he found patches of scorched earth spattered with bodies that were either dead or unconscious. He had lost track.

To his disappointment, it was Flowing-Hair and one of his companions who were hurling most of the Fire at them. Dancer knelt and rummaged through her sack of stolen goods. She took out a helm and put it on.

"I'll be fine," she shouted over the roar of Fire and Storm. "I can heal myself."

"I'm not going to let you run into the flames," said Bard.

"I'm mostly covered. Don't worry about me." She smiled underneath her helm. "If you don't start frying them, we'll both be dead."

Dancer was right.

The Hounds were advancing, weapons drawn, and if Bard kept up his shield, they would be able to overpower him soon. He saw no other choice. "On my count, then," he shouted over the roar. "Three … two … *one!*"

He lowered the shield as Dancer made a run for it, disappearing in the flames with her sack of assorted weaponry.

Here goes nothing. He took a deep breath and gathered his senses.

A moment of silence.

Then the skies erupted in a flash of lightning, cracking at the seams. Everything around it turned dark as the elements sucked in all light. Whatever that got caught between Fire and Storm splintered, whether tree or bird or Bard's mind, and Bard found himself hideously out of practice. His hands were starting to ache, but all he had to do was think of Morian to bridge his resolve. *One more.* He took a deep breath.

Soon, all he felt around him was heat. Even the ground shook in sympathy as he fought back four or five Hounds, none of whom were Vet. He wondered how many of them he would attract from the neighboring villages if he kept this up. If Bard lost, the Fire would melt the flesh from his bones. The gods only knew what they would do to Dancer.

He took another deep breath.

And screamed.

A surge of Storm erupted in the sky. Its force knocked his assailants back. The Fire stopped, if only for a stunned moment, as the Suits tried to regain sure footing. Bard stretched an arm out towards them, knocking them out one by one with a single surge. He just wanted the sounds to stop, for the sky to turn back to its natural color—not this red fog that swept over the camp, not the dirt and ash it pushed into his eyes.

Bard had no desire to move. He had to find Dancer, but it was impossible. The tents were still on fire, and the trees leading back into the Greenwood had been reduced to angry, red swirls. Being surrounded by fire was his worst nightmare.

A wave of relief swept over him when he heard her voice, glib as a song. "Franco!" she yelled, mostly unharmed. Whatever scrapes or burns she had sustained mended before his very eyes, leaving behind a rash that would wash away with time.

"What are you doing over there?" he asked, deciding it was safe to lower his guard. As soon as he did, he felt strength return to his forearms.

"I have a score to settle." She pointed to a crouching lump of a man Bard had once called Freckles. Dirt had concealed the splotches on his face, but his orange hair gave him away.

Dancer had clearly beaten him down while Bard warded off Flowing-Hair and his companions. Multiple times, it seemed.

Freckles grimaced, this time toothlessly. Blood was still trickling down his chin, but he took Dancer's dagger from the ground and waved it wildly at her.

"Stay down and I'll let you live," she said.

Bard wondered why no one ever took her up on that offer.

"Who … who are you?" Freckles demanded with all the authority of a Hound with its tail tucked between its legs, but all he managed to do was stammer as he gazed upon the blood-smeared, tattered thing of beauty he had once called tavern wench.

"I AM BRUNHILDA," bellowed Dancer, a battle cry that would surely ring throughout the ages. Bard tried not to burst into laughter.

Gathering the rest of his strength, Freckles lunged, not wanting to be bested by a foreign whore. He thrust the blade towards her.

Dancer sighed. Instinctively, she grabbed onto his forearm and twisted until the blade was pointed away from her. The grotesque angle of his arm forced its owner to twist along with it, and soon, their arms were intertwined—until her other arm swung upwards, grabbing past a tangle of limbs before latching onto his jawbone.

She snapped his neck, and for a moment, it looked like she was cradling his in her arms. "League of gentlemen my ass," she muttered as she released.

The blade dropped to the ground long before Freckles' body did, and she picked it up and sheathed it. "If my count is correct, we only killed two people. And you killed one first."

Bard doubted they only killed two but didn't feel like arguing. They watched the burning camp wordlessly, the destruction they had made. It was almost romantic. A story to tell the grandkids.

"They're planning on attacking the Iceborne, then?" she asked after a moment of silence.

He nodded absently and kept his eyes fixed on the fire, feeling like they were missing something. He hadn't seen the golden-haired Northerner in battle, nor had he seen …

Oh. Fuck, he thought when he saw it: that monstrous silhouette that grew in the firelight, dominating the landscape of scorched earth and shambles. It had donned armor in the chaos. Not that it needed that extra layer of intimidation.

Vet emerged from the flames wielding a greatsword he didn't bother to lift. Instead, he let it drag behind him as he trudged in their direction. It etched deep scars into the ground. The flames barely touched him as he walked past the carnage—instead, they seemed to bow to his presence. Some even parted to make way.

"THUNDERBORNE," Vet's voice boomed through the face-guard. It was like nothing Bard had heard before, and he almost vomited when he took a closer look at the mask. Metal claws had wrapped themselves around Vet's jaw, attaching themselves to his face. As in, someone had bolted the face-guard to his skin.

It's not there to protect his face, thought Bard with dread. *It's there to hold it in place.*

Bard definitely didn't remember him. Vet's voice didn't even sound human; it was a low roar that echoed in his ears, and talking seemed to cause him pain.

"Dancer," said Bard, gripping the hilt of his sword. "Get out of here."

But when he turned, Dancer had already gone.

Bard cursed himself for being surprised.

Every woman for herself, he thought. Her words stung his pride.

But Bard had no time to waste. If Vet had indeed been a Spade, even Bard would be no match for him. In a clash of Fire, Storm, and steel, the beast would eat him alive.

"THUNDERBORNE," repeated Vet.

"That's me," said Bard. There was no witty retort for circumstances like this; Dancer had left him with this tower of a man, and it was Bard's fate to brave him alone.

"VALERYA'S. THUNDERBORNE." The man's eyes bore into his, and Bard forced himself to stare back.

"Do we know each other?" he asked, making peace with the Fates as every memory that ever mattered shot through his mind. Flashbacks of his parents. Valerya. The Falcons. Artis ...

Dancer.

"I. NEVER. FORGET." Vet pointed to Bard's face.

At least they won't be able to say I went down a coward. Bard readied his element hand just as a depressing realization hit him. *Who would even know?*

Vet let his hand drop to the side and made no motion to lift his greatsword. "I. SERVE. THE REALM," he said. "NOT. THE. KING."

"You're in the King's Command," said Bard, marveling at his own willingness to speak to this creature. But Bard figured that he was confused by so many things that he should at least clarify a few of them before he died.

"VALERYA'S. THUNDERBORNE," repeated Vet. "DIE. ANOTHER. DAY."

"Who are you?" demanded Bard, realizing that the beast's fight was not with him. A stupid question since he already knew the man's name, but Vet clearly recognized him.

Before he could get an answer, he heard the sudden clashing of hooves behind him as Dancer reappeared with a destrier.

"Bard," she called, and Bard could see an arrow jutting from her shoulder. She had already snapped it at the shaft, but blood was trickling down the side of her cuirass. "We have to go." She reached an arm towards him.

He had never been so overjoyed to see anyone in his life.

Bard took one last glance at Vet as an arrow sliced through the air, barely missing his face. He turned and saw Pretty-Boy take another arrow from his quiver.

"Come on," said Dancer, this time more urgently, and he took her arm, lifting himself onto the back of the horse.

He almost laughed when he saw her sack of stolen goods tied to its side.

Finally, the destrier had come in handy.

Dancer swerved as the arrow whizzed past them. She urged the horse forward at full gallop towards the mouth of the forest. Vet halted his companion and watched them flee.

Bard saw the splintered shaft lodged into Dancer's shoulder. He leaned forward and saw that it had struck her at an angle, perhaps even deep enough to puncture a lung.

"I'm fine," she said before he could ask, but her face had turned a shade paler.

"Where are you going?" asked Bard. "The border's the other way. We need to get help."

"I will," she said, determined. "But I need to send a falcon first."

"What?" asked Bard incredulously. "You'll bleed to death!"

"I'll be *fine*. And given your line of work, I thought you might want to send one, too."

"What do you mean *my* line of work?"

"Oh, come on," she said. "Don't you think I know a Falcon when I see one?" She gave him a weak smile. "You still owe me a secret. I want you to tell me all about the … Citadel, and Valerya." She passed him the reins. "But you're right … we may have to go to the border first."

Bard took the reins, confused. "Why did you …?"

His arm swung out instinctively as her body swayed to the side, unconscious.

21

THE FORESTS
FIRE REALM

At night, Gryff couldn't tell the difference between the black-woods and the surrounding sprawl of land. The trees were so dark that they looked like stone, petrified shapes that twisted into the stuff of nightmares. His eyes were used to the night, but it was hard to concentrate when exhaustion bore holes into his resolve. Thoughts of the Red Citadel filled them, especially when he remembered that beautiful, broken voice.

"You'll come back for me, won't you?" No doubt Lyra thought he couldn't see the bruises in the moon-lit corridor, but she didn't know he had lived his whole life in darkness.

For all his awkward attempts at conversation, she still thought he was a Spade. Even when she saw him heading out with all his belongings strapped to his back, armor-clad in the dead of night, she was convinced of it. *A fantasy of hers, just like it is mine.* He thought of all the kind things he could have said to her. He could have said she was beautiful, that her smile lit up the darkest corners of the castle. But those words were reserved for someone else.

Gryff sighed. Maybe Lyra was the reason he had gotten off so easy. There had been enough cruelty to go around, and now he was leaving her to take the full brunt of Morian's amusement. No, that wasn't entirely true—they were also leaving *Valerya* behind to brave Morian's birthday alone. But the Summoner General could take care of herself.

Lyra, on the other hand ...

He shivered. Everywhere around them, it was silent and still. He didn't know how long they had been riding, nor had Valk bothered to tell him where they were headed. They had journeyed and slept and ate with such inconsistency that he had lost all sense of time.

Still, at least he didn't have to worry about starving. His companion was a good hunter, and they feasted on meat every night. Gryff couldn't complain. It packed his body with muscle, wrenched the softness from his face. They often passed by scouts and messengers traveling between towns, but no one showed interest in causing trouble with a Spade—even Gryff, who trailed behind Valk on a pony.

Valk had warned him of the sore muscles that came with riding, so Gryff wasn't surprised when everything started burning from the inside. But no one had warned him about the dark thoughts that came once the woods grew still, the hoof-beats steady. His companion took care to break the silence whenever it threatened to consume him.

"I find it hilarious that we left our General alone at the Citadel, and so close to our King's birthday," Valk had mused after their first, fifth, or fiftieth day on the road.

Gryff grinned despite the pain. He could imagine few things that would displease the General more than realizing Morian had survived another year. But for the others, it wasn't so bad. All throughout the Firelands, the Sun-sworn priests offered free food at the temples, and for one day, gambling was openly encouraged. It was the one time of year that he and Dove could eat as much as they wanted, and at night, Fire-sculptors competed to see who could create the most beautiful shapes. To Gryff's knowledge, the General had never taken part in the fighting, but Valk said she had been strongly considering it this year—if anything, to avoid spending the day at Morian's side.

Gryff reckoned she would even go in without armor to avoid *any* time at his side. Her pain made his tickle in comparison.

"Have you taken part in the tourneys?" he asked.

"Yes," said Valk. "I came in second last year. Jousting."

Gryff blinked. *"Second?"* The shock resonated in his helm. Jousting was a game, but everyone played to win favor from their sovereign. That meant blood. "Wait, what? VALK." He pulled his pony up beside him.

"Yes," said the Spade. "I thought I had a shot, but I almost broke my neck going against this beast of a man called Vet."

Not much of a swordsman my ass. "I didn't think you were the type to compete in these events," said Gryff.

"I'm not, really. But I welcome any chance to take down Greaven. I believe you've made his acquaintance recently."

Gryff wondered what had transpired between them to warrant such a rare grimace on the Spade's face, but he understood. There was something off about Greaven that he couldn't quite place. He was a vile creature who always trailed behind the king, but it wasn't a servitude born out of respect. Part of it must have been fear, but the king's scraps were still better than a peasant's riches, and Morian let him have all the leftovers. Life wasn't fair.

They rode on in silence as Gryff tried to imagine all the things he would do with Valk's powers, his name. *I would take all of them down,* he thought. *Everything the Hounds took from me, I would take from them.*

He glanced at his companion with unease. Valk was part of the company that razed through his village, tore his life apart. When all was said and done, they were enemies.

"What made you decide to join the Swordsworn? You mentioned duty before," said Gryff, distracting himself. It made no sense. Valk was patient and kind, the opposite of what he imagined a Hound to be.

"The same thing that *inspired* you to be a scribe. I suppose you could say it ran in the family," said Valk. "And I was a young man too, once. Being a Swordsworn isn't particularly held in high regard, but I was told that First Cloaks had all the girls running after them. Lies."

Gryff laughed. "What, no luck?" he asked. "I find that hard to believe."

Indeed, Valk seemed to be well liked at the Citadel, and on the rare occasion they stopped by a guest-keep, he garnered more than several shy glances from the women in the crowd. Maybe they liked that rugged, serious sort of look.

Valk smiled and kept his gaze fixed on the road ahead. "Do you know the term *mereyn?* Of course you do. You read a lot," he said. "It's the sacred circle in Lancistierre. You see, unlike the Swordsworn, Waterborne fighters are paired for life. One man, the *temereyn,* and one woman, the *mereyna.* You can see where the word *Temereyna* comes from."

"Both halves of a greater whole," said Gryff, reciting its translation.

"Indeed. Very good," said Valk. "But the concept of the *mereyn* can be found in our Scrolls, as well. They believed that a person was born into this world with the sole purpose of finding his or her other half. Most of us never find ours, and that is why we are doomed."

"You believe that?"

"For me, there was only the one," said Valk. "No one else came close." He gave a quick laugh to ease the tension. "Besides, when it comes to winning the affections of other ladies, I'm afraid even our General has more luck than I do," he said.

Gryff blinked, then decided he wasn't surprised.

His mind flashed to the castle, to the bricks of sunken sand and stone that had become his home. The General must have been bored to tears without her most trusted confidante and taking it out on the trainees, but she could deal with it fine. It was Lyra he was concerned about.

Lyra and Dove and all the people he couldn't protect.

Thinking of the castle smith's daughter helped, as much as it hurt to admit, because when he thought of Dove, the pain grew unbearable.

"You're still thinking of her." Valk jolted him out of his daze, and for a split-moment, Gryff didn't know who he was referring to.

Gryff supposed it didn't matter and nodded.

The Spade grimaced, aware of Morian's welcoming ritual. "It will pass. Lyra is from a decent family, after all. Our King lavishes them with attention, then leaves them be. And I'm sure our General wouldn't let the poor girl meet an ill-fitting demise, especially after the last one."

"The last one?" asked Gryff, struggling to keep up.

Valk nodded. "The last one was a Fireborne girl he made his squire, but she came from … let's say more *humble* origins. Nothing to her name. He grew bored with her after a while and had her killed."

That did nothing to soften Gryff's guilt. Anger flushed underneath his helm. "Killed? What did she do?"

"Exist," said Valk. "He lavished her with attention too, but she had the ill fortune of being born a commoner."

"Couldn't he have just let her go?" It seemed so unnecessary, this loss of life. *I am a commoner, too,* Gryff realized. The distance between him and Valk widened.

"I suppose. But I'm afraid if he couldn't have her, no one else could." Valk shrugged. "He placed our General in charge of her execution. Couldn't even do it himself."

The rest of the journey was marked with silence. At times, boredom prompted Gryff to ask questions that lingered in the back of his mind.

"Valk," he said as they were plodding along yet another road that refused to end. "Who will take over after Morian?"

Valk laughed as he glimpsed a brighter future. "Our King has no heir, no siblings. His uncle Eithander left behind no sons or daughters. If he falls, families will want to put one of their own on the *throne.*" He said throne, but Gryff knew he envisioned an empire. "His only hope is marrying and siring a child. Or a bastard. It's been done before."

"Why don't you just take the throne for yourself, then?" asked Gryff, half-joking. "I'm sure you'll do better."

"I have no heir."

"Sire a bastard."

Valk laughed at the thought of doing something unlawful. "Never felt the urge to rule."

"What about our General?"

Gryff couldn't help but feel envious when he recalled the slaughter, the utter desolation she was capable of. All the things that came into being—the sun and stars and the life they breathed—reduced to dust and dreams. Whatever connection she had to her beast had the power to divide voids, crack worlds. He wondered what he would do with the same power.

Justice, most likely.

No, he corrected himself. *Vengeance.*

They crossed a water-carved bridge when the sky was nothing more than a cold, gray canvas. Salandra's light was losing its intensity, which meant that the Rhysar would show itself soon. Its ascension, at least, would signal the passing of time.

"Valk," he said. "What's the Otherworld?"

To his surprise, Valk halted, glared. "I told you not to talk to the skin-crawlers."

"What? No. I read about it in the library," Gryff said hastily. He shrugged. It wasn't a lie.

Valk's eyes narrowed, saw truth in Gryff's eyes. Finally, he said, "Sorcery. That's all you need to know." He cleared his throat and threw him a warning glance. "I think it's time to treat ourselves to a warm meal and nice beds."

Gryff was too overjoyed to ask further. His muscles were in agony. His stomach burned. He was used to not eating in Myrne, but he was beginning to grow into his limbs, and grow, period. It was as though the Ice had set off a chain of reactions in his body that made it impossible to control. With each step, his pony was looking more and more appetizing.

"Where are we?" he asked.

"In the heart of the Greenwood." The villagers looked kind enough, but when they spoke, Gryff wondered if they were still in the same realm.

Are they even speaking Sinthean? he wondered, but realized that their accent was familiar to his ears. It was harder, sharper, but at its core, he knew it. He turned again to ask Valk where they were, but the Spade was already tying his steed to a tree outside a stone house. Children had carved letters into its trunk, and next to the tree, the gardens were neatly trimmed.

Gryff dismounted. If anything, he had gotten good at that, at least. "I don't see a guest-keep," he said, rubbing his arms. He didn't quite understand the logic of his pains. Riding had carved notches into his lower body, but it was his backside that was killing him now.

But the slumbering greenlands made him forget the pain. He had missed being in a village. It made him feel safer than a castle surrounded by guards. People actually smiled and talked to each other—unlike at the capital, where everyone assumed the worst in each other.

"It doesn't matter," said Valk. "No one turns away a couple of travel-weary Spades."

Valk halted a cloaked villager who was carrying a large sack over his shoulder. The old man looked hassled from carrying such a heavy load, but he wielded a walking stick that looked hefty enough to bludgeon a troll.

"How fare the times?" asked the Spade.

The villager sighed underneath his hood. "Oh, you know," he said, sounding fatigued. He shrugged his thin shoulders. "The harvest is good, the forest is quiet, and my day was marred by a ruffian trying to purloin a ham from the roof beam."

"A travesty," said Valk.

The man set down his sack, and the two stared at each other before bursting into laughter.

"Valk!" said the old man, and Gryff was surprised to see his companion's face break out into a grin. And a *laugh*. "You're about five years late."

Gryff was at a loss for words. "Are you … are you Valk's father?" he asked.

"Gods, no," said the old man, still laughing. "I would have had twenty heart attacks by now if I was." He pulled away from the Spade and contemplated Gryff with conflicted amusement. Gryff wondered how often mongrels found themselves in this part of the Realm.

His heart stopped in his throat. "Are you *Valerya's* father?" he asked as Valk snorted.

"He loves drama, doesn't he?" asked the villager. "I suppose he is at that age where everything's dramatic." He cleared his throat and straightened. He rolled up his sleeves to expose thin arms. "No, dear boy. I am *not* Valerya's father. Do I look like a smith to you?"

Gryff felt his ears redden as Valk and the old man chuckled to themselves.

The man turned back to Gryff, still smiling. He was short and lean, but his eyes betrayed strength, warning. "But I did teach her a thing or two during my time at the Citadel. And it has come to my attention that you need the same training."

Gryff's eyes widened. The answer surprised him even more. "Who are you?" he asked

"My name is Artis," said the man as he pulled down his hood. "Welcome to Genovel."

***

Gryff soon concluded that Artis' kind-hearted face was a farce, his old age a trap. The man *blinked* Fire, and he didn't even need to use his hands. He wasn't much bigger than Gryff, but the shadows cast by his flames made him taller than the trees.

Are they sure he's not Valerya's father? thought Gryff bitterly.

They had gone deep into the Greenwood to practice beyond the eyes and ears of the village, and it took all of five seconds before Gryff found himself engulfed in flames. His will swerved into an agony beyond words.

Valk stood by idly, arms folded as he watched. A smile stretched across his face. "I believe I have earned the right to laugh," he said.

"*Cast!*" Artis commanded.

Gryff's vision returned. He braced himself for the next wave, but it never came. Instead, Artis towered over him, a complete dragon disguised in the frail body of an old man. His fire-bred eyes burned cold. "What drives you?"

Gryff tried to sit up but couldn't speak. It was such an undignified way to go, and he wondered what in the hells the General had in mind when she sent him here.

***

Meanwhile, from atop the Citadel watchtower, Valerya laughed.

***

Gryff found himself gasping for air. His armor shielded him from the attack, but the smoke stung his lungs. "Survival!" he found himself screaming. It was the first thought that came to mind, and it sounded like a good answer.

A blast of Fire knocked him flat on his back. For such a small man, Artis' presence was everywhere. "Survival?" Are you *struggling* to survive?"

"I was forced to come here," Gryff found himself saying. He had said it so many times, they could carve it on his grave-marker. He threw a desperate glance at the Spade, but Valk, true to his character, pretended awkward situations didn't exist. "And then I was sent here."

Artis' expression didn't soften. "Your horse is tied to that tree," he said coldly. "You may choose to go and never return. Neither Valk nor I will stand in your way."

Gryff struggled to his feet. "I ... I can't."

"Then you were not *forced* to be here," said Artis. He was not angry, which made Gryff even more uncomfortable. He was not used to all this freedom. Before, daylight determined where he went, and at the Citadel, it was the General who told him what to do. But now?

Another blink, another blaze.

"This isn't about survival," said the old man. "Now, consider your words more carefully. What *drives* you?"

"I ... I want to find the people I love." Gryff felt the last of his strength leave his limbs. His sense of balance disappeared into an abyss.

"Then go," said Artis. "That is no answer. It makes no sense why you're still here. *WHAT DRIVES YOU?*" He hurled another blast in his direction, angrier and more powerful than the last.

Gryff screamed. It didn't seem like Artis would relent until he got a satisfactory answer, and he was out of excuses. Panic drove truth to the forefront.

"*I DON'T WANT TO GO BACK!*" yelled Gryff, crying, begging, *hurting* all in one as the Ice in his blood surged to the surface. It shot up from the ground around him, sparkling white crystals that rose to his height and protected him from the flames. For a moment, at least. The Fire melted it away almost instantly, but Artis released his hold.

"You don't want to go back," Artis repeated as Valk unfolded his arms in interest.

Gryff blinked, surprised. "I … I'm the son of a scribe," he began, marveling at how easily the words came to him. "Daylight burns me. I've lived my entire life in the darkness. I … I stood by and saw everything I loved burn and couldn't do anything about it. And when they took her away, I couldn't … I couldn't …"

"The Swordsworn gave you a different life. A chance to fight," said Artis, nodding. "A chance that was nothing more than a fantasy in your mind. Until recently."

Another blast. Without thinking, Gryff flung his element hand in its direction.

It was weak, but he saw the half-blade form in the air. It was rough like an icicle, but its tip was as sharp as a sword. Before he could stop it, it flung itself at Artis, who melted it away with a blink of an eye. "I think we're done for the day," he said, satisfied.

That night, they ate around a cooking spit they had built, though Gryff didn't understand why. Two of them had the ability to cast Fire. Valk could have *held* the rabbit over the flames, but there was something calming about eating over an open fire. As a child, Gryff was never allowed. The fire-light would have pelted welts across his skin.

There were so many things I couldn't do. Dove had always done them for him. She had looked out for him for so long that he didn't know what he would do without her. Maybe now, it was his turn to take care of her. If he kept up his training, they would never have to live in the backwoods again. He imagined all the new things he could show her and wondered how she would react to living in a big castle, in a *library.* Imagining her happiness gave him strength.

The smoke and ash didn't bother him, and he ate ravenously as soon as the meat charred.

"Well done," said Artis, back to good manners and propriety.

"I didn't die," said Gryff, shrugging as he bit into the rabbit leg, holding his helm half-open to shield his face from the fire-light.

"We all had to start somewhere. Even Valerya."

"Did she have trouble casting Fire?" Gryff asked between bites.

"Gods, no," said Artis, laughing. "I'm afraid she needed more help *stopping* Fire. Whenever she had a nightmare, we had to evacuate the tower. Sometimes, she got so angry that everything she touched turned to ash. There's a reason why I stopped tending the Citadel gardens, you know. Whenever she got startled, there went my rosebushes."

Valk laughed. "It wasn't just you. I remember when they brought in a proper lady to teach children their manners. For girls, it was mostly sewing and playing harps. Poetry, that sort of thing. From what I heard, Valerya brought her to *tears* after her second day."

Gryff imagined the General burning the Citadel spindles in rage and wondered why they had even attempted teaching her poetry to begin with.

Artis chuckled to himself. "I rarely meet someone stronger than me, and there she was. She didn't even want to be there."

Gryff stared, stunned. He supposed it came as no surprise that

Valerya was the stronger caster, but he couldn't imagine it being much fiercer than what he had just experienced. His skin prickled uneasily.

They ate in silence. Valk and Artis reminisced about days past while Gryff listened to their misadventures. He imagined having some of his own soon, full of colors and sound. He smiled softly, lulled to a half-sleep by the crackling flames.

***

When they got back to Genovel, Valk excused himself. It was the dead of night, but Gryff was too tired—and sore—to ask where he was going, lest the Spade want company. He rubbed his arms. His wounds would sing tomorrow.

"He was a curious boy," said Artis, breaking his concentration. They had reached his house. "Preferred staring at the stars all day. But he grew into a good man." He made sure Valk wasn't in sight. "And even then, Valerya was constantly ordering him around."

They shared a moment of laughter, lost in a different time.

"So you know him well," said Gryff.

"I did, to my great joy and dismay," said Artis. "He was in love with my daughter once, but duty drives us to do what we must. She was given to another."

Gryff was taken aback. "*Your* daughter?" He wasn't expecting that. He thought back to Valk, to all the times his companion had withdrawn into himself on the road, to the dreadful silences Gryff couldn't break. "But Valk said she was wed to a traitor."

Artis gave a sad laugh. "Oh, I doubt even Valk believes that." He picked up Gryff's helm from the table. "He and Lucien may not have always seen eye to eye, but they were still brothers, bound by blood."

Gryff was at a loss for words. *If Lucien was a traitor, that means Morian had her killed, too.* He had only met Morian once, terrifying and whimsical as he was—but dull minds weren't capable of such calculated torture.

"I suppose you could say I resigned after that," said Artis.

Gryff couldn't believe his ears. "How could you …?" It was incomprehensible to him. He had speared three people at the thought of Dove lying dead somewhere, discarded like trash. "Why didn't you fight …?"

"Me against the entire King's Command?" Artis chuckled to himself. "If I died, Morian would still be alive, one way or another," he said, "but the Falcons will have lost something far more valuable." Artis saw Gryff's reaction. "Don't think I haven't thought about it every day since it happened. But one shouldn't sacrifice the fate of thousands for a ruined man's revenge."

Gryff stared. He wanted to tell him that his father had been a Falcon, but before the words could escape his lips, Artis cleared his throat.

"Well, that's enough idle talk." Artis rose and handed him his helm. "This is fine work. I see infusions have come a long way since my days at the Citadel."

Gryff wished him a good night. He made his way to the guestroom and collapsed onto the bed farthest from the window, a habit that wouldn't die. It was the only room that didn't look regularly cleaned. The doors of the wardrobe across from him were blackened and splintered, and there were too many things for such a small room. Artis never threw anything away.

Gryff turned to his side and let his arm dangle from the edge of the bed. It knocked over something that had been leaning against the wall.

Cursing, he groped for it in the darkness. His fingers gripped around a blunt wooden shaft, and when he pulled it close, he saw that it was heavier than he thought.

With both hands, he brought it close to his chest.

Odd, he thought. *Why would Artis have a crossbow here?*

22

SINTHEA
THE FIRE REALM

The streets of the capital spilled with banners of red and dark red, and for once, they didn't mark the rallies of Morian's blood campaign. The communes and cobblestone roads were impeccably scrubbed. The guest-keeps and brothels were overflowing with patrons, and the citizens of Sinthea donned their best smiles to accommodate the hordes of visitors that graced their city. Anyone did anything for a few extra crowns, even if it meant associating with the lower castes. *And not just on the streets.*

"Valerya, look happier!" Morian scolded, as he liked to do when others were watching. Valerya didn't care. It bothered him most when she didn't react, and it was no lie to say she was a black thorn in his golden wreath of nobles. "Don't you agree, Greaven?"

"Yes, your Highness," Greaven answered next to her. Disgust coiled under her skin. As Summoner General, she had the authority to send him away for the afternoon, but she might as well stage an uprising. Morian liked keeping them close on his birthday, and Greaven's absence would raise questions. Instead, she took care to make sure Greaven was always at her side. Never behind her, never outside her field of vision. *Never again.*

All the Swordsworn posted in the capital were commanded to wear full-plate armor today. It was one of the few occasions that so many great names gathered in one place, and Morian didn't want them to dress in inferior garb. Even her elite had to don crimson. Citizens were always on their best behavior when they saw red steel.

Valerya knew her men hated the king's birthday almost as much as she did, but they would swallow needles if she commanded it— because they knew she would do it for them. *A leader must lead by example. Their pain must become your pain. Their joy must become your joy.* That was what Avander had said. Now they stood guard in front of the dais like perfect, blood-colored statues, because they knew Valerya was suffering right behind them.

She scanned the crowd through the fresh gleam of swords and spears, newly forged in the king's honor. She wondered how many soldiers had spent their families' livelihoods on such lavish displays of wealth, only to forfeit their new gear in the wagering rounds.

At least the whores are ready. They lined the streets but watched the crowd with half-hearted interest. They knew gold shone brightest at night. *And they think I have a lot of it.* They eyed her with curiosity, taking in every piece of her armor. Calculating its worth.

Valerya's armor cost more than a commune, but it had been a gift from Avander when she joined the Spades. Ceremonial, mostly; most of the pieces, she never used. She had only dusted off her shield that morning. It bore no sigil of her own—only the red shades of her donned allegiance, a constant reminder of the oath she had sworn.

A pauldron with an exaggeratedly large blade-breaker was strapped to her right shoulder. It was a piece of art made to intimidate, not shield, and each plate was carefully crafted and Fire-forged.

It was a luxury many people killed for, but she could do without it.

The only thing she cared about was the sword. It had no decorated pommel, no intricate hilt, but the blade remained flawless after years of use. Avander had it etched with a dragon and his family name: Pyrrheas. It was something Morian had always envied but could do nothing about, so she had made it a point to carry it around until she no longer noticed its weight.

But his wrath is greater.

It had become Morian's goal to make each birthday more unbearable than the last, so he had a second throne placed by his side: a wild—yet symmetrical—mess of ivory that must have taken months to carve. Valerya had very nearly suggested that Greaven take it, but she bit her tongue and sat, rueful that Morian had survived yet another year. It did not make sense to anyone with eyes that a She-Jackal, the Summoner General of the Swordsworn, would sit on a *throne.*

Perhaps Morian was trying to tell her something.

Valerya sighed as she glanced at the king to her left, and sighed even more heavily when she glimpsed Greaven to her right.

It was going to be a long day.

To cope with the unpleasantries, she had made the tailor's apprentice her cupbearer. His sole task was to provide her with wine when the occasion arose, and she was going to need a lot of it today. She hated the taste more than the dulled senses that followed, but she made a consistent exception for Morian's birthday. While they were waiting for the joust to begin, Valerya motioned Marcus over.

"M'lord!" said Marcus proudly as he presented her with the flask. Wordlessly, she drank and thrust it back against his chest. She waved a hand dismissively, to which Marcus beamed and strutted off, enthralled with his heightened status. Plenty of trainees had competed for the honor, but she wanted someone simple, and *common.*

Valerya had seen the tents of competitors who had traveled far and wide to take part in the games. Of the hundreds of sigils, she recognized maybe four as she walked through the camp. It was a colossal waste of her time, but Morian wanted everyone to see her. Especially now that he had beautified his city, he wanted everyone to bask in its glory—and its legends.

As usual, Rhysia was underrepresented. The people up there were as stern and mysterious as the woods they worshipped, but it was a breath of fresh air whenever she considered Morian's trail of sycophants. She would rather pray to a tree than to her sovereign.

They would, too. Since the Cleansing, Rhysia sent one or two representatives as a formality, but they often elected not to take part in the mock battles. The lone huntsman flew over a sea of lions, shadow-bears, and night-wolves.

Valerya sighed and threw a glance at her sovereign, but Morian was busy receiving trinkets and well wishes from his admirers. It was the same every year. A few books he never read. Chests of premium grain he never ate.

She recognized a particularly rotund man and his wife when they approached. The woman, Reya, was a distant cousin of Morian's. She had been comely, but the good life rounded her features, softened her resolve. Bad intentions took care of the rest, and her looks crumbled with her character. Their servants presented a silver goblet for the third year in a row. *Great,* thought Valerya. *One for Morian, one for Greaven, and now one for me.* Reya and her high lord husband approached like dogs with their tails tucked between their legs.

Kingsbridge. Valerya's eyes narrowed. No wonder.

She never liked Kingsbridge. Its people had rallied to Morian's cause like rats after Avander's death, but after the victory, they were nowhere to be found. While other cities sent manpower, grain, and coin, they kept their soldiers to themselves, ate their own bread, and spent on their own vanities. Well-known purists who enjoyed clearing the Realm of the lower castes.

And inbred, most likely, thought Valerya, trying to make sense of the high lord's face. Eyes looked in different directions with a mouth that told nothing but lies. They knew Valerya had been a common laborer—dirt, in other words—but that didn't stop them from running to her whenever they needed protection from local bandits or builders to reinforce their battlements.

"We are fortunate to greet you on this glorious day," said the high lord, avoiding her eyes. His voice lost confidence with each passing year, and with good reason. For a city of purists, his only remaining heir, the golden boy of their house and name, had run off to join the insurgents. They hoped it was a phase, but the boy had already made a name for himself among the Spears. *Haden. Haden of Kingsbridge.* Once they found out, they disowned him.

If only they knew. Valerya glowered. *That fucking idiot.*

As much as she hated Kingsbridge, Valerya had no mercy for rebels. They fought for dreams much greater than they were, and only fools wanted something they couldn't define. People didn't need dreams. They needed leadership. Lofty ideas did not fill their bellies or keep their bodies warm. They needed clothes and food and a stable livelihood, things to get them through the winter. They needed medicans, weavers, builders. Not more idealists. All these insurgents did was cry for equality, for *freedom,* but how would the Firelands feed a nation of dreamers? *If left to their own devices, most people would sit around and pick their asses.*

"Thank you, Lord Danyel!" Morian said graciously, but Valerya saw cruelty flash across his eyes. "I am sorry to hear about your son, so *sorry* …" He threw Valerya a winning smile, but she couldn't be bothered to return it. Instead, she nodded courteously to the high lord and lady of Kingsbridge. *If only they knew.*

"Your Highness." Lord Danyel bowed his head. "Between you and me, the Realm could use another Purge soon." He turned to Valerya, and the two men shared a hearty laugh. *I'm just a guard-dog to them,* she thought, wondering how they would react if she actually did bite off those fat, bejeweled fingers.

"Too right you are!" said Morian as Valerya summoned Marcus over for another swig. "I *have* been considering that lately. It's been over half a year since the last one …"

Valerya turned her attention to the crowd. It was taking a long time to set up the games, and the people were getting restless. *Everyone wants blood.* It was a never-ending cycle. The Fireborne may have been cruel to the losing side, but no less so than what the Glasgérians and Lancistierreans had done to them. Morian was blind to the dead and dying, but so were their enemies. So many blind forces, unable to see anything but each other. If those were the choices, it was better to be at the top. At least she would never be at anyone's mercy.

Still, the company could have been better. The heralds boasted of valor and courtesy, but that was all a lie. Bad blood was brewing among the Trueborne, and with each passing year, talks of succession spread. Clans groomed their sons for rulership. More and more young women from the higher castes attended the affair, but their hunger for the king made them no different from whores. Men eyed each other in distrust, flexed their sword arms. Their aggression would manifest itself in the fighting.

Valerya wasn't paying attention when the heralds announced the names of the first challengers. All she saw was a banner of pigeons pitted against two-headed goats before realizing it was supposed to be hawks versus twin rams. Her eyes glazed over.

So useless. In what battle would a mole—three, even—challenge a sabre-cat? What in the natural world would ever prompt a woodpecker to attack a mammoth?

After an hour, Morian remembered she was there. "I would encourage you to join, Valerya, but what sigils would you bear?" Another glint of malice rippled across his eyes as Marcus approached her cautiously with the flask.

And so the circus continued until the herald announced a name that pulled Valerya's attention back to the tourney. "Greaven of Blackmont!" he cried, followed swiftly by, *"Venturon of Heavensward!"*

At first, Valerya thought it was the wine she had been downing since dawn. Seeing Vet in the capital had become as rare as sighting an elephant in the Firelands, but there was no mistaking the face-guard strapped to the back of his head, the crimson banners of a shadow-bear flung across his horse's flank. And when he turned and gazed upon Valerya with eyes nearly dead, he pointed his lance in her direction.

Morian shifted uncomfortably, as did hundreds of onlookers behind them. Vet had that charming effect on people. She waved a hand dismissively and took another swig from the flask.

Interesting turn of events. She almost snorted when she remembered that Valk had gone up against both men last year, how he had flown like a rag doll across the list. She had never seen anyone soar like that before. *Vet went easy on him.* An absolute beast who was more than capable of human wreckage. But despite his appearance, he kept to himself. Even under her command, he obeyed under the sole condition that he could do as he wished during peacetime.

Curious that he decided to show up on the king's birthday.

On the other side of the list, Greaven was preparing. He yanked the lance impatiently from one of his squires and positioned it under his right arm.

When the two titans charged, the crowd grew still. No one wanted to get caught in the middle. Both lances met their targets, and fractured wood erupted like a jag in every direction. Vet barely flinched as Greaven wobbled uneasily in his saddle; he didn't even bother replacing his lance when they charged each other a second time. Instead, he threw his weapon down and grabbed onto Greaven's as the man thrust it out in front of him.

Valerya almost smiled when she saw Greaven's body flip graciously over the barrier, wondering how many bones snapped as Vet dragged him along for a good stride or ten before letting go. Greaven lay defeated, pride more wounded than body.

With remarkable resilience against a man of Vet's size, Greaven rose and drew his sword. He may have been bested in a game, but she had seen him on the killing fields. He had been her team commander when she was just a drudge, and they had toughed it out in the Glasgérian wastelands for half a winter. It was meant to be a training excursion, but nothing about it had been designed to teach. They had set up camp where there was no food, but she later found out it had been intentional. *The things people do when they're hungry,* she thought grimly. *The things he made them do to each other.*

Greaven couldn't touch her, of course. A Summoner always outranked the highest general, even at seventeen, and Avander would have had him hanged if she came back like the others. But she was not exempted from the cruelties Greaven made her see. The stench lingered after they had returned to the capital, and she could not stand the sight of meat for months. *He and Morian deserve each other.*

Vet threw a threatening glance at Valerya and pointed his blade in her direction. For a split-moment, the two men faced off.

Greaven made the first move. He was still disoriented from his fall from grace, but he swung his blade outwards. It met Vet's with a deafening clash. Greaven twisted under its impact and retracted it at his shoulder. Its weight forced him to drop before he twisted his hip, driving the sword full force to his opponent's ribs.

Vet had anticipated the fake, and he sidestepped to block the attack.

Clash.

Valerya frowned. Vet may have been a tower of a man, but they had fought together on several blood campaigns. He was capable of moving faster than boys half his age and a fourth his size, and blocking was not his style. She had seen him split an armored man in half with a battle-axe and crush a man's rib cage with a single-fisted blow to the chest. Maybe he was feeling tired.

Unless ...

Greaven swung clumsily.

Clash.

Vet lunged forward with his back leg, heaving his sword and bringing its back edge to his opponent's shoulder. *Clash.* The impact knocked Greaven forward a few steps, and when he turned, Valerya could see his pauldron was dented.

"USELESS," boomed Vet's voice, and he flung his blade to the ground. He would never fight a man at a disadvantage. Greaven lunged forward and aimed his sword at Vet's head, but Vet ducked and twisted, driving his elbow into his assailant's chest. It was enough to knock an already unbalanced man to his knees.

In a spectacular lapse of judgment, Greaven let his sword drop to the floor and flew at the man's face in an attempt to rip off his face-guard.

This should be good, thought Valerya, not even bothering to hide her glee.

Vet bellowed. A surge of Fire exploded from the ground in fury, and with absurd strength, he flung his opponent off him and punched him full-force. His spiked gauntlet met the man's helm, and Greaven screamed.

Morian sighed and rose, casting a warning blast in their direction. Onlookers watched as Fire expanded into a wall between them. It was vaguely translucent, but it burned fierce and drowned out the light at its edges. Valerya often forgot he could do that. Morian's Fire was strong, but he rarely cast it in public.

Damn. She sighed, disappointed. Reluctantly, she rose with him.

The king glowered in disapproval as Vet stepped in front of them, greatsword in hand. The Swordsworn who had assembled themselves in front of the king's platform drew their swords, but the crimson statues made no move. Vet ignored them and bowed his head in mock deference. "HAPPY. BIRTHDAY," his voice boomed.

He trudged back to his destrier and passed a dejected Greaven, who had only now managed to stand. One of his squires had pried off his helm, and Valerya could see a fist-formed dent at its side. A wonder the blow hadn't killed him.

Perhaps his skull was already dented before the fight.

The onlookers clapped, still under the impression that giant, armor-clad men could not get hurt. The king took his seat with a laugh, back to the natural order of things.

"I'm out of wine, m'lord," stammered Marcus when Valerya sat back down.

She sighed, exasperated. "You had one job, Marcus," she snapped, sending the boy off to fetch more. *At least it's over.* The jousting was done for the day, gone with Valerya's patience.

Greaven resumed his position at her side, and she was disappointed to see that he had not sustained severe injuries. The graces on the field had sewn up the side of his head, but it was no different from how he normally looked. He drew his blade and set it in front of him, resting both hands on its quillons.

Morian sighed. "A poor display, Greaven. What would our General think?"

"Yes, your Highness," answered Greaven as Marcus darted past him, flask in hand.

Valerya grabbed the flask and took another swig.

"Why, Valerya, I didn't think you indulged," said Morian, feigning surprise.

"Yes, your Highness," she said courteously, echoing Greaven as more admirers arrived at his feet. She rose as she felt the wine take its course and brushed past Greaven, rueful that she didn't think to kick the sword out from under him. Marcus scrambled after her.

"M'lord?" he asked uncertainly as Valerya strode ahead of him. There was only so much she could take of Morian and his golden circle. Any longer and she would have stripped off her armor and challenged Vet to a duel.

Where *had* Vet gone?

She scanned the crowd, parting it as she passed. In a sea of metal, she caught a flash of auburn.

Lyra, she thought. *Fuck.*

The girl watched the fighting in admiration. She even halted passing Swordsworn in their tracks to ask about their armor, and the men seemed all too glad to converse with her. *Marry one,* Valerya urged her silently. *Marry one and he won't touch you anymore.*

Valerya held out a hand to stop her cupbearer. "Marcus."

"M'lord?"

"Make sure Lyra stays away from our King tonight."

She sent him on his way and continued in the other direction, where the crowds thinned. *Three clashes,* she recalled. *Three clashes before Vet ended the brawl.*

The man may have looked like a beast, but there was always a reason behind his savagery. Three clashes meant thirty men. A hit to the shoulder was far from the heart, which meant that thirty men had set up camp near the border. And the blow to Greaven's helm was nothing more than Vet's desperate attempts to keep his face-guard in place.

A wise choice. The world might not have been ready for what lay hidden behind it.

Then the trumpets blared, badly. The mock battle was set to begin, and after that, the feast. Morian would be looking for her now. She sighed, preparing herself for the next phase of misery.

Where the hell was Valk when she needed him?

***

Valerya never thought she would make it back to her chambers alive, given the shitstorm she had endured at the feast. Instead of sitting at the head of the Spades' table like last year, Morian had her seated next to him. Her men threw her sympathetic glances from across the hall, but the drudges at the lower tables smirked and gawked when they saw. Ale made them braver, but she would remember their faces. They would run laps around the Scarlet Cities tomorrow.

At least boar, fowl, and fish were aplenty, and eating all of it had saved her from hours of talking. She had gone so silent that nobody noticed her slip past the grovelers and catch the Spades' caravan back to the Citadel. Her men had gotten irrevocably drunk and boisterous by then, but they were like family. A bunch of uncles who spat and cursed and talked about good times. The stable boys had to guide them back to their quarters, but Valerya managed on her own. She hated strangers on her floor. A single serving girl had access to her chambers, and even then, only at certain times. Anyone else would get thrown out the window.

Indeed, her room was stark and uninviting, but nothing looked more glorious to her than her bed. She immediately unstrapped her pauldron and groaned when it fell to the ground. The sound slammed against her skull like a hammer. The rest of her armor followed.

But when she unbuckled her scabbard, she leaned her sword against the wall, almost lovingly. It was the only thing of value to her, the one thing she could not replace.

Then the knock came.

It was neither forceful nor bumbling, and Valerya frowned. Most who stopped by were either one or the other. She considered ignoring it until she heard a meek voice from the other side. *"General?"*

Valerya's head screeched in protest when she opened the door, but she supposed she had a soft spot for smiths' daughters. "Lyra," she said impatiently. "What is it?"

"Marcus ... he, erm. He wanted to see if you needed more wine,

General," said Lyra awkwardly, keeping her gaze down and ignoring the various pieces of armor strewn about on the floor. She held a flask in one hand, and in the other, a slab of metal nearly as tall as she was. She held it up with more than moderate effort. "And your ... your shield ..."

"Where is he?"

"Well, he sort of ... got drunk at the feast. They were peeling him off the ground when I last saw him, and he asked me to make sure you had more wine, and..." Her smile died on her lips. She tried to kneel but fell forward trying to keep the shield steady.

"On your feet." Valerya sighed and took the shield. In truth, she was counting on the pickpockets to scavenge it when she left. It would have fetched a good price, and Valerya wouldn't have even reported it missing. "I need no more wine, girl. And neither do you."

Lyra rose and bowed her head, reddening. "General," she said hastily, taking her leave.

"Lyra," Valerya called after her as something else flashed through her mind.

The girl stopped in her tracks. "Yes?"

"What happened to your face?"

"Oh, nothing," said Lyra, glancing to her right. "Hanging around the kitchens has proven to be dangerous, what with the feast, and all. The cooks, they don't even notice someone like me." She smiled. "I'm just clumsy, that's all."

Sweet girl, thought Valerya dryly. *Can't lie her way out of a potato sack.*

"Does our King know of your quarters at the Citadel?" she asked.

"Yes," answered the girl as her body tensed. "He knows I'm sleeping in the guest quarters. He's never visited, of course, I mean, he's our King and all, so … he just … sends Greaven sometimes, when he … when he needs me."

Damn it, thought Valerya. More wine did not sound like such a bad idea after all. "Girl, do you know where the Spades' Quarters are?" she asked.

Lyra nodded. Her face brightened; dimples returned to her cheeks. "Of course! I follow them around all the time. I re-forge their swords and adjust their armor, and they give me tips on how to incapacitate people. I was hoping to run into Valk, but …"

"He will return soon," said Valerya, cutting her off. So many words. Her head was spinning from the conversation, and she just wanted the evening to end. "Do you know where his chambers are?" she asked. "At the far end."

Lucien's old room.

Lyra nodded. "I think so."

"You may sleep there until his return." Valerya closed her eyes and wondered why she even bothered. "And if my men give you problems, tell them I'll skin them alive."

Lyra's eyes widened. "My General is too kind," she said, but her face betrayed relief.

Valerya waved a hand dismissively. "Now go before I change my mind."

Lyra opened her mouth to say something but thought against it. Instead, she bowed her head and smiled awkwardly.

Valerya sighed. "Speak plainly," she said.

"Um, General …" said the girl, shifting uncomfortably. "Will Spade Gryff be back soon?"

Fucking hell. Valerya reminded herself to never enlist the help of children again. *Useless, all of them.* "That's the plan, regrettably," she said. "Now leave me."

"Good night, General!" exclaimed Lyra. Her face lit up as she took her leave.

Valerya closed the door with more force than intended. Its slam echoed in her skull, and she collapsed in bed, not even bothering to change out of her clothes. *Sian will have a field day tomorrow.* Valerya liked to keep her things orderly, but it was about time her serving girl had something to do. She slung an arm over her eyes. *If only I were twenty again.* The pain had only lasted a moment then. Now, she could no longer envision a pain-free future.

She turned over and tried to sense her dragon, but the connection was faint. It was probably slumbering beyond the stars, something she should be doing. Her hopes vanished when she heard a knock at the door. She cursed into her pillow.

Damn it, she thought as daggers stabbed at the back of her eyes. "Enter," she snapped.

The door opened, and she vowed to buy a deadbolt when she heard the voice that followed. "Why, General. Is that any way to talk to your king?"

"Your Highness," she said, forcing herself to stand and bow, feeling her insides lurch. Her evening had taken the worst possible turn. "Forgive me. I'm afraid I've had too much wine."

"Nothing to forgive, Valerya. I'm glad you enjoyed yourself," said Morian cordially as he entered, stepping over pieces of armor in distaste. "*Simply impossible,*" she heard him mutter. He sat at the edge of her bed, and she took care not to curse openly. "I must admit, that was an enjoyable birthday."

"Many families from all over the Realm came to pay their respects, and the common-folk were entertained," said Valerya. She had said the same thing every year for the past twenty years. "Only twelve were severely injured in the games."

"At least you had a good time," he said as his gaze fell on her hair. "Though I didn't know you could move so *quietly*. I didn't even notice you leave until you were gone." He smiled, and she felt his gaze linger on her underclothes. "Tell me, how *did* you find your way back?"

"With the other Spades," she said. Had he come to torment her on any other day, she might have taken care to soften her expression. Instead, she was sure she looked exactly how she felt: tired, and angry at everything for being so loud. Morian's voice boomed thunder in her ears.

"You shouldn't glare so much, Valerya," he scolded as he rose. "You know, sometimes I think you're missing the finer points in life." He fussed over her hair, straightened it with his long, thin fingers.

A sneak-thief's fingers. Even his hands held no honor.

Morian paused as if pretending to think. "Today, it was brought to my attention by many a lord and lady that they would find it a shame if my line ended."

"They want to make alliances. There were many eligible ladies of noble birth present at the festivities."

"Oh, you know they bore me so," said Morian, distracted. He frowned. "You know, you're not bad-looking. Strong eyes, a nice, solid … jawline … and only two scars!" His fingers traced down the lines that ran along the left side of her face. "And you're … tall." He leaned in, much too close for Valerya's comfort, and she could see herself in his eyes of gray and green.

"You really must relax," he said in her ear, and she caught a glimpse of her greatsword against the wall, neglected and forgotten. And when he kissed her neck, she was convinced that a sword through the bowels would be the perfect birthday present. Pulling off Vet's face-guard would have been preferable to the madness that was unfolding before her eyes.

His hand moved her face towards his, and when their lips met, Valerya backed away. "Your Highness," she said, biting down bile. "It would be improper."

"I am your *sovereign,*" he said, leaning in again.

Instinctively, Valerya grabbed onto his arm and pushed it away from her, a gesture that would have had her killed had she been anyone else. "I'm quite drunk."

Morian stepped back, wounded. His mood soon gave way to something else, as it often did with him. But this time was different. She saw in his eyes the pain that hardened into cruelty. "You know," he said, his voice wrought with spite. "Things have been getting … predictable as of late. You know how I hate *predictability.* So when my guests told me how another Purge would be *just* what the Fire-lands needed, I believe I may just take their advice to heart."

Valerya forced herself to look back into those eyes, wondering how long it would take Greaven in his half-bludgeoned state to notice Morian's absence should she slit his throat in her chambers.

"If that is what you command, your Highness," she said coldly.

"Then get your men ready. You are to ride in a fortnight," he said as he made his way to the door. It had always fascinated her how little sound he made as he walked. Like a snake slithering across stone.

"Where are we heading?" she asked.

Morian didn't even bother looking back as he flung the door open. "Genovel," he said.

23

GLASGÉRIOS
ICE REALM

The high walls stood half as old as the world. Beyond them lay nothing but townlands and snow-cloaked fields, and Dove wondered what it must have been like being born in a place that defied cultivation: cold, bleak, and surrounded by glass.

By the fourth night, Salandra had faded, but Rhysar was nowhere to be seen. Dove did not like that. Whenever the ascendants turned a blind eye, she found herself fearful that something would happen. With hundreds and thousands of children, they were bound to overlook one or two. Entire villages, even.

Dove shivered as a gust of wind starved her lungs of heat. She was not supposed to be outside. Climbing the crags was not particularly safe, but that small, narrow ridge she found tucked halfway up the mountain kept her hidden from prying eyes. It was the only time she let her hood down. No one saw red up here.

She took one last look at the horizon before beginning her descent. It was a long climb, but her body had gotten stronger. She found herself matching Merc and Decker at the dinner table, but food burned away inside her almost instantly. She even *grew*. A little.

She pulled up her hood and darted past the crowds, but she was not wary of getting caught. It was the turning hour—for some, the day was over. For the Nightkeepers, like Marv, the day had just begun. Torch-light was encased in dim glass when the sun went down, but it was a slow start. Half the city wanted to sleep, and the other half had just woken up. In the collective exhaustion, no one paid attention to her as she slipped in and out of the alleyways.

Dove took care to stop by the bakery, hoping she could at least catch the last cart. Every night, the baker's girl loaded a cart and took it into the keep to feed the Nightkeepers of the castle. She was the only Glasger Dove had met who was smaller than she was, and she rarely spoke. They were meant to be friends.

To her fortune, she arrived in time to catch Zeya closing shop. Recognition flashed in Zeya's eyes, but that was all that broke her expression. They were not too far apart in age, but their worlds were so different that words would not have helped them, anyway. Zeya stuffed a bread roll in Dove's hand and wheeled the cart in the opposite direction.

Glasgérians never waved. They did not know what it meant. They intuitively knew the encounter was over and left the conversation. Sometimes they would mutter a quick *segnes,* but more often than not, they just walked away.

And so Dove continued, eating all the way to the Court of Queens. She made it to the Underground without attracting any attention and wondered if the others were finished with dinner. It seemed like the perfect night for a kitchen raid, but she stopped dead when she reached the entrance to the guest-keep. The room was lined with armed men. Her companions huddled around a long table, and they definitely detected her.

"Where were you?" Wolff growled. His dark eyes regarded

her with disdain, and even in the tinted torchlight, she saw them narrow. "You better not have gone above-ground."

A quick glance around the hall told her that the others had been looking for her. She had never seen so many people glare at the same time.

Wolff cursed. "Merc, can you keep a better eye on …"

"The Sintger was eating with me," said a voice behind her, irritatingly confident. "I was showing her around the … *sunmaehr'ius,* and we lost track of time."

Dove turned to face its source, but Marv returned her confusion with a smile. Bear made his way to her side and pressed his snout against her hand. She felt his fangs graze her palm. The gap between her and the others widened.

"Yeah?" Wolff ignored the night-wolf. "What was your favorite part, then?"

Without thinking, Dove turned back to him and mouthed: *glow-flies.*

Decker came to her rescue. "See? Told you there was nothing to worry about. She's only been hanging around night-wolves."

"Let's begin," said Tomá before Wolff could reply. The domeric's hair looked even more tousled than usual, like someone had attempted to rip it from its roots. The atmosphere in the room darkened.

"A rider came today," Wolff said, glowered. "The Swordsworn have been spotted close to the border. Thirty men, thereabouts. More coming, most like, knowing Morian."

Dove wished she could have been more surprised. She felt everyone's stares shift towards her hair and pretended not to notice. *No wonder they were looking for me.* Whenever Morian did something stupid, the Fireborne abroad were in grave danger.

"It is time," said Tomá decisively. "We fight."

"Just like that, huh?" Wolff asked. His disposition soured. "Us and what army? Them?" He glanced around the table. "No offense, but every one of us in this room can burn, save for one. And she's not coming with us."

His decision was so quick that Dove blinked, surprised.

"Don't look at me like that," he growled. "It's too dangerous."

"Hey, whatever happened to free will and all that?" asked Merc. His hair flamed above indignant eyes. "She wants to go, in this … incredibly hypothetical situation."

"Shut up, Merc," Wolff snapped. He turned back to Tomá, and Dove sighed. She might as well have been invisible. "Has your queen been informed?"

Tomá kept his hands folded across the table, but Dove knew to be wary. Bad things happened when he hid his palms, and it was when he did not move that he was most dangerous. "This message was sent by a Falcon's hand," he said, "despite the somewhat dubious spelling."

"Remember your vows. All of you," warned Wolff before anyone could say anything. "We can't pass this onto the Crown. But *we* can do whatever we want."

Merc grinned. "So we're going?"

"Hah." Wolff scoffed, but his laughter was only half-convincing. "They'll sing songs of our doomed venture before we begin. But that doesn't mean we can't buy our boys and girls some time. This could be just what we need to revive the Order."

Tomá gave a grim smile. "I have some friends at the border. I will send word."

"For thirty men?" asked Merc. "What harm can thirty men do to Glasgérios?"

"What can seven?" snapped Wolff. He pointed a finger around

the table. "Remember that, all of you. Seven Glasgers was all it took. And their actions unleashed a dragon that set the world on fire."

Dove glanced at him, looked sad.

"Don't even think about it," said Wolff without looking at her.

"C'mon, Wolff," said Decker. "Falcons have always found themselves in places they don't belong. I can't think of anyone who matches that description better than her."

"A sign, then," said Sirian. His hoarse voice interrupted the tension that spilled between words. "Do you not see? It is the will of the *domeras*."

Dove nodded in agreement, feeling a sudden burst of gratitude. If there was one thing to be said for fanatics, it was that almost anything could be seen as a sign from their savior.

"Might be," said Wolff, unfazed by their higher power. "But the *domeras* won't save us from the Swordsworn."

His response caught Dove off-guard, and she bit back resentment. Anger pierced through her fear. If anything, she had *more* of a reason to fight against the Firelands. Airship traders saw the carnage from afar, but she had been in it.

"Send word out to whatever allies you have. Whoever else wants to come along will ride northwards." His tone sharpened as he turned. "But she stays. Will of the *domeras* or not."

Wolff dismissed the rest of his onlookers without even looking at her. It was Tomá who did, and she wanted to scream. His eyes were bloodshot, red veins against white marble. The cold rings around his pupils narrowed.

"Prepare the caravans and ready the horses," she heard Wolff say as people began clearing the hall. "Take only what you need. We ride at daybreak."

Dove waited for everyone to leave before gathering herself. They were keeping something from her. Wolff may have been a good liar, but Merc had been bursting at the seams with secrets. Maybe Morian would be there? *No, that would be stupid.* If he was, he would surely think to surround himself with more than thirty men.

"Hey, Sintger!" a voice called, pulling her back from her thoughts. She turned and found Marv leaning against the wall, arms folded in amusement. He reminded her so much of Gryff, even though they looked nothing alike. "I'm no liar, you know."

And he made less sense. Dove frowned. *What are you ...?*

"Earlier. When they didn't know where you were." He unfolded his arms. "That wasn't a lie. That was just... a truth from the future. How do you say this ... a *premonition.* Now you really do have to eat with me, unless you plan to make a liar out of me."

Dove tried vainly to look indignant, but a soft smile slipped through the cracks.

"It's also a promise that you'll survive. That *we'll* survive." He glanced over his shoulder, making sure no one else was in the hall. "But first, come with me."

Without warning, he hooked an arm around hers and led her into the tunnels. It was not the subtlest of abductions, especially with a night-wolf at their heels, but they went unnoticed. Word had spread quickly in the Underground. Some were excited for a new dawn, while others planned a quick getaway. The news had prompted an old soothsayer to wander from chamber to chamber, demanding sinners to repent.

Three turns gave her an idea of where they were going.

Merc and Decker had already been waiting for them when they entered. What Dove saw would have garnered a bounty on their heads in the Firelands—the mess would have driven Morian *insane.* Contents of their sacks had been emptied onto the ground, and Dove could barely make out the floor. She did not remember them bringing so much stuff.

Merc shrugged. "Could be worse," he said as Marv shut the door behind them.

"Most of it's his," said Decker, sitting up. It was obvious they had started packing before dawn. His blade leaned against the wall, freshly sharpened, next to a tower shield that looked Fire-forged. A flaming skull was painted on it, which did not match Decker at all.

Decker followed her gaze. "Beggars can't be choosers." He swung down from the top bunk. "I'd rather take on a horde of Hounds looking like a swashbuckling pirate than burn."

"It's about time for some action," said Merc as he pulled out another bag from the wardrobe. "Wolff's been a bit off to all of us lately. I don't know why he's so against you coming. You probably remind him of ..."

"His wayward youth," interrupted Decker graciously.

"So Tomá had something made for you. I think he's quite fond of you," continued Merc. "Ha, can you imagine him and Sirian being friends? I mean, what do they even talk about?"

Dove nodded. She imagined it would be difficult sustaining a conversation when the only topics were the She-Jackal and the *domeras.* A wonder they had not killed each other yet.

Merc pulled out a gleam of ivory twisted unnaturally into a bow. It was not a perfect arch, like she was used to, but it had a slight indentation where the grip should have been. "Tomá even had the shaft of every arrow carved with the mark of the Falcon, hoping each one would find its way into a Hound's heart."

Dove felt oddly moved, if not disturbed. She took the bow in her hands, feeling unworthy. It was smoother and lighter than a practice bow and did not splinter at the edges. She set it down and took an arrow out of its quiver, examined the tip.

"And don't forget this." Merc strapped a bracer around her forearm. The buckles were wider than her wrist, but the leather wrapped neatly around her thumb. Straps covered the first three fingers of her hand.

Merc cleared his throat, almost embarrassed. "I, ah ... so, I used to be a smith's apprentice during *my* wayward youth," he said, ignoring her skeptical glance. She knew that he once apprenticed under a smith, a tailor, a builder, and an artesan, though not necessarily in that order. It made her wonder what his parents did for a living. "It's not perfect, but it was something I was working on at the smithy. Realms, do you know how hard it is to just... *not* talk out there?" He paused. "Oh, wait ..."

Dove ignored him. He talked before thinking, but he said things no one else would. That sort of made up for it.

"If we get there and all hell breaks loose, you're heading for the high hills. But *some* protection might prove to be useful," said Decker, unwrapping something from cloth folds. It looked like a dagger at first glance, but it was not one that she had seen before. Instead of a hilt and pommel, there was a cross-grip lodged between two side-bars. The double-edged blade was flat and horizontal.

Merc grinned. "That was Decker's idea. It's what Lancistierreans use."

"Folks in that part of the world live to be over two hundred," said Decker. When he stretched, his fingertips reached the ceiling. "They must be doing something right."

Dove's fingers clenched around the cross-grip. *This can kill,* she realized.

"It's not the *best,*" said Merc before she could react. "But it's enough to open someone's throat if you hit fast and hard enough. And you won't drop it as easily." He smiled. "What about you, Marv? Are you gearing up?"

"I've never been much of a fighter," said Marv. "Bear takes care of all that for me."

You are going? Dove asked with her eyes.

"Of course he's going," said Decker for him. "Elayne may be a Healer, but we need all the help we can get. Marv is one of the best medicans around. Knows all the weird herbs and venoms in exactly the right combinations ..."

Her eyes widened. A *medican?* He was smart and peculiar enough, but she imagined medicans to be old and ... *old.*

"Spending all my time indoors as a child gave me the opportunity to study all sorts of things." Marv shrugged. "I figured if I couldn't hold a sword, I might as well have other uses. I'm good with my hands, you know."

"And his giant dog might come in handy," said Merc. "When it's not sleeping."

Bear had made a bed out of a pile of clothing on the floor, but his ears perked at the attention. He gave a low growl but grew quiet when Marv threw him a dead rat.

"Seriously? Over my favorite ...? Yeah, not wearing that again," Merc said, disgusted. "Can't he go hunt in the wastelands or something?"

"Better rats than people. He would die out there before dawn. Packs don't trust a lone wolf." Marv watched Bear tear into the rat's bones.

"What happened to him, anyway?" Merc asked.

"I found him next to a tree. He was abandoned when he got injured by a Glasger elk. I guess he doesn't trust packs, either."

"*Speaking* of lone wolves," said Decker when he turned to Dove. "Have you ever been in a fight before?"

Of course I have, thought Dove, pretending it was no big deal. He had been a big man, too, even bigger than Decker, and loved giving Gryff a hard time. She had seen him again in the Purge, that bull of a man she had punched in the face. Benno, his name was. But he did not recognize her. Perhaps he had been too preoccupied with other things, like burning alive.

"What about you?" asked Marv, straightening, and Dove frowned. She did not realize how tall he was when he did not slouch. "When was the last time you had to fight?"

To Dove's surprise, the two laughed. "Well, there's one thing to be said about this ridiculous plan," said Decker. "We'll have a better story the next time someone asks."

"It wasn't *that* bad," said Merc. "Just … unintentional. We'd gotten spectacularly lost in the Firelands. Imagine our relief when we stumbled upon Fort Townstead, hoping someone could point us in the right direction. But we found ourselves in the middle of a battle."

"Just imagine. Folks started attacking us from both sides, and we had no idea who we were fighting and why."

"So we just hacked away at whoever we could, hoping we weren't helping to overthrow a lord, or something."

"But you're so good at unseating them, Merc."

"Don't start with that stupid seawall again …"

Dove liked hearing their adventures. She smiled when she realized her own list of stories was growing. It may have been shorter than the others, but sailing to Glasgérios on an airship had been a good start.

"We'll be loading a caravan tonight," said Merc. "It wouldn't be a bad idea to hide behind a pile of blankets and cloaks that will magically appear in the corner ..."

They gathered their belongings and loaded the caravans, making sure Dove stayed out of sight. Whatever they left behind would be a gesture of good faith for the next traveler, though Dove wondered what use they would have for empty bottles and dirty clothes. Rat bones.

Decker excused himself to get Elayne, who was finishing up at the infirmary at the other end of the city. Marv retreated to the *sunmaehr'ius* to pack up a few things, which left Dove alone with Merc. That had never happened before.

"Come on, then," said Merc. "And be quick. We can't be seen."

It was not difficult. By then, the Daykeepers had gone to sleep, and none of the Nightkeepers above-ground recognized them. It was only Wolff they needed to avoid. Dove trailed behind Merc and tried not to look too conspicuous. The giant bow made it difficult.

And when they turned into a pub, she sighed.

But much to her surprise, it was not ale he was looking for. Merc scanned the crowd before his eyes fell on the golden-haired bar-maid she had seen more than a few times in the guest-keep. The bar-maid's face lit up, brighter than the tinted torchlight in the tavern.

Dove felt awkward standing there while they kissed and laughed, but she could not help but feel a spark of something not wholly fathomable to her. She wondered how often it happened to them—finding something, someone—only to leave it all behind at a split-moment's notice. She had never been with anyone before, but she could imagine what it was like.

Merc was strangely silent on the way to the caravan, but he remained in good humor for the rest of the walk. "C'mon," he joked. "I thought you'd have an easier time here, what with no one talking, and all. There are lots of eligible grim-faced boys your age in Glasgérios."

Dove admired Merc's smooth talking.

Merc shrugged without a drop of grace. "Nan goes crazy for them. I don't know what your generation finds attractive." He threw her a playful glance. "Let me guess. You're more into the Hound type. Strong, solid, *serious.* Scarred and soulless and all that."

Dove blinked. *Well ...*

He gave her a good-natured shove as he continued his musings all the way to the caravan. His voice dropped to a whisper when they reached it, making sure no one else was around. He helped her on, practically shoving her inside.

"Elayne will ride in the back with you," he said. "Decker should have told her by now, and I don't imagine the rest minding much, but just ... don't get caught by anyone large, imposing, and whose name rhymes with Bolff, yeah? He'll kill us all."

Dove nodded as she shifted towards the front of the caravan. As promised, there was an unexplained pile of cloaks and blankets in the corner, which was more than enough to hide behind. *Always a stowaway,* she thought, but she was getting used to it.

Excitement stirred inside her, but something else fought for room beside it. Was it terror? She closed her eyes, listening between heartbeats until she heard nothing.

And when the coming of day shattered the sky into curious bursts of violet and blue, they were gone.

24

WAYFARER'S BARROW
ICE REALM

"I left my crossbow," Dancer said when she woke up, the first words that left her lips since they arrived at the border. Her face had become as dry and gray as the stone that surrounded them.

"We'll find you another," Bard promised in his most caressing tone. He tried in vain to hide his relief, lest she thought he cared. So much light and fire confined to a broken body. But behind that weakness lay a spark. She was still alive, and that was all that mattered.

"You'd better." Her voice creaked like rusted iron. Nightbloom made her body frail—and temporarily, her state of mind. He took advantage of it by pressing her cheeks together while she slept, contorting her face into comical expressions. He would pay dearly for this later.

"We'll swipe one from the next Hound's corpse," he said, holding her hand.

The attending graces didn't understand their words, but they suppressed shy giggles as they scuttled past his field of vision. They probably thought they were whispering sweet nothings to each other, dreaming of brighter futures.

Only the medican could speak Sinthean, or at least some variation of it. He had studied his craft in Sinthea for eight years, and his efforts were rewarded cruelly with large chains that weighed him down like shackles. His days of serving were far from over.

The medican's name was Grey-Bum. In truth, it was Graybym, but Bard found the former much easier to remember. He came in every so often to check on Dancer's injuries, but they kept disappearing; internal wounds were hard to treat once the skin above them had healed.

Upon seeing that she had woken up, the graces rushed off to fetch the medican. Grey-Bum ordered Bard to leave the room while they took over, speaking in their accursed tongue and leaving him to wonder where in Wayfarer's Barrow one could procure a crossbow.

The village was uneventful, to say the least. Outside, no one talked to him, and the rows of stone dwellings slid without resistance into the back of his mind. The anonymity was crushing, but the villagers gazed upon him with calm curiosity—a reminder that he was no longer in the Firelands.

He had certainly attracted the attention of a little boy, who followed him around wherever he went. He barely came up to Bard's knee, but he would likely tower over him in ten years, seeing how his clansmen were built. His mother tended the livestock; she was already as tall as Bard and didn't seem at all concerned that her son was poking at Bard's weaponry.

Bard loved children, as much as it pained him to admit. If he hadn't thought so little of this shit world, he would have liked to bring one or two into it. This one didn't smile or laugh, but that was how they were. All Bard needed to do was look into his eyes to know how he felt. He decided to call him Ram, if for no other reason than his mother's occupation.

While Bard was waiting, he carved him a wooden dagger, and the kid ran off, swinging it at anyone who walked in his presence. The villagers pretended to disapprove, but the pride in their eyes was unmistakable. There weren't a lot of children in the Icelands. Their numbers never recovered after the Battle of the Shadows, and the younger ones didn't live long without their parents. The ones that survived, however, were protected at all cost. Even bastards and street rats were treasured commodities.

Bard *should* have continued into Glasgérios, he knew. That's what the past forty or so years had conditioned him to do. But instead, he decided to hang around the border village, waiting for a sign. And when he grew bored, he made signs out of anything, predicting the end of the world when a crow shat on a wheelbarrow.

He wasn't quite sure how anyone managed to live in such deafening silence, even in a place like this. They had nothing. The Hounds had taken everything from them, yet there they were, thanking some divine shadow for whatever scraps they could salvage. Orphans replaced their children. Houses were patched but never rebuilt. They resewed and repaired and shared. One member's success was the village's triumph.

Good for them, thought Bard.

Boredom nearly drove him to sneak up behind the sentries and cut their bowstrings, but before he could stand, Grey-Bum emerged from the infirmary. "You may see her now," he said and gave him a slight nod. He had a kind face, and Bard wondered how many people he had pulled back to the waking world with his bare hands. Medicans weren't mages, after all, and he had to make do with what he had.

Bard re-sheathed Dancer's dagger and smiled innocently as he headed back inside. The medican told him she had bled on the inside; they had to cut and re-cut her skin to let it out.

Maybe self-healing had its disadvantages after all.

The cold in the infirmary sliced deep when Bard entered the room. Dancer's cot was in the far corner, half-draped in curtains. Her eyes were closed, but he knew she was pretending—a suspicion confirmed when she opened her eyes weakly and croaked, "I'm thirsty, Bard."

But Bard was prepared for her wiles. He handed her a flask, but her head dropped to the side. Sighing, he propped her pillow up and moved her head towards his, uncorking the bottle and placing its nozzle at her lips. He tilted it with care, and she spat out its contents.

"Ale?" she asked indignantly. "Where's the wine?"

"A rare commodity here," answered Bard. "They do have grog, though."

Dancer cursed, and her head dropped back to the side. She smiled playfully through closed eyes. "You still owe me a secret, Bard," she whispered, as though she would slip back into unconsciousness if he refused. "I promise I won't tell."

Another one to add to her collection. "What do you want to know?"

"A lot of things." She opened her eyes at the invitation. The rings around them disappeared instantly. "Tell me about the Citadel. About how you knew all that when the Hounds asked you those questions. And don't lie. I can tell if you do. Hell, anyone can tell if you do."

"It's Franco who's a terrible liar. Not me."

They giggled to themselves.

Bard sighed. It was harder thinking back to what once was. Much easier being someone else. "I was a Guardian once," he said, "as hard as that is to believe."

"Not really," said Dancer, to his surprise. "You fight well, and you determine exactly when you want your opponents to die. That's quite a rare gift." She smiled. "And you didn't even cast Storm until we were surrounded by flames." She gazed into his eyes. "Cutthroats don't have that code to live by, and neither do aimless, drunken mercenaries. Only those trained in the art of proper warfare."

"Proper warfare?"

"Don't play dumb, Bard," she said coyly, seeing through his act. "I'm not talking about skirmishes and rebel uprisings. I'm talking about proper wars. *Elemental* wars."

Bard nodded. "Well, what do you know about it? The last one involving Lancistierre was fifty years ago. Between Sinthea and Glasgérios, eight."

Dancer blinked innocently. "I know nothing of such affairs."

"You know enough about war conduct," he said, suddenly wondering if Dancer had been alive fifty years ago. He made a mental note to ask her age if he won the next game. "It's considered improper to cast elements in the first wave of battle. One can only begin using them after the third wave."

"Or unless your opponent casts it first," she said. Her eyes gleamed like silver.

Bard nodded, grinning. She was sharp, if not unconditionally insane. He continued. "So I was a Protector stationed in Sinthea. Guarded all sorts of important people. That was around the same time Morian had all those Glasgérians slaughtered."

"So I've heard," said Dancer, throwing him a playful glance. "But surely I wouldn't remember. That was twenty years ago, after all."

Bard's heart melted. "After that, I was sent to escort a convoy of Glasgérian officials out of the Firelands. The other men were typical Hounds, you know the sort … save for one. His name was Lucien."

"You were friends, I take it?"

"You could say that. We dropped off the officials at the border, and turned back to see …" He paused, trying to put chaos into words. "We just saw this *beast* tear a hole in the sky, and for a moment, it was like the world had broken."

Bard remembered how the clouds had caught fire, blanketing the world in red flames. The sun had tried its best to shine, and with it the stars and the moon, but when the dragon departed, there was nothing left. Only darkness. "The men and I rode into Genovel expecting to find this absolute beast of a warrior. Three meters tall, long, braided beard, part dragon."

"Instead, you found …"

"This *kid*. This kid who'd never even left her village before it disappeared." Bard's thoughts took a dark turn. "We brought her back to the Citadel. Morian had taken an interest in her, so I put a sword in her hand."

Dancer laughed. "I can see that," she said.

"She was good. We threw her in with the drudges, but the others were scared of her. If not of her powers, then of her fists. The girl could punch something fierce." Bard smiled, almost nostalgically. "I was called to the Highlands after that. Lucien took over her training, then."

"So you were a Protector," Dancer teased, "and you discovered the Blood Queen."

"Don't say it like that."

"And who trained the She-Jackal's trainer?" she asked, eyeing him playfully. Her finger traced along the scratches in his armor. "And don't give me that nonsense about having a soldier's training."

Bard grinned. "Oh, you know. Fighting folks here and there. Even ran across one of your Blue Knights not too long ago."

"One of them?" she asked skeptically.

"What, you don't believe I fought one?"

"I don't believe that you fought *one,*" she said. "*Temereyna* always come in pairs. Where one goes, the other follows. It's a bond stronger than matrimony, you know."

"Really, now?" asked Bard, playing dumb. "Perhaps he lost his better half."

"Then he is no longer a *temereyn,*" she said. "It's common knowledge. One cannot fight without the other. One cannot exist without the other."

Bard blinked, moved. "Is that what happened to you?"

Dancer laughed. "Oh, Bard," she said. "I already told you in the forests. I lost *some*thing, but I didn't mean that someone close to me died. Besides," she smiled. "Do I look like an honorable knight to you?"

"It's all honor and propriety with your people, isn't it?"

"Not *all,*" she said, giving him a warm smile. He would have been hers then and there, but her hand shot up to her chest. "Bard …"

Bard's eyes widened. "Medican!" he yelled, jumping from his chair. "Grey-Bum!"

"Wait," she said, but her grip on his arm loosened.

"MEDICAN!" he screamed as Grey-Bum rushed in.

"Her heart beats irregularly," said the man, feeling her wrist. "But there is no pulse."

"WHAT?" bellowed Bard. "Fix it! Fix it!"

Grey-Bum opened her mouth and breathed into it twice. "Does she have any metal on her?" he asked, pressing against her chest.

"Why is this relevant?" asked Bard incredulously. "I took her dagger, but …"

"We must stop her heart, lest it burst," he said. "Quickly, Thoryn."

"What do you want me to do, rip it out and hold it steady?"

"You must shock her. Do it now!"

"WHAT?"

Grey-Bum grabbed Bard's hands and placed them on her chest. He had gone through this exact motion countless times in his head, but under vastly different circumstances. And there, Grey-Bum had been nowhere near them. "A light surge!" ordered the old man. "Do it, Thoryn!"

Bard wondered if he needed to shock his own heart into stopping when he cast Storm into her. He felt it leave his fingers, felt his strength become her own. Her body stirred, and the medican shoved him out of the way. *"Saestren!"* the man screamed, and the two graces rushed back inside, harried and disheveled. *"Ven braehen zeahrkhen!"*

It made Bard's head spin. The senseless words pouring out of their mouths. The smell of death that draped over the infirmary. Everyone doing something absurdly different at the same time. Fighting was the same, but this was different. This was …

"Thunderborne! *Thunderborne!*" The medican's voice brought him back to reality, detached, resounding off the walls like an echo. "Once more!"

Bard obeyed. Grey-Bum pushed him aside and listened to her heart, feeling for a pulse. "It's weak," he observed, and his eyebrows furrowed. as he contemplated Bard with curiosity. "Leave us," he said. "We must cut her open again."

"WHAT?" asked Bard as the graces pushed him off to the side. They were cute and sweet and shy, but not when they gripped those surgical knives. He watched as Dancer opened her eyes and leaned to the side. She tried to vomit, but nothing came out.

"Is that normal?" asked Bard, overcome with the urge to vomit, himself.

"Leave us!" the medican, and one of the graces ushered Bard outside. Bard could barely feel his legs, but they moved without him somehow, carrying him forward with unease. He was used to seeing blood and entrails—once, he had seen a man explode from a rogue jag—but the thought of someone cutting and recutting skin made him uneasy. That was how they used to torture Lancistierreans back then. They just skinned them over and over again until they succumbed or killed themselves.

Torture at the hands of Grey-Bum, thought Bard, shuddering. Perhaps the medican lugged around that massive chain for a reason.

Bard took a deep breath and started walking to regain the sensation in his legs. He didn't make it very far before he sensed that something was off. It might have been something in the air, or in the trees. Or the five outsiders who readied their battle axes when he stepped outside.

They didn't look like vagrants or pillagers, but something put them on edge. The four younger men with flaming orange hair abandoned their axes, opting instead for their bows. They aimed arrows at Bard's head.

Bard found it hideously unjust. He had just come from one bout of chaos, only to stumble headfirst into another. *All because that fucking pigeon told me to fly.* "Easy, now." He raised his arms and kept his voice calm. No reason to provoke them. The youths, he could take on easily; he could singe their arrows to a crisp before they got anywhere near him. The stocky one closest to him, however, would pose a challenge. His eyes told of a greater pain.

And of course it was that one who approached him first. Anyone would have spotted the Hound from miles away. His beard looked like it was on fire, and he appeared to be the leader of the group. Maybe it was his grim demeanor that made him look so intimidating, or the ritual scars that sang of blood battles.

Or the giant battle-axe he wielded with ease.

"Greetings," he said gruffly, eyeing Bard with suspicion. His accent placed him in the Firelands, but it was so rough around the edges that it sanded off the end of his words. "You look like your wife's just gone into labor." He extended his right arm.

"Not quite," said Bard as his fingers clasped beneath the man's elbow. He was not prepared for how forceful the stranger's grip was. The bearded man's arm was twice as thick as his and layered with plates of muscle. He may have been a head shorter, but it did not detract from his overall size. Wherever he came from, he knew how to swing that axe.

"Who are you?" asked Bard, lowering his guard.

"Thornbeard, they call me. And these're m'boys, Bruin, Bayne, and Boar. That one over there is my sister's boy, Ivan. Ain't much of a man, I'm afraid, but he's a good kid."

The fire-headed youths waved as villagers threw them disapproving glances for speaking. They looked nothing like Thornbeard, save for the hair, but at least three of them looked like they'd seen their share of adventure. Bruin had long hair that was turning white, while Bayne and Boar kept theirs short. Bayne sported a beard while Boar was clean-shaven, but Bard could see that the two were twins.

I really must shave, thought Bard suddenly. As for Ivan ... Bard frowned. No, try as he might, there was nothing remarkable about him.

"I've seen your face before," said Thornbeard before letting go of his arm.

Bard had never seen Thornbeard before in his life, but he never remembered faces. He had seen so many of them on his travels, and after a while, forgetting them was the only way he could sleep at night.

"Ah, yes," said Thornbeard after a solemn pause. "I know who y'are."

Why does everyone know who I am? Bard thought, annoyed. He made a mental note to start remembering names. "Let's not burden ourselves with the past," he said. He'd had enough memories thrown in his face for one day.

Bard widened his audience, turning to Thornbeard's kin. "My name is Bard. My companion, Brunhilda, and I encountered a Swordsuit camp not too far from here."

"Thirty men, was it?" asked Bayne or Boar. Whoever had the beard.

"Thereabouts," said Bard. *And one face-guarded behemoth of doom.*

"Then it was you who sent word t'Glasgérios," said Thornbeard.

"Indeed it was."

"Then we fight together," Thornbeard nodded. "Where's Brunhilda?"

"She was caught by a Hound's arrow when we escaped."

"I am sorry for that. Those bastards will pay," said Thornbeard, throwing another glance at the infirmary. "But at least she escaped with her life."

Bard nodded grimly, though he didn't know for how long. "Do you have wine?" he asked. An opportune time for a change in topic.

Thornbeard and his three sons laughed heartily. "A woman's drink, they say!" He slapped Bard on the back, throwing him forward. "Maybe Ivan does, now that I think about it."

The boy reddened as he offered Bard his wineskin, and Bard nodded in gratitude. "Thank you. Now if you'll excuse me, friends, I must tend to my companion."

"There'll be more coming," said the beardless twin, and Bard frowned. Strangely, they all sported different accents. "Maybe you can join us for some ale when you're finished."

Now you're talking. Bard gave a courteous wave before heading back inside.

***

It didn't take long before Grey-Bum caught Bard slipping Dancer some wine and chased him out of the infirmary. By then, night had fallen, and an ascendant star was being born. In Divisorya, they just called it the fifth month, but it was different in other parts of the world. In Glasgérios, the white star meant the space between air and earth. In Lancistierre, it was the most celebrated, as it was not a pairing, but a collision of all colors. The Fireborne, on the other hand, named them after their dragons, but Bard couldn't keep track of which one was what color.

Whatever it was called, Bard was glad it was being born. He was growing tired of black, featureless nights. Any time would have been a shitty time to die, he supposed, but there was something insulting about dying in a place so dark that not even the stars could see.

Ram sat by Bard's side, poking at his leg with the wooden dagger. Some of the villagers sat around the fire they had made. It took Thornbeard and his kin more than several attempts to get them talking, but once the ale settled, they made exceptions to their rule of silence. Not that it helped much; few spoke their words, but laughter was a welcome sound.

More and more outsiders came in, some stealthier than others, armed with bows and spears and whatever had gotten them that far. Some settled in the fields, propping up tents when no space was left in the village. The first who had arrived—among them Thornbeard and his kin—huddled around the fire. It was nothing compared to the cold in Glasgérios, but warmth was still a distant memory.

He found himself wishing Dancer could join. She would find amusement in their company. In a gesture of good faith, Thornbeard stepped inside the infirmary to offer her wine, much to Grey-Bum's dismay. The medican may have been able to throw Bard out, but no one said no to a large, braid-bearded man wielding a battle-axe.

"Brunhilda is splendid company!" said Thornbeard as he emerged from the tent, smelling like tavern. He and his sons left no bottles to chance. Bard suspected ale made up the bulk of their supplies, but they shared willingly with newcomers.

Most of them were Realmborn, but Bard's face softened when he saw the sigil-less colors of those who spoke with his own accent. Divisoryans had a much different air to them, in all sense of the word. He supposed they had not yet withstood the passage of time that produced beautiful civilizations like Lancistierre or the stone-bound traditions of the Scarlet Cities. Yet it was time that had separated the Realmborn from each other, driving a wall between them so deep that anyone standing on the other side was an enemy.

No, life was better in the air. Everyone came from somewhere else, and things were more peaceful—unless, of course, one counted that mishap with the archemages. But no one talked about that anymore.

Bard didn't recognize any of the Divisoryans, but he felt at peace when he heard their voices. It brought him back to happier times, and when he closed his eyes, he could almost see the Blackstone again. How his father had taken him high, high up the tower until he was overlooking the Realmlands and beyond.

Bard hadn't been home in a long time. That day atop the Black-stone was the last good memory he had of his father, the man who just said "fuck it" and snuck a child past a hundred mages so the boy could know what it was like being the tallest man in the world.

Bard sighed as he took a swig of ale, thinking of home.

And when he opened his eyes, he saw Ram's little hand reaching for the flask.

"No," he said, setting the boy down. He pointed to himself. "Bard," he said. "Baaaaard."

"Baaaaahd," the boy repeated.

"Bard."

"Bahd."

"Close enough. Now go whack Thornbeard with your dagger," said Bard, making a stabbing notion towards the fire-bearded man. Ram ran off and Bard laughed, clinking tankards with Bayne, the un-bearded twin.

"Where are you from?" asked Bard.

"We're from the outskirts of Rhysia. Good land. But then we settled in the mountains north of the Huntsmen Woods." Bayne took a swig. He took care to speak slowly. "Ivan is from Fort Townstead. Or *was,* rather … the last I heard, it was called Pillage Run. No wonder he's so confused." He shrugged. "What about you? You sound Divisoryan."

"Yep," said Bard. Of course he was. It would have been easier catching an ogre in the wastelands than a Thoryn in this part of the world. "Not such an interesting story, I'm afraid."

"Can't help where we're from," said Bayne. "Only where we're going. And when Da said a falcon came from Glasgérios, we knew where we wanted to be."

"Even if it means raising arms against your own?"

"Especially if it's my own," said Bayne. His eyes narrowed against the smoke. "Everything that had once made the Firelands good died with Avander."

Bard took another swig. *Everything* good had died with Avander. "Excuse me, friend," he said, rising. "I've had too much ale."

"We've got plenty more!" shouted Thornbeard, raising his own flagon.

Bard grinned as he stumbled towards the fields. Several tents were propped up along the road, and travelers were huddled around the cooking spits. The Falcons may not have shared the same words, but food and drink made for good bonding. They all said something different to him when he passed.

"Cheers," said Bard, but he avoided their glances. If his suspicions were true, most of them would die before the turn of the next star. No need for more faces to forget.

Bard was in the middle of a much-needed piss when he saw two caravans halt in the distance. Riders set up perimeters around the encampment. *Smart.* He washed his hands with water from the well before he approached them, trying not to look as drunk and downtrodden as he felt. Some of the silent villagers even came to their aid, grateful for their arrival.

Bard weaved through the newcomers and inspected the contents of their satchels. This group was even more eclectic than the others— if anything, because they had a *domeric* with them. He may not have been wearing their armor, but Bard knew one when he saw one.

Bard was terrified of domerics. Not because they looked inhuman—which they did, and this one especially—but because he could never, ever tell what they were planning. Their movements were silent, and their eyes betrayed nothing. When they became shadows, they became shells.

The domeric wielded a bow of tortured ebony, crafted from the trees of the Blackwood. And a greatsword was strapped to his back.

Wait, thought Bard as his eyes tried to make sense of the combination. *I know that sword.* The face of its wielder had twisted and scarred past recognition, much like the bow, but Bard knew him. They fought for the same side, but they weren't allies, and though they had known each other for years, he was hesitant to call him friend.

Bard decided to postpone their happy reunion and turned, keen on staying out of view.

Instead, he saw another fire-haired man with curiously large pauldrons. It had more straps than functions, more blade-breakers than blades, and where shoulder connected to chest, a makeshift sigil of a burning hound.

"Nice pauldrons," Bard pretended to be impressed.

And when the man turned, he did a double take before his face broke out into the broadest grin Bard had ever seen on the face of Fire.

"OH, SHIT!" he said, rousing every slumbering giant within a five-mile radius. "SURGE! What the hell are you doing here?"

"Could ask you the same thing," said Bard as the two embraced like brothers. He had almost forgotten that nickname. He had donned far too many for his liking, but he figured it was better to keep people confused. A hundred bounty hunters with a hundred names would not get very far. "Glad to see those pauldrons are being put to good use."

"Still hurts, don't it?" teased Merc. Bard hadn't seen him in years, but he looked almost exactly how Bard had left him: flaming hair, a smile that cut through half his face, and the ability to attract attention wherever he went. "Don't be a sore loser. I won them fair and square."

"Yep," said Bard. "Can't wait to win them back. They're still too big on you."

"You're not nearly drunk enough," said a familiar voice behind him, and Bard turned.

"Decker," said Bard, clasping elbows. "Strange seeing you on land."

"We all have to make sacrifices," said Decker. The Ice in his blood was unmistakable now. The last time Bard saw him, he was a head shorter and far less sure-footed. The boy had always been mistaken for Lancistierrean when he was thin and slight in build, but that was over ten years ago. Still, aside from that, Decker barely looked like he had aged.

Bard, on the other hand ...

"Damn, I almost didn't recognize you," said Decker. "What happened to the fresh-faced, clean-shaven Guardian of the Realms?"

"He became old, bitter, and bearded." Bard said. "But he can still kick your ass."

"It's been what, ten years?" asked Decker, laughing. "Last I saw you, you had to smooth over matters in Fort Townstead. Of all the people to handle it, they send *you*. They might as well have asked Merc to represent us in the trials."

"Your bodies would have hung from the towers the next morning," said Bard. "Wouldn't have been surprised if you two started the uprising."

"Prolly did," a voice spat behind him. "What the hell are you doing here? We were expecting you in Glasgérios."

"Got held up," said Bard innocently as he extended his right arm.

Wolff took it. "Where were you?"

"I've been a bit busy," said Bard.

"For twenty years?"

"I've been very busy."

The two stared at each other and burst into laughter. Wolff pulled him into a bear hug, crushing every bone along his spine, and twenty years vanished between them—something he wished he could say for his back as it screamed in protest.

Bard felt like he was on the airship again. Rickety thing, a wonder it hadn't burst into flames or swayed into the side of a mountain by now.

"How's the *Smuggler* faring these days?" asked Bard.

"Seen better days," answered Wolff brusquely. "Good to see you in good health. We were wondering if you'd come to us in pieces."

His words sparked a dark thought in Bard's mind. "I know it's in poor taste to ask a favor after such a long journey, especially after twenty years," he said, trying to sound calm and composed. It didn't work. "But is Elayne with you?"

"Yeah," nodded Wolff. "Elayne!"

Bard turned his gaze to the back of one of the caravans, where a girl—no, a *woman*—stepped down, carrying a heavy satchel. Her robes may have carried with them all the grace of the mages, but to him, she was still the same brat who had followed him around all day, asking for tips on how to throw punches—a skill she had practiced all too eagerly on Merc.

Only this time, she could probably kick *his* ass.

"Surge," she said, smiling sweetly as she pecked him on the cheek and pulled him into an embrace. "What's wrong?"

"Elayne," answered Bard. "I hate to ask, but my companion got hit by an arrow. The medican is doing all he can in the infirmary, but her wounds are … *inside* her." He tried to keep calm, but a deaf man could hear his concern. "Do you think you can help?"

"A companion, eh?" asked Merc, grinning. "What *kind* of companion?"

"The kind utterly lost on you," Decker snapped.

"Of course," said Elayne, ignoring them. Despite the exhaustion, she smiled. She always had a soft spot for underdogs. A Healer, in all meanings of the word. "Stay here and catch up with the crew. The infirmary shouldn't be too hard to find, and you might need to sit down yourself, soon." She punched him on the shoulder. "But we'll catch up over a tankard, promise?"

"You have my word," said Bard, trying not to look too baffled. It was Elayne—*Elayne*—the big sis of the *Smuggler* who used to beat up all the boys who misbehaved. Bard had even thought it would be a good idea to introduce her to Valerya, before Valerya became the face of evil and all. Now Elayne was a *Healer.* Grey-Bum would have to take orders from her.

"Don't you wish you had some pauldrons to ward off Elayne's punches?" asked Merc.

"Shut up, Merc," said Wolff before turning back to Bard. "The rest of these clods and I will get settled in. After that, I've got a raging domeric to calm down." He sighed as he pointed a finger at Bard. "Then I want to hear all about your hare-brained schemes."

"Yep," said Bard. He felt like a boy again.

Merc cleared his throat at the mention of hare-brained schemes. "Hey, um … Surge… you should, ah … help me unload the caravan," he said after Wolff wandered out of earshot. Bard frowned, wondering if Merc had taken out another seawall. Merc never lost his confidence whenever he did something stupid—only when he had to talk about it.

Bard peered into the caravan. "Damn, how many cloaks do you need?" It was the first thing he noticed. Decker never got cold, and neither did Elayne.

Decker ignored him. "Dove," he said, dropping his voice to a whisper. "Come out."

Bard was half-expecting a white pigeon to emerge from the darkness, but it was girl, no older than seventeen, who peered out from behind the clutter. She approached them uncertainly, half-eager to stretch her arms and legs. *Fireborne,* he thought immediately when he saw deep red peering out from under her hood. Her eyes were unmistakable, too. Like Dancer's, but in them, Fire came to life. Pure, most likely. And Realmborn.

The girl regarded him with the same curiosity, throwing a cursory glance at the blue—no, *azure*—of his hair before her eyes locked onto his own.

"She's not supposed to be here ..." began Decker, but Bard cut him off.

"I like her already," he said, trying to remain in good humor. He didn't know her, but simply being Fireborne—as in, from the *Firelands*—made her a walking target in present company. He wanted to slap Merc.

But when the girl winced under his tone, it became clear: she was voiceless. He smiled regardless, extending his arm. "Surge," he said as she took it reluctantly. "Dove, was it?"

The girl nodded.

Bard turned to the others. "How long were you planning on keeping this up?" he asked. "Until Wolff sees her flailing on a burning battlefield?"

"C'mon. She needs Uncle Surge," Merc wheedled. "I'm sure we can hide her away for a while. At least until Wolff is relaxed enough to not break our bones when he finds out."

Bard turned to the girl, who was trying not to smile too broadly. She fit in well. "This is the least of Uncle Merc's stupid schemes," he said to her. "And now Uncle Decker and Uncle Surge will have to clean up the mess he's made. Just like … oh, I don't know. *Every time* Uncle Merc has an idea."

He supposed it could have been worse. The girl didn't seem like the sort to attract trouble. Not intentionally, at least. He grinned and turned to his companions. "Well, boys. Best get some rest. Who knows how long it'll be before Morian sends reinforcements." He looked away, pretending not to know anything about the newly demolished Swordsworn encampment.

"Come, Merc," said Decker. "Let's go distract the big, bad Wolff."

Bard saw them throw her sympathetic glances before they wandered off, leaving Bard alone with her. It was like hanging out with Ram, but taller and fire-headed. And bow-wielding. And … girlier. *Damn it,* he thought. He wasn't cut out for this sort of thing. He had spent the last several months of his life hanging around foul-mouthed Hounds, gamblers, brothel whores, and Dancer. He could deal with all sorts of children and adults, but not the creatures in between.

She glanced at him, waiting for him to say something. He raised his flask.

"So," he said. "Ever try grog?"

25

GENOVEL
FIRE REALM

They came at night, clearing paths with blades that shone like crescent moons. Gryff and Valk crouched behind the trees, careful to stay out of sight. Now that Rhysar had bound itself to their world, its rays laid bare the moving shadows of the woodlands. The other side of the heath trembled. They were no longer alone.

The white star made nights grow especially cold, but the Swordsworn brought with them warm winds. Fire radiated from their core as they marched, signaling tension. Probably from the younger drudges. Gryff always felt a spike of cold whenever something frightened him, rattled his elements. He made sure to stay calm.

He and Valk scouted the premises, keeping track of how many Swordsworn had poured into the Greenwood since sundown. There were none Gryff recognized, but Valk knew immediately that they were not all sent on the same mission. Those with heavy-loaded caravans were headed for the border. There were over a hundred of them.

"What about the others?" asked Gryff. Valk raised a hand to silence him, but his eyes said it all. *They're purging the town,* Gryff realized as his companion turned back to the horses. But Valk didn't seem to be counting. His eyes darted from one caravan to the other, trying to piece together what could have happened for Morian to order the Purge of Genovel. It didn't take a medican to figure it out.

"Bastard," Valk whispered before turning. "Come. We have to disappear."

They slid out of the forest, hiding their tracks as they went. When they reached the village, they started packing their satchels, ready to flee at any given moment. As much as Gryff wanted to warn the villagers, Valk was adamant about keeping it to themselves.

"If our King found out the village was empty, that would put our General in a precarious situation," said the Spade, stuffing clothes into his satchel. Gryff frowned, certain half the things didn't belong to him. "Sometimes, the only thing we can do is choose the lesser of two evils. One day, you'll understand."

Gryff loaded the saddlebags and paused to watch the sleeping village. *They have no idea what's coming to them. How familiar,* he thought bitterly. *Only now, I'm on the other side.* He shivered and headed back inside.

"Are you finished, Artis?" he asked when he saw the old man sitting at the table. He hadn't seen Artis gather many things at all— only a few belongings here and there, and whatever he took from his room, he placed in Valk's already overloaded satchel.

Artis stared thoughtfully at his cup. "I'm not joining you."

Gryff halted in his tracks. "What?" he asked.

The old man coughed. "I'm tired of running, and I can't burn. What they do to me cannot possibly be worse than what they have already done." His face broke out into a resigned smile, broken at the tips.

Gryff was overcome with the bizarre urge to laugh. "Are you

serious?" He had grown fond of the old man. It seemed like such a waste for him to stay here.

"I'm always serious," said Artis. "Are you still questioning my judgment, boy? After everything you've seen?"

"But—"

"You have a good heart." Artis swirled the tea in his cup. "Better than many. But evil often comes from the best intentions. Your General is a prime example." He coughed again and took a sip. "And without proper care, a good heart can wither and die."

"What ... what does that have to do with staying?"

"It's a warning," said Artis, setting his cup down. "You're a good boy, but the shadows are in you. I see the anger." He straightened in his chair. "Now, go on and help Valk pack."

Gryff opened his mouth, but there were so many things he wanted to say that no words came out. At least, not in any order that made sense to him. "Artis," he began.

And then the knock came.

"If you please," said Artis as he turned back to the window. Their conversation was over.

Frustrated, Gryff headed towards the door. "Valk, talk some sense into him," he said as he swung it open. But instead of the Spade, a hooded figure stood in the doorway. There was no wind, but the cloth wavered. Black silk spilled slowly to the ground, and it brushed past him without a word of apology.

ARE YOU JOKING, Gryff thought to the gods as the air around him tightened. His vision blurred at the edges, and sweat collected at the base of his neck.

But when the figure pulled down its hood, Gryff was overcome with relief and terror. The General looked past him and extended her right arm towards Artis.

"I was wondering when I would see you again," said Artis softly, taking it. "The years haven't been kind to you, have they?" The air around them loosened its grip, but it was no heartfelt reunion. Recognition turned into something else. The world must have been a different place the last time they saw each other.

Gryff lowered his guard, but his heart leapt to his throat when she spoke.

"My men are setting up camp in the Greenwood," she said, not one to waste time. Indeed, she looked like she had just marched straight from Sinthea. "You would be well advised to leave before they finish."

"How many are there?" asked Artis.

"My Spades number thirteen. Twenty more from the King's Command."

Artis nodded. "The standard number for a Purge, I hear."

Valerya shrugged.

"I'm sure you've heard of the thirty men at the border?"

"I have."

"And our King's reinforcements?"

The General nodded. "How many?"

"A hundred, thereabouts, from what the boy and I saw," said Valk, emerging from the guestroom with a sack slung over his shoulder. Instead of bowing, he and the General clasped arms. "They've been coming through the Greenwood every night."

If the news was troubling, the General hid it well. Gryff couldn't imagine her losing sleep over one hundred foes; she needed rest for the other thousand.

"How have you been?" she asked.

"Splendid," answered the Spade. "His training has been fruitful. He can now cast Ice at will, but emotions still get the best of him."

The General's lips drew back into a thin line at the mention of Ice. Or emotions. "Get your things ready, boy," she commanded.

Gryff was done packing, but he bowed and retreated to the guestroom. He began to strap on his armor, grateful for the reprieve. His helm lay on the table, but he would put that on last. He much preferred breathing without it, and precious few were the moments he could afford to.

His blade leaned against the wall, and he curled his fingers around the hilt. *Emotions,* he recalled, feeling them course through his body like a warming flame. He sat at the edge of the bed and held his blade downwards, resting his head on his hands.

Love, duty, honor, revenge, hate ... Gryff had heard every possible reason for why people fought. Carried on. And there he was, surrounded by seasoned fighters. Yet one fought for revenge, one for duty, one for honor ...

What about him?

What would Dove think of me now?

A bang at the door jolted him back to his senses.

The General came in, letting the door shut behind her. It felt oddly invasive. Not once had she stopped by the library during his stay at the Citadel. She either had him summoned to her quarters or met him in the training hall. Aside from that, she couldn't be bothered.

Gryff fell silent as she examined the contents of the room. "Move," she said, and when he rose, she took his place at the edge of the bed. Awkwardly, Gryff bowed and headed towards the wardrobe, emptying its contents. He pretended they were his. He felt her eyes on him but forced himself not to falter.

"This is my first time back in twenty-one years," she said after a courtesy pause, and Gryff blinked in surprise. The normalcy was unsettling. "They rebuilt this entire village from the ground up. Most of this house was rebuilt. I'm surprised much of it survived."

"You've been here before?" asked Gryff, aware that it was a stupid question before it left his lips. Genovel was even smaller than Myrne. If she had spent the first fifteen years of her life here, of course she knew every stone and leaf in the village.

The General looked at the walls and rose slowly. "This was my house," she said. "This was my room."

Gryff nearly dropped his helm in shock as she made her way to the wardrobe. Her hand traced over the spots that had long since blackened and splintered.

"When I was four, I had a nightmare," she said. "The wardrobe burst into flames." She almost smiled, as though setting something ablaze amused her. "My father ran in before I could burn the house down. Big man, more brawn than brains." She laughed, bitterly. "I told him I had dreamt of ogres and trolls. I didn't have the heart to tell him that it was flying ponies and harps that plagued me that night."

As hard-pressed as he was to believe that he was standing in the General's childhood home—in her *bed*room, of all places—Gryff had a harder time convincing himself that she had once been four years old. Yet he had no trouble imagining her being afraid of harps.

"The wardrobe's smaller than I remember," she said, removing her left gauntlet as she traced along the edge of its doors with her fingers. He saw the scars that ran across her palm and down her arm but kept silent. "Remind me again. How old are you?"

"Nineteen," said Gryff, half-guessing. He was certain his birthday had passed once in the past seven stars.

"Do you still remember your kin?"

"Yes," he answered truthfully. "Like I'd just seen them yesterday."

"You would be wise to keep it that way," she said. Her voice was deep, dangerous. "I stopped thinking about mine one day. And now I can't remember what they looked like. Big and brawny, but faceless. My mother was golden-haired and comely enough. But that's all I remember."

Gryff stared blankly. He couldn't imagine ever forgetting his parents' faces. Even Dove's haunted him every day. Even if he wanted to, he wasn't sure she would let him forget.

"General," he said, forgetting himself as she turned. "Have you … have you ever wondered what life would have been like if you'd never arrived at the Citadel?" He frowned but stayed his ground. Now, more than ever, the question seemed important. "Can you imagine leaving it all behind?"

The General paused, and for a split-moment, she looked as though she wanted to snap at him for asking such a stupid question. Instead, she said, "Valk asked me the same question." She closed the wardrobe. "There was a time I could have left it all behind. But that was before I made promises. Decisions that couldn't be reversed. And one must always face the consequences."

She regarded him solemnly. "I have made my peace with the Fates. I will live and die by my sword. But you are still young, and you will face many choices. Some good, some bad. None free of consequences. And you've already made one when you decided to stay."

Gryff nodded. "Forgive me for asking, General," he said.

But the General ignored his apology and cast one last look at the bedroom that had once been hers. "Keep packing, and make your choice," she snapped as she took her leave. Gryff suspected she would be faced with a difficult one tonight.

He sheathed his blade and slung his satchel over his shoulder, collecting his helm before joining the others. He found his companions seated around the table. The silence between them screamed louder than words. Indignantly, he let his satchel drop to the floor.

"Will you really purge Genovel tonight?" he asked, deciding it was high time he be made privy to the plans involving him.

The General turned to the others. "Valk," she said, almost playfully. "How common is it that deserters of the Crown flee to the border?"

The Spade could barely suppress his glee as he answered. "Not unheard of, I would imagine. Especially after a battle."

"And if we just so *happened* to be informed of deserters, would it not be our sworn duty to bring them back to answer for their treachery?"

"I suppose so." Valk pretended to ponder. He stroked his beard.

"Get the men ready," she commanded, and the Spade stood at attention, brimming with enthusiasm. The idea of not burning a village to the ground seemed to appeal to him, and he nearly knocked Gryff over as he ran out the door.

"Valerya," said Artis after he left, taking her hand in his. "If my suspicions are true, everything as we know it will change. I'm afraid the decisions you make will be even more difficult than before."

"I'm aware." Valerya's expression did not soften. "But if I go, perhaps more than one village may be saved tonight." She laughed dryly. "My squire is a Glasger, and here I am, trying to save a Glasgérian village. I'm cursed."

Artis smiled. "One thing has been proven by the histories, my dear," he said. "Our allies change almost as much as our foes. Why, sometimes, they even switch places." He brushed a lock of her hair behind her ear and sighed. "Do remind me. How long, again, did the lady of the castle last with you?"

"Two days," she answered bluntly, and the two laughed, much to Gryff's surprise. "I would have taken down the entire castle before they made me *sew*."

"I remember," said Artis fondly. "Lady Gwynne ran from the sewing room in tears."

"Why they have an entire room dedicated to sewing still eludes me."

"I suppose not all girls have a talent for beating up boys. Or grown men, for that matter." He smiled. "That sparring match with Lucien did not end well for him, did it?"

"No. I imagine it didn't. But he looked better with a broken nose than he did before."

Another pause.

"It will no longer be safe for you here," said the General firmly, not one to linger too long in the past. "Do you have anywhere to go?"

"As I told your squire, I'm tired of fleeing. Let them come."

"I can't let that happen," she said. Gryff found himself moved by her concern. "What about your Falcon friends? Glasgérios? You'll even be safer in the Sore." She cringed when she said the name.

"Don't you worry about me. I've still got a few tricks up my sleeve." He sighed. "I'm afraid after tonight, we may not see each other again."

"But …" she began, as if backed into a corner. Gryff wasn't sure he had ever heard her utter the word in protest. Finally, she said, "Let me help you."

"There are others worthier of saving," he said, kissing her on the forehead before he rose. Gryff was certain that anyone else in the Four Realms who attempted such a maneuver would have gotten a swift sword through the bowels.

"Quickly, now," urged the old man. "You mustn't linger."

"Artis," said Gryff. He couldn't believe his ears. "What do you intend to do?"

"I can take care of myself," said Artis. "Now off with you both."

"Come," commanded Valerya. Whatever trace of emotion he thought he had seen in her vanished the instant she spoke. Gryff rose reluctantly, wondering where it all went. Even he felt more upset than she did.

Valerya extended her arm.

"Until the tides, my dear," said Artis, clasping it.

She barely nodded, casting aside his Falcon greeting. In the end, she hunted down his kind and would burn through their ranks if she had the chance. "May the Fates aid your journey," she said and broke away.

Gryff picked up his satchel and began to follow, but Artis stopped him. "Best of luck to you. And keep in mind what I told you." He extended his arm. Gryff clasped it, at a loss for words, and ran out the door.

"General!" said Valk, who appeared just as Gryff pulled his helm over his head. The General turned to the Spade, already irritated at whatever news would come pouring out of his mouth. "The King's Command has pushed ahead towards the border. The Spades await your command."

The General cursed, though she didn't seem entirely taken aback. She nodded when Valk glanced towards Artis' house.

"Make haste," she said, and the Spade rushed back inside to bid his farewells.

Valerya's destrier stood waiting, armored and looking more primed for battle than Gryff did. Gryff blinked, surprised, when he realized she hadn't even bothered tying it to a tree. He wasn't sure he had ever heard her utter a name for it, either, but he assumed she refused to name it. Like her greatsword.

"It's a sword," she had snapped when he asked. "It won't come when I call it."

The horse, on the other hand, had been trained to respond solely to her voice, and Gryff wondered if her childhood fear of ponies had prompted her to get the biggest warhorse she could possibly find. It donned no cloths to bear colors, and it looked like it would murder anyone who tried forcing it into one. Valerya's steed, without a doubt.

Gryff reddened underneath his helm as he approached his own mighty stallion, which was a pygmy-horse compared to the beast that stood next to it.

His pony was already saddled, and the General frowned when she saw it. "If you're still alive tomorrow, we'll see about getting you a proper horse," she said. "You will not drag down the name of the Spades riding that mule." She mounted her destrier as Gryff looked on, puzzled.

"Oh, yes," she said sarcastically as she sensed his confusion. "Lyra sends her regards to *Spade* Gryff."

Valk emerged from the house just as Gryff climbed hastily onto the back of his pony, pretending to ignore her quip. The Spade was fully armored in red plates for the first time since they had arrived.

When they were ready, the General led them through the mouth of the Greenwood until they reached a half-erected encampment. The Spades were already standing in a dutiful line as though she had commanded them to guard the forest.

"Diebold," she called, halting her horse. A heavy-set man with more scars than a pell post stepped forward, breaking the line. He was the oldest of the group, but his hair was still thick with the color of ash. "What happened?"

"The other soldiers rode ahead. We managed to ... *subdue* a few of them. At least long enough for them to squeal that a hundred men were waiting for them," he said, grimacing. Scars rippled down his face like a wave. "Unfortunately, they didn't quite make it past the rest of our questioning."

Gryff glanced beyond their formation and saw to his own revulsion several men sprawled on the ground, throats cut and limbs severed. No one else seemed the slightest bit concerned.

"For all that is important to know, they defied my orders. They will count as deserters," said the General. "And what do we do with deserters?"

It was almost disconcerting how the men grinned, straightened in formation. *The Realm's most elite killers.* Adrenaline wiped the exhaustion from their eyes. Fourteen fists, including Valk's, pounded against fourteen chest-plates as they cried, "NO MERCY!" in unison.

"And with any man who refuses to fall back from the border?"

"NO MERCY!"

"And if they beg and plead and cry?"

"NO MERCY!"

"Leave what can be spared," said the General. "We ride."

Fourteen fists rose to meet fourteen chest-plates, and Gryff realized he wasn't the only one relieved that Genovel wasn't being cleansed that night.

The General led the line through Genovel. Even the dwarf-horse seemed excited, and it charged much faster than Gryff had anticipated.

Gods, he thought, more exhilarated than frightened. He really, really wished Dove could see him now. *Am I really riding off to battle with the Spades?*

26

WAYFARER'S BARROW
ICE REALM

Dove decided that she quite liked Bard's company. He had given her a choice between a curious array of nicknames: Bard, Surge, and for some reason he refused to explain, Franco. She liked Bard best. Surge was too typical for a Thunderborne, and Franco sounded like the name of some beastly Hound. She must have come across four or five Francos at the Citadel, and she was sure they were all related.

Bard was fine.

Somehow, he had convinced Greybym to keep her housed in the graces' quarters, away from Wolff's eyes and ears. Marv vouched for her, and graces always listened to the medican. He taught her how to read their words, and as soon as she began recognizing the symbols and matching them to their sounds, she could help the graces change sheets and fetch herbs from the cupboard. Elayne showed her how it was organized and explained what everything did.

"I'm sure you've seen this before," she had said, pulling a jar from the shelves. The plant inside it writhed in pain, its violet glow dying in the daylight.

The nightbloom. It was Dove's favorite flower. Deceptively tantalizing, but lethal, much like a certain someone she had gotten to know.

Dove had grown quite fond of Brunhilda. The woman did not seem overly concerned with what was happening around her, and social propriety was a chore, not an asset. In her moments of boredom, she resorted to giving Dove tips on how to shoot arrows with her own bow—much to the other patients' dismay. A Glasgérian farmer who had injured his leg in a wheelbarrow accident promptly asked to change cots when he saw Brunhilda demonstrating the best way to snap a man's jaw.

Elayne worked her wonders in the morning. As a healer, she owned the infirmary. She could have asked the graces to cook her meals, and they would have obliged. When she was done with Brunhilda, no one could tell she had been speared in the heart.

Dove could not leave the infirmary, so she and Brunhilda spent their days together. At first, it scared her, but Brunhilda seemed to like her. "Everyone else talks too much," she had said nonchalantly, swiping a helm from the table. "It's what people *don't* say that interests me."

For reasons not entirely known to Dove, Brunhilda insisted on wearing a face-guard and a helm whenever she braved the world beyond the infirmary. Bard also found himself donning various items he had pilfered—temporarily, he added—from his companions. His favorite by far had been Thornbeard's helm, which covered most of his head and sprouted horns from the side.

Dove wondered if Thornbeard head-butted his assailants when he grew tired of swinging his battle-axe. The horns looked sharper than his blade.

"Dove, eat with me," said Bard one morning, suddenly leaning against the doorframe of the infirmary. He had a talent for appearing whenever it was most inconvenient, usually when Dove had a hundred things in her hands. Still, she preferred his company to tidying up the supply cupboard and pocketed them for later.

They ate a late breakfast in the infirmary canteens. Bard preferred to have the food to himself, so he ate at odd hours. In truth, Dove was not sure he was allowed to be there, but Greybym had long since given up trying to reason with him. She only ate there when he accompanied her, or at the turning hour when Marv woke up for his shift.

"Stop apologizing," Bard said suddenly, in the middle of breakfast.

Dove glanced up from her bowl of porridge and blinked.

"I can't hear you, but I can feel you apologizing all. The *time*," he said.

Dove opened her mouth uncertainly.

"Stop!" Bard put his hands to his ears. "You're doing it again!"

He rose and made his way across the table. She backed up along the bench, but before she could get very far, he grabbed her by the arm and pulled her forward.

"C'mon," he said, pulling her forward forcefully.

Dove cringed. She hated being touched. Every second felt like a stain on her skin.

Without thinking, she raised a hand and slapped him across the face. When she realized what she had done, her hand shot towards his head.

"See? You keep doing it!" said Bard incredulously. He had not even felt the blow. "I was grabbing you. *WHY* are you apologizing?"

Dove blinked, unsure of what to do.

"My advice? Apologize for the things that *matter*. Tell you what." He dropped his voice to a whisper. His eyes specked with mischief. "Apologies are good and all for avoiding unpleasantries, blah, blah, blah. But it's a load of bullshi—ahhh, nonsense, if you make everything your fault. So here's what I want you to do!" He grinned, and Dove braced herself. "Whenever you want to say sorry, just spit. A nice, big, unapologetic wad."

Dove eyed him skeptically.

"Oh, but observe," he said. Curiously, she trailed behind him. She stopped just in time to see Bard crash into an unassuming passerby. He spat to the side.

"See? It's easy!" he yelled to Dove, bumping and spitting. "Come on, give it a try!"

And so they continued, crashing, mostly into each other, and spitting, garnering bewildered looks from the locals. She swiped Thornbeard's helm and spat before putting it on her head. It slipped down and blocked her vision. After a stunned pause, Thornbeard gave a hearty laugh.

"Fits perfectly!" He slapped her on the back and sent her crashing into Bard.

"Isn't it liberating?" asked Bard. "Wait, where are you …? Ah, shit."

Dove threw him a curious glance, but when she turned, she wished she still had the helm to cover her face. Not that it would have helped much, but at least she would not have to see Wolff's eyes erupt into flames. Or worse, the domeric next to him. Tomá's mouth pulled back into a grotesque smile. The Ice was in his eyes again. They saw everything.

She turned her attention back to Wolff. Until then, she had never thought a man could turn purple. His face puffed and his mouth opened, but no words came out. "MERCURO!" he bellowed before Bard or Dove could get the chance to run.

Merc trotted over, happy as could be, until the smile deflated on his face.

"Oh, uh … hey, Dove. Fancy seeing you here!" he said unconvincingly.

"Shut up, Merc." Wolff cursed in several tongues, unleashing a stream of profanities that caused more than a few bystanders to halt in their tracks and head in the opposite direction.

Finally, he took a deep breath and turned to them both. "WHAT do you two have to say for yourselves?" he asked.

Dove and Merc looked at each other and spat. Bard tried not to burst into laughter.

Wolff opened his mouth to say more but stopped himself when he saw the black peregrine descend from the skies. It landed softly on Tomá's shoulder.

Silence fell as Tomá leaned in and whispered to it. Everyone else stood by and watched, like they expected the bird to talk. After a moment, he sent the peregrine back to the skies.

"My *Raehys* has sighted the Swordsworn."

"Fuck," was all Wolff said before he turned to the rest of the encampment. "GET OFF YOUR ASSES!" he bellowed. "The Hounds have been sighted!" He moved from tent to tent, urging everyone to make haste.

Tomá's face twisted into another hideous smile as he retreated into the mob. But he was a shadow; Dove had no such luck. She tried to find an opening, but people jostled her left and right until she no longer knew where the infirmary was. Finally, a hand grabbed her arm.

"Follow me!" shouted Bard as he pummeled through the crowd. When they stopped, he sighed and took a swig from his flask, feeling smug.

"Well, boys and girl," he said as she, Merc, and Decker leaned back against the outside walls of the infirmary. They had already strapped on their leather armor that morning and could not be bothered to join the excitement. "Looks like they're going to eat each other, doesn't it? Back in my day, we were prepared before dawn."

Dove rushed into the infirmary to get her bow. By then, Brunhilda had already strapped on a curious assortment of armored pieces.

"Don't worry, love," she said coyly through her helm. "I plucked these from the bodies of dead Hounds." Dove blinked, wondering how that could have possibly comforted anyone. Dove slung her bow over her shoulder, but Brunhilda stopped her before she could sheathe her dagger. "Where did you get that?" she asked.

Dove paused, looking at the curved blade Decker had given her.

"I only see these back home," Brunhilda said, but her concern lasted all of two seconds. "You *must* tell me about it later." Her tone changed, conveniently ignoring the threat of battle that had swept over their encampment. "All you have to do is not die."

Brunhilda swung her own bow over her shoulder, and Dove followed closely behind her. The paths had cleared, and the smell of rain was in the air. Some footsteps led away from the action, but she did not blame them; no one wanted to die in the middle of nowhere, and dead Falcons were never mourned.

When Tomá emerged from his tent, Dove's mouth dropped. *Midnight forged.* The Scrolls did not exaggerate. His armor was overlapping plates of darkened steel, some newer than others. Something left deep claw wounds in the metal, but he wore it with pride. Scales flowed with his movements.

It would have taken a madman to cross him, especially when she saw the blades jutting from the outer side of his gauntlet. When Tomá saw her, he turned his right arm over. A strange-looking plate was strapped to the underside of his gauntlet, extending just before his palm.

"What do you see when you close your eyes?" he whispered. "Watch closely." Without warning, he flung his arm towards a tree. A blade no bigger than half a dagger shot from his arm and embedded itself in the bark. In truth, Dove did not even see it—only splinters of wood where steel met tree.

The others looked at him with admiration and fear. Their morale increased.

Wolff did not even bother donning armor. "Haven't seen that in a while," he said gruffly as he approached. "I'd clasp elbows, but …" He glanced at the blades in Tomá's gauntlet. The domeric laughed and swung his greatsword over his shoulder.

"You stay in the back with the archers, kid," said Wolff. "Should things take a turn for the worse, promise me you'll get the hell out of here."

"She'll be fine," said Brunhilda playfully, dragging Dove to the back. Wolff frowned, trying to make sense of the pieces that made up her armor. Dove was overcome with the urge to laugh when she realized that every piece of it had been crafted for the Swordsworn, which might have explained the bewildered looks they were getting from the others.

The sun was high above them when Dove saw the first Swordsworn on the horizon, gathering at the top of the hill. Rags shielded their faces from the wind. They were less intimidating than she remembered, but circumstances had changed considerably since then.

The Swordsworn halted. They had not expected to encounter resistance from the other side, but they had the winning odds. They numbered well over a hundred, facing villagers with pitchforks. For them, it was an easy victory.

They charged.

They came at them with no apparent order, save for causing as much mayhem as possible. *This is fun for them,* Dove realized. Hooves clashed against earth, pounding trails of dust behind them. She tightened the grip on her bow.

Merc and Decker drew their blades. "You got this?" Merc shouted over the noise.

"More than you!" yelled Decker. "Just pretend there's a high lord over the hills waiting to be unseated!"

The two broke out into boisterous laughter. Adrenaline hung from their every word.

Bard stayed behind, keeping Dove at arm's length. "Ready?" he asked, taking a deep breath. He seemed excited. "Stay close to me!"

Brunhilda emerged next to them and gave Dove a playful wink as she nudged Bard.

"Shall we then, Bard?" she asked, readying her own bow as he drew his sword.

"SHIELD-CASTERS TO THE FRONT!" bellowed Wolff as Tomá translated for the Glasgérians. "MONGRELS, STAY CLOSE TO THEM! HORSES GET READY!" He turned to Dove and nodded, binding her to her promise.

Dove nodded back, feeling her heart rise to her throat as she felt the ground shake. Wolff turned back to the rest of the line. "ALL RIGHT!" he screamed. "This is how history is made! Let's give the bards something to sing about!"

The line burst into a chorus of mixed battle cries as everyone dedicated their final moments to whatever mattered to them. Some shouted family names. Ideals. Freedom was a popular one, along with death. Dove felt their bond tighten.

"ELEMENT-CASTERS!" bellowed Wolff, raising his longsword high before pointing it forward. "CHARGE!"

Dove heard the sound of Thornbeard laughing maniacally as he and his sons rushed the battlefield. "C'MON BOYS! LET'S MAKE YOUR MOTHER PROUD!"

The first wave of men and horses clashed in a fury of elements that hated each other. The air around them split into a thousand unbound particles, and for a moment, it looked like it rained glass. She shielded her eyes from the brightness.

Dove barely saw Thornbeard swing his battle-axe before Bard pushed her aside. "Stay close to me!" he repeated, and Dove realized he was the only Thunderborne on the field.

"If you dare," smiled Brunhilda underneath her helm.

"ARCHERS!" shouted Wolff. "NOCK!"

Dove and Brunhilda drew their arrows.

"AIM! *FIRE!*"

The sky erupted in a sea of arrows volleyed from both sides. Dove's arrow clipped a charging Swordsworn. It was not enough to pierce his armor, but its impact slowed him down.

"Well done!" said Brunhilda as hers hit a man in the face.

A wall of Storm rose from the ground as Fire came to claim them. Dove felt her hair stand on end, but it fell back to her shoulders when Bard lowered his shield. "DON'T TOUCH IT!" warned Bard. Dove decided she would stick close to him from now on.

Decker and Merc crouched behind their tower-shields. Black-wood consumed the oncoming flames. "OHHHH YEAH!" Merc's voice rang above the chaos. She saw them push their shields forward to block, advancing as they thrust their swords forward.

"HIDE!" said Bard when the first Swordsworn breached the line.

Dove glanced about wildly and crouched, tripping a Hound as he charged towards her. His foot dug into her side when he tripped over her, but adrenaline numbed its impact on her ribs. Instinctively, she turned and curled her fingers around the cross-grips of her dagger. She punched at him wildly.

The blade hit the man in the cheek, tearing through it like paper. He screamed as the side of his face flapped against the wind.

Dove spat on the floor unapologetically and struck again, this time hitting him just above the collarbone. He grabbed at his throat instinctively as blood spurted from it like ink.

Bard laughed morbidly. "That's it!" he said as he warded off another Hound's advances. "Keep tripping them!"

And so she did, rushing in front of oncoming soldiers and curling into a ball when they attacked. Bard took care of the rest and cut them down before they knew what hit them.

Brunhilda, on the other hand, was in another league of her own. Blasts of Fire deflected smoothly off her armor, and she brought down attackers with her bare hands. One had the particular misfortune of being deceived by her appearance. When he cut at her with the back edge of his blade, she ducked and grabbed onto both of his wrists.

She leapt in the air, and for a split-moment, their arms formed a circle. Even the Swordsworn stared, confused, until she lowered herself through their loop, gliding down his back and flinging her body forward—ripping his arms from their sockets and shattering his spine.

Dove did not even have time to be amazed.

But as more and more Swordsworn filed in, she found it difficult to keep track of her companions. She pulled a round shield from a corpse and thrust it between her and an oncoming arrow. When she peered above it, she saw a Swordsworn raise his blade above her.

Oh, shit! she thought, making her peace with the Fates.

But before she could react, a blade of Ice exploded through his chest, spraying her with blood. She looked for its caster, only to find Wolff standing behind the man with his arm outstretched. He flicked his wrist, and the blade flung to the side, pinning her assailant to a tree.

"Remember your promise!" Wolff bellowed, sword in hand. "GET TO SAFETY!"

She ran to a tree, picking up quivers from fallen allies along the way, and began to climb. From atop, she could see the entire battlefield. The snow had melted into crimson waters. It looked like there were still over a hundred Hounds against their own dwindling numbers, but her friends were holding their ground.

Dove aimed and shot, taking care to stun the ones attacking them.

An arrow clipped one who was fighting Decker, and Decker used his moment of surprise to drive his blade through the man's heart. Merc was hacking away at his opponent, aiming for the space between pauldron and chest-plate. She almost vomited when she saw the soldier's arm drop from his shoulder. Wolff was not joking when he said they could hold their own.

Dove caught a glimpse of Tomá and lowered her bow. He was surrounded by four men, but none of them managed to hit him as he twisted and turned like a shadow in daylight. She could see on the men's faces that they bitterly regretted taking on a domeric, but even that only lasted a few seconds. Tomá swiped his arm through them, severing their throats with the blade-breakers on his gauntlet. She shuddered. *He does not need any help.*

Wolff was sending shards of Ice left and right, bringing up crystals from the ground to ward off Fire. He volleyed boulders at the other side, and she watched in awe as they exploded into a hundred fragments that tore through everything they touched. When she saw him draw his sword, feinting this way and that and cutting back with the agility of a man half his age—and size!—she vowed never to defy him again.

Focus, thought Dove to herself, raining arrows down below. It was uncanny how easy it became the more she did it. In the midst of all the chaos, no one had a face, much less a name. And it was disconcertingly easy to kill a nameless thing.

Dove had just the presence of mind to duck as an arrow barely missed her face. A golden-haired Hound had breached the line and reached the mouth of the forest. Instinctively, she swung her bow over her shoulder and hopped to another branch. She made a wild jump into nothingness, grabbing onto the branch of the next tree and hiding herself in its crown.

Damn it. She closed her eyes and waited for the next arrow. As it whizzed past her head, she peered out from the side of the tree and fired. She did not have time to see if it hit its mark; another arrow shot past her, barely grazing her field of vision.

Dove slumped back against the tree. He was bound to run out sooner or later.

Another arrow. And another.

She took a deep breath and shot. Her arrow hit the man's leg, bringing him down to one knee. Without hesitating, she shot another, but this time, she missed.

It was Bard who came valiantly to her rescue. "FUCK YOU, PRETTY-BOY!" he screamed as he brought his blade down on the man's neck.

Dove found it troubling how quickly a head could fall from a body—even more unsettling how he stayed on his knees before his body fell to the side.

Shit, shit, shit, she thought, pressing her body against the tree.

"DOVE!" Bard screamed, breaking her out of her daze. "GET OUT OF HERE!"

Dove climbed down as a burst of Fire hit her in the face. Instinctively, she crouched as a soldier emerged, crazed, from the flames. He stumbled over her, cursing as his sword flew from his grip. She drew her dagger and flung it at him wildly, but he grabbed her wrist and knocked it out of her hand. With his free hand, he hit her across the face.

Dove staggered, thrown against the tree. Her brain rattled in her skull as she tasted blood. Sensing a quick kill, the man pulled her back and threw himself on top of her. He grabbed her throat, clenching until she could feel the blood surge behind her eyes. He was the ugliest man she had ever seen, with scars and teeth that were either chipped or missing.

And he had no nose.

Seriously? She reached about wildly for anything that could help her. *This cannot be the last thing I see.*

"You little *bitch,*" he said as Dove's fingers curled around the Nightbloom she had pocketed at the infirmary.

She screamed inside as she stuffed the flower in his mouth. She used his moment of shock to drive her hand upwards, slamming his jaw shut. She heard a sickening crunch as the man bit down on the petals. When his grip on her neck loosened, she gasped for air.

Her hand shot up to her throat as she saw his eyes widen, *deaden* before her. The veins in his cheeks turned black as the poison coursed through them, etching dark webs into his face. The veins in his neck burst from the inside, and he coughed out black blood.

Oh. So that is what it does. She kicked the man away from her as he died, and in her panic, she made a mental note to kiss

Greybym and Marv and Elayne should they all survive the day. She collected her dagger and massaged her wrist as she stumbled back into the clearing.

"GO!" Bard shouted at her as Storm burst from his fingertips. It collided against Fire, creating a deep red fog that blurred her vision. The land around them was cratered by the clash of elements, barren ground that made the bodies all the more visible by contrast.

Gods. The rats and crows would grow fat tonight. She cast one last look at it all before turning back to the mouth of the forest.

And she ran.

27

FORESTS
THE FIRE REALM

Gryff heard the screams long before they reached the hill just before the Icelands, but it was only when they halted that he saw the sky erupt into shades of red and gray.

He had never seen dying before. Of course, he had seen corpses—he had made three, after all—but never what happened before that. The distance between life and death was so vast that seeing people severed from the waking world so quickly didn't make sense to him. Scattered limbs looked like pieces of dolls strewn about the field. It didn't even look like it hurt.

Gryff suspected that the Falcons knew of the Swordsworn's plans long before their arrival. It was what they did, and he couldn't help but wonder: if his father had been alive today, would he have raised arms against the Hounds? Would *Gryff?*

Guilt ate at his nerves, but he remembered the General's words. Now was not the time to question his allegiance. This was the path he had chosen, and he had to brave the consequences. There may have been a time he hated the Hounds, but that was back when he was weak. Scared. That time was long gone now.

The General and her men formed a line along the hill. She rode out in front of them, pacing back and forth along the formation. "Remember, men," she said as she drew her sword, unaffected by the battle down below. "End only those who defy us."

Fifteen fists clashed against fifteen chest-plates, and Gryff was surprised that he had joined in their salute. *These men love her,* he realized. They would follow her anywhere.

The General halted her horse and raised her sword towards the killing fields.

"Who do we fight today?" she shouted.

"THE DESERTERS!" the Spades screamed in unison.

"And what do we say to those who defy us?"

"NO MERCY!" screamed her men, and Gryff found himself shouting with them.

"If you die, *I WILL BUTCHER YOUR CORPSES,"* she screamed. "YOU WILL NOT FALL AT THE HANDS OF MORIAN'S MEN. THERE IS NO GREATER EMBARRASSMENT."

"NO MERCY!"

The men cheered as she turned her horse and pointed her sword towards the battlefield.

"CHARGE!"

28

WAYFARER'S BARROW
THE ICE REALM

"**I** think we're doing splendidly!" Bard shouted over the chaos that had erupted in the killing fields. The Swordsworn present today were not in top form, and some of the Falcons were holding their ground. He had seen worse odds, much worse.

Dancer shrugged as she hooked a leg around the neck of a Hound from behind and tumbled forward, taking him down with her. "I suppose," she said curtly as she sat, cradling his head between her legs as she watched the light leave his eyes. She was in another one of her moods. Something sharp had grazed the side of her forehead, but she didn't notice. Slowly, she let the man's head drop to the floor before she rose, brushing dirt off her gauntlet.

Bard cast a quick glance around the battlefield and saw Merc, who had abandoned sword and shield and resorted to a full-blown fist-fight. Bard laughed despite himself, recalling fondly all the pub brawls they had found themselves caught in the middle of … or caused. The details were fuzzy now.

Bard made his way towards his companions. Dancer trailed behind him, swerving to avoid arrows and blades. Injured Swordsworn were struggling to rise, but she hopped from one to the next, ending them swiftly before they could scramble to their feet.

Bard saw a shroud of darkness dart past his field of vision, and he turned just in time to see Tomá warding off surrounding Hounds—or the Hounds warding off Tomá. The domeric's cloak flowed behind him, taking on a shape of its own. It twisted and turned to avoid the Hounds' blades. Tomá swung his arm out towards them, sending dart-blades in their direction.

Bard watched, stunned, as dart-blades lodged themselves through full-plate armor. It happened so fast, the men barely knew they'd been hit until Tomá soared past them, collecting his blades from beds of flesh and steel.

Then they screamed.

Yeah, not getting anywhere near him. Bard cringed. He dodged an incoming blow from a frenzied Hound and back-handed the man, cutting across the back of his leg. It wasn't enough to sever it at the bone, but Bard was tired. Dancer would finish what he started.

"HEY, BOYS!" he shouted to Merc and Decker, who had just ended their opponents and stopped to catch their breaths. "Great show, eh?"

Merc grinned as he leaned on his tower shield, but he froze when his eyes fell on something in the distance. Some *things* in the distance. Bard followed his gaze past the savagery that had cloaked the killing fields in red—and saw why.

A formation of men plated in crimson had formed along the horizon. They had been the stuff of legends for so long that their presence in a village skirmish seemed absurd. Just one of them could subdue the Falcon side, easy.

Bard's heart leapt through his throat when he saw Valerya in the distance, less disfigured than he had imagined. But there was no trace of the girl he once knew. Hope vanished before his eyes when she pointed her sword towards the field and led the charge.

Some of the Falcons dropped their shields in shock and ran towards the mouth of the forest. Strangely, some of the *Hounds* dropped their weapons and made for the trees.

"Well, *we're* royally fucked, aren't we?" asked Merc with as much grace as he could muster. He squinted. "Is that a fucking pony?"

"Shut up, Merc," muttered Decker, but his hands shook around the hilt of his sword. He was constantly at a disadvantage when it came to elemental brawls, but he was always the first to fight. Even when he was a kid. Even when it left him bleeding in the gutter.

Bard reached for Dancer's hand, but she hooked her arm around his. "Well," she sighed. "At least we can say we got murdered by the She-Jackal."

Bard forced himself to face the oncoming charge and nodded in agreement. "We'll just have to give them one hell of a fight, then!"

Dancer smiled, and when their arms broke apart, they screamed and charged the killing fields. Bard hacked his way through a line of Swordsworn, and Dancer leapt onto the ones that hadn't quite died. He screamed as a surge of Storm erupted from his wrists, aimed at the line of Spades. Blocks of Ice flew past him. Bard wasn't the only one with the same idea.

Valerya flicked her wrist, blocking their paltry attempts with a rush of Fire.

Fuck me, thought Bard. This was the monster Artis had created. He didn't teach her how to control the beast—he taught her how to understand it. And if she summoned it now, not even his shield of Storm would be enough to save them.

But the dragon didn't come. Instead, Valerya sent bursts of Fire towards the skies. A warning signal.

"FRANCO!" a familiar voice bellowed.

"What?" Bard spat as he turned, irritated. He decided that he no longer wanted to be a Franco anymore. He cursed when his arm didn't respond. Casting elements after such a long break had been draining, and his sword hand was killing him after all that hacking and slashing. His training may have come in handy in the first moments of combat, but the horde had quickly degenerated into a hysterical mess. He was foolish enough to get swept up in the chaos.

Flowing-Hair emerged from the flames. "You killed my cousin!" he screamed.

"Who?" Bard squinted, pretending to care.

"The archer!"

"PRETTY-BOY?" Bard raised his sword to stop the man's blow. "HE ALMOST KILLED DANCER!" he bellowed.

"What the fuck are you talking about?" Flowing-Hair asked through gritted teeth. The Hound may have been younger, but Bard had manlier hair, and far more years of wielding swords than this whelp. The thought depressed him far more than it encouraged.

"Come on, old man!" Flowing-Hair taunted, not helping at all. He brought his element hand up to his face, prepared for Fire.

Several Swordsuits had surrounded them in an attempt to support Flowing-Hair, and Bard wondered where the hell they all came from. They sprouted from the ground like dandelions.

Bard was exhausted, but when he saw the flames erupt from Flowing-Hair's wrist, he decided that now was the perfect time to do something he hadn't tried in decades. *This got me kicked out of the service,* he thought, suppressing a grin. He flung his right arm upwards and screamed as Storm exploded from his hand, curling towards the skies as far as the eye could see.

It caught his assailants by surprise, and it was that moment of shock that Bard needed. When the Storm straightened, he heaved his arm to the left, catching them in a colossal whiplash. Flowing-Hair had cast a Fire-shield around him, but the others had no chance. It was enough to halt both friend and foe in their tracks. Not many of them had ever seen Storm before.

Bard screamed again, feeling the energy drain from his bones as he whirled his arm back and around, catching others in the second wave.

Storm was soon engulfed by Fire as a charging Spade rushed past them, and its impact threw Bard back. There was an unpleasant ringing in his ears that drowned out all sound, and when he got to his knees, he stumbled. That little show had wrecked his sense of balance. Fighting figures swirled around him. Sharp teeth tore through his left arm, and when he looked down, he saw that some of the flesh had burned and curled away. He wanted to vomit.

He fell to the side, cursing. It depressed him how out of practice he was.

In the chaos, he lost track of his companions. The Spades soared past him on charging steeds, and he frowned when he heard them scream orders at the Hounds. "DRIVE YOUR MEN BACK!" they warned.

"Bard!" screamed Dancer as she shot an arrow through a Swordsworn's face. "What, are you in love, or something?"

Bard blinked, remembering where he was. He would have liked to witness the absurdity of the Spades slaughter their own drudges, but his senses had died, drowned in the mud surrounding him. The slight ringing in his ears turned into full-blown hammering in his head. He could no longer tell between screams and sobs, Hounds and Falcons …

Except for one.

"BAAAHD!"

Fuck. He tried to stand, wondering how the hell the boy had managed to get this far. He squinted, forcing his eyes to adjust past the pain. They focused on Ram swinging his wooden dagger at Flowing-Hair, who laughed.

"What the fuck is this?" the Swordsworn taunted cruelly. "They've got toddlers fighting for them now?"

Bard reached out his arm but stopped himself from casting. He was disoriented beyond repair, and any Storm could hit the boy instead. He let his arm drop and clutched at his sides.

Bastard. Bard watched on, imagining all sorts of ways he could flay the man alive. He hoisted himself to his knees, feeling like his insides had ruptured inside him. He glanced up just in time to see Flowing-Hair raise his sword, and Bard yelled out a string of profanities, both at the Swordsworn and himself.

But the Hound's efforts were hindered by a red-stained blade that had erupted through his mouth, driven through the back of his skull. His arms fell limply at his side, and his face wavered in the air, open-mouthed, as if sticking a metal tongue out at Bard.

Bard was overcome with the urge to thank whoever had thrust the sword through Flowing-Hair's flowing hair, but when it withdrew, Valerya glanced down at his body in disgust.

"Run back to your mother, boy," she said coldly as she turned to Ram.

Ram didn't know her words, but he understood, making his way instinctively back to Bard. As she watched the boy leave, her eyes locked onto Bard's. Any hint of recognition he thought he saw in them soon gave way to something cold.

I'm a fucking dead man, thought Bard, finally managing to stand.

"Tell your men to fall back," she said. She had aged, but she was still in good form. Enviably so.

She broke their gaze and sighed, deflecting a blow from a charging Glasger who had just realized who he was attacking. She raised her sword to discipline, not end, and after beating back a few of his swats, she heaved the flat end of her blade against the front of his armor—and then, with disconcerting speed, the back. "FALL BACK," she spat at him as he struggled to his knees. His cuirass was badly dented from both sides. A wonder the blows hadn't crushed his lungs.

The Glasger didn't even bother collecting his weaponry as he ran for the forest, and Bard passed him the boy as he ran.

"VALERYA, WHAT THE FUCK?" screamed Bard.

"Tell your men to fall back!" she shouted back, making her way towards him.

Perhaps it was their past friendship that had inspired her not to drive her sword through his heart, but she turned, distracted by a Swordsworn who was locking blades with one of the Falcons. *"DISENGAGE!"* she screamed.

Bard no longer knew what to believe when the Hound turned and spat as his opponent fled for dear life. *He must be drunk off his mind.* Bard blinked, trying to make sense of the madness unfolding before his eyes.

"I answer to our King. NOT you." The Hound grimaced, somehow convinced that mentioning Morian would work in his favor. But his face quickly swerved into fear as she turned and approached him, slowly, allowing him time to make his peace with the Fates.

The Swordsworn raised his blade, shaking. He must have realized he was doomed either way, because he swung it at her with little regard for his own safety.

Valerya sighed again, irritated, and heaved an arm out in front of her. She stepped back, catching his sword between the blade-breakers of her gauntlet.

Bard gaped. Valerya had just stopped a sword with her fucking *arm*.

"I bet you parry with the edge of your blade," she said coldly, twisting her arm at the elbow until the Swordsworn could no longer pull it back. She threw him a disapproving glance.

"I ... I apologize," he stammered. "I don't know what I was thinking, I ..."

But Valerya was having none of it.

"Never parry with the edge of your blade. Did Diante teach you nothing?" She drew her arm back slowly. Metal screeched until her blade-breaker was closer to the tip of the sword.

Bard cringed. He hated that sound.

"You really must take better care of it." She jerked her arm back and snapped the blade. The man looked on as though she had just snapped his neck. He fell to his knees, begging, stammering, sobbing for his poor decisions.

She lifted her greatsword and swung, slicing through his neck.

Bard had never seen a head fly from its body like that before. *Royal executioner indeed,* he thought, wincing as his neck hurt from secondhand pain.

The Blood Queen turned back to him.

Well, can't say I died a coward. He limped as he raised his own sword against her.

Instead, she threw him a threatening nod. "I know your face, but have no problem carving it out," she said.

Bard grinned, laughed at the absurdity of his situation. "I told you that once," he protested, biting back pain, and he swore he saw the corners of her mouth curl into a smile.

"ALL RIGHT, BOY?" bellowed Wolff, stepping up beside him. The man flinched when he saw Valerya before them. "Fuck me," he said, drawing his own blade.

Valerya frowned. Another hint of recognition flickered across her face, but it vanished, rippling out into the killing fields. "Tell your fucking drudges to fall back," she said, unaccustomed to repeating herself. "I will do the same."

Wolff nodded, but Bard knew he was afraid. "Very well," he said.

Bard saw beyond her a curious sight that convinced him he was hallucinating. Her destrier was crashing left and right into Sword-sworn and Falcons alike, taking them out like it was stamping on flowers. He blinked several times, certain he had gone insane.

Fucking destrier.

"Surge. Surge!" Wolff's voice brought him back to reality. He felt the man's arms under his own, hoisting him back to his feet. Bard wasn't even aware he had fallen again. "Let's go!"

When Bard looked up, Valerya was screaming orders at her men. Whoever heard her obeyed without hesitation, and those who lingered didn't linger very long. Falcons were running into the forest. The Spades circled back and herded their own men to the border.

Suddenly, Wolff's relief swerved into surprise—and dread. Bard followed his gaze, and blood froze in his veins.

"No," said Wolff. "Don't do it, old friend."

But the domeric was not to be stopped.

"VALERYA," he called.

The Blood Queen turned, irate. Her expression hardened into disgust. "I know you," she said. "The domeric who tried to take me on at the Battle of the Shadows. A *stupid* battle."

Tomá's lips twisted upwards. "We aimed to unseat that *bastard* you call king."

"Tried and failed. And we retaliated. Hence the battle," said Valerya, tired of words. "Do you fault me for avenging my king?"

"Did your king command you to cut down civilians, as well?"

"My men and I did no such thing, but I cannot speak for the others." Valerya smirked. "You should have made it easy on yourselves and surrendered the domerics responsible."

"A craven move," said Tomá.

"Sacrificing hundreds hardly seems logical," said Valerya. "My men and I withdrew after those responsible were cut down. A wonder we didn't go on to besiege the capital, but our King is ... *fair*."

Bard swore he saw her cringe at the word.

"More civilians fell in that battle than did domerics," said Tomá.

"More innocents suffer than soldiers, and they suffer for far longer," said Valerya coldly. Perhaps she had experience in that regard. "Such is the way of it, domeric. Perhaps your queen should have considered that."

"Let us settle this, then. Once and for all," said Tomá, pushing past Wolff's attempts to stop him. "No elements. Only swords and shields."

"Think of what you're doing," urged Wolff.

"Listen to your ally, shadow guard," said Valerya, but she gripped the hilt of her greatsword with both hands. "You will not get another chance."

The domeric drew his blade.

Valerya raised her hilt to the side of her head and pointed her blade downwards into a queen's guard.

The one stance I told her not to do, thought Bard, insulted. For a moment, he wondered if she was doing it on purpose, but he didn't have time to find out.

Tomá made the first move.

Bard stared in awe. The domeric soared through the air, twisting to avoid the Blood Queen's blade. When she swung her sword down and upwards, he bent, sometimes backwards. Valerya wasn't nearly as agile, but she changed guards faster than even Bard could process his moves. Her distaste for unnecessary words spilled into her fighting, and she did not fall for his attempts to misdirect her attention. Not once did she aim for his cloak, nor did she let his feints in the air fool her.

Everyone around them—those fleeing and fighting and crying and dying—stopped to watch. A glimpse of history replayed in a barren wasteland village. If Bard hadn't been convinced that their aim was to rip each other's hearts out, he would have thought they were dancing. Tomá flipped backwards as she whirled her blade towards him, and she attacked and defended, almost obediently. Darkness forged versus the Dragon Summoner.

What followed was a wonderful melee of clashes and blocks as each anticipated the other's strikes. Bard could see the strain on their faces as they twirled around each other. Even the brawniest fighters grew tired after a few minutes on the field. Greatswords weren't heavy, but each swing added a brick to its weight.

Valerya blocked and attacked with calculated repetition. She heaved her sword towards Tomá, but he leapt back before she could bring it back down.

He dropped his sword and flipped over her, kicking her in the face. And when she turned, surprised at the domeric's decision to resort to street-fighting, he used her split-moment of surprise to fling his arm towards her.

The dart-blade shot from his gauntlet, but Valerya had probably fought off enough domerics to know it was coming. Still, it was too fast for her to avoid it completely, and there was a sickening *clang* as it embedded itself through metal and flesh, just below where collarbone met shoulder.

Valerya staggered. Her insanely large pauldron had taken much of the impact, but she glared as though it had wounded her grievously. Even her men jeered, showering the domeric with insults. Swords and shields did not include the use of dart-blades.

Blood spilled down her shoulder, but Valerya held up a hand to silence the crowd. She cracked her neck as if waking up from a nap and didn't bother wiping the scarlet stream trickling down her armor.

And when Tomá lunged again, she planted her own sword into the ground and punched.

Tomá avoided her gauntlet, but the move had caught him off-guard. Valerya used the momentum of the hit to bring her body forward, down and back again, leaving her other arm to drive up with more force.

Her left gauntlet hit him in the chest, and Bard heard Dancer gasp in admiration next to him. Tomá grunted and shifted his weight unsteadily, and when Valerya kicked his leg in—the same one he used to kick her in the face—his knee cracked. He bit back his tongue, lest he show too much pain.

Bard found himself oddly proud as he glimpsed the shadow of Valerya's former self, breaking Lucien's nose in a sparring match. Tomá had expected her to fight with all the courtesies of a court-bred swordsman—not with the crudeness of a common tavern brawler. If only he had known how many taverns she had cleared out as a teenager …

Valerya spat blood and picked up her sword from the ground. "Enough of this nonsense," she said. "Draw your blade."

Without the use of his leg, Tomá wasn't nearly as quick, but

Bard had to admire his resilience when he lifted his sword and swung. Both fighters were exhausted, but one of them was going to die. Better tired than dead.

But it was clear that the domeric's skill was in the air, for he seemed to linger somewhat clumsily on land. Perhaps a grounded falcon was nothing compared to a raging jackal, and she flung her blade at him full-force, allowing him no time to use his dart-blades.

Tomá staggered, and she heaved the flat end of her blade down on his wrists. He screamed, letting his own blade drop to the ground.

As the domeric lingered on his knees, Valerya wrenched a round shield from a fallen Falcon's fingers. The man dared a half-frenzied attempt to launch more dart-blades in her direction, but she held up her shield to block them as she advanced. After the fourth, she lowered it and swept her shield arm over him, driving the steel plate directly into his collarbone.

A wonder the blow didn't behead him outright, but Valerya liked to allow people time to make their peace. She pulled the shield from his flesh and flung it to the side as Tomá fell, gasped for air. She took her sword in both hands and drew back into a queen's guard as she approached him.

"Any last words?" she asked. Spoken like a true executioner.

"The … the *domeras* … will have its revenge," said Tomá between gasps.

Valerya paused. "Tell your shadow friends I said hi," she said cruelly, and swung down.

29

THE WAYFARE FORESTS
ICE REALM

Dove had no idea where she was. The trees formed the last barrier between man and beast, but they were falling like flies. The air crackled and tortured the leaves, trapping sound within the forest. When the burning grew louder, she headed in the opposite direction, hoping it would lead her away from the bloodshed. But when shouts erupted from the other side, she thought twice.

The fight did not end in the forests.

With no immediate threat in sight, her body decided it was the perfect time for her to feel the pain that had erupted in her jaw. She clenched her teeth and traced her tongue along the inside of her mouth to make sure they were all there. Then her ribs exploded in pain. Tripping the Hounds had cracked each one in her body, and her limbs began to ache from climbing. She felt like a doll falling apart at the seams.

Before long, she saw Boar helping his twin back to the village. Bayne looked like he was missing the lower half of his leg. "C'mon!" she heard them urge, but their words did not make sense to her. Pain and exhaustion swirled in her head like a ship in a violent sea.

She started to follow them, but a Hound darted past her, herding her in the opposite direction. In truth, he barely even noticed her, but by the time she came to her senses, Thornbeard's sons were nowhere to be found. She sighed and continued into the forest, wondering where it led. She glanced around for something that looked familiar, but the forest was featureless. Everyone in it seemed to have vanished.

Dove readied her bow when she entered a clearing, ready to shoot at anyone who approached. She may have been one step closer to the hells, but that was no reason to drop her guard. And when she heard footsteps running parallel to hers, she turned.

She caught a glimpse of a running Swordsworn in the distance and sent an arrow in his direction. The first one missed, but the second dented his armor. The force was enough to knock him down. Immediately, she nocked and drew as she approached him.

The Swordsworn grunted in pain as he pushed himself to his knees. He twisted his body over and backed up towards the shade of trees, thrusting an arm out in front of him. Dove tried to make sense of the Ice that had solidified mid-air but had just enough presence of mind to drop to the ground when he sent it rushing towards her head.

Dove heard the Ice-blade lodge itself in the tree behind her, and she recalled with unease how Wolff had speared a Hound with one not too long ago. She leapt in the air, throwing herself forward and to the side as more and more blades soared past her. One managed to graze her thigh like a needle, but it still stung.

She tumbled forward as she landed, biting back the pain that seared along her sides. She sprang up in defiance, prepared to go another round, but the man had stopped attacking her. Instead, his eyes watched her intently through the slits in his curiously forged helm.

She drew an arrow from her quiver and aimed, but the Hound formed a circle shield with a triangle down the middle. When she fired, her arrow disappeared inside it. *What in the hells?* She drew another arrow and aimed.

"Wait," said the Swordsworn as his shield disappeared. He pulled off his helm. "Dove?"

She lowered her bow.

The Hound's hair was blacker than the shade that gave him cover, a wild swirl of thorns against the snow that blanketed the clearing. Half his face had been burned away, but fire still burned in his eyes. Without thinking, Dove slung her bow over her shoulder and ran towards him. The man rose to his feet, but she was quicker.

He opened his arms to catch her.

Dove embraced him, burying her face against his chest-plate. He had grown since they last saw each other, and she actually came up to it this time. She traced the side of his face with her fingers. Scars had patched his wounds together, but he looked healthy. For a moment, it did not matter that the world was burning around them.

"Well, I didn't recognize you either." Gryff wiped the blood off her face with his gauntlet. "I knew you were still alive," he said. "There's so much we have to talk about!"

Dove smiled, surprised to see him in such good shape. He was bigger and taller and did not buckle when she dove into his arms. His voice had deepened considerably, and he stood straight—not like the boy who crouched in the Scriptorium all day, poring over manuscripts. Whatever happened between then and now, he did not need her to throw his punches anymore.

"I'm so glad," he said. "Now you can come back with me."

Dove's smile faded. Realization hit her like cold water to the face.

"I'm sure they'll take you in at the Citadel," he continued, oblivious to the horror that had settled on her face. "You won't have to fight anymore."

The armor ... the blade ...

It was all wrong. None of it made sense in her mind. The throbbing in her head returned with a vengeance as reality sank in all around her. Her eyes fell on the dragon sigil on his sword.

What is this? she thought, breaking away. Her eyes fixed on the blade.

What, this?" asked Gryff, reading her thoughts. Like he always did. He grinned sheepishly. "You'll never believe it. They caught me in Edenn sending off falcons, and before I knew it, I was our General's squire. Can you imagine? Me!" he beamed. "Come on. Say you're proud of me. Or at least tell me how lucky I am."

Dove was certain she could hear the sound of her own heart breaking. Or perhaps that was her mind. *What is this, Gryff?*

"What's wrong?" he asked. He stepped forward and touched her face, but she backed away instinctively. "Are my hands cold?"

She stared, bewildered. In the excitement, she had forgotten he had cast Ice, very nearly spearing her with it. That he even could ...

Then again, she thought, shrugging to herself. *I did shoot him down.*

"Don't worry about the others," he continued, interrupting her thoughts. "I'm sure our General wouldn't mind ... I mean, sure, we'd probably have to hide you from Morian and all, but I guess that's ... hey, what's wrong?"

Dove wanted to back away until she fell off the edge of the world.

Gryff followed, his concern genuine, but stopped when he stepped beyond the shade. He grunted in pain as the light hit his face, and he stepped back immediately. "Dove!" he called after her, massaging his forehead where a red welt had begun to form. "What's wrong?"

You ... She threw her arms towards him, indicating his armor. *You are one of them.*

Gryff looked down at his chest-plate. "What, you don't really think I'm a Spade, do you?" He laughed. "Our General just had this made so I can walk in daylight. *Me,* can you believe it? Walking in daylight?"

Another Spade emerged from the trees and halted his horse. "Boy," he called. His wild tangles had also grown into dark waves, but she knew his face.

"Our orders are to fall back," said Valk. "Where's your horse?"

"Lost him," said Gryff, distracted. The Spade's eyes followed his gaze and locked onto Dove's. Instinctively, he urged his horse forward, but it did not seem like he intended to attack. Quite the opposite; his face broke out into slow recognition.

"Dove?" he asked.

Dove did not know who was more taken aback—her or Gryff.

"You know her?" asked Gryff incredulously.

You know him? she thought to Gryff and pointed, somewhat brazenly, at the man.

"You know each other?" asked the man. He frowned. "Look at me, girl," he commanded, and she obeyed. It was definitely Valk. She would recognize him anywhere.

Before he could speak any further, she caught a familiar shade of blue in the corner of her eye. She was almost grateful to have him there. His presence anchored her into something familiar, something real. Not this nightmare that did not seem to end.

"There you are," she heard Decker's voice as he appeared behind her. "The Hounds are falling back. We're to ..." His eyes fell on Gryff and his Spade companion, and he drew his sword. "Get back." He shoved her behind him.

Dove could not help but admire his resilience in the face of an Ice-blood and a Spade, both of whom had the power to end him with their elements. "Run," he urged.

No, thought Dove, grabbing onto his sword arm. It bent at the elbow.

Decker glanced down, confused.

"What is this?" Gryff demanded. "Who's he?"

"Hey, *kid,*" warned Decker, keeping his voice steady. "Both sides have been ordered to fall back. Just walk away. *Now.*"

Dove stared, trying to hide her awe. She had shared enough time and words with him to know that he was not made of stone. He must have been frightened, but he refused to let it show. He kept his sword raised, hiding Dove behind him as he stared down his opponents. The situation would have been heart-warming had it not been so terribly disturbing.

"You chose *him?*" asked Gryff in disbelief.

Dove blinked. *What?* she thought.

"What?" asked Decker. It had not been the battle threat he was expecting. "What the hell are you talking about?"

The shard was not long, but it was thick like the blade of a long-sword, and quick. And when Gryff glared, it soared through the air, lodging itself just beneath Decker's ribs.

Dove screamed inside.

"Fuck." Decker staggered as he threw Gryff a furious glance. "What's wrong with you? *WE'RE PULLING BACK!*" he screamed, bleeding. Instinctively, Dove knelt beside him, pressing her hands against his wound the way Greybym and the graces had shown her. The Ice seemed to have missed his heart, but it was stuck inside him, protruding from the other end.

Shit, thought Dove, panicking. She had never seen that before.

And when Gryff moved forward, unfazed by the daylight, the Spade thrust an arm out to stop him. "What are you doing, boy?" he asked sternly. There was a soft crackling sound as another blade of Ice formed in the air, much bigger and sharper than the last. As it sliced towards Decker, the Spade stopped it with Fire.

Decker took a deep breath and rose, but Dove saw the color drain from his face.

It was all terribly confusing, and Dove did not know who to aim an arrow at. Gryff, to stop him from hurting Decker? Decker, to stop him from attacking Gryff? The Spade, who was a Spade?

For a wild moment, she was grateful that they were interrupted by the sound of hooves clashing against earth.

And then she ate her words.

"Why are you standing there?" said a voice, cold and unforgiving. *That voice.* And when its owner appeared, Dove was certain that she had died and descended into a bizarre sort of hell that could have only been designed by the most malicious of Fates.

"I told everyone to fall back. That *includes* you." The General halted her destrier. Even the horse screeched in anger, reprimanding the Spade. Red trails and entrails coated her armor, and Dove was surprised to see that some of it was Valerya's. She could remember everything from those stone-colored eyes to the scars that ran down the left side of her face.

"General." The Spade nodded solemnly towards Dove.

The Blood Queen frowned when she saw her. It was hard to tell what went on behind that stare, what sort of thoughts it masked. But Dove was still standing, so perhaps the General thought a lot.

"This is what you've chosen, then?" she asked. Little had changed. They were simply continuing where they had left off.

Dove blinked, surprised. *I* ...

She stepped forward despite herself, but Decker made a mad grab for her arm. "ARE YOU INSANE," he demanded, straining under the Ice-blade inside him, but she wrenched her arm free. "Come back!"

The General sighed, irritated. "I said, stand down," she said, flicking her wrist and sending a blast of Fire at his blade. The flames did not touch him, but its impact hurled him back, forced him to drop his sword.

"DECKER!" Dove heard Merc's voice shout as he ran up to them. He fell to his knees. "OH SHIT!" he screamed when he glanced up and saw the General. "DECKER!" Deciding quickly, he swung Decker's arm around his neck and rose, supporting his weight with his body. "OH SHIT!" he screamed again when he saw the General.

Dove's head was spinning, and for a wild moment, she wanted to vomit. Her hands were covered in Decker's blood, which was already hardening around her fingers. And Gryff, that soft-spoken boy she had grown up with, that boy she had come to consider brother, had become little more than a … a ….

A murderer. A man who killed not to defend, but to destroy. Eliminate.

Dove," said the General.

"OH SHIT!" screamed Merc, and Dove nearly punched him in the face.

"Get your men out if you want them to live." She turned her horse, whose armor was also stained with blood. It had probably done its fair share on the killing fields. "Come, Valk. Boy, find your horse or *walk.*"

Gryff glanced at Dove once more and bit his lip before he pulled on his helm.

None of it made sense. As Dove saw Merc scrambling to get Decker to safety, she heard his voice, dulled and echoed, ordering her to follow. It was that curious combination of feelings that began its course throughout her body, trickling through her like poison. By the time she realized it, it was too late.

No, no, no, she thought desperately. *Not like this.*

Decker crouched to grab her arm, but she shoved it away from him.

GET AWAY FROM ME. She fell to her knees as Fire consumed her from the inside, coming to her aid where mercy and reason had abandoned her.

And when it finally cooled in her veins, she knew she had lost.

Her companions stood, scared but mesmerized, as the air tightened around them. It was much fiercer than before, which meant that Valerya must have been drawing power from the ascendant star. *Gods,* thought Dove. Now her friends would die a terrible death, and all because they ran into the forests to find her.

But it was not the General they were looking at. She looked up and saw a pinprick soar to the skies, barely noticeable against the flames. And when its glow began to alter past the highest tree, turning whiter than the brightest of stars, everyone but her knew.

Oh, thought Dove. *I did not expect that.* And she screamed inside her.

30

WAYFARER'S BARROW
ICE REALM

"**I** can't fucking believe we're alive," said Bard as he and Dancer went through the bodies of fallen enemies, inspecting them for anything valuable. He found it strangely endearing that the Spades had reassembled on the hill, doing absolutely nothing as he and Dancer looted the dead Swordsworn. They even laughed when Dancer turned the bodies over with a stick, lest she gets her hands dirty.

"Once a man dies, he starts … *festering,*" said Dancer, shuddering.

Bard didn't know how that made any sense, but her words took a dark turn in his mind.

Tomá was barely breathing when Valerya left him to die, and the Falcons carted what was left of him back to the infirmary. The domeric wasn't Bard's favorite drinking companion by far, but imagining him dying, *festering* like Flowing-Hair, was inconceivable. Soon he would be dead and in the ground—or stuffed in a hanging coffin off the side of the mountain, if they chose to follow Glasgerían burial rites.

Bard sighed when he turned to the cratered wasteland they had made. It was only when the fighting died down that the extent of their destruction became evident. *And this was only a skirmish.* The Falcons had already begun collecting their fallen from the field.

No one wept for the Hounds, however, and Bard was all too willing to leave their corpses to the night-wolves. It would be a shame if they were hindered by armor, so Dancer salvaged everything she could. Good steel was always needed, and after the chaos they had both endured, a new blade seemed more than an adequate reward.

Bard wrapped his arm with cloth he had torn from a fallen Hound's cloak. Elayne would have healed him in a heartbeat, but he thought he would let her tend to the dying before he made his way back to the infirmary.

That, and he didn't want Dancer to get all the good toys.

"Did you ever think you'd be caught up in all this?" Bard asked. "What would you be doing back in good ol' Lancistierre, anyway? Eating guavas?"

"I fucking hate guavas."

Bard frowned. He didn't know how anyone could hate guavas. "Well, we're alive."

"A modest effort," she said, smiling and waving at the Spades. Some waved back.

"I killed Pretty-Boy for you," said Bard suddenly, clearing his throat. He steadied his voice to make it sound less boastful.

"I know," said Dancer nonchalantly, replacing her elbow-guard with one she had plucked from a dead man's arm. "I heard you from across the field."

Dancer had sustained minor injuries, or so she claimed, but the blemishes on her skin had already healed. She had gone back to her normal self now that the fighting had died down, filling her sack with secondhand things.

Bard glanced up at the Spades. He felt a strange alliance to them, as they had likely slaughtered most of the Swordsworn on the field. They fought well. Disciplined and calculated, much like their leader.

Fuck, I had no idea. Bard thought back to Valerya. He had lost count of the times he stood there, gawking at her and the Spades like a halfwit.

His thoughts were interrupted by laughter that had rung continuously through his eardrums since the battle began. He barely noticed it until it drew near.

Thornbeard approached, rejuvenated from all the fighting. "Good to see you both alive!" he said as though they had just run into each other at a tavern. He handed him a flask. "Boar caught a couple o' arrows. Bayne came out a leg shorter, but he's a tough one. Ne'er had much use of that leg, anyway. Was ne'er much of a fighter, but damn it, he tried." He took a swig from his own flask. "Their mother'll be none too pleased."

"Lady Thornbeard didn't want them to come out and fight?" asked Dancer playfully.

"HA!" Thornbeard spat as though she had just told a joke. Ale dribbled down his chin in streams. "I mean their mother'll be none too pleased she *missed* the fight." He wiped at his beard, ineffectively. "Anyway, they're resting up. I think Ivan's passed out from shock."

Bard laughed. He had seen Ivan on the battlefield, but the poor kid didn't last very long. He fainted at the sight of the She-Jackal, and the Swordsworn probably assumed he was dead.

"What about Tomá?" asked Dancer.

"Recovering, or dying. Though if y'ask me, dying would be easier." Thornbeard shrugged. "Don't know what he was thinking."

Bard sighed and handed the flask to Dancer. To his surprise, she drank.

"Ale," she said, wrinkling her nose. "Whatever I can get at this point."

Bard grinned, but it was short-lived. Something cold and familiar crept down his spine, and he cast a glance over his shoulder. The winds ceased completely as they fled the forests, but the trees still swayed and bowed before a ball of light that had risen above them.

When the fire flooded towards it like moths to a flame, he knew.

"Dancer, get close to me," he said, surprised at the urgency in his voice.

Dancer's eyes widened when she saw the flames in the air, the angry, red tides that made it look like a river ablaze.

Until the tides. Bard finally understood. And then he lost himself. "VALERYA'S DRAGON!" he bellowed at the top of his lungs. "GET TO SAFETY!"

"Cast your shields!" shouted Dancer.

"CAST YOUR SHIELDS!" screamed Thornbeard after her.

As the others fell into panic, Bard knew those who weren't Fireborne were doomed to a terrible end. A cruel joke, if he ever recognized one. They had fought until they shed blood, tears, and innards, but it had all been for nothing. He had never been a religious man, but if he died tonight, he would surely give the gods a piece of his mind.

The dragon cast a brilliant glow across the skies, born from the light of the ascendant star. It fed off the flames of the battlefield as it came to life, screeching at everything in its field of vision. But it didn't roar.

And it was white.

"Rhysar," said Thornbeard fondly beside him, and Bard was surprised to see his eyes threaten tears. He pulled off his helm and cradled it in his hands.

"I thought the dragon's name is Avantys?" Dancer frowned.

"It is," said Bard as he struggled to understand.

He closed his eyes and made his peace with the Fates. Twenty years ago, he had been half a day's ride away when it happened, so the flames had missed him completely. Now there was no such distance between them. It would send a sheet of Fire as far as the eye could see. A beautiful thing, really. It could have been worse.

Even the Spades stopped talking and watched on, confused. This wasn't the dragon that had carved their General's name into the Scrolls.

But then who ...?

The White Dragon writhed in the air, unaccustomed to being pulled back from slumber. It stretched its limbs, its screeches still incapable of a full roar. Bard stared, enamored. It was kind of cute. But when it opened its eyes, it turned its fiery head towards them like they were intruders. It screeched again, empowered, twisting and arching its back. Its wings unfolded for the first time, looking for the first signs of prey.

They were going to die.

It flew higher and looked down, threatening to swoop down on them all. A white light blinded him, searing through the space behind his eyes. It felt strangely invasive, like he was being watched. The dragon seemed to sense life all around it, the stirrings inside his head, guiding it to its first kill.

Instinctively, Bard reached a hand out for Dancer, but she tugged on his arm.

"Bard, what ... is that?" She pointed to another glowing shape, this time blood-red against the night sky. That, Bard definitely recognized. The newborn looked at it, curious but undeterred, as the orb took on a life of its own.

Bard's eyes couldn't decide if they should widen or frown, so they simply closed. He was getting too old for this shit.

Another one?

It was like seeing an old friend, albeit in a blood-crazed, mortifying sort of way. From the ball of light, it formed, exactly like the one he had seen all those years ago: fire-red and twice as immense, with a temper twice as short. It snapped at the smaller one, angered that it had just been born.

Valerya's. Of that there was no doubt.

Bard could see Fire trace the scales around it, and it was much more defined, *grown*, than the other. The White Dragon tried to howl, but Avantys reared its head in fury and roared, drowning out its attempts. It spread its wings and towered over the newborn, covering the light of the moon as it tore scars into the skies. Their world was splitting at the seams.

Avantys snapped at the other, but it hissed back in defiance, unwilling to give up its freedom. Bard almost felt sorry for it.

True to its Summoner, Avantys was having none of it. They faced each other, howling with the war cries of a thousand and more men and women they had ended—a bestial roar that made his skin crawl. Avantys soared effortlessly around its challenger, cutting it off at every turn, warding off its clumsy attempts to bite back. The newborn struggled to break free, but its predecessor was relentless.

And when the Red Dragon finally lunged, tired of their games, they clashed in a battle of their own. The sound threatened to burst Bard's eardrums.

And then suddenly, it stopped.

A glorious bout of silence, enough to convince Bard that he had died or gone deaf, before the sky erupted in the most spectacular display of Fire he had ever seen. The impact threw them on their backs and brushed his hair back with hot air, but he couldn't breathe any of it in. His heart clenched. The collision swept dirt into his eyes, and he could feel the beasts' energy dance just beneath the surface of his skin.

This was the end. This was his last moment in the waking world. If one dragon's descent was enough to wipe out entire cities, he could only imagine what two could do.

But instead of sweeping through the ground, their battle had cast a blanket of Fire in the skies. White and red covered the stars when their jaws locked, and Bard wondered if they could be seen from Divisorya. They split into a thousand and one rays that flew from impact, sending stars of fire in every direction.

Inside, he screamed as the land all around them sprang to life, but as sudden as it came, it stopped. A shroud of darkness overcame them, desolate of comfort. The air was bathed in Fire in its purest form, and the sky glowed warm like hot coals before they cooled.

The beasts may not have descended, but their flames had grazed the outer layers of the forest. Smoke rose from fire-seared leaves like a soft mist, but when Bard squinted, he saw the trees start to burn. He threw a quick glance at the Spades, who were trying in vain to calm their steeds. It was obvious they hadn't expected such a thing of beauty.

But through the confusion and chaos, one thing remained clear.

There was another summoner in their midst.

THE
OTHERWORLD

For a moment, it smelled like sand.

Not like sand in the desert, but sand-leaves that blossomed along the coast of the Dragontail whenever the moon blocked out the sun. Dove did not know what they were really called, but Gryff always called them sand-leaves. She used to hate how they scratched her arms whenever she climbed, but now, it was the most welcome smell in the world. Even with her eyes closed, she knew she was home. *It was all a dream,* she thought, stretching, feeling the warmth of sleep fade. It had been the first harvest night in Myrne, and she must have fallen asleep somewhere in the star-lit fields. It had always been where she felt safest, cocooned between the tallest trees at the hill's edge that overlooked the Dragontail villages.

But when she opened her eyes, all she saw was black. It was not dark like night, or the way shadows could be dark, but black, as in the absolute absence of everything. It drained her surroundings of light, of sound. Of feeling.

Am I ... dead? she wondered, bringing a hand to her face. None of it made sense. There was no source of light, but her fingers were as clear as day. She saw nothing save for her own body and the patch of ground she was lying on, but beyond arm's length, the earth had faded into blackness. When she turned to the side, the patch shifted with her. *I must be dead,* she thought. This must be what the other side was like, where shadow and light exchanged places. The throbbing in her head had disappeared completely, and when she traced her fingers along her ribs, there was no pain. She felt something at her side and brought it to her face.

An arrow? She frowned when she recognized the falcon carvings. *No. My arrow.*

"It took a while to find you."

The presence of another startled her, and she sat up. It required less effort than she thought; strength had returned to her limbs, and it felt like she had just woken up from a long nap. The cut from the Ice-blade was still there, surrounded by burnt cloth, but she no longer felt anything. It was like she had never gotten hurt at all.

Dove turned but found herself unafraid. If she had indeed died, nothing could harm her here. But when she saw the source of sound, she realized she had never been so wrong.

The General glanced around them as if searching for a way out. "Have you gone dumb as well?" she snapped. "Make it quick. I hate being in other people's minds."

That got Dove's attention. Fear clouded her judgment, settling just below the surface of her skin. *We are in my mind?*

The ground beneath her began to tremble. Cracks formed along the walls of her mind like glass, held together by a blinding white light that seared her vision. Her defenses were crumbling before her eyes.

"Calm your mind," said Valerya. "If you panic, this will shatter, and I won't be able to find you. *Concentrate.*"

Dove closed her eyes and tried to block out the crackling sound that replaced the silence. She had to think of something calming. Like a lake, or a puppy. Or …

The sand-leaves. The star-lit fields in the Dragontail. That one time of year when the moon blocked out the sun and cast a shadow over the village. *It was as dark as this.* But when the darkness had reached its deepest depths, it called the fireflies to action. It was exactly like … like …

When the ground stopped shaking, she opened her eyes. *Like this,* she thought, feeling the sand-leaves between her fingers. She was back in the blossom-fields, lit only by the deep green bulbs of the fireflies.

"Seriously," said Valerya, recognizing nothing. "Where are we?"

I am dead, thought Dove miserably. It was not like anything she had imagined. She thought her life would simply end, that she would cease to exist; she certainly did not expect her conscious mind to carry on, especially in the presence of another. For a horrible moment, she did not know if Valerya made it heaven or hell, but she was glad that she was not alone.

"Speak," said Valerya sharply. Her tone cut through the silence, startling the fireflies. "We're in your mind. The only thing you can't change here is me."

"I can't …" Dove found herself saying, and stopped as though a knife had slammed into her throat. Her voice was scratchy, but soft. Barely a shade above a whisper. "Am I talking?"

"That's pretty much how I expected you to sound," said Valerya, turning her attention back to the fields. "Where are we?"

"The … Dragontail," said Dove. *My home. The thing you burned.*

Valerya barely reacted. "I need you to come back to the waking world."

"How …?"

"This is *your* world. You can speak if you want to."

"No, I mean … how are you … here? In my mind."

"You passed out. I came to get you. I don't understand the confusion."

"But why you?" asked Dove before she could stop herself. "I mean … why … you?"

"You would prefer someone else?"

"No," said Dove, too fast for her own liking. "I'm not used to talking. I can't … I mean … I don't understand."

"Then try harder. It's really quite simple," said Valerya impatiently. "And make it fast. Being in someone else's mind is my worst fucking nightmare." She paused and glared when Dove's confusion made no motion to clear itself. "Stand," she commanded sharply.

Dove obeyed. Even in her mind, she had lost. The General's hand slid down past Dove's hair, brushing it back and resting on Dove's chest, just over her heart.

"It's here, now," said Valerya coldly, and Dove felt it beat, *hiss*, within her. Pain shrouded her senses, but then it was gone. The General released her grip and unstrapped her gauntlet, pressing her hand against skin. A ball of glowing scarlet burst in Dove's mind, spreading as each point of contact sent Fire coursing through her.

The connection, Dove realized. She did not know if that was the answer she was looking for, but it was the only word that came to mind.

"Some believe that dragons live behind the stars, that Summoners create a connection to another world." Valerya's eyes narrowed. She was unaccustomed to explaining things. "But the *mereyn* creates a connection between dragons, past and present. The Otherworld."

"So … I really did summon a dragon?" Dove asked. "It wasn't just a bad dream?"

Much to her surprise, Valerya laughed. It was bitter, not unlike Tomá's, but it laughed at herself more than anything else. "Oh, how the gods favor irony," said Valerya. "A skirmish becomes a battle etched into the Scrolls. A shadow rises from the darkness and falls in the light. And a voiceless girl roars in the skies."

Dove paused when she heard the General's words. "A shadow falls?" Suddenly, she wondered where the domeric was. Her eyes widened when they fell on the dart-blade embedded in the General's pauldron.

The General did not have to follow Dove's gaze to know what she was gawking at. "Fucking domeric," she cursed, spitting. "Your … *ally* … challenged me to a duel."

Valerya released her grip, and Dove staggered under useless legs. There were so many questions she wanted answered that none of them came out. Suddenly, she felt her senses sharpen. Something new came into being all around her. She began to hear the crackling of the forest, to see the scorched wood of the trees. The smell of smoke. The taste of fear.

No, she thought as she felt the beast in her heart, pacing back and forth inside her.

The General leaned in closer. *"Control it,"* she said faintly, a near whisper. "Or I will."

Dove tried to calm herself and felt her connection to the beast weaken.

The General pulled back. "My squire," she said, straightening. "Do you know him well?"

Dove began to nod, but the thought of it was enough to tear at her insides.

"I suppose you did once," said Valerya. "But don't delude yourself. Once unveiled, a man's character never wavers." She turned to the blossoms. "Perhaps your closeness once forced you to share interests, but no longer."

The Blood Queen's words cut deep, but Dove did not protest. Perhaps the reason why Gryff's reaction had devastated her so much, was that it did not surprise her. Not in the least.

"Save yourself the pain," said the General, reading her face. "Now that you understand, you must wake up."

"I do not want to."

"Wake up?"

"Go back."

At first, there was no reaction. "The dragons are still in our world," said Valerya. "When they leave it, our connection will be broken."

Dove paused. "Does this mean I can ... enter your mind too?"

"Do you have a death wish?" snapped Valerya.

"No, I just ..." Dove smiled shyly. "I have never spoken to anyone before."

Valerya swatted at a firefly, not bothering to hide her distaste. "Why this place?"

"I used to ... come here," said Dove. "When the moon covered the sun, and everyone ... hid in their houses, it was the only time I felt ... safe ... being outside." Dove frowned. "What are you doing here?"

"Your manners need work."

"But ... how ... I mean ..." Dove collected herself before continuing. After being voiceless her entire life, she never had to think twice about which words to keep to herself. "I just ... never thought I would see these fields again. I thought you would kill me."

"I still can."

"But why didn't you?"

"I'm asking myself that now."

"I mean, before. When we … in Edenn."

"Are you complaining?"

"No, I …" Dove said. "I was just … wondering." She closed her eyes. "What will … happen when I wake up?"

"It will take time for you to readjust to the other side," said Valerya. "Your dragon will fight for its place in our world, and until you gain control over it, you will experience the worst pain you have ever felt."

Dove sighed. Even in the coldest, loneliest depths of her mind, the General could not say anything comforting. "I am scared," she said before she could stop herself.

For the first time, Valerya's expression softened. "Yours is young, but it will fight for control," she said. "When it does, you will feel your skin being torn from your bones. It can dig into your deepest memories and show you things that will make you want to die." Her eyes narrowed, all sympathy gone. "There is only one piece of advice I can give you."

Dove did not know how any of this could be salvaged. "What?" she asked.

"When it feels like it has the upper hand, when you feel close to giving in, just remember," said Valerya. Her lips drew back into a thin line. "It *needs* you. You are its only connection to our world. You will love it. And you will hate it."

"What about you?"

"I will be gone when you wake up."

"Gone?"

"This was a courtesy, girl," said Valerya. "We are still on different sides. I will still be the Summoner General of the Firelands, and you will have joined the insurgents. For your sake, I hope we will not see each other again for a long time."

Dove did not know if that made her happy or sad. "I ... can we stay here a little longer?"

"The connection will break soon." said the General, ignoring her. She spat blood. "Well, girl. It appears that you will find out who your true allies are soon. A *lovely* experience." She grimaced and looked at her again with all the intensity of the burning forest that was slowly returning to her field of vision. "Do you remember what I told you in Edenn?"

Dove nodded despite herself. The Purge of Edenn seemed like it had taken place worlds away, far beyond the realms of man, but she remembered. It was not a particularly cheerful memory, but it was not one she was willing to let go.

The General closed her eyes as if wishing away a headache. "When you wake up, I urge you to run," she said when she opened them. "If I catch you in the forest, I will show no mercy. I will end you."

"But ..." Dove began, but she knew it was not a negotiation. "I do not want to go."

"*Weakling,*" said Valerya cruelly, spitting more blood. "We've chosen our paths. And we must live with our decisions."

Dove did not know what else to say. Even if she did, her voice had left her again. The forest around her began to take shape as their connection faded. She felt her senses dull as if waking from a dream, faster and faster until she could no longer think straight. The blossom-fields and the fireflies sank back into the depths of her mind, and when Dove opened her eyes to the waking world, Valerya was gone.

KERSTIN ESPINOSA ROSERO

First edition 2020.

Book Interior Design: © Franziska Haase - www.coverdungeon.com
- using motifs from pixabay.com -
Cover Design: © Franziska Haase - www.coverdungeon.com
Book Interior Graphics: © Kerstin Espinosa Rosero
Instagram: @k.e.rosero
ISBN 978-1-7361041-0-1

Lightning Source UK Ltd.
Milton Keynes UK
UKHW040046180123
415533UK00018B/269/J